WHERE BODIES FALL

Sheila Kindellan-Sheehan

WHERE
BODIES
FALL

Véhicule Press

Published with the assistance of the Canada Council for the Arts, the
Canada Book Fund of the Department of Canadian Heritage, and the
Société de développement des entreprises culturelles du Québec (SODEC).

Funded by the Government of Canada
Financé par le gouvernement du Canada | **Canadä**

Cover design: David Drummond
Typeset in Minion by Simon Garamond
Printed by Marquis Printing Inc.

LIBRARY AND ARCHIVES CANADA CATALOGUING IN PUBLICATION

Sheehan, Sheila Kindellan, 1944-, author
Where bodies fall / Sheila Kindellan-Sheehan.

Issued in print and electronic formats.
ISBN 978-1-55065-427-1 (paperback). – ISBN 978-1-55065-434-9 (epub)

I. Title.

PS8637.H44W44 2015   C813'.6   C2015-903067-6
C2015-903068-4

Published by Véhicule Press, Montréal, Québec, Canada
www.vehiculepress.com

Distribution in Canada by LitDistCo
www.litdistco.ca

Distributed in the U.S. by Independent Publishers Group
www.ipgbook.com

Printed in Canada on FSC certified paper

For
Dad and Mom,
Michael, Kathryn, and Thomas
Always near, forever loved

And to be wroth with one we love
Doth work like madness on the brain.
–Coleridge, "Christabel," ii.

Characters

Major Crimes: The Team

TONI DAMIANO: 43, lieutenant-detective, lead on the Sanderson case; tough, the 'whole package,' but haunted by her last difficult case; trying to regain her balance.

PIERRE MATTE: Detective Damiano's partner, an observer, almost a digital recorder, determined, quiet, complex.

RICHARD DONAT: chief of the Crémazie Division, demanding and crusty, but mellowing with time.

MARIE DUMONT: head of the Crime Unit, working rain-washed evidence.

The Family

TREVOR SANDERSON: accomplished, high-profile lawyer, prominent in Montreal, father and husband.

SHARI SANDERSON: psychologist, successful, gentler than her husband, partial to her son.

TAYLOR SANDERSON: 22, university student, spirited, adventurous, spoiled and secretive.

MATTHEW SANDERSON: 17, a techie, egocentric like all teenagers, a nuisance to his sister.

CAITLIN DONOVAN: university professor, a target, facing dilemmas at home and at work.

AMIRA CUPID: university student, Taylor's roommate, intelligent, studious and vulnerable.

JOSH GOLDMAN: the third roommate, cocky, bold, unlucky with his female roomies.

ANDREW WESTON: Taylor's ex, sincere, true, caught in the vortex of murder.

GLEN GARDINER: the 'tunnel man,' knowledgeable, confident and sly, a jokester.

JEFF SHEA: Damiano's husband, pediatrician, wise and firm, a match for the lieutenant.

LUKE SHEA: 15, handsome, vulnerable and cunning, a normal teenager.

JOSEPH CASTONGUAY: a rooted man and father, husband, a man of good heart.

LIAM CASTONGUAY: 14, a young man of standards and conscience, learns the cost of adventure.

CAMERON MILLER: 14, Liam's friend who looks out for himself.

Chapter One

Thursday morning, Liam Castonguay stretched across his bed, raised the blue vertical with the back of his hand and saw fog and drizzle. He reached for his phone and texted Cameron Miller. *Nothing's changed. We go today at three.* He didn't wait long for a response. *Are you nuts? It could snow.* Liam ignored the return text. He had done his research. The city planned to demolish Montreal's Wellington Tunnel in a few weeks, so the summer plan was blown. Thursday was a pedagogical day. Their parents were at work, and the fourteen-year-olds were alone! The bike tires were pumped, and the backpacks were secretly stored in Liam's father's garage at the end of the driveway, a short distance from the house. It was almost noon. He wished they could leave immediately, but he needed his father's hacksaw for the lock, and four in the afternoon meant fewer risks of being arrested by patrolling police. Cameron was their lookout. Worse case, who could catch a kid on a bike? They'd be home before their parents. The plan was simple. Liam was jacked with excitement.

In the shower, he stood under the full spray of the nozzle. Soaping down quickly didn't stop nagging thoughts at the back of his head. Towelling off didn't help. When he turned fourteen in February, his father had shaken his hand. *You'll be a good man, Liam. I have confidence in you.* At six foot, Liam was almost as tall as his father, but without his muscle. His mother joked that he was a younger and better version of his father. For that, his father gave her a whack on the behind. Liam remembered hiking with his dad on Mont-St-Hilaire, fishing on Lake of Two Mountains, climbing Mount Washington, building wooden shelves in the garage and painting them last summer – a lot of stuff together. If his plan blew up? If? Liam ran his hands through his brush of dark brown hair and shook his head. He had strategy. *Officer, there's no sign, I mean.* But the hacksaw! That was a problem. He rapped his forehead with his knuckles. Where the hell was Cameron? Liam wanted this adventure, his fingertips tingled. He'd be back in time.

Cameron came around to the door at the side of the house. Shorter but heavier than Liam, Cameron had come from Toronto last September. His parents bought the most expensive house on the corner of 39th Avenue in

Lachine, not the usual brick job but stone, two doors down from Liam. He had deep-set blue eyes and kinky red hair that he hated. Somehow he'd managed to develop his father's paunch, so he carried a grudge against both parents, added to the anger for having to leave his friends in Toronto and the first girl who ever checked him out. After seven months at Lachine High, he had one friend, Liam, and he went to Collège Saint-Louis on the French side. Liam didn't bother with girls. His focus was the tunnel. Cameron never missed the three girls at school who timed Liam's approach like clockwork, turned their heads, smiled over at him, and giggled. A rush of jealous blood always rose in Cameron's cheeks, but Liam didn't seem to notice. Cameron thumped the side door.

'It's almost two. Where have you been? Never mind, get in here. My Mom left us egg sandwiches.' They ate in silence. 'You're not backing out, Cameron. Don't be a wuss.'

'I said I'd go. But if it snows?'

'We can do snow. When we get there, I'm sawing – you're lookout, so be alert. I'm the one breaking the law. This has to be quick and fast.'

'I got that, ten times ago,' Cameron shot back, pulling at the cuff of his work shirt. Both boys wore remarkably similar clothes: bright, heavily-worked sneakers, saggy jeans that hung on their bottoms, tees under checkered work shirts, dark hoodies, and jackets they grabbed ten minutes before they walked out to the garage. Cameron reached for his bike helmet. 'No!' Liam said adamantly. 'Not cool.'

The pecking order was established. The boys shouldered the backpacks, slouching by habit with the weight, pulled up their hoodies, walked the bikes out and Liam locked the garage. They raced down 39th Avenue to the bike path bordering the Saint Lawrence River and turned left.

The afternoon was heavily overcast. Mist rose from the roads. It was seven degrees on the good side of zero. Drizzle had turned to rain, and the afternoon appeared later than three o'clock. The dark figures pedalled hard on strong legs. Birdhouses marking the path and the stone Fur Trade Museum went unnoticed. The boys rode over narrow wooden bridges at full tilt, but slowed down past the first locks of the canal when they reached the four corners of the path that had taken out pros. The bike path veered onto St. Joseph Boulevard into the center of Lachine's new infrastructure. Lachine had re-established itself and was buzzing with energy. The boys zigzagged past pedestrians carrying umbrellas and regained their speed once they were back on the path.

Forty-three minutes later they braked. Mounds of wet slippery ice stood between them and the tunnel. 'There's no path?'

'Do you see one?' Liam answered harshly to mask his apprehension. The ice was everywhere. 'Follow me, slide your feet along the ice and use your bike for support. Don't lean too heavily on it, or you'll wipe out.'

'You should have thought of skates.' The jab went nowhere. Cameron slid one foot forward, almost falling. 'Man!' He tried the other, clutching his bike, and inched ahead unsteadily.

'Nobody's around,' Liam called back, for he was well ahead of Cameron who almost fell a second time.

'Only dumb asses would come here today,' Cameron mumbled, slipping and sliding.

Liam reached the old road leading down to the tunnel. His heart slumped. 'Damn!' Just seven days ago his online friend Glen had told him the gates were secured by a simple lock! The tunnel lay stunted, deep in the grip of ice and neglect like remains of antiquity. It was choked, not by a lock, but by three-foot cement blocks, piled on top of each another. Three at the base, two on the center and one on top. 'Shit!' Liam growled.

A minute later Cameron joined him; relief spread behind his eyes. 'Look at the graffiti on the side walls. Epic!'

They laid the bikes down, took off their backpacks, unzipped them and grabbed their phones. Liam took his father's new lithium flashlight. Getting to their knees, they snagged photos. 'This is neat, but I'm climbing those blocks. The graffiti is even better inside. Seen it online.'

'You're crazy. You don't even know if there's ice on them.'

When Liam turned to Cameron, he saw that he was soaked. The hoodie, like his own, was plastered to Cameron's head. 'I'm going down.'

Cameron watched as Liam half slid half ran down the embankment.

'No ice! Comin'?' Liam climbed easily to the top cement block and flashed his light through the bars. 'You should see the walls. Come on. It's like a movie set. It's probably been used for that. This is more than epic.'

'I don't have a death wish.'

Liam smirked and worked his way slowly back up the hill. 'You're not out of this. Remember the towers I told you about. One's on either side. We just have to get there.' Liam took his bike, hoisted his pack and began his slip and slide towards the first tower which was surrounded with treacherous ice. Liam slid down to the side of the tower wall and held on for support. Another cement block barred their entrance to a wide wooden door. *Ha!* 'Get over here! There's hope.' On the top right side someone had sawed a square large enough for a climber to get through. Dangling from a tree was a cable that ran through the opening. 'That work is new, has to be. I hope we're alone.'

'What?'

'Do you see the cable? There's no ice on the cement. I'll wait for you. I'll hold the light, you shoot the pics.'

'I'm not climbing into a hole.'

'Just get your ass up here.' Liam offered his hand and pulled Cameron up beside him. 'Good. I'm taking the first look.' He shone the light at the top wall and then he angled it down. 'Oh shit! Oh shit!' Liam leaned inside for a better view. His right foot began to kick the door. 'Shit!'

'What?'

'There's a dead chick at the bottom,' Liam whispered, backing off.

'Are you juicin' me? Give me the light.'

Liam began pounding the door.

'Wow! Jees! A body. Is she dead? I can't tell if she's moving.' Cameron lost all fear in avid curiosity, aimed the light on the face and found eyes looking right back at him. He shot back so quickly he dropped the flashlight, scraped his arm and fell off the block. He yelped in pain. 'We are in some deep shit!'

'You fucker! You dropped my father's flashlight.'

Cameron had scrambled to his feet. 'I'm outta here. My father's gonna kill me if he finds out. I'm outta here,' he repeated. He didn't see Liam jump and grab him.

'We have to call the police, Cameron – we can't just leave. She might be unconscious. It's not right – we can't just take off.'

'Those eyes that looked back at me were dead. They were dead! I'm gone.'

'What about the flashlight?'

'How can the cops trace it back to you? We're not in the system. I'm done if my dad finds out.' Cameron crawled up the incline. 'I really hurt my knee.' He wasn't aware of his arm. 'We gotta get out of here. This is wicked bad.'

Liam followed. 'We are both in shit!' The boys ran and fell as they left the ice, jumped on their bikes and flew back across the path home. They never spoke another word. Liam fell, striking his head on the corner of the last wooden bridge. He got to his feet panting.

Cameron braked hard to miss a collision. 'Your chin's bleeding.'

Somehow, Liam felt better about the blood, felt good he'd hurt himself. He got on his bike. Three houses from home, he saw his father's truck in the driveway. Liam began to cry. He knew instantly what he had lost. His father's words stung his ears before he heard them. *How could you leave...* Liam wished he was thirteen again.

Chapter Two

Liam dropped his bike by the side door. He was crying. 'Pa!' he shouted. 'Pa!'

Cameron was no fool. His parents weren't home, and he wasn't about to take the blame for Liam's plan. He caught up with Liam before he could shut the door and pushed his way through behind his friend.

Joseph Castonguay ran up the basement stairs. He saw drenched bodies that looked like wet groundhogs, then blood, then Cameron, and switched to English. 'What happened, Liam?' There was an alarming calm to his tone. He turned instinctively to eight-year-old Alexanne who had run up the stairs behind him. He had fetched her from a friend's on his way home. 'Dans ta chambre, Pouce!' He watched Alexanne stomp up to her room in full pout before turning his attention to Liam.

'Pa, Pa, we found a dead body, I banged my head…' Liam's words ran headlong into one another. He couldn't breathe or recognize his own voice. The sounds rasped and raced.

'Arrête!' Joseph wanted to speak his own language, but he needed the full story. 'Take off those wet clothes. Don't take another step on your mother's clean floors.' Liam shed everything but his boxers and undershirt. Cameron followed suit. Joseph raised Liam's chin with his hand and took a good look at the cut. He left the boys huddled by the door, guilty and forlorn. He returned with a wet facecloth and suture Band-Aids he had left over from a cut at work. 'You'll live. Get up to the kitchen, boys. Liam, take your time and tell me exactly what happened.'

'Cameron lost your flashlight and…' The words ran together in a garbled mess.

'Stop, Liam. A dead body? Start with that. Now.' Dread crept into his father's voice.

Liam's left leg began to shake. 'Okay, Son. Calm down and speak slowly.'

'We found a dead woman in the Wellington Tunnel,' Cameron interjected quietly, looking down at the floor. The top of his knee had a good size bruise. The boys sat, clasping their arms and shivering. 'My arm's scraped.' Cameron said, hoping the bruises could excuse their actions.

Liam ignored that. 'We don't even know if she's dead – we just ran. I wanted to call, but…'

Cameron was crying now. 'I saw dead eyes. I saw them, Mr. Castonguay. I just wanted to get out of there. She had to be dead, right? I mean if she was moving, I would have... There was brown stuff at the side of her mouth. She had to be dead...'

'You chicken-shit!' Liam lashed out. 'You just wanted out – you didn't care.'

'Have either of you ever seen a dead person?'

The boys dropped their heads.

Joseph looked at his son. '*You* didn't call for help, Liam?' he asked incredulously. Joseph reached into his back pocket for his phone. 'I'm calling 911. You'll speak to the police immediately, Liam.'

'But, Pa.'

'You abandoned a woman who might have needed your help, might still need help. I am ashamed of you.' His father's voice was flat. He tapped in the emergency number and handed Liam the phone.

He stood rigidly on his bare feet, wiping his tears with the back of his hand. He looked young and lost. What could be worse than his father's shame?

'911. Is this an emergency?'

'Yes.'

Nicole Lambert was the most valued responder. She tweeted, texted and tracked all related news. The senior shields often told her she should have been a cop. Lambert was fifty-seven and bytes beyond her juniors. 'Go ahead.'

'Me and my friend found a woman's dead body at the bottom of one of the towers at the Wellington Tunnel an hour ago. She wasn't really old.'

'Name, address and the location of the body.'

'Liam Castonguay.' He gave his address and described the tower beside the Wellington Tunnel, and the ice.

'Stay on the line while I transfer the call. It might take a few minutes.' Nicole had one of her bad feelings. A Concordia University student had been reported missing that morning. No other such reports had been issued in the last two days. She put the call through to Major Crimes.

Lieutenant Detective Toni Damiano picked up and listened, pushing aside a mound of paperwork on a fatal stabbing that had occurred behind a bar on St-Laurent Boulevard. The suspect had been arrested, and she was closing the file. 'A body of a woman has been found at the Wellington Tunnel. And we have a student, a Taylor Sanderson, reported missing this morning. Does the name Trevor Sanderson ring a bell?'

'The lawyer on the construction investigation?'

'Yes. Taylor is his daughter. We don't treat the rich better, so we say... I think it's worth a look. I've dispatched a bus and Crime, and alerted them about the ice. I hope it's not the twenty-two-year-old. I have one of my feelings. If it is the girl, I thought you'd want to be on it. I'll put the kid through.'

'Lieutenant Detective Damiano. Please repeat what you told the responder.'

Liam looked at his father and the support brought about a transformation that only kids can accomplish. He was concise and thorough. Joseph gave his son a nod, but he was alarmed.

'Is a parent with you now?'

'Yes, my father.'

'Hand him the phone.'

'Joseph Castonguay.'

'Lieutenant Detective Damiano. I must interview the boys in your presence. Please keep the friend there with you and contact his parents. Crime will need to collect the clothes the boys were wearing. To save time, I'll come to your home with a technician for the clothes and the elimination prints.'

'The boys are not involved. I don't see...'

'Routine procedure, Sir. I appreciate the call and will see you tonight.'

'Any idea of the time?'

'I will try to be there around eight.'

'I see.' Joseph put the phone back on its station and turned to the boys. 'You took a hacksaw, my hacksaw? The detective is coming here tonight to interview both of you. Did you use the hacksaw on that opening? This is serious, boys.'

'No! Pa, Glen told us we would need it butI never took it out of the backpack.'

'I know you're both scared, but I need the truth.'

'No! I swear!'

'Okay. Cameron, call your parents.' Joseph covered his face with both hands. When he did speak, there was a marked weariness to his voice. 'Boys, this adventure is a very serious matter. It's far from over. Taking my things without permission and deceiving us will be dealt with later.'

'It was all Liam's plan, all he ever thought about – I didn't even want to go.'

Joseph was thirty-eight years old and he could recall the risks he'd taken as a kid. Liam was definitely his son. 'Cameron, let's settle down. You decided to run – Liam wanted to call. I'd say that squares things. For now, we wait. Your mother's had a long day. She didn't need this.' Joseph began to pace. 'Do you know this Glen character?'

'No, Pa. He was on a site. He rock climbs and searches for tunnels. I tweeted him and he answered. We emailed a few times. He told me about the lock and that I needed a saw. That's it, I swear. I never met him. I only know his site.'

'He could have been dangerous, still could be. We've told you about hazards on the Internet.'

'I never met him! I swear, Pa.'

'I thought you and I had something special, Liam. I'm disappointed.' Joseph left the boys. As he climbed the stairs, he heard the scurrying of little feet. *Pouce.* A shower would feel good, but he didn't want his wife Isabelle finding the boys alone and frightened. He soaped his hands and forearms, and splashed water on his face. He toweled his goatee, grabbed a handful of curly hair, and began to twist bits of his hair, a twitch that helped keep his fiery temper in check. Not every man suited a goatee, he did. Joseph's eyes were clear; his face and hands had the color of a man who worked outdoors, had the energy and warmth of sun and rain. He knew life differently from men who shuffled papers or wore three-piece suits. Joseph managed two cemeteries in the West Island. He knew how to build with his hands and tend to cemetery gardens. Isabelle once said, 'When I jump into your arms, I know you won't drop me.' His wife and children were his love. The dead had taught him the value of minutes. He oversaw the burying of infants, teenagers, young adults and seniors. Death was random. Ends were final. He never forgot the words on a woman's monument: *Live and Love Fully.* He quickly gathered clothes for the boys and headed back down.

From what he could see, they hadn't said one word. Liam was picking at the side of the table. Cameron was chewing his little finger. Joseph put the clothes on the kitchen table. 'Use these for now.' He laid his hand on Liam's shoulder. 'Is this the first time you went to the tunnel?'

Liam's eyes blurred. 'I swear, Pa. It's the first time and the last.' Tears rolled from his eyes. Cameron's eyes teared up.

'We're past tears, boys.'

Chapter Three

Lieutenant Detective Damiano sat in her glassed-in office behind her desk, bent over, rubbed her arm and winced. Exhaling, she sat back up and picked up the phone. When she was through, she called Detective Pierre Matte and brought her partner on board.

At the Crémazie Division of Major Crimes, she was the only detective with a measure of privacy. The large room was open plan. She made certain there were no personal items in her office. Curiosity came with the badge, and she offered up nothing for the gossip mill. Men weren't as tight-lipped as people thought. That day nine detectives were at their desks. Three had called in sick. Four had rolled their chairs closer to each other to share dirty jokes Damiano couldn't hear. Two new shields kept their eyes on files and tried not to smile. The room reeked of bad coffee and men's cologne. They all wore jeans and sweaters to protest Bill 3, the Pension Reform Bill the government was determined to pass that would impact police officers, fire fighters and other city workers. Jokes mitigated their anger at losing money they felt they'd already paid. They wore red caps that read *Libre Négo*. Officers had also begun taking turns calling in sick.

Detective Matte worked at the far end of the room. He was on his feet before Detective Damiano reached his desk. His gelled hair was closely cropped with just a hint of gray at the temples. His features were sculpted and almost too smooth. He had lively blue eyes and a wary smile. He liked Damiano – she was an easier fit than the jocks. He wore jeans and a coordinated blue denim shirt, but there was always something too neat about Matte.

Casual looked good on Damiano with her tight black jeans and a fitted scarlet shirt open at her neck, and black Sketchers sneakers. She carried a Michael Kors bag on her shoulder, with the red cap tucked inside it. Her thick dark hair was pulled behind her ears. She wore little makeup, but was definitely 'a package.' The guys never noticed her bling. Whether she liked it or not, at five foot ten, she had a commanding presence and drew eyes whenever she left her office. Her gait was elegant and provocative. As she walked over to Matte, one of the older shields got brave.

'Detective, do you practice that walk?'

Damiano answered with fine precision. 'It's all natural, gutter minds,' she fired back without turning her head.

'Wow!' One of the new shields couldn't help himself.

Damiano rolled her eyes when she reached Matte.

'Are you up for this case, everything considered?' asked Matte.

'Are you suggesting I've capped my career at street stabbings and easy files?' They had both left the room and were heading to Chief Donat's office.

'It's another young person, might be too soon is all, Toni.'

'I'm dealing with the aftermath,' she said adamantly. 'I won't be lost on the sidelines either. Anyway, we might be looking at an accidental and then we'd be out of it. Still, it's strange that anyone but a homeless person would climb alone into the tunnel. CTV's *Hidden Montreal* series revealed the city's three hundred tunnels. My son Luke was talking about tunnels a few weeks ago. Some info should stay hidden.'

'Let's run this by the chief. It's his call.'

Chief Donat was in the hall talking to another detective. 'No protest stickers on our cars! That's final. We deal first-hand with the public at difficult times. We're professionals. If the boots are not serving tickets, we'll be included in the backlash. Still, we can't interfere.' He was wearing a small red cap that sat on the top of his head because it added three inches to his meager five-foot-six frame. Chief Donat was burdened with *small man* twitches: shouting, hand motions, brusqueness and grudges. He was also a good cop and a decent man. When he saw Detective Damiano, he slipped into his office and sat on the tall chair behind his desk. He felt any man standing beside Damiano appeared shorter than he was. He waved them inside with two fingers, pointed to the chairs and felt better when they were seated. The jacket of his suit hung on a rack by the door. He wore red suspenders over a crisp white shirt. Damiano thought he looked smaller with the suspenders. The chief was wiry and never seemed to gain a pound. He had a sallow complexion, and cheeks that bore the scars of old pockmarks. The walls boasted a collage of photos of Donat and the mayor, important functionaries and professional athletes. Damiano looked briefly at his diplomas and commendations that hung on the wall behind his desk.

The chief wasted no time. 'I do want a team at the tunnel. Detective Matte, will you give me a few minutes with Detective Damiano?'

Matte nodded diplomatically and left, closing the door.

Chief Donat leaned forward. 'How's the arm?'

'Lets me know it's there.'

'It's been eight months since you lost that kid. It'll eat you alive. You gotta let it go. Sleeping?'

'Better.'

'Where'd you put the medal from Ottawa?'

'Under sweaters in a bottom drawer.'

'Good. The guilt?'

She admired and hated that Donat understood her. 'It's an ache in my conscience,' she admitted. 'Not all the time.'

He leaned closer. 'What were you thinking when you lunged to grab the kid?'

Tears welled in her eyes. 'He was so pitiful, so lost. I thought I could pull him back inside and... but I didn't and that...'

Chief Donat had the answer he wanted from his detective. 'Hindsight is overrated and not always accurate. Guilt is selfish and *ifs* a waste. We work with facts, Detective. Remember this. If your arm hadn't imploded, you wouldn't be here today. You risked your life as well as the kid's.

'Now, we may be dealing with a homicide here. A dead university student from a prominent family – I'm hoping to avoid national media attention. I want you and Matte to work the case. Get out to the Wellington Tunnel and keep me informed.'

'Always, Chief.' Matte was on his phone in the hall. 'We're on, Pierre. Will you drive? Is the Decarie Expressway the fastest route?'

Matte chose not to correct Damiano on the spot. Instead he waited until they were in the black Buick in the underground parking. 'The quickest and most direct route is south on St-Denis and through Old Montreal.' As they drove under the Metropolitan Expressway, Matte turned on the flashers and hit the siren.

'You know that from your GPS?'

'No, I was checking out the tunnel. I worked as a courier while at university and got to know the city.'

'Ah, that's where your detail radar began.'

'More admiration for detail. Old Bernie was my tutor. I heard about him on my first courier job. I had three in all. The story was that he had dropped out of school at fourteen and was a messenger for CN delivering telegrams in the 1950s. If you give me an address, I can get you within a few blocks. Apparently Bernie could tell you who lived there! When he got sick and began losing weight, guys kind of helped him out, did some deliveries and got him food. He died of cancer, still trying to work and earn. Always happy, that was Bernie's legend.'

'You're his disciple, carrying on his tradition. But enough history. Let's gun it! I want to get to the tunnel!'

Rue St-Denis was a traffic bottleneck. Affected by adjacent street construction, pot holes, double-parked delivery trucks and drivers pulling out into the traffic without signaling made for a hellish commute. Flashers and sirens had little chance to make headway. Matte knew how to ride the road. 'Calm down, Toni. We're almost in Old Montreal.' He also knew there were closures along Avenue Viger, so he took the slower Rue Notre-Dame and ignored Damiano's grumbling.

Damiano bit her lip and felt the buzz of a new challenge. She began to formulate her questions for Marie Dumont who led the crime unit. The two worked well together. Matte picked up speed in Old Montreal. The bad weather had kept diners home. When they passed the Steak Frites restaurant, she knew they were almost there. Matte made a few illegal turns on Ottawa Street and parked.

When Damiano opened her door, she swore. 'Ice and rain!'

'I have boots and a huge umbrella in the back of the car – want them?'

'You would, and yes.' The boots were loose, but they'd do just fine.

As they neared the embankment, Matte took Damiano's arm. She was about to pull away when she saw the field of ice. They used their flashlights, and Damiano saw that one of the city trucks must have spread sand. 'Over there!' she steered Matte.

In the near distance, they saw lights and white makeshift tents and worked their way over. 'They built this tunnel in the 1930s...'

'Never mind the history lesson.' Ahead, trucks and an ambulance were parked on the ice. Two Crime techs, clothed in white from head to toe, appeared to skate on the ice. No one seemed to be speaking. The scene was quiet and surreal, like a distant carnival of tents. The rain had turned to a fine mist. Lights had been set at the sides of the tunnel. Both detectives gawked at the arresting display of graffiti on the outer walls, which continued with a massive display inside the tunnel. But it wasn't the time for artistic appreciation. They were there to investigate the crime scene at the base of a tower, where a young woman had met her death. 'Marie must be in the tunnel,' Damiano whispered.

Chapter Four

As Detective Damiano and Detective Matte entered the tunnel, the spectacular graffiti continued. It was almost like entering some ancient tomb, Damiano thought. Marie Dumont of Crime, in white protective gear, met them outside the tower and handed them white booties. The forensics techs had completed their work of marking, gathering and bagging, and stood by quietly as the detectives performed their own investigation. The Crime photographer had videotaped the scene, taken stills and the customary two Polaroids.

'Sanderson?'

Marie nodded.

They approached a T-junction in the tunnel. With the kid in her head Damiano worked to get a grip on herself. Around the corner, to the right of the tunnel, the graffiti ended. Tripods of high-intensity lights illuminated a dark, sullen tower. Paramedics, two patrol cops, and techs stood outside the tower to allow Damiano and Matte needed space. Dumont followed. The body was eerily lit and the chalk outline around it visible. Damiano walked carefully until she stood at the foot of the body. Sanderson had landed flat on her back. Her right hand was caught under her buttocks; her right leg was twisted at an unnatural angle, folded under her left knee. Her eyes looked straight up but milky, frozen and dead. Damiano felt a buzzing behind her eyes, felt her vision blurring, *saw the kid falling from her grasp, saw him looking up at her when...* The terror rushed back and she gasped.

Matte had been watching her. 'You'll be alright,' he whispered. He pointed to a backpack a few feet away and the flashlight which lay beside the girl's foot.

She touched Matte's arm in thanks. 'The flashlight belonged to the kids who found her. One of them dropped it when he saw the body.' Damiano studied the girl's clothes. The blue ThermoBall North Face jacket was stained at the collar with blood that had left a trail down the side of the girl's mouth. The jacket was hitched up on the right side of her hip. Damiano looked up at the opening of the tower. The jacket must have caught on the jagged wood. She recognized the boots, the popular Australian Uggs the kids wore. Still, there was so little visible body damage that she felt the girl would get up and walk away. She appeared to be sleeping – not dead, just still. Damiano walked around to the girl's head, slipped on white gloves and reached for a pen. She raised the thick, matted blonde hair to calculate blood loss. She didn't need Dumont to tell her the girl was still alive after the fall, still breathing, and choking. Damiano's scalp began to itch.

Matte was taking notes for both of them.

Damiano rotated her head around her shoulders, heard the grind of calcium and took a deep settling breath. She needed the control she had lost eight months ago, and the confidence. More significant, Damiano felt the death of someone so young somehow had to be more than an accident. 'Okay, Marie, tell us what you have.'

'The paramedics pronounced at the scene. The TOD is just an estimate. Couldn't find a watch.'

Damiano couldn't help herself. 'Marie, kids don't wear watches today – they use their phones.'

'Fine, but her phone is still working, so that was no help. The pathologist, most probably Belmont for this case, will better determine the LTD in his *post mortem*. The temperature fluctuated a lot over these last three days. She's not ripe yet due to the two cold nights. *Rigor* has come and gone, so that's at least thirty-six hours. The voicemail on the phone is full. We found cash and cards in her bag, and she was wearing a Pandora charm bracelet fully loaded. It wasn't robbery. First viewing, I don't see any sexual assault, but Belmont might find something. Genital injuries are not immediately apparent.'

'I know from the blood she survived the fall – the landing, I mean. Why couldn't she help herself?' Damiano asked, guessing she already knew.

'I'm Crime, Toni, not Pathology.'

Matte offered what he sensed. 'She broke her neck and the spinal injury paralyzed her from the neck down. Is that your thought, Marie?'

'Yes, and the paramedics as well. She couldn't move her head and suffocated on her own blood.'

No one spoke. Damiano rubbed her eyes, Dumont and Matte looked down at the body, sharing the right mix of anger and empathy. *What a terrible way to die, alone and helpless.*

'Marie, is there a chance this was an accident?'

'That's the question.'

'And?'

'Her hands show no signs of struggle. Her face isn't bruised. It's not a suicide. The drop is not high enough for certain death. I have…'

'Damn, I told MsPers it was our call. Was I wrong?'

'Hold on, Toni. I have three initial findings. First, a blood smear on her Lauren backpack. I'd expect to see blood spatter, blood droplets that flew when she struck her head, but not a smear. She'd have to have touched the pack, and I don't think she could move. Had she been able, she would have sat up to cough, or simply turned her head to the side and prevented suffocation. Prelim on my part. Belmont will certify after his autopsy.'

'Suspicious then?'

'I'm not through. We've cut the cable and we'll check for prints, hers and others.'

'There shouldn't be that many because the cable has been up for less than a week, Marie.'

'Good to hear. We found blood on the wood at the top of the opening and a slight trace on the bottom. If she struck her head while trying to climb down…'

'You said it wasn't an accident.'

'Calm down. Secondly, if that was the case, blood would not have seeped through her thick hair that quickly. My theory for now is that our victim may have been struck outside the tower and dumped. We now have to find the *locus* of the assault. We've cordoned off the area outside the tower and we'll be back tomorrow with heat blowers for the ice. Leave a patrol officer tonight to preserve the crime scene. If the weapon was discarded, we'll find it. Water doesn't get rid of blood.'

'Will do. Did you find evidence of trespass inside the tunnel?'

'The cliché squatting derelict? No, we didn't. The cable wasn't set up by a homeless man either. It was high quality stuff and secured with good material. Adventurers, twenty-somethings or younger, I'm guessing. I was saving my last point. If we don't find the victim's prints on the cable, then we pretty much know she was dumped.'

The girl had officially become the victim and lost her identity.

Matte had the evidence neatly written and recorded. He knew he'd be sharing his notes with Damiano who did make a good stab at the process, but habitually gave it up midway through ta case.

'We need a tech. Matte and I have to interview the kids who found the victim. I want swabs taken and their clothes sent to the lab. We then have to inform the parents.' The photographer stepped forward and handed over both Polaroids.

'You can tell the parents that we are treating the death as suspicious for *now*. I don't envy you the job of informing them. Losing a child – nothing's worse.'

Chapter Five

The rain was falling in sheets by the time the detectives, huddling together under the umbrella, made the treacherous walk and slide back to their car. It was an ugly night. Damiano sat sideways on the front seat, handed Matte the boots and with a few twists and pulls was back in her sneakers. She flipped the sun visor down and did the best she could with her hair. As soon as Matte was seated, she asked, 'You wouldn't happen to have a towel in the trunk?'

'I have a cotton blanket that might do, and water.'

'May I use it and beg some water? I want to appear presentable tonight and that's not easy in this weather. How did you know to have all that stuff?'

'Prep – one never knows, right?'

Matte was good to have on the team, she had to admit. When she finished towelling off her hair and brushing it into place, she reached back for her jacket and folded it on her knees. 'Thanks for the support tonight, Pierre. I thought I was past the nerves.'

'We could hand off if that's what would be best.'

'Dammit no! I want the case. I'll get by the mess in my head. I have to move on, or quit, and that's not an option. Understand?'

'Think so.' Matte removed a phone from a plastic bag that was in his pack. 'It's been dusted. We can go through her last calls before we meet the parents.'

'*I* should have thought of that. Part of me is still stuck in that hospital room – I can't pull myself out. There's something wrong with me, but I want the case. I want my life back. I should have let things go by now. Dammit to hell!'

'There's always been something wrong with you.'

A roaring belly laugh escaped Damiano. 'You're right, you are right.'

'Any good cop is screwed up in one way or another.'

'I accept the compliment, I think. At least, I'm out of my funk for now. I'd like you to interview one of the boys, I'll handle the other. Can you see if the tech is still behind us? I gave him the address.'

'He's with us.'

'Alright. I see two major issues with the boys. First, is this their first time at the tunnel? Second, did either one of them climb down to the victim? Obviously our victim was dead before the boys got there. It's too bad we're in a business where people lie to us, for whatever their reasons. Teenagers are pros at that game. We also have to know everything they touched for elimination and transfer prints. That's why I need the swabs, prints and clothes. Matte, you know that old cop adage, the clean get cleaner and…'

'I know it.'

'Let's also see if their stories correspond.'

Matte made a left turn up 39th Avenue. The home was the fifth on the right side. No home looks good in fog and rain, except for the tri-color brick house with the pitched roof and lighted windows where they had just parked. It was cosy and solid and somehow hinted at a time long past. 'My mother kept her *Dick and Jane* readers. This house could have been in it. Do you see the little girl up there, looking down at us? Oops! Too late, she ducked down.' They noticed the long driveway and the black truck as they walked up the path to the porch. Matte held onto the railing, but the shovel by the front door with traces of snow told Damiano that the walk had been cleaned for them.

Joseph Castonguay opened the front door and the brown screen door before they rang. His eyes were wary with concern. '*Bonsoir, entrez s'il vous plaît.*'

Damiano snapped out of her reminiscing mood and felt a familiar energy surge. It was mandatory to understand every piece of evidence. Her French was good, but she admitted only to herself that she still missed the odd word. 'Lieutenant Detective Damiano.'

'I'm Detective Matte and this is Jean Lepine from Crime.'

Joseph's eyes opened wider and he took a step back when he saw Damiano. Tension and fatigue dropped away, and he managed a smile. 'Please follow me. Don't bother with your shoes. The floor's been wet three times today.' Joseph switched to English because of Cameron and his father. His wife stood at the bottom of the stairs with her arm around her daughter. Both were near tears and tiptoed up the stairs, but the girl looked back at Damiano. Joseph led them into the kitchen that smelled of Kraft Dinner, toast, and wet socks. Damiano felt a twinge of emotion for the life reflected here – one she had never known, a life she had not created in her own home.

The boys sat with their elbows on the table and their faces cupped in their hands. Both cast a side glance as Damiano led the threesome into the room. Cameron's father, Stephen Miller, introduced himself.

Damiano got down to business. 'Boys, we appreciate the call. That's the first thing. Now our Crime officer will take your prints and mouth swabs and gather your clothes. We'll have them back to you as soon as possible.'

Stephen Miller stepped forward. 'Isn't this extreme, Detective? The boys didn't do anything. They alerted *you* to the accident, and they're not involved! I fail to see why…'

'Necessary procedure, Sir. We want to eliminate the boys from the investigation.'

Damiano stared Miller down until he stopped protesting. 'When that's done, I'd like Detective Matte to interview your son in your presence, Mr. Miller.'

Joseph admired Damiano's presence. He respected strength in a woman. 'I set up a table and chairs, in case.'

'Thank you. Good thinking.'

'We fathers must be present during the questioning,' Joseph said with authority. 'That's the law.'

Damiano signalled for Crime to get to work.

Cameron, with tensed fists, called out to Damiano. 'I scratched my arm on the opening when I dropped the flashlight. I got some blood here.' He pulled up his shirt and held out his arm. 'That's all I did, I swear!' He gave Liam a sharp kick under the table when Lepine was taking their prints. Its message was clear. *Snitch!*

Liam didn't move. He'd settle with his hang-buddy. He breathed easier when his father sat down beside him. Damiano sat across from them, and Liam squirmed when she turned on her digital recorder to record his answers. He identified himself and waited for her questions.

'Lying to a police officer is very serious, Liam, so consider your answers carefully. Did you ever cycle down to the tower before today to check it out, even a quick check? Remember, people always leave trace evidence for Crime to find.'

'Never!'

'Why today?'

'They're going to demolish the tunnel soon and today is a ped day. My parents weren't home, so we had to go today, or miss it.' Liam stole a glance at his father.

'Did you touch the cable?'

'Yes. I wanted to see how strong it was.'

Damiano lowered her voice to a whisper. 'Did you climb down to have a better look at the body?'

'NO! NO!' Liam shouted. 'I only had one quick look. I wanted to call for help, I did, honestly, but we freaked. Cameron fell off the block and we ran.' He hung his head.

Lepine appeared with the bagged hacksaw.

Damiano spoke emphatically. 'Did you cut the opening and set up the cable?'

Liam's shoulders stiffened. He looked back at his father before answering. 'I'm sorry, Dad. I thought there'd be a lock. That's what that Glen told me. But we found those cement blocks instead. I never used the saw, Detective. I didn't need it. The opening and the cable were already there. I swear that. I never used the saw! You can tell, right, at your labs, you'll see it wasn't used.'

'You were ready to break the law, Liam?' Damiano changed tack.

'Glen said it wasn't a big deal 'cause there was no sign. We thought we could outrun the cops. I was so stupid. I thought no one would see us.' Liam seemed to shrink when he heard himself.

'Who is this Glen?'

Liam explained his online friend who found and explored tunnels. 'I was surfing and found his website, glen&tunnels.com.' He was going to be with them at first, but he had to be in New York for work. 'He told me about the lock. He works downtown and he offered to check out the site for us over a week ago.'

'Do you have a number for him?'

'No, just the website – I never met him.' Liam wished he'd had his phone that was still in his backpack because he'd find the website right then. Prove what he was saying was true.

Damiano noted down the link.

'Did you touch the body?' She was almost whispering again.

'We never went near it. Well, not till Cameron dropped Dad's flashlight. He fell and then we ran.'

'Do you want to add anything, Liam? Now's your chance.'

Liam dropped his head into both hands. 'No, except I fell coming home, but that doesn't matter much now. I'm sorry – I'm sorry, Dad.'

Matte had finished and waited by the front door with the Millers. Joseph had forgotten about Damiano's appearance. He saw them to the door, locked up and came back to the kitchen.

Liam was wiping away tears with his fists. 'Dad, I'm sorry.'

'Go to bed, son.'

Chapter Six

'The kid looked so much younger than Luke. He's almost sixteen, going on twenty. Liam is just a kid.' Damiano stared out at the rain and mused. *The dead grab hold of us like gum on new shoes.* 'The other kid is a piece of work, Toni, so let's wait for the elimination prints.'

'You're right. I'm just...'

'A little lost?'

'I don't recall people getting to me like this, Pierre. Did they?'

'Keep in mind you almost died! You're vulnerable, but you're easier to be with. Did you ever go to that counseling?'

'Do you think I'd let anyone screw around with my head? I may be off, but it's my off.' Damiano flicked him the finger and tapped in the chief's number. The chief listened and didn't give her a hard time. Was the chief going soft on her too? She'd set him straight. *I'm good or damn near it!*

'Suspicious for now then.'

'Yes, till the lab checks for her prints on the cable and works with the smear on her pack.'

'See the Sandersons tonight.' Chief Donat said. 'I can't risk leaks getting out before you inform the parents. You have photos for ID?'

'Polaroids.'

'They're easier on them than actually seeing their daughter. Text me later.'

'Of course.'

Matte took the opportunity to type in their destination on Summit Crescent in Westmount, just to be sure they got it right. They drove back into the city without talking. He looked over at Damiano. He'd never seen her silent, almost morose. He thought it best to leave her be.

These visits were never easy for Damiano. Tonight's was the most difficult she could recall. There was a need, she understood, to follow the ritual that would mark the end of hope, and the onslaught of grief. She looked up at the deep, dark clouds that hung above the city. The rain had turned to a dirty mist. Grief, she'd read, was a worthless emotion that picked at the heart and severed futures. Damiano was a believer – eight months later, she still woke sweating and shaking. Grief was a cancer. She and Matte would search for answers for the *how* and *why* and *who*. But what would they change for the Sandersons? There was no closure for the death of a child. Their only daughter, Taylor Sanderson, twenty-two years old, was dead.

Summit Crescent wound its way up behind the city to a world of luxury homes hidden by a forest of trees and carefully tended shrubbery. One might even feel he had found a country road in the city until he had a peek at the hidden mansions, their lights twinkling in the dark. These city lords looked down on Montreal from private marble balconies. The Boulevard, famous for its old English and luxury stone mansions, lacked its subtlety. Summit Crescent had hidden secrets.

Matte parked. Damiano picked up her bag. 'There's a bird sanctuary right behind us.'

Damiano made no comment. Instead she stopped at the beginning of a winding path that led to a black wrought iron gate, the entrance to a spectacular home. As she opened it, Damiano looked back at Matte, her detail guy.

'European style,' he said, 'with a host of windows for better views.'

'They chose the right road for that.' Damiano stopped short of the door.

'I can do this if you want. Give the bad news quickly and clearly – that's the lesson, so the family doesn't build up false hope.'

She stepped forward and rang a bell that made no sound they could hear. 'I know that, Pierre. I'm ready. I just noticed we're on camera.'

Matte lowered his head.

Trevor Sanderson opened the front door himself. Damiano didn't think he was fifty. He was six foot at least, still in the pale blue fitted shirt he must have worn that day, sleeves rolled to the elbow, with a loose dark blue tie. Tall and slightly hollow-chested, he looked every bit a lawyer – a lean and hungry face, pinched with stress. He was startled momentarily when he saw Damiano, but immediately read Matte for a cop. 'It's good to know the police are involving themselves personally.' He saw the wet shoes, and stalled before he changed his mind. 'Doesn't matter, come on in. These bloody floors should be able to survive a little water. Shari and I have been doing our part.' They left Matte's umbrella at the front door. 'We called hospitals – I even called the morgue. Now, we're contacting neighbors who keep an eye on a few homes we own.' There was no stopping Sanderson. 'These kids! A gap year, gap time. Who ever heard of that nonsense when we were in university? Sorry to be going on, please, sit.' He called out, 'Shari, come to the living room.'

Matte was listening carefully, at the same time taking in the Wedgewood-tiled fireplace with vintage mouldings. He didn't miss the double wood panel doors or the panoramic windows overlooking the city. In the rain he could make out the lines of a spectacular terrace. He didn't waste valuable time on the art, but was waiting for Damiano to break in soon. Was she waiting for the wife?

When Sanderson's wife walked into the room, Damiano and Matte eyed one another. Mother and daughter looked like sisters. It was unsettling. She had to be in her forties, but appeared years younger.

'Good of you to come,' she said formally. Shari Sanderson was about to sit beside her husband on the white plush sofa, but then sat apart. Fidgiting at the cuffs of her tight-fitting black cashmere sweater, she was about to add a thought when she detected something in Damiano's expression that silenced her. Crossing her arms, as if she could protect her heart, she sat up rigidly, and waited. Her eyes never left Damiano's.

Damiano spoke to her. 'I'm very sorry to inform you that we have found your daughter and…'

'And what?' Sanderson shouted, jumping to his feet. 'What? Not possible, we've just begun looking for her.'

A sudden rending scream caught them all off guard. 'TREVOR! For once shut your mouth.' Shari had not taken her attention from Damiano. 'Go on,' she whispered with dread. 'I need to know.'

'For the time being, we are treating her death as suspicious. We're detectives from Major Crimes.'

Sanderson took a step back, as if he'd been punched twice. He turned towards his wife, shook his head, then whipped back around to confront the detectives. His face drained of color, but he fought on. 'Do you know how many times you guys fuck up? I know, not just from this corruption file, but from years enduring the mess you make of due process. I mean…'

'Trevor, please, for me,' his wife pleaded. She had managed to get to her feet and put a hand on his shoulder. 'Look at me.'

'Shari! It can't be. It just can't be. We can't give up.' He pulled away from her.

'We have these photos, Taylor's phone and her backpack.' Damiano thought she'd seen a flash of color disappear from the doorway. Their son Matthew?

Sanderson was stubborn. 'I'm not looking at those. Do you know how many girls look somewhat alike? Look at them Shari! I'm not identifying my Taylor from a photo.'

Shari Sanderson opened her hand and took the photos, trembling. Her groan didn't sound human. The photos fell to the floor as she backed to the sofa and collapsed. 'What happened?' she moaned. 'Tell me what happened.'

Sanderson tore on. 'I want to see my daughter – do you hear me? I have to see her and not from behind some small window. I must be in the same room with her. Shari, you have to come with me. I can't do this alone. We can't just abandon Taylor and accept photos, for God's sake.'

This was not the time to see what she might learn from the Sandersons, including their son. Damiano allowed them their grief and anger, but she fought for control. 'That might not be possible because...'

'Call your chief – set it up! My daughter has been taken to the morgue, right? Contact someone there. I won't accept anything less. I'm leaving with Shari!'

Damiano stepped in his way. 'Mr. Sanderson. You're in no condition to be behind a wheel. If you insist, we will drive you, and have a car take you back home.'

'Shari! Get up.' Sanderson marched over to his wife and pulled her to her feet.

'Matthew?' she wailed.

'He's almost seventeen. I'll speak to him.' Sanderson turned his head toward the door. 'Matthew, I saw you a few minutes ago. Get in here.'

The boy slouched around the corner with his hands in his drainpipe jeans pockets. He was tall and slight and he wore the smallest designer lenses Damiano had ever seen. 'Dad?' he said fearfully. Damiano sensed the teenager was holding something back.

'Son, we haven't time. I'm sure you heard enough. We'll talk when we get home. Right now...'

'So go. I'll be okay.' But he obviously wasn't. His nose was running and his eyes were watery. *They have the phone! Oh man.* Matthew disappeared up the stairs like rising smoke.

Shari Sanderson appeared lost when her husband threw a coat around her shoulders, guiding her out the front door.

Damiano saw Matte throw his hands in the air. Her expression answered *what the hell could I have done?* He lingered behind them, called the morgue, and advised the examiner what to expect. When the overnight examiner complained, Matte cut her off. 'We had no choice,' he whispered.

No one spoke in the car for ten minutes.

'Where did you find Taylor? You keep referring to her as my daughter – she has a name. Try to remember it.'

'In the Wellington Tunnel.' Damiano purposely did not add more information.

'Christ! She's claustrophobic, like Shari.' He slammed his fist on the side door. 'Why didn't you cops think of looking there? Over the years there have been stories. The cops called the tunnel the hole where bodies fall. Ah Tay…' He fell against his wife. The city was still hustling and noisy, but inside the car, the mood was rigidly quiet for the rest of the way.

Chapter Seven

Chief Richard Donat was not a man to waste time. He put a home call in to the morgue's senior pathologist, Michael Belmont. Belmont was the product of a French-Irish marriage. At fifty-seven, he was past trying to influence the politics that came with the job. Apart from his work at the Parthenais Morgue, he had shifts at the Royal Victoria Hospital. The body count at the city morgue stood, on average, at forty-one per year, not enough work for a full-time job. 'It's almost eleven, Richard. I had a busy day.'

'You've heard of Trevor Sanderson.'

'He's part of the Corruption Commission. What's your point? I'm tired.'

'We just found the body of his daughter in the Wellington Tunnel. My detectives informed the parents that we're treating the death as suspicious for now. Sanderson demanded a personal ID at the morgue tonight. Detective Matte is driving the couple there as we speak. If you rush, you'll be there to meet them. We should have the senior pathologist there.'

'My assistants know how to prepare a body. You're rushing us.'

'More than that, Michael, I need you to pull an all-nighter. I don't want media making it appear we're not on top of this case. Joe Public is not supporting our pension protest or many of our tactics of late. We have legal problems as well. I can't afford bad press. We need them on side. Sanderson is distraught and angry. He has powerful connections. I'm not your boss, but I need your help.'

Belmont groaned loudly enough for Donat to hear. 'You owe me, Richard, big time.' Belmont's wife put down her book; she was not pleased. 'Please, Kathy, not you too. I don't have a choice. I'm not happy about this either.'

His wife tossed her book aside and went upstairs fuming, appearing a few seconds later. 'Here, change your shirt.' And tossed it from the landing.

Belmont ran to catch it. *Great!* He packed six Nutri-Grain bars from the kitchen, filled the old thermos he'd used for twenty-one years and took two bananas and an apple. He threw the food into a pack, took his coat, ran his hand through the wispy hair on his scalp and hurried out the door without an umbrella. He kept his head down as he walked the four blocks to the morgue and let himself in by the back door. Vans brought the bodies there, hoisted them onto a steel cart that was wheeled onto a scale before being taken inside the primary examination room.

Belmont spotted Marie Dumont from Crime, standing outside the small room and knew the body had arrived. She was on the phone asking Damiano to stall Sanderson.

'Good of you to come, Michael,' Marie Dumont commented.

'It's not as though I had a choice.'

'I wanted you to see the blood before your assistants cleaned her up for the ID.'

Belmont walked into the room and spoke briefly with one of his assistants. Dumont had followed him. Belmont turned back to her. 'Your prelim, Marie?'

'Blunt force trauma to the back of the skull, but the blood from the mouth suggests she was still alive and then suffocated. I think the victim couldn't move once she hit the tunnel floor. Had she been able to turn her head, she might have survived the fall. When and why are your domain.'

'Rigor?'

'Come and gone.'

'Good work. Shoot me your photos tonight.'

'Of course.' Photos and recordings were never taken with phones. They could be hacked and destroy a case – and careers. 'The Sandersons will be here any second. Damiano had trouble stalling the couple.'

Belmont was about to change into his meds when he heard the whoosh of the elevator door from around the corner. He wished the Chief Coroner were there. He was good with people. Belmont rubbed the bridge of his nose and saw Dumont eyeing his discomfort. He rushed across the room and pulled the green curtain closed. The techs worked quickly and backed into one of the pale yellow autopsy rooms.

Belmont and Dumont hurried from the room and closed the door just as Detectives Damiano and Matte led the Sandersons around the corner. The introductions were brief and muted.

Along the morgue's gray walls and narrow halls, the Sandersons missed the stacked fridges that occupied two rooms, the first for bodies waiting for autopsies, the second, for those already completed. The autopsy rooms stank of plastic and sapped most emotions, even anger, from those who were determined to make personal IDs. Belmont wondered, not for the first time, why humans had to howl at fate, shout out their anger, cast blame and often destroy one another before they accepted reality. We're all doubters like the biblical Thomas, he thought, reaching out to finger the wounds. Rushing down to the morgue had changed nothing. Their daughter was dead.

Although Sanderson supported his wife, to Damiano he appeared fragile. She heard his quick breaths and observed the glassy look in the couples' eyes. She turned directly to them. 'Take a minute before we go inside if you need it,' she said gently.

Sanderson folded his wife into his arms and began weeping. 'I don't want to see Taylor because then I'll know she's gone.'

His wife kept her head buried in Sanderson's shoulder.

'If a photo is easier...' Damiano whispered.

'No!' he cried. 'We can't abandon Taylor. Can't you understand that?' he said hoarsely.

Belmont spoke quietly. 'I'm sorry, but once we're in the room, I can't allow you to touch the body. I'll take you in now.'

Sanderson flinched at the word *body*. The room was small. Matte and Dumont stayed near the door. Covered with two white sheets, Taylor lay on the examining gurney wheeled to the left side of the room. Sanderson caught his wife from falling and almost lifted her towards the gurney. Belmont waited a few seconds, then reached across and slowly pulled down the sheet with both hands.

Sanderson let go of his wife, and Damiano caught her before she fell. 'My little girl – my little girl.' The techs had hidden the greenish-blue markings around the victim's neck. Her eyes had retreated into the skull. There was nothing they could do with the gray, tight, waxy skin, although the cold had helped preserve the remains. Had it been summer, the Sandersons would not have been able to recognize their daughter. Sanderson's shoulders shook in spasms. Belmont had to raise his arm for fear Sanderson would lift his daughter up in his arms, hold her one last time. He was biting his fist when he turned. 'If this wasn't some freak accident, if someone hurt my daughter, find the bastard, Detective! I'll kill him if I get my hands on him first.' He saw his wife. 'Oh Jesus, Shari, I'm sorry. Let's get out of here – I can't bear it!'

Belmont watched. *Kathy wonders why I can't talk about my work. She'd never sleep if I told her of the grief and the horror.* Matte walked back with the couple. Damiano and Dumont had stayed with Belmont, but his thoughts were elsewhere. He had long ago given up questioning. Life was random. What faith he'd salvaged was answers, detailed clues and facts of *how* and *why* some of the mortally wounded had died. His findings mattered because he discovered peace in facts that horrific crime could not destroy. The dead told their story and he wrote it up to avenge them.

Damiano watched Belmont walk back into the examining room. 'Are you up for any overtime tonight, Marie?'

'I'm done – I'm wet and cold. Look, I'll give you two hours and start early tomorrow. Are you hanging around for the autopsy?'

'I'll wait out here. Can't be in the room. I will never subject myself to the grating sucking sounds as Belmont removes a skull. It's too much at this point in my life. Know what? I still see that kid landing on the hood of the car.'

'You have a case of the "creeping ghosts." You're not alone.'

'Do they fade?'

'Don't hang onto things – learn to let go, though most of us can't. This kid Sanderson deserves your best, Toni. Hand off if you're still somewhere else.'

'I am here! I want the fucker who shoved this kid down a hole and left her to die.'

'Well then, do your job.'

'You know I will. At base, I'm okay. Text me anytime with news.' Damiano shivered and walked into the room with Belmont. 'Michael, I'm going to wait outside for your results.'

'Get out and eat first. I don't share my bars. I should have something for you in a few hours. Call me on my private line – I'll open the back door. Let yourself out.'

I need a double vodka straight, a shower, a change of clothes, then food. Some of the tension lifted when she was back in the rain, calling a cab. She'd call Matte and tell him to do the same, minus the vodka, and to meet her back at the morgue in two hours. She'd begin to detail her notebook when she was back at the morgue, time and dates were critical. She was not going to rely on Matte this time out. If called to court, she wanted to read from her own notes. She wanted all in on this case, but for the moment, she wanted to leave the acrid stench of plastic behind. She texted Chief Donat: 'We have a homicide – will be in early tomorrow for the press/media release.'

Belmont opened the door at the end of the room and wheeled the corpse into his 'shop.' He dressed slowly and carefully in his surgeon's meds and laid out his snacks in rows beside the tray of saws and scalpels. He adjusted the lighting, reached for the microphone and pulled it down beside his cheek. He liked working alone, and the silence. To him his work was art. He found his ear buds and iPod in a bottom drawer, and began his ritual by repeatedly playing *Il Silenzio* and *Hallelujah*. A plaintive trumpet for the victim – a remembrance of lost joy for him. A balance.

Chapter Eight

Damiano had the cabbie drop her on the corner of Sherbrooke and Clarke. The rain didn't bother her. A hot shower would fix the damage. She walked up the steep hill and turned onto Anwoth Road. Their home, not far from Greene Avenue and Westmount Park, had been one purchase she and Jeff had agreed upon. Damiano liked the natural stone contrasted with the Kentucky blue grass and yellow begonias, especially in late May. It was kind of a fortress she thought at first, until she felt it was a prison. During their trial separation eight months back, freedom was more compelling. Standing outside in the rain, she wished she was back at the condo which she hadn't seen for months. But there was no way for her to even hint at using it. Jeff had cared for her after the surgery, and they had begun to reboot their marriage. It wasn't the right time to be alone just yet.

It was almost midnight. The home on Anwoth was dark, but that didn't mean Jeff wasn't awake and ready with questions. He should have been a cop and not a pediatrician. She opened the front door as quietly as she could. She didn't notice Jeff until he turned on a lamp behind the french doors. He had been waiting for her in the dark.

'You've found the missing student.'

'Yes.'

'This late must be bad news. I know I can't ask you about the case.'

'I have to shower, change, eat and be back at the morgue asap.'

About to launch into a lecture, he had a change of heart. 'Do your thing. I'll make you a couple of chicken sandwiches.'

Damiano smiled at him. 'I love you for this.'

'Hidden motives; we have to talk.'

It didn't take her long to be standing under the full shower spray, towelling off and blow-drying her hair. She chose a navy business suit and a white camisole. Twenty-five minutes later, she was at the kitchen nook with Jeff, wolfing down a sandwich.

'One day, you'll choke.'

'I'm with a doctor, clever me. Okay, what's up?'

'Luke's been skipping school for the past few weeks, not the whole day, just the last two classes. He forged notes using your chicken scratches that no one can ever read. Luke said he was in therapy for a shoulder injury. His math teacher caught on. He didn't make it home till eleven tonight. That's probably because he knew I'd be waiting for him.'

'Luke's been "up" lately. I thought he had a girlfriend.'

'Well, he's down now. Swore it's not drugs. He's sullen and angry. Teenage angst, I guess. Can you talk to him?'

'You're his father.'

'You're the "hip" parent – he might open up to you. He promised to be back in class and attend all of them.'

'I have to get back, Jeff.'

'I know! I'm just asking you to touch base with him. I'm sure he's not asleep. You're one noisy chick.'

Damiano checked the time on her phone. 'Pack up the other sandwich. I'll brush my teeth and speak to him.' Composing herself for a few seconds, she opened the door, not bothering with the poster *NO VISITORS*. She didn't turn on the light. The hall light cast enough illumination for her to see that Luke was on his side and therefore not asleep. Had he been on his stomach with one foot stuck out, he'd have been long gone. 'Luke, I only have a few minutes.'

Luke grabbed his pillow and crushed it over his head. 'I'm going back to school, isn't that enough?' he mumbled hoarsely.

He's been crying. 'I just want to know you're okay.'

Luke shot up out of the bed. 'I did a stupid thing – now I'll go back to being my boring self at a boring school! This is the first offence, Detective – a good slap on the wrist is all I need. Happy?'

'You don't want to talk.'

'Wow! Another medal for my detective mom.'

'I want a hug – then I'll leave you alone.'

'Since when? I'm almost sixteen! I'm not a fucking baby.'

'Watch your mouth.' Damiano marched across the room and grabbed Luke in her arms. She was surprised he didn't pull away. When she reached the door, she turned, 'I trust you to work it out.'

Luke was still standing watching her. She couldn't tell if he was crying. *Some girl broke my beautiful son's heart!* Her heart ripped for him. 'Love you.'

'Yeah, yeah.'

Her eyes teared up.

'Figured pretty much the same – first broken heart. Fifty years from now, he'll smile about it,' Jeff said.

'Maybe, maybe not. I gotta go. Give me a hug, you hunk.'

She drove her red Mini back to the morgue. *The nerve of that bitch hurting my boy!* She couldn't dwell on that thought because she spotted Matte at the morgue's back door and rushed over to go in with him. The door buzzed and they let themselves in.

'Pierre, were you able to find out from the Sandersons when their daughter was last in touch with them?'

'They were in shock – trying to grasp their daughter's death.'

'You didn't ask them anything then?'

'Toni, I was looking back at zombies. Sanderson was gasping and rocking back and forth. And it was like his wife wasn't there. Then it started, or I caused it. I did ask when they had last spoken with their daughter. The wife became hysterical and Sanderson shouted at her to stop crying. He demanded to know when she had last spoken to her daughter. She wasn't certain. She thought Sunday. He scolded her, and she reminded him that they both worked and he was Taylor's father. The blame game began. *She* should have called more often. The wife flew back at him with the fact that their daughter was twenty-two, and independent. No one spoke after the tirade. They were spent by the time we reached their home, and they slammed the door in my face. Questioning the son was out.'

'Too bad. Questioning works best in weak moments, but we'll be back there tomorrow.'

'You should have been born a wolf with big teeth.'

'I'm not partial to blood. Let's wait for Dr. Belmont. He should be here soon.' They moved two stools in the first examining room against a wall for back support, sat together and entered notes in their murder books. Matte looked over at Damiano's page and smiled. 'I'm perfectly capable of writing, you know, Pierre.'

'Thought you had an aversion to pens.'

'Ha! High time I did this work. Might still need the odd borrowing – you're such a neat sponge.'

'Anytime.' They wrote for the next hour.

Belmont startled them when he opened the door. He slid his blue mask on top of his head and began to pull off the long rubber gloves. Matte didn't miss the iPod in his right pocket. 'Let's go to my office.'

His office was located on the other side of the hall away from the clinical theaters. Three walls of the office were packed to the ceiling with files. There didn't appear to be any order, but Matte guessed that Belmont knew exactly where everything was. Before the detectives sat in the wooden chairs close to the desk, Belmont opened a drawer, took out a towel, wiped his face and dropped Visine into his eyes.

Damiano placed her recorder on his desk.

'I'll begin with the most salient point. You're dealing with a homicide. No possibility of suicide or accident. No evidence of sexual interference. No evidence of a struggle. We have to wait for the Tox screen. TOD or LTD – I cannot pin down, due to temp fluctuations. Closest I can estimate is between forty-two to forty-eight hours from the time the kids discovered the body. The fatal attack took place on Tuesday between three and six or seven in the afternoon. As I've said with Montreal's weather – a positive estimate is not possible.'

When Belmont paused, the detectives refrained from asking questions. They were waiting for the cause of death.

'The victim sustained two blunt force traumas to the back of the skull. The first blow with a blunt instrument was struck on the left side of the victim's head, so we have a right-handed assailant. Not a hammer or a board. From the indentation in the skull that rendered the victim unconscious, my guess is a rock, the size of a hand. The second trauma was sustained when the victim landed on the tunnel floor. Both wounds fractured the skull and sent splinters like shrapnel into the cerebellum. Further, the victim sustained a fracture of the cervical vertebrae C5 that caused paralysis but left breathing limited but intact. The brain struggled to survive, but the paralysis was the cause of the asphyxiation. In layman's language, she drowned in her own blood.

'A healthy young woman, the victim weighed one hundred fifteen pounds. She was not conscious in the final hour of her life. Small solace. Questions?'

'When will you release the remains to the family?' Damiano said.

'In a few days. I have Dumont's photos, but I want to study her forensic findings before I make my final report.'

Matte had walked out, put on his white gloves, and then removed the victim's phone from the plastic bag. With the approximate TOD, he tapped into the victim's directory, taking note of the names. Matte scrolled Tuesday's calls, the last the victim made. He stopped at one, and waited for Damiano who was thanking Belmont for his overtime.

When they reached the back door of the morgue, he tapped Damiano's shoulder. 'Our vic's last call was to her brother.'

Damiano's eyes brightened. 'I say press this advantage. Go back to the house. The kid was squirrely at their home when he peeked around the door. He's vulnerable. We use that.'

'It's after two. Not a good move. You know the chief won't back us.'

'Damn! It's also too late for Marie. See you tomorrow, eight sharp. I'll take the phone.'

Chapter Nine

The rain finally let up. The night air smelled fresh as though the rain had rinsed the city streets. On her ride home Damiano played Cohen's 'Boogie Street.' The soft rhythmic beat and bluesy sound helped ease the burn throbbing in her arm. The pain was worst at night. Blood pulsed around her elbow, shooting darts of pain up to her shoulder. She had one Dilaudid in her purse. Damiano had sworn off liquor and meds during work hours, but she owned the nights. When she arrived at the house she parked the car on the street, used the side door and made a real effort not to awaken Jeff or Luke.

Tiptoeing into the spare room at the end of the hall, she stripped off her clothes, closed the bathroom door, opened her purse without a sound, found the pill and swallowed it. Carrying the purse back with her, she left it with her clothes and crawled into bed, with Sanderson's phone. She didn't dare turn on a light. Jeff was a light sleeper. The directory attracted her attention. It provided a contact list. Damiano went to the victim's posts on Facebook, but there wasn't much there. Kids had turned to Twitter, Instagram, and Pinterest. Since Damiano was a tech novice, she scanned Taylor's last calls. There were only four on that Tuesday. She checked the directory for the first. Missed calls were next on her list. Odd, she thought, after three on Tuesday, their vic had turned off her phone. She was about to listen to the voicemail when the narcotic began to take effect. She put down the phone, pulled up her covers and surrendered. The throbbing in her arm softened. Before Damiano fell off, she recalled something she'd read. Every now and then an extremely dangerous wave breaks so viciously against the rocks that it's called "the rage." Dr. Belmont had said Sanderson was struck from behind only once. Was rage behind this murder?

Matthew Sanderson had waited up for his parents. He had discarded his glasses, paced the floor, sometimes in shock and pain, then in blistering anger. Once Taylor left the house, she never bothered with her nerdy brother. He hadn't expected more from 'Princess.' When she deigned to drop by on weekends, all he ever got was, 'Hey you!' None of that neglect mattered then. He was cooked – better to own up now before the cops told his father. He practiced his confession, but it all fell apart when his father slammed the front door. Matthew liked words – 'skeletal' was the word for his father's face – 'aggrieved' for his mother. They didn't notice him. He began to back out of the living room.

'Wait a minute, Matt. You were listening as usual. You know then that Taylor's dead.'

His father's words stung him because he heard their anger. He could only imagine what he'd hear when his father learned Taylor had called him. He hung his head, 'Yeah, I know. I'm sorry.' Matthew wanted to run from the room. He didn't dare.

'I hope you are a lot more than sorry. She was your sister, your only sister!'

He tried crying then. 'What do you want me to say? It's fucking awful.' He stumbled into his question. 'How did Tay die?'

'Die, DIE! She was dumped like garbage into a tunnel. That's how.'

'Trevor, leave Matthew alone. We don't know anything yet – except that Taylor's gone.'

'What's wrong with the two of you? You know Tay would never have gone into that tunnel – we all know that. She was murdered, for Christ's sake! I don't have to be a cop to know that. I need a drink. Oh my God!'

'Matthew, get your father some scotch. Sit down with me, Trevor.'

'I can't, Shari. You and Matt are going to grieve quietly. What's the matter with you two? We have to rage for Tay. I'm not taking this quietly. She was my little girl, and yours, and your sister, even if she wasn't perfect. How can you be so quiet? Matt all you could say was, "Yeah, I know."'

Shari looked into her husband's eyes. 'I can't shout with a broken heart.'

'Me too, but I can't give up. I'll crawl on my knees if I have to, but I won't accept this.'

Shari sat alone quietly. Matthew returned with two glasses of scotch.

'Leave the bottle.'

'Dad, I have to tell you something.' Matthew had gulped some scotch from the bottle. His glasses were back on. He wanted a clear view of his father when he spoke.

'Not now, son. I just can't hear anything else.'

'But…'

'Leave me alone.'

Matthew didn't leave. 'Taylor called me on Tuesday to ask me to meet her – I told her I was in the middle of a war game…'

'What are you saying? Tay called you?'

'Yes. And I didn't go to help her. Have you heard that? Is it clear now, Dad?'

Trevor caught Matthew with a vicious right hook that drew blood and sent him flying back out of the room. Matthew stood back up and reached down for his glasses that had survived his fall. 'Hit me again, Dad. I'd feel better if you did. Think I don't feel like shit! But Tay never helped me with that math, and she was home that weekend. All I needed was fifteen minutes and she blew me off. Not going to meet her was just payback. I didn't know she was in trouble. I didn't know.' But Matthew did. His father might kill him if he knew the whole truth.

His mother looked at him with such despair that he fled to his room.

'Tay didn't have to die,' Trevor rasped. 'She didn't have to die, if Matt had…'

Matthew began to trash his room – smashing his games against the wall, stomping on his laptop, kicking his desk over, throwing his chair against the wall. He didn't hear his father run into the room.

'Enough!'

Matthew pushed his father aside and ripped the pages of a textbook, tore off his posters, threw his iPhone on the floor.

Trevor grabbed his arms and pinned them. 'Enough, son.'

'I'm so fucking sorry.'

When Matthew stopped shaking, Trevor released his grip. He wanted to tell his son that he forgave him, but he couldn't and didn't believe he ever would. Matthew had betrayed his sister. He grabbed Matthew's shoulders. 'Tell me exactly what Tay said when she called you.'

Matthew wasn't prepared for this question. He thought he'd have time to think of answers; that it would be the police doing the questioning. 'We didn't talk long. I don't know.'

'Are you lying to me?'

Matthew backed away. 'I'm not lying. She…'

'SHE! Your sister for God's sake! I want the truth.'

'Taylor said she had to meet someone. Could I go with her? Like I said, I blew her off.'

As a lawyer it was Sanderson's job to read people. Matthew was not telling him everything. He spoke very slowly. 'I'm giving you one more chance.'

Matthew panicked, but he couldn't tell the truth, not after the first lie. He looked down at his father's fist, and lied again.

'I wasn't really listening – I was just waiting to sling her, just like she did to me a lot of times.'

'You're lying!' Sanderson pushed Matthew back and he almost fell.

'Did you go down to that tunnel?'

'No, I swear.'

'Did Tay sound nervous – be honest about that at least.' Sanderson was loud and threatening.

'I'm sorry.' Matthew had covered his face.

'I'll beat the truth out of you,' Sanderson cut in.

'Fuck, fuck! Alright, she was scared, and I didn't help her. I let her die.' At least he'd told some of the truth.

Sanderson didn't strike Matthew with his fist. He used words. 'What a miserable example of a son and brother.' He stepped on the broken pieces of the iPhone on the floor and left.

Matthew threw himself back on his bed and blubbered like a two-year-old. 'I'm sorry.'

Sanderson found Shari in the massive hall dragging a blanket toward the study. 'I'm not fit to sleep with now because I want the truth,' he hissed, following her.

'You're a bully, Trevor. When we first met you were a man who got things done, confident and strong, and that attracted me. I loved you then and I love you now, but I can't stand the sight of you tonight.'

Sanderson ignored the words. 'Know what, had I gotten my way, with your support, Tay would still be alive. I wouldn't be in this state tonight. Her room is a goddamn self-contained apartment, and she left that for a hole on Lincoln Avenue!'

'She's twenty-two.'

'Wake up, Shari. *Was* twenty-two. You side with the kids – you always have! Tay was twenty-two. With today's kids that's a mental age of sixteen! Apparently, Tay was not ready to leave. What the hell was she doing at the Wellington Tunnel? Girls are at high risk today. How many times do we read of abductions and worse? Now, Tay's dead, and our coddled son could have helped her and he blew her off.'

Shari dropped the blanket and shouted. 'The truth, Trevor? Is that what you really want? Can you take it? Well, here it is –Tay wanted to get away from you, you and your rules. That's why she left. That's why she'd come to feel her room was a prison.'

'How do you know that?' Trevor winced.

'She confided in me.'

'Right, touchy, feely Mom.'

'I'm a psychologist!'

'Yeah, and you're all nuts!'

A chair flew over the bannister and crashed on the white marble floor gouging a good chunk of the floor. 'Shut the fuck up! It's *my* fault Tay's dead. It's my fault. I might as well have killed her.' Matthew sank to the floor.

'Go to him, Trevor. Please, I'm begging you. You'll destroy him if you don't,' she whispered.

'I can't, Shari.' Sanderson turned his back. Tears had begun to fill his eyes. 'I can't.'

Chapter Ten

Detective Damiano woke before five-thirty to a dry mouth and crusty eyelids. She remembered she hadn't removed her mascara or washed up. It was too early to shower without waking up her men, so she stole into the kitchen. She opened a cupboard without allowing the magnetic sucking sound and slid her hand behind the second row and eased the vodka out, gulped once and returned it before she stole back to the bedroom, the spirit spreading through her limbs. *Three hours of sleep! Who wouldn't need something? My work day begins at eight, so I haven't broken my promise.*

She read the notes she'd made in bed the night before and swore that was a stupid move. She couldn't make out a single word. She showered quickly, wavering in the doorway for a few seconds, and then ran to the master bedroom in the buff carrying her clothes and bag. No time for ghosts. She had a full day ahead of her: media, Crime, the phone, family interview. Most important, she and Matte had to learn of their victim's movements the day she died and why she ended up at the tunnel.

Jeff rolled her way. 'I'm awake. Your story's out – just caught it on my phone.'

'Great! The chief will be pleased. Leave me alone while I dress and think. Will you see to Luke today?'

'Yep. You've got to eat though.'

'Still have that second sandwich you made for me.'

'Here we go again.' Jeff was up and gave her a peck while Damiano raced around the room.

'It's my job. Tell Luke I love him.'

'Will do.'

Damiano heard Luke in his room. She entered without knocking.

'Mom! The posters – you gotta knock.' He yanked up the sheet and crumpled it, trying to hide his morning boner.

'Oops, sorry. I changed your diapers. You have nothing I haven't seen.' She planted a kiss on his left cheek. It didn't seem possible, but Luke looked worse, lonely and lost. *He hasn't slept.* 'Give it a few days, Luke. I know you won't talk about what's bothering you.' Luke looked at the wall behind her. A twinge of guilt followed her out the door.

Detective Matte was outside in their city car. She was grateful and rushed to get in beside him. 'You know the case is out?'

'Me and the rest of the city. The chief will be at the boardroom waiting on us. Want to bet?'

Damiano wasn't listening. 'Some girl has clobbered Luke. At least that's what Jeff and I think.'

Matte pulled away and drove toward the Crémazie Division. 'Women sometimes think they own broken hearts – guys suffer as much.'

'This coming from my gay partner.'

'You know what I mean.'

'I do – I'll concede that. Crazy thing is my pride is hurt for him. He's one beautiful kid – hard to imagine anyone would want to hurt him. He's the heart-breaker. Nobody broke my heart. When I felt a crack – I ran. Maybe last year's problems with Jeff, but that's it. Luke? Doesn't figure.'

'This is not about you.'

'You know what I mean.'

'Gotcha! Toni, if Luke didn't see it coming, and who does with the first love, he's devastated. Age doesn't come into this equation. It hurts, but he'll get over this – we all do.'

Damiano didn't want to hear any more of Matte's analysis of love and pain. 'How the hell do you not swear at the road closures and orange cones? It's only April and they've already started. Step on it, Pierre. I know the chief will be there before us. That goes for the media as well.'

'Calm down. Did you check out the vic's phone?'

'It's a redo. My brain was mush by that time. It was almost three, remember?' She glared Matte's way. 'I should have driven today.' When he pulled into the Division's underground parking lot, Damiano didn't admit they had made good time.

They didn't make it to their lockers before a colleague caught them. 'Boss wants you both downstairs. So this file is not a 'missing.' You guys managed to catch yet another good case. Should have been born a pretty woman.'

'Bad taste, bad joke, Patrice,' Damiano said.

'Lighten up!' Detective Patrice Dagenais strode off.

Damiano stopped at a washroom. 'We don't have time, Toni. You look fine.'

She was thinking of her mouth spray. Well, Matte hadn't noticed. It was one swig – no damage.

The chief was freshly showered. His cologne assaulted her nostrils as it always did. 'They're inside. I'll run this briefing, but I do want to introduce you. I'm not taking questions. Ready?'

They nodded and followed Chief Donat into the room. The usual suspects were there: local TV stations, radio networks, a few anchors she recognized and a tangle of mics and wires. She and Matte stood to the side of the chief, and he mounted a box to the microphone where he appeared as tall as his detectives.

The chief cleared his throat and placed his briefing sheet on the podium. 'Good morning ladies and gentlemen. I am Chief Richard Donat of Major Crimes at the Crémazie Division. This is an official briefing. I will not be taking any questions. Yesterday afternoon police recovered the body of Taylor Sanderson, the Concordia student reported missing a few days ago. This department can now confirm that we are dealing with a homicide. Lieutenant Detective Toni Damiano is the lead investigator with her partner, Detective Pierre Matte. The investigation is underway with all our resources at work.

'Further details will not be forthcoming at this time. We are in the preliminary stages and will not engage in speculation. When we have something concrete to report, we will meet with the you. The Sanderson family has requested that you respect their privacy at this difficult time. That is all, thank you.'

'Who found the body at the Wellington Tunnel?' a *Gazette* reporter who obviously knew something more called out.

Chief Donat enjoyed a mental swear word he rarely used, gave the reporter a steely-eyed admonition and left with his two detectives and closed the door on the media. 'They're all jerks, vultures. Some of them will prey on the Sandersons.'

'Chief, your office door is open,' said Damiano in a low voice.

'Let's get back upstairs to my office. I want to know exactly where we are on this case.' They stepped into an elevator. The chief's anger didn't subside. 'One thing that has always bothered me about the work we do is the lack of decency for the victims of violent crime, murder in particular. If this kid had committed suicide, we all know the press could not reveal the name or any of the lurid details. Suicides are granted that privacy. But this kid will have every facet of her life dissected for public scrutiny. Eventually, some asshole will make a joke of her death. Her parents' lives, the brother and all the other people we have to investigate will see their secrets and flaws laid bare by us and bits leaked to these vultures. It's a wretched circus.'

'We have to find who took her life – that's what we do. Dr. Belmont cuts them open – we probe everything and everybody she touched. If we didn't – who'd speak for her? Retribution begins with us,' Damiano interjected.

'Sometimes you get on my nerves, Damiano, but you know what my rant means and you agree with it. Platitudes – who will help if not us? Reality stinks! Times like this I smell the stench. By the way, I had an officer drive to the morgue for the kid's personal effects. Belmont forgot to hand them to you last night. The meager contents of that brown envelope sparked my rage. I'm glad I still feel it. '

'Well said, Chief,' Matte agreed and received an elbow in the ribs from Damiano who looked up as she struck.

Damiano discussed her plans for the day with the chief. 'Crime needs time to work on the blood smears and type them. We have the phone. The calls should help track her movements. Sanderson called her brother the afternoon of her death. I want to return the personal effects, interview the brother, see the vic's room to get a feel for her, obtain her address on Lincoln, and speak to the Sandersons again. I need more information from them.'

'What are you waiting for, Detective? Pierre, you stay back and work on the phone. Access as much information as you can. Meet me back at the office in a few hours. Go, Damiano.'

Chapter Eleven

Detective Damiano regretted not calling the Sandersons before she pulled up beside their home; she stood a full minute after ringing the silent bell. When Trevor Sanderson finally opened the door, his appearance did not catch her off guard. She'd seen it before in similar situations. Unshaven, in yesterday's clothes, he reeked of sweat. His shirttail hung out of his pants and his eyes were bloodshot. 'I'm sorry to disturb you, Mr. Sanderson, but I have some questions for all of you. They simply can't wait.'

'Well, don't just stand there.' Sanderson turned and left Damiano to close the door.

She had wrestled with the problem of who to question first. Going for the son was going to add another blow to the Sandersons. To hell with it! Damiano caught up to Sanderson. 'Sir, I'd like to question Matthew first. I didn't have the opportunity last night.'

'We know, Detective. We know that Taylor called him. Do whatever it takes to get the whole truth out of him. I couldn't, even when I threatened him. I'll fetch him for you. The study is two doors down.'

'Mr. Sanderson, a minute please.' Damiano opened her case to retrieve an envelope. 'I think you will want Taylor's personal effects.' She handed Sanderson the envelope.

He winced before taking the envelope with both hands. The gentleness with which he took the effects and held them against his chest touched Damiano. She remembered her childhood hero, the young Roman, Tarcisius, who had been stoned to death, guarding the sacred host. 'Thank you,' he said. 'I'll never let these out of my sight.' His tears fell easily, she thought for the first time.

The sour smell of liquor on Sanderson's breath she understood. The living room was empty.

'My wife's in the bedroom, but she's not asleep. I'll get my son.'

After nodding, Damiano saw paneled walls in the study lined with what she assumed were first editions in oak bookcases. Damiano pulled a heavy burgundy padded desk chair around the side of the desk, laid her recorder on the edge of it and took out her notepad. So they knew of the call. The kid must have told them.

'Well, here's our hero.' Sanderson's gentleness was short-lived. He steered his son into the study. The boy's cheekbone and eye were swollen and deeply bruised. The boy too hadn't changed.

'Mr. Sanderson, did you strike your son?'

Matthew, sullen and angry, responded before his father could answer. 'No, I trashed my room and was clumsy. Where do I sit?'

'How about pulling up a chair closer to the desk, Matthew?'

To his father's disdain, Matthew purposely dragged it across the polished oak floors.

'Your son is a minor. You or your wife must be present for the interview.'

'I can be alone. I want to be alone.'

'I'll get his mother – I don't trust myself.'

Damiano motioned the boy to sit and turned on the recorder. 'Detective Damiano, Major Crimes. Interview with Matthew Sanderson in the presence of his mother, Shari Tellett- Sanderson. The time is nine-twenty, Friday, April 3, 2014.' She turned the recorder off and waited. Matthew sat hunched, brushing his cheek with a fist. 'You should get some ice on that.'

'Butt out!' He stared her down. 'Think this matters? Think I matter?'

Before Damiano could say anything else, Shari Sanderson was guided into the room by her husband. 'Matthew wanted you, Shari.' The wife was in the same shape as her husband and son. She appeared almost frail. Her cheeks were gray and smeared with mascara.

She said only one thing when Sanderson closed the door. As she pushed her hair back with the palm of her hand before she sat and whispered, 'I love you, Matthew.'

Matthew's Adam's apple rose and fell.

'We know the time your sister called you Tuesday afternoon – please tell me about the conversation.'

'Taylor's always early…'

His mother's head rose, but Damiano shook her hand, signalling not to interrupt him.

'She wanted me to meet her at the tunnel. I blew her off. Payback.'

'Did she say why she needed you or why was she going there?'

He sniffed loudly. 'Can't you all just let this go? I never went there – my sister died. What's the point of anything else? She's still dead – I'm still the fuck who didn't help her.'

'You can help us find who hurt her, Matthew, if you tell me what you know.'

'She's dead. If I add anything – I'm just going to fuck her up even more. That would be all she needs now.'

'No, you won't. Your sister still needs your help.'

'Are you for real? Taylor is DEAD. What more can she need, especially from me?'

Shari Sanderson laid her hand on Matthew's shoulder and he jumped up. 'You don't know what you're asking, Mom.'

'Matthew, sit back down, please. You will help your sister by telling us the truth. You don't want your sister's murderer to walk away.'

'I'm right here.' He began to moan and kick the legs of the chair and he almost fell off.

'Matthew, sometime detectives spin the truth to get the truth. I'm not spinning anything. I'm telling you we need to know the facts – I want to know who left your sister to die alone in some godforsaken tunnel. You are not the one who murdered her. You're only guilty of letting her down. We all betray someone at one time or another. You're not a hero – none of us are! So please…' *Finally, she had admitted what she'd felt for eight months – she was no hero. The boy had died. Damiano felt as badly as Matthew Sanderson at that moment.* 'Help your sister now, Matthew.'

He whispered through his fist. 'She said she was in deep shit – she might even be arrested. I told her to handle her own shit and I hung up.'

Shari Sanderson rushed from the room.

'Did she say what for, Matthew?'

'No, nothing. Are you deaf? I hung up on her.' He knocked the chair over when he got to his feet and stormed out of the room, opening the door with such force it slammed into a side table.

Damiano packed her things quickly and went looking for Matthew's mother and found her slumped against the first of two ultra-white leather sofas in the living room. 'Mrs. Sanderson, Matthew needs help. You all do. Did your husband strike him? Is your son in danger?'

She laughed hysterically before she broke down again. 'I'm a psychologist. Don't you find that amusing? Trevor says we're all nuts and he's probably right. Taylor was a young woman. I thought she needed to stand on her own, to find herself. Last night I was thinking when I was twenty-two, I felt sure of my way. The reality is that we thought we did, but we know nothing at that age. I'm forty-six and I still don't know much. I thought we were a conventional family, but we're not. I don't know my husband – I obviously didn't know my daughter. I did know that Matthew lived in Taylor's shadow, or felt he did. I thought if she were on her own – he'd find himself. Instead, Tay is gone and Trevor hates both of us, blames us for losing her. Maybe he's right.'

Damiano couldn't involve herself in Shari Sanderson's psychological musings, yet she heard what the woman was saying. Damiano had to worry about Sanderson. He was dangerous, but could she take him to the station? He struck his son, but she couldn't prove it. Charging Sanderson with abuse the day after he learned his daughter had been murdered seemed wrong to her. The chief would have her neck. It was a judgment call and there was never surety in that. She decided to stay with the Sandersons, things might simmer down. 'May I sit with you?'

Shari Sanderson didn't object.

'Was your daughter seeing anyone?'

The woman had retreated into herself. 'Mrs. Sanderson, was Taylor seeing anyone?'

'At Christmas Tay broke up with Andrew Weston, a boy she'd been seeing for almost a year. They were students together. She never told me why. Kids stop telling you things, and I stopped asking.'

'Was she seeing anyone lately?'

'For a few weeks Tay was excited, happy, but she didn't tell me anything. The last ten days, she was edgy. I thought it was exams, and I didn't see much of her. I didn't last year either at exam time.'

Damiano was taking notes. 'May I see her room, please, to give me a sense of her?' The question brought the horror back.

'I can't – it's all we have…'

Trevor Sanderson has been standing by the door listening. When he walked in on them, Damiano saw that he had showered and shaved. There was an elegance about him she hadn't noticed before as he stood in the center of the room. 'Tay took after me.' He spoke through the tightness of pain that Damiano felt was sharp and brutal. 'She was beautiful, arrogant, bright, outgoing, spirited, secretive, friendly, intelligent, and also impulsive. My girl was spirited. Tay was always early for any event. She aped everything I did since she was three. Shari and Matthew are the gentle souls. I'm sorry, Shari.' He stood pleading for forgiveness.

'Sir, would you take me to Taylor's room?'

Sanderson looked at his wife, who was shaking her head.

'I need to examine the contents,' Damiano said more forcefully.

'Not today, Detective. When can we claim her body?' Sanderson was back in control.

'In a few days. I'm certain you don't want a full search team here tomorrow. I must see the room.'

Shari Sanderson shrieked. 'Trevor, take her up, but don't you dare touch anything! Trevor, you explain what needs to be explained. Detective Damiano is not to touch anything!'

Damiano agreed, for the moment. She wasn't ruling out a team, but she remembered the girl lived on Lincoln. She asked Sanderson for that address when they were safely upstairs. Sanderson grimaced as soon as he opened the bedroom door. The pastel painted room was airy and bright, full of space. Clothes were strewn on the floor, shoes, underwear, notes, though Damiano saw two open walk-in closets, a shoe closet, two desks, a laptop and a Bose iPod station. The only tidy area of the room was the carefully arranged color-coded files on the second desk. Above it were posters of old radio shows: *Zero Hour*, Ray Bradbury, and Orson Wells's *The Shadow*. 'What's that all about?'

Sanderson hadn't actually stepped into the room. 'Every man wants a son – I certainly did, but a daughter changes a man. Taylor crept into my heart and stole it. When she locked her baby arms around my neck, I was done for. She used to play shave beside me. She'd watched Shari, so she'd pretend to shave her legs. As they grow, it's the energy, the beauty, the fluid graceful movements, feminine, and captivating. I couldn't quite believe that little girl was mine. Matthew may be quiet, but he can take care of himself, like Shari. They are both deceptively strong. Shari blamed me and my rules for Tay moving out. She was right. I wanted to protect my girl as long as I could. Tay was so free that she could never sense danger, but it found her.'

Damiano needed to move along. 'What are all those files?'

'My father got her into that, *Radio Classics*. Tay wanted to write a good mystery. She listened to all the old shows, mesmerized by the excellence of that early work. I can hear her now: "You should hear how they used music for drama and scene changes, classical music, great prose and all the old actors like Charles Boyer, Marlene Dietrich, George Sanders, Vincent Price, some directed by Cecil B. De Mille…" she'd tired me out. That old world excited her. But that was a year ago. That stuff hasn't been touched since. Kids just grow up and move on.'

'How often did she sleep here overnight?' Damiano checked the ensemble bathroom. There were no prescription drugs. Then again, Sanderson would have hidden them. 'Sorry?'

'Never this past year. She popped in to grace us with her presence, changed clothes, as you can see, dropped them on the floor, and popped right out. Shari was determined not to clean her room – she was old enough to do that herself. She didn't want Taylor to treat our home as a drop-off center.' Sanderson turned away before he spoke again. 'There's nothing recent here. You have to go, Detective. We'll be alright. I was out of my mind last night. I still can't believe any of this. I need time. Leave me in peace.' Detective Damiano chose to trust Sanderson and headed downstairs. Sanderson watched her and he thought about the day his daughter died. *It was a very busy session at the Commission, if Tay had called me...* He crushed that thought, almost breaking the door handle.

Damiano left by the front door, once she'd scooped up her case, and closed it behind her. What had Taylor done that was cause for an arrest? Why the tunnel if she was claustrophobic? Had she been forced to go there? Who else had she called to go with her? Damiano was eager to see what Detective Matte had learned from the phone. He'd have examined the photos as well.

Three media slogs, like pelicans on a wharf, sat in cars with cameras in hand, two brazen enough to let them hang out the windows. Damiano's temper erupted. She strode out to the middle of the road. Waving her badge, she shouted, 'Move out of here!'

Not a single engine fired up.

Damiano put her case down and took her phone. 'Send assistance to...'

They left.

'Assholes!'

Damiano thought of calling Jeff to see if Luke had gone to school, but Jeff would have called if there were problems. Luke was more mature and self-reliant than Matthew. Like her, he'd take care of himself. She knew her son.

Chapter Twelve

Detective Damiano called Matte en route to the Division. 'Quite a morning. I do have a lead. How are you doing with the victim's phone?'

'I have good information as well but one of our vic's four calls is to a throwaway.'

'It's not uncommon with kids to buy those. Just makes it more difficult for us. What about Marie?'

'Soon, actually she might be here by the time you arrive.'

'I have to pick up something to eat. My day-old chicken sandwich died.'

'We received a call from an officer in Ville Marie Ouest – PDQ 20.'

'About?'

'A Professor Donovan from Concordia University filed an assault charge against Taylor Sanderson a few days before her death. I'll save the report for you rather than reading it – it's interesting.'

'Does it have legs?'

'Might well. Don't forget food! I don't want to hear your stomach all day.'

'Where are the food trucks when you need them?'

'What?'

'Nothing. I'm hanging up.' Schwartz's Deli was out – an hour later the smoked meat would feel like a carry-on in her stomach. She settled on chicken in a bun and a coffee, had the sandwich wrapped and burned her tongue on the coffee before she left the restaurant. She was lead detective – she could eat where she wanted. Sanderson had committed an offence, something big enough to cause an arrest. Lucky break for them. Communication between cops wasn't an everyday event. Good teamwork, she thought. Damiano eyed the sandwich, but it was too much of a job to pull out snips of chicken from aluminum wrap as she drove. She couldn't see neat freak Matte curling his lip when he spied the food and her intent to eat it in the office.

After dropping her coat jacket in her locker, she saw from a distance that Marie Dumont had not arrived. Matte was working alone. Once she was inside her office, she understood, not for the first time, what a valuable partner she had in Matte. He was a walking, intelligent laptop, an accountant, a reporter and an organizer. Photos of the friends the vic had called were pinned to the bulletin board on the wall of her office, under them, their phone numbers and addresses, a question mark for the throwaway. The Sandersons were posted there as well, and the professor who had filed an assault charge against their vic. Caitlin Donovan, Concordia Professor, address and phone number. To the right of the board a large photo of their vic and neatly printed below in bullet points, her address on Lincoln, which Matte must have found on a reverse phone search, and all the information Dr. Belmont had given them. Matte had worked non-stop.

'I should have picked up two sandwiches. Great work.'

'Toni, I packed my lunch last night.'

'In the three hours before we had to be back?' Damiano checked his face. No lazy shave for Matte. Sometimes she wondered if he missed a few chin hairs, would that disrupt his world.

'Works for me. Watch the crumbs.'

'It's my office.'

'That I cleaned. We can also expect the chief.'

'Alright, Pierre, I'll be careful. Matthew Sanderson said his sister was freaking because she might be arrested. Didn't know for what. He didn't pump her – I believe him, for now. Considering their condition I couldn't not subject the husband and wife to a tough interrogation. It is too soon for them. What's the story with the professor?'

'She filed an assault charge against Sanderson last Thursday. Claimed Sanderson barged into her home on Wood Avenue arguing for a third chance on some school paper. Plagiarism was involved and Donovan wouldn't change the failing grade. Sanderson left threatening a charge against *her* at the university. Our cop said he didn't ask what the charge was because Donovan never saw Sanderson throw the brick through her front window. Claims she was almost struck and waited a few minutes before opening her door. By that time, she saw no one.'

'We have legs. I'm thinking out loud. We could ask her to come here. However, I'd like to question the two tenants. They're both in the same Lincoln Street area.'

Matte pointed to the board. 'These two are the two tenants along with our vic who share the apartment. It must be one of those old mansions that's subdivided into rental units. Sanderson called each tenant. We should go to the vic's apartment today. We don't know who has keys.'

'Whatever our vic has in her apartment I want to see before someone else makes off with information we need. Pierre, would you make the calls and set the times? The vic's apartment first, Donovan, followed by the students. Actually, I'll call Donovan myself. I want to get a feel about her before we meet. Where is Marie? I'm going to call her now.' Damiano used Dumont's private line.

'Toni, I'm sorry. We're still busy here. We might as well do this by phone. My unit is still working the scene. They have two good-sized rocks, but Luminol didn't reveal any trace blood. They're widening the scope pf the search. At the lab, we have identified passive blood spatters on the body, plus projected blood spatter resulting from the fall. It's the transfer stain that most interests us. We may have a partial print, but we are not optimistic about identity points. I want to send it to an American lab that specializes in this kind of work. That will take time, but we might get lucky.

'From the opening it is clear the vic was pushed through. We have blood trace on the bottom of the wood – it's new, too new to be directly related to the day of the murder. We're running a match with one of the boys who found the body. You said the kid scratched his arm, right?'

'Cameron Miller.'

'From the top of the opening, we have another transfer stain that we are examining for skin cells. The blood's from the vic, but I think it may have been transferred to the assailant. We can do that work here. I spoke to Belmont, and he confirmed my theory that the woman was struck outside the tunnel and then shoved into it.'

'Keep on it, Marie.'

'You know it.'

Chief Donat had stood at the closed door until Damiano was off the phone. Matte was still busy with calls, so he knocked on the glass and motioned her outside.

Damiano stepped out and gave her boss a detailed account of their progress. 'We're heading out to the vic's apartment.'

'How are the Sandersons holding up?'

Damiano told the chief about the bruises and her exchange with them.

'Are you certain the son is not in danger? Not good, not good at all. Still, I would have acted as you did. The kid won't press charges, but we have to know he's not subject to further abuse. I'm going to call Sanderson myself.'

Damiano was about to object that she wanted to manage her own inquiry, but relented. 'May I listen in?' Chief Donat gave her his best glare, but Damiano stood firm. He marched down the hall into his office. She marched right behind him and waited while he made the call.

Reluctantly, the chief used the speaker phone. The phone rang several times and stopped. Then it rang again before it was finally picked up. 'Trevor Sanderson?'

Sanderson sensed from the Private Caller on the ID it might be the police, so he took the call. 'Yes?'

'Sir, this is Chief Richard Donat, Crémazie Division. You have been dealing with my lead, Lieutenant Detective Damiano.'

'She's left.'

'I know that, Sir. I want you to know that we are working overtime on this file. It's a terrible time for all of you.'

'What's your point? I haven't the time, nor do you, for idle talk.'

'My detective has some concerns…'

'About my son.'

'Yes, Sir.'

There was a pause. 'None of us were sane last night – how could we be? This morning, we're grieving. There's no need to worry about our safety. We are a loving family who has lost their only daughter.'

'Do I have your word on that, Sir?'

'As a man and as a father.'

'We are doing our best, Mr. Sanderson.'

'See that you do, Chief Donat.'

Donat turned to Damiano. 'He had to have the last word.'

'He's a lawyer.'

'The situation remains troublesome, but you said the kid won't admit the truth.'

'He's guilt-ridden – I think he welcomed the punch. I don't think Sanderson will ever forgive his son. We'll keep tabs on them. That's all we can do because we don't have a case. I have calls to make, Chief.' Damiano headed back to her office.

Matte was busy on the phone when she got back. Damiano copied Professor Donovan's number from the bulletin board, grabbed her iPhone and signalled to Matte that she was about to make the call. He could use her office. She found a quiet place in an interview room on the Division's main floor behind the cells. That room was locked. To enter the room she tapped in the code.

Caitlin Donovan was sitting in her office clearing up some paperwork when the phone rang.

'Professor Donovan.'

'Lieutenant Detective Toni Damiano, Major Crimes.'

Caitlin's cheeks burned. 'I've been expecting a call about the charge.'

Damiano heard the catch in her voice. 'I would like to meet with you as soon as possible. Could I come by the office?'

'I'm in my office in the Hall Building.'

The voice was definitely clipped, on edge.

'Would it be more convenient for you to have us come to your home on Wood? We could be there shortly.'

So they knew. They even have my address. 'Yes, I'd rather you come to my home. I'll leave now.'

'Good, we will see you soon.'

Caitlin slouched back in her chair for a second. Then she was standing, grabbing her phone. 'Carmen, *they've* called.'

'You knew it was just a matter of time. Caitlin, get in touch with your father.'

'He's in court in New York.'

'I can't leave work, Caitlin. I have a huge quote that has to go out today, *sans faute.* I'll be over tonight.'

'If I'm not in some holding cell!'

Chapter Thirteen

As Lieutenant Detective Damiano and Detective Matte drove to Wood Avenue, Damiano could see that Matte was thinking, tapping his temple with his middle finger. 'Have we forgotten anything?'

'We've worked together for almost ten years and something clicked in the back of my brain, from that time.'

'And?'

'Something about this street and the name rings a bell. I'm going to run the name, specifically in 2004 and 2005, and see what I come up with.'

Damiano had driven, so his thoughts wouldn't slow him down, as they generally did when he was at the wheel.

'Well! In 2004, the professor's brother was a DUI fatality at the corner of Wood Avenue and Sherbrooke Street. It was front-page news. Prestigious family on The Boulevard. The kid had just graduated from Harvard and then he was killed. Detective Claude Remay made the arrest. He's working out of Place Versailles. If we need more on the professor, he can give us the back story. Her father is some high-profile lawyer.'

'Two lawyers to get into our faces – great for us!'

By that time, Damiano made a left off Sherbrooke Street onto Wood Avenue. Parked cars had claimed the entire side of the street. She double-parked in front of the house and slapped her official ID on the dash and told Matte to do the same. Wood Avenue was a quiet wooded street bordered on one side by what used to be the motherhouse of the Congrégation de Notre-Dame nuns. The century-old religious building became Dawson College. 'Do you know that there are graves in the basement of the old Grey Nuns Motherhouse a few blocks east of here now occupied by Concordia University that cannot be dug up because some of the nuns died of typhoid fever? Do you think there are dead bodies here too?'

'Nice thought, Pierre. Don't get lost in details that go nowhere. Are you as well prepared for Donovan?'

'Have I ever let you down?'

Damiano took a good look at Donovan's expensively-renovated home. 'Quite a home for one person, but it makes sense now that I know about the moneyed Irish clan.' The brick used for most of the homes on the street had been replaced by natural stone, the windows were new, probably double impact, she thought. The home was solid and warm. At least she could hear the bell when she pressed a bronze square tab.

The professor opened the door and invited them into the living room to the right of the entrance. Damiano was surprised to find a woman her height. She appeared to be around thirty, maybe a few years older. She was a fox as Luke would say, tall and fit with a mass of dirty-blond layered hair and large hazel eyes. Her male students must have enjoyed her classes. The introductions were made smoothly, and Professor Donovan offered them coffee which Damiano grudgingly refused. She wanted the professor on edge. The professor was too intelligent to fall for the buddy routine. With her father a lawyer, she gave the professor 'cred' for brains.

'Professor Donovan, we're here regarding Taylor Sanderson. We have some questions for you. She was one of your students, and you filed an assault charge against her a week ago Thursday. Would you mind if I recorded the questioning to keep the record straight?'

Caitlin was her father's daughter. 'Is that routine?' She looked from one detective to the other. 'I'm very upset to learn of Taylor's death. The recording of our conversation caught me off guard.'

'This is not an interrogation, Professor. We just want to ensure we get the facts straight. My partner is almost perfect, but we both can miss and forget important points that might assist in the case.'

'Should I have consulted a lawyer?'

Damiano was right, Donovan wasn't naïve, but neither was she. 'Suspects request lawyers – it's your right, Professor Donovan. If that's what you'd like, we should continue the questioning at the Division.'

'Are you considering me a suspect?'

'Not at this stage. Recording keeps questions and answers clearer for both parties.'

'Alright then.' *Do not add anything that is not asked. Keep it simple.* Caitlin could hear herself breathing.

'Can you tell us about Ms. Sanderson's assault and what was behind it?'

'Taylor handed in a plagiarized copy for her last assignment of the year. I called her to my office. I told her how such an infraction could impact her reputation and score. She begged me not to report it and pleaded for a second chance. That was my first mistake.'

'How so?'

'Our families know one another. I capitulated, acted outside the purview of the University's Rights and Responsibilities guidelines. I made that same mistake in my first year. A student came to my office – same story. His fourteen-year-old dog had died the night before. He couldn't concentrate, couldn't sleep. Big tears, heaving shoulders – the whole bit. He handed in a decent paper four days later, but it turned out his dog had died two months before.' Caitlin laughed in spite of her nerves. Damiano and Matte smiled.

'Did Sanderson produce a proper assignment?'

'Another "bought" paper. She admitted she thought my TA would read it when I met her in the hall.'

'Go on.'

'I handed her the assignment and walked away. There was nothing left to say.'

'Was that the end of your exchange?'

'Last Thursday, I didn't have a class till eleven. I opened my front door to fetch the *Gazette*, and Taylor pushed past me into my home. She must have been waiting on the porch.'

'Did you ask her to leave?'

'Of course I did, and I stayed by the front door. In student jargon, she went ballistic. It was eight o'clock in the morning. Taylor was dressed as if she were going on a date. Students usually appear sloppy and tired for early classes. Apart from her state, that struck me as odd.'

'Please continue.'

'She wanted a third chance. I explained to her, I shouldn't have given her the second. The only concession I was prepared to make was a simple "incomplete." She'd be spared the plagiarism charge. I again requested her to leave.

'She didn't. Taylor was about to knock the papers from my sitting chair in the living room, but changed her mind. I was still at my door, but I can recall exactly what she said: "How dare you ruin my life! You're not God – you're supposed to be teaching me, guiding me. You don't know anything about my life. I have stuff to deal with!"'

'Did she indicate what stuff?'

'No. Our parents are acquaintances, but I don't know anything about Taylor. I just wanted her to leave. She gave me one last chance to help her. I said I couldn't, but she could drop the course and pick up another in the summer session. Taylor started up, "Alright, alright..."' Caitlin could hear her father telling her to stop there, but she had gone to Concordia's Senior Director of Rights and Responsibilities. No doubt these detectives would meet with the director.

'Professor, it's not in your interest to hold back. I can see this is difficult, but go on, please.'

'Taylor rushed to the door and stood face to face with me. "Screw up my life – I'll screw with yours. Let's see how you fight a sexual harassment charge." I couldn't figure out if I saw more hatred than fear in her eyes. Her whole face was blood-red. She stopped on the veranda to catch her breath. Her bag was by the door. I scooped it up, threw it at her feet, slammed the door and locked it.'

'Where's the assault charge, Professor?'

'I sank in my chair, shaking. I guess about a minute later, half a brick crashed through my front window. Had I been sitting up straight, I would have been struck on the head.'

'What did you do?'

'I got out of the living room in case she intended to throw the other half. I stood in the hall, fuming and in shock. I couldn't muster the nerve to open the door. When I did, there was no sign of Taylor.'

'You have no proof Sanderson made that assault.'

'Simple deduction for me, but I understand it's not proof.'

'You called the police then?'

'I called my window installers and I waited two-and-a-half hours for a new window. I stormed down to the Rights Office and spoke to the director. She suggested I call the police since the incident occurred off university grounds. I asked her if Sanderson had filed a charge against me. She told me she could not reveal contents of any charge, but she could speak in hypotheticals. She listened to me. But she also told me I should have followed protocol and reported the first plagiarized assignment. I felt I could do better with the police. I left and called them. I'd file a charge later, but I saw that I had no viable proof for the police, or a charge I could make with Rights and Responsibilities. Taylor was right. In her words, I was screwed. I did keep her first assignment and made a copy of the second, just in case. I see Taylor only twice a week. When she didn't show up for class, I thought guilt was the reason. I don't think she would have told me what the "stuff" was, not in that frame of mind. I feel very badly.' *Dad would be proud. I've just handed these cops a suspect!*

'Professor, where were you this past Tuesday afternoon?'

'My last class on Tuesday ended at two. When I'm troubled, I drive to Mount Royal Cemetery, to the mausoleum where my brother is buried. Years pass, but the hole in my heart is still wide. I'm not that far gone that I talk to Chris, but I feel his presence. He comforts me, and the grounds are peaceful, away from the jungle. It's a good place to be, at least for me.' *Why don't I tell them my whole story?*

'What time frame are we looking at?'

'I was there at three. I didn't bother with the time till I was home. It was four thirty-five.'

'Did anyone see you?'

'No cars passed, workers might have, but it's April. Apart from clearing snow, they're not on the grounds much. I'm a regular. I'm guessing that Taylor died on that Tuesday.'

Matte knew when to stand – it was part of their tag-team routine. Damiano stayed seated. He walked casually out into the hall. Caitlin had an idea what he was doing. With a quick eye sweep, Matte took in a good part of the kitchen and the exercise room. He noticed the specialized mountain bike, carbon no doubt, the Soloflex exercise machine, a towel rack mounted on the far wall beside a blue sink. They signaled quietly to one another at the four pairs of hiking boots on a piece of brown carpet.

'Professor Donovan, thank you for your time. We may need to meet with you again.'

Matte walked out before Damiano and waited until they were inside their car. 'Our prof has no alibi,' Damiano remarked. 'Do you see sexual harassment here?'

'Don't sense that, at least for now. I'll run her. Still, the professor could also easily lift 115 pounds. Her Soloflex is not for amateurs.'

Chapter Fourteen

The detectives again found no parking on Lincoln Avenue, a popular venue for student rentals and professors who taught at Concordia but lived out of town. Damiano edged their car up onto the sidewalk. Times like this, Detective Matte didn't appreciate being a passenger. The apartments and old mansions Matte guessed were well over a hundred years old. From appearances, little renovation had ever taken place. The street smelled old. Windows and frames were shiny, cemented with the grime of years. The atmosphere on the narrow street was heavy and dour. Pedestrians, mostly students, gawked as they edged around the car, but didn't touch it because of the police flashers.

'You're asking for trouble parking like this, Toni.'

'We don't have time to waste. The chief will understand.'

'Sure he will.'

'Our vic's apartment is up there on the left. Students have begun the flower vigil.' A small group had gathered on the sidewalk, talking quietly. 'Who do we see first?'

'The owner said he'd meet us with our vic's key.' When they stood at the well-worn oak door, Detective Matte rang the bell. A man in his sixties, paunchy and balding, opened it. He handed over the key to apartment number 3.

'That belongs, belonged, sorry, to Ms. Sanderson.'

'Did you go inside the apartment after the news broke?' From the way the owner looked – his jacket shredded at the collar and wrists, his pants worn white at the knees – he might have helped himself to the apartment's contents. The man obviously hadn't cashed in on current rental profits.

'No. I drove in from LaSalle half an hour ago. It wouldn't be right after what happened. The place belongs to my mother, and she won't sell. I can't stay around either; I have to get back to work.'

'What do you want us to do with the key?'

'Give it to Amira Cupid. She's very reliable and around.'

'Cupid?'

'Yep, nice name and well suited. Apartment 2.'

Damiano took down the owner's name and phone number and waited until he left before pointing to number 2. 'If she's generally around,

Ms. Cupid must know the goings on better than whatshisname.'

'Josh Goldman. You're terrible with names.'

'Not really, I just don't listen. I allow you to take care of that end of things,' Damiano answered with her best smile.

Matte scowled. He wasn't her secretary. He knew that Damiano respected him, but she took advantage. While she treated him as her equal, she was just *more* equal.

One knock was all it took for the tenant to open the door. Both detectives were taken aback by the stunning young woman who stood by the opened door. The girl had been crying. Her soft dark eyes were watery with tears. Her complexion was flawless, dewy. Dark curls fell over her forehead, and her hair was shiny with light gel. Damiano thought of Luke. If she wasn't six foot, Amira was very close. 'I haven't much room, but you can sit on my bed, and I'll use my stool.' She had spoken directly to Detective Damiano, catching her eye and holding her gaze. Amira wore navy jeans, tight and sylishly creased at the knees and ankles. She was barefoot. A light blue cotton sweater revealed she was at that age when a bra was unnecessary. The detectives followed a lovely light scent and Amira's body swaying into the smallest room ever dubbed an apartment. The forties suddenly felt older.

The room had a suggestion of an alcove. A bed on one wall, an architect's desk spilling with drawings against the other left only inches to pass between them. 'I made that desk myself – I couldn't afford the price of the real ones.' There was no kitchen to speak of. A second-hand mini fridge, a hot plate on the floor beside a toaster and two boxes of Bran Flakes, a clothes cupboard, another cupboard above the single sink, a shower stall with a clothes hamper beside it, the bed and desk. Drawings and books were piled high on the floor. A laptop lay under the desk. 'You don't find it claustrophobic in here?' Damiano probed.

'It's my first place, my lair, no sharing.' Without warning, Amira began to weep. 'I am so sorry for Taylor. I can't go to class, I can't go to work. I have no place to go – no family here. I'm from a small island, Mesopotamia in St. Vincent, you know. My sisters are in Toronto.'

There was soft music in her voice. When Damiano caught Matte's eye, she winked seeing *he* was still admiring the girl. Beauty was beauty – sexual orientation was irrelevant. When he saw Damiano, he shrugged and took out the recorder.

'Ms. Cupid, I'd like to record our conversation for clarity if you don't mind.'

'Am I a suspect then?'

'This is simply routine. I record everyone we question.'

'I see.'

'How long have you known Taylor?'

'Two years.'

'Are you friends or neighbors?'

'Both at different times because of our schedules.'

'In the last eight months?'

'Close friends in September and part of October, then neighbors. I hardly saw her.'

'Schedules?'

'Yes, and Taylor was often out. I drop dead asleep at ten when I come in from work.'

'No falling out?'

'We just don't see one another. Josh often stays in Hampstead with his parents, for holidays, and Jewish people have many holidays. The apartments are so close to one another, but we might as well be living on different streets.'

It was odd, Damiano thought, kids could look you in the eye and lie without blinking, but they still blushed, like Amira. There had been some sort of falling out, she was sure of it.

She asked the next question pointedly. 'Are you seeing anyone?'

Amira laughed heartily. 'I've been forced to beat a few men off with a stick, but I made a decision. Both my sisters married before twenty, and they are unhappy with the husbands who are rarely home. I want my education – men can wait.'

Damiano was hoping for something more. Matte was busy scoping out the room. 'Taylor called you the day she died.'

Amira covered her face with her hands, ushering in another rush of tears.

'The call went unanswered?'

Amira nodded.

'Were you here when she called?'

'Yes.'

'Why didn't you take the call?'

'You will think me terrible.' Again that velvet voice.

'Taylor's death was terrible, Amira.'

'It didn't matter that I didn't take her call because a book fell from my desk. Taylor must have been in the hall then and heard it because she began to pound on my door.

'I had to open my door. We have each other's keys. Taylor was furious about some mark, but she was also very hyper, bouncing off the walls.

'Taylor told me she was in some real trouble and she wanted me to get dressed and go to the abandoned Wellington Tunnel with her right away. She said it was a weird place but we had to go. And we had to be early. I will never forgive myself for not going.' Fresh tears.

'Why didn't you go? Wouldn't you have an interest in the tunnel itself for the architecture alone?'

'I had to study. We are in exams. I must obtain good marks. I can't afford to fail. It's not an option for me."

'There's more, I think, Amira.' The question dangled before Damiano heard the answer.

'I will not speak ill of the dead. Taylor is past her problems.'

'She still needs any help you can provide. She would want the truth from you.'

Amira wiped her tears with long artistic fingers. Damiano wasn't certain, but she thought she saw the hint of a smile that was gone before it appeared. 'In two years, I cannot remember Taylor doing anything for me, not ever. She even joked about it. Friends helped *her*. Taylor and Josh have wealthy families. I do not. I work hard for my food and education. I do not expect anyone to do my bidding. On Tuesday, I said I could not go with her. I had to study, and she bolted. Two minutes later, I put on my coat and ran out to the street, but she had disappeared.'

'That was the last time you saw Taylor.'

'Standing at my door, yes.'

'We may be speaking to you again, Amira. One more question, did Taylor have any close friends?'

Another pause. 'We were friends for a few months. Taylor didn't look for long-term.'

Outside the apartment, Damiano wanted Matte's take. 'Do you believe her, Pierre?'

'No one ever tells us the whole truth. I saw two painted rocks she uses for paperweights, but they were dusty.'

'That's not so rare. I've used rocks for paperweights.'

'Still.'

'Note it. She has no alibi, and she has secrets, I suspect. Maybe Goldman will know something.'

Chapter Fifteen

Josh Goldman surprised them by hurrying through the front door of the apartment building, and the detectives saw a look of relief when he spotted them. 'I had something to finish up. My place is Number One beside Amira.'

Josh was short, expensively dressed in a cashmere pea coat, a large multi-colored scarf knotted at the neck, tight jeans and Doc Martens boots. His black curly hair was thick and unruly, for effect. His eyes were small, but steely blue, and he had perfect teeth. Josh raised his arm and waved them inside.

The kid must have hired an interior decorator to make the best use of small space. multi-colored shelves were mounted on the wall adjoining Amira's. The laptop, the iPod station, books, an array of pens and sundries filled brass pots. His parents had invested in a Murphy bed, so that gave Josh room for a neat teak table with two chairs that were cut for a side wall. He also had room for a captain's chair. A large-screen TV was mounted on the wall as well, and below it a red leather loveseat.

'Nice,' Detective Matte commented.

'Not bad,' Josh said, 'for a start-up. Sit down.' He sat in the captain's chair and crossed his legs at the knees, a tough man's pose. He threw his right arm behind the chair. With a different face, Damiano saw the chief imitating tall manoeuvers. 'We're all talking on campus about Taylor. I guess you have all the house news from the resident spy.'

'Amira?'

'Who else?'

'You're not friends then?'

'Schedules, library, buds – this place is just my drop.'

Damiano took out the recorder, and Josh straightened up.

'What's that for?'

'Routine.' Damiano sped into her next question to distract Goldman from thinking of a lawyer. 'I'd have thought that a guy like you might have felt he'd died and gone to heaven having two attractive women so close by.'

Josh was about to agree, when the expression on his face soured. 'Bitches…'

'Excuse me?' Damiano cut in.

'You can use that word positively. You guys must be cool.'

Detective Damiano tried to supress the instant dislike she took to this witness. 'I'm going to take a stab in the dark here, Josh.' *Keep it friendly.* 'You're a guy going places, so you hit on both women and, and what?'

'It was mutual.'

'What do you mean?'

'Whatever.'

Damiano smiled over at Matte. Goldman bit a nail and spit it across the room. *A genuine little prick!* 'Taylor called you the day she died. We have the phone records.'

'How was I to know it was a life and death call?'

'Point being, you didn't bother picking up.'

'Whenever Taylor called, there was a favor at the other end. I quit taking her calls.'

'Was anyone here friends?'

'Amira and Taylor were tight at the start of the school year. I know 'cause I heard them laughing and talking. Over time, when I was here, the place was quiet. Happens. We're just tenants when you come down to it.'

'Where were you the afternoon she called you?'

'I was here actually, totally wiped. I'd pulled an all-nighter. I'm pre-med.'

'So you knew where she was going. The walls are thin, and she was standing in the hall.'

'She woke me up actually. Put in my buds, and turned over. What time did this happen?'

'You were here the whole night then?'

'Slept like a baby. Anyhow, I did the right thing. Those are my red roses on the steps. Seemed right.'

'You have no alibi, Josh.'

'Don't need one. I had nothing to do with this. Taylor got herself killed all on her own.'

'That's pretty rough talk. At some point, I think Taylor may have dumped you. Am I right?'

Josh Goldman rose and opened the door. 'She was a user. Now, please leave.' He slammed the door after them, but they both clearly heard Josh's last words. 'Fuck her!'

'What a weasel!' Damiano whispered under her breath as she walked the few steps back to Amira's door. Detective Matte didn't move. He took out his phone and tapped in the number of the throwaway. They listened.

'It was worth a try. It's pretty clear that whoever had the phone disposed of it. Let's hope we have better luck with Taylor's apartment.' Before opening the door, the detectives reached into their pockets and put on their white gloves. Sanderson's apartment was double the size of the other two. Hers had a complete bathroom. Matte spotted the tiered makeup case.

'Is that what I think it is?' He used his pen to pull out the first of four drawers. 'Who could use all this?'

'Take a wild guess.' Damiano was opening the medicine cabinet. No meds at all. *Nice to be young!* Beside the bathroom a cupboard was stuffed with designer clothes. At least they were hung up. Her father must have had the apartment painted. The pale yellow was fresh and clean. There was a small kitchen with a fridge and stove. When Damiano opened the fridge she found energy drinks, fruit, a loaf of six-grain bread, Skippy peanut butter, Smuckers raspberry jam and unopened butter sticks.

Matte had gone to Sanderson's laptop and was looking there. Damiano began opening the drawers of the desk, with only a mild hope Sanderson had kept a diary. Kids blogged. She was on the edge of disappointment when she spied crumpled paper in the yellow plastic wastepaper basket. 'Matte, I may have something.' Damiano reached in and lifted out two crumpled sheets by their edges. She dropped them on the desk.

Using pens, they did their best to unfold the first sheet. Sanderson had written a name, but she had crossed it out so many times that the sheet had torn into bits and the name was unreadable. What was left on the sheet was legible, though it too was crossed out: *How could you have done this to me?*

Matte pulled a plastic bag from his inner pocket, and Damiano dropped the note into it. She opened the second, hoping for a name. There was none, but the words were not crossed out: *I was in love with you – I was in love – what a fool I've been…* 'Bag this as well. We can send the notes and laptop to Crime.'

'Ominous words.'

'I finally agree with your vocabulary, Pierre. I wonder if Marie will be able to recover at least part of the name.'

'I doubt it. We also don't know when she wrote this, Toni. I need more time with her phone. Kids keep their lives on their phones. The notes humanize Sanderson. She was probably no better or no worse than the rest of us. She was in love. She didn't deserve to suffocate in a dark hole.'

'True. Every flaw is exaggerated after a murder. We'll need techs here for prints. Crime will be thorough. We'll take the key with us and send it with the package. I wonder if the love in her life is the person with the throwaway phone. We have to trace it.'

'We can learn where the phone was bought. That's it, unless the buyer used a credit card or debit.'

'We have more people to see: the director of Rights and Responsibilities at the University, the boyfriend, the caveman who corresponded with the boys who found the body, Detective Claude Remay, and all our suspects to date. Right now I need food before we head back to the office.' Damiano winced.

'The arm?'

'Yep, early throb. You can choose the eatery.'

'Hurley's on Crescent.'

'I'm a detective. That's where you met Dylan.'

'He called early this morning.'

'No, no, Pierre.'

'We can talk when we get to Hurley's.' Matte veered off the subject – he knew what he'd hear from her. 'Keep in mind the sexual harassment charge filed against the professor. From what we know, she's a possible fit.'

Chapter Sixteen

Hurley's Irish Pub on Crescent Street was a favorite of Montrealers and tourists. Detectives Matte and Damiano chose a table beside a black radiator and sat back in the red leather chairs. Damiano liked the cozy brick walls and carved wood, the eclectic mix of Irish coats of arms and trophies. She ordered the beef stew, Matte the fish of the day and a coke and bottled water, both wishing they could enjoy a Guinness.

Damiano checked the time. 'If we rush, we just might be able to speak to that director at Concordia if she finishes at four. I'm interested to see how she handled the case. You shouldn't have ordered the fish. Extra time wasted. I'm assuming the beef stew is already prepared.'

'Calm down. I think we can make it. Let me call her.' Matte stood and walked to a quieter part of the restaurant, checked his notebook and made the call. He must have gotten through because she could see he was listening. He gave her a thumbs up. 'We have thirty-five minutes to eat.'

'Piece of cake. So Dylan called.'

'He misses me. He wants to come back. Before you trash him, I still love him, Toni. I'm tired of the odd one-nighters. I'm only a year younger than you. It's not easy – it's been nine months. I want Dylan in my life. Whose life is perfect? How are you and Jeff?'

Damiano was aware of Pierre's utter loneliness and it pinched her heart. 'With Jeff and me, it's at that *don't-ask-don't-tell* stage, but we're trying. He knows I want to be at the condo. Jeff doesn't trust me as much as he once did, with reason. It's always a war between my job and him. He can't forgive me for that. If I leave again, I don't know where we'll be. He allots me one painkiller at night for my arm and keeps an eye on the alcohol in the house. So far, I'm hanging in. I want you to be happy, Pierre. You're like a brother to me. Dylan's left you twice, broken you up in pieces. You love him because the relationship wasn't over when he left, but love gets tangled with hurt. I lived those months on the job with you. I remember what you went through. You believe the love survived. Maybe it did, but it's fragmented now; it's less than it was. We're both at the same place – in a cop's life.'

'Less is more than nothing, Toni.' Pierre wiped a tear as though it wasn't there.

'Does Dylan love you, Pierre?'

Matte smiled sadly. 'Dylan loves himself, whatever is left over he offers up. I envy him. He's impulsive and daring. Let's face it; no normal person wants to marry a cop. We're not neurosurgeons, but we have their hours. I know my limitations. I'm not an exciting man. I've never met one person really interested in details, my specialty. I'm lonely. I'll settle for Dylan's leftovers. I'm sick of sitting alone on a bar stool.'

'Then go for it. Moments are all we have in life, at least that's what I'm beginning to see.' The dinners and drinks arrived at the right moment. They ate quietly. 'I'm glad you backed me, Toni.'

Damiano nodded. 'Dinner's my treat.'

'It goes on the account. You want Donat's job, Toni.'

'Sounded good to the waiter. And I'll be sitting in Chief Donat's chair one day!'

The detectives went first to the washrooms before they set out for Concordia University's Hall Building in downtown Montreal. Damiano relied on Matte to find the office of the director. Susan Wyman was on the phone with her door open, and she signalled for them to enter. They stood until she finished the call. 'Lieutenant Detective Damiano and Detective Matte, Ms. Wyman.'

'Please sit down. This is a terrible tragedy. We are prepared to help the grieving family in any way. It's a very sad time for the Sandersons and the university. We value and support our students.'

The detectives read the spin job and nodded appropriately. They knew the information they needed was not going to be easy to gather. Wyman had no doubt spoken to her superiors, and, Matte also guessed, to the universityès counsel, undoubtedly kept on retainer. Universities as large as Concordia were tightly regulated. Wyman, like Damiano, was in her forties, well-dressed, confident, and kept a meticulous office. She was also a party-line administrator who had worked to achieve her position and maintain her mandate. Damiano went for the jugular. They had no time to waste. 'Ms. Wyman, it has come to our attention that Taylor Sanderson filed a charge of sexual harassment against a Professor Donovan. We also know that Professor Donovan informed you about Ms. Sanderson's plagiarized assignments. We have questioned the professor. This is a murder investigation. Our job is bringing the perpetrator of this crime to justice. We need one answer from you. Did you quash or move forward with the charge?'

'I have been advised…'

'Ms. Wyman, we understand there are issues of privacy. Above and beyond those rules and regulations, Taylor Sanderson is dead – please assist us in helping to find the person responsible for her death. We haven't the time to secure a warrant, but we can have such an order issued.'

'I would have gone forward with the charge on the Friday…'

'Did you?'

Wyman appeared anxious to do the right thing. 'I did not, but that does not mean I will discard it, given the tragic turn of events. I am consulting the general counsel tomorrow morning.'

'You're not giving us an answer.'

'It's the best I can do.'

'Can you tell us if Taylor Sanderson had filed charges against other professors?'

'What I can say is that I deal only with the charge as it is presented to me.'

'No background check?'

'My job is handling the immediate charge or complaint.'

Damiano was taken aback. 'Do you inform the professor involved in the charge?'

'Again, no, according to my mandate, I deal only with the charge.'

'May I ask how many complaints or charges you receive a year?'

'In the vicinity of three hundred, give or take.'

'On average, how many do you put forward?'

'Perhaps around thirty.'

'If I understand you correctly, you have not checked to see if any other charges have been made against Professor Donovan in the past?'

'You are correct.'

Detectives Damiano and Matte rose together. They had worked together long enough to know they had reached a stalemate. 'Thank you for your time, Ms. Wyman. I appreciate the constraints of your position.' In the halls, Damiano's head was thumping and she was uncharacteristically quiet. Was it regret Damiano noticed in Wyman's expression, or the reflection of her own? Neither detective spoke until they were outside the building in the fresh air.

'Don't start, Toni! Every institution has its rules.'

Damiano didn't have the chance because her phone chirped.

'Toni, we have prints from the vic's bag.'

'Are you talking the blood smear?'

'No, that's been cut out and sent off to the States. Doesn't mean what we have is not a match. We've no matches with the prints we have.'

'Sanderson had handed in two bogus assignments, but wanted another chance that was refused. According to her professor, Sanderson burst into her home, and later that day, the kid files a sexual harassment charge against the professor. I'd like to know if Sanderson's prints are anywhere else in the house. We don't have the vic's side of the event. You may need a warrant. The professor's not stupid. Matte will drop off a package for you that has the key to Sanderson's apartment. You might want to be present for both.'

'Fine, I can't obtain a warrant this quickly. We'll try the elimination approach with the professor and mention a warrant. I can be pretty convincing.'

'Good. We're driving back to the Division. You'll have the package within the hour. Matte has a hotfoot when he's pressured. We have more people to interview as well. Donovan is interesting because we have only her word about the time and place she picked up the bag. Only her word that Sanderson, essentialy, invaded her home.'

'That's a start.'

'You bet.'

Chapter Seventeen

Caitlin Donovan parked outside one of the three garages at her parents' home on The Boulevard. She used her own key in the red, solid-wood door. The beloved pug, Monsieur, was already sniffing on the other side of it. He jumped as high as he could and performed a pirouette, a shadow of his past performances. 'Mom?' There was no reply. 'Mom!' Caitlin called louder. She ran through the house to the back garden, with only a vague hope of finding her mother. Donovan's nerves were already raw and her tension rose. Returning from the garden she found her mother sitting in the dark at the end of the spacious living room. Exasperated she asked, 'Why didn't you answer me, Mom?'

'Why haven't *you* called, Caitlin? I've been worried to death.' Maggie Donovan rose and turned. She was taller, perhaps even more graceful than her daughter. 'I've been trying to reach you.'

'The police were questioning me this morning. I had afternoon classes.'

'Taylor's death must be so devastating for Trevor and Shari – we know what it is to lose a child in terrible circumstances. Are the police talking to all of Taylor's professors?'

Caitlin knew that her mother had been to the hospital and did not wish to talk about her condition. She didn't want to add to whatever problems her mother had chosen to face alone, though she felt like crying and talking everything out for her mother's reassurance and guidance. 'They have to gather as much information as they can. It's all routine. Taylor was one of my students.'

'Have you called the Sandersons to express your sympathies?'

'No, I haven't. It's you I want to talk to, Mom. Will you please tell me what's going on? Finding you all alone in the dark is heart-breaking. What happened at the hospital today? Not knowing is killing me.'

Maggie Donovan, once a vivacious, animated, loud laugher, had changed the night her son was killed. The surviving family members were never the same again. Caitlin and her father had thrown themselves into work, and Maggie had become solitary and quiet. She looked over at her daughter. 'None of this gets back to your father. I can't cope with his sympathy or his guilt or the lectures that undoubtedly will come. I have a mass, Cait. They won't know if it's a cyst or a tumor until they have the results of the biopsy. That's all I can say.'

'Oh, Mom. Can I take you to the biopsy?'

'I've had it done today.'

'Jesus, Mom. I would have taken you and been with you.' Caitlin hugged her mother and tried not to cry. 'I'm sorry I haven't been around more often. It doesn't matter how much time has passed. It's hard for me in this house – I still see Chris everywhere. The grief suffocates me. I have to get on with life. That doesn't mean I forget him, but I work.'

'I like feeling him close by. It's a comfort. Maurice drove me down to the Royal Victoria Hospital today and waited for me.'

'He's your chauffeur, Mom.'

'He's become a friend to me, Cait.' Caitlin had stopped listening. A cancerous mass had insinuated itself somewhere in her mother's body, and it might threaten her life. How could she compound her mother's fear by revealing anything about Taylor Sanderson? She turned on the lights; the room brightened. The dusty-blue leather sofas and white-linen natural fibers of the single chairs blended softly with creamy white walls that were home to artwork worth hundreds of thousands of dollars. The huge stone fireplace was dark.

'I know what you're thinking. I don't want you calling your father. I won't know the results for at least two weeks.'

'But Mom…'

'Come over here, Cait, and hear me out. If this mass is not a cyst, I have pancreatic cancer. I remember too well the two-year battle my friend Rosemary endured: the pain, the chemotherapy, the infections, the nerve blocks that didn't work, the daily narcotics and finally the diabetes. Yes, she's beaten the odds, but for how long? My heart is tired – I haven't the energy for a war. I lost a chunk of my heart when Chris was killed. You and your father are off on your own. I yearn for peace. Try to understand, Cait.'

Caitlin was crying. 'You're only sixty-two. I know you have the idea that you'll be reunited with Chris. He won't be on the other side, Mom. There is no one on the other side.'

'You don't know that, Cait.'

'I know I don't want to lose you – I know that! Let me help you. I can make the appointments, and I'll take you to all of them. You have to be brave, Mom. You were once.'

Maggie smiled at her daughter. 'I got lucky when I had you. I haven't anything for dinner, but there is homemade soup.'

The front doorbell rang its tune. 'Who could that be?'

'I invited Carmen over.'

'No talk of the mass.'

'Alright.' Caitlin hurried to the front door. Monsieur couldn't catch up to her. 'Hey, what's all this?'

'Salad and pizza from St-Michel, all natural. It's about time I treat for all the meals I've eaten here.'

Caitlin took the food, laid it on the floor and used her foot to keep Monsieur away. 'Mom's not well. Say nothing about Sanderson.'

'But…'

'But really – nothing.'

Monsieur was pirouetting without results. Miffed, he ambled off.

'Mom, Carmen brought pizza. Do you prefer soup?'

'Hi, Maggie. It's so great to see you. I want a hug.' Carmen walked over and got her usual fix.

'Salad and pizza are fine. No need to fuss. We'll eat in the kitchen. Caitlin, will you set up and I'll chat with Carmen.'

Caitlin rushed through the work, unwrapped the heavy brown paper stapled around the slab pizza, watching out for the staples, and laid it on a pan before she shoved it into the oven. She set out the glasses, knives and forks, salad bowls and plates and chose a rosé from the fridge. With a quick toss, the salad was ready. Leaning over the table, her limbs shook as she thought of Taylor. *That damn little bitch!* She ran some water and splashed it on her face. 'Alright, guys, come and get it. We'll begin with salad. The pizza will be ready soon.'

'I like it cold,' Carmen said, and Caitlin sent her a look.

'Tonight it's hot.'

'Good enough.'

Once they had begun the pizza, Maggie smiled. 'It's so good to be together, such good memories.' Caitlin looked at her mother and felt better. It was Carmen who heard the phone. 'I think it's yours. I have mine with me.'

Caitlin found her phone in her bag by a chair in the living room and answered. 'Yes?'

'Professor Donovan?'

'Speaking.' Caitlin guessed it was the police, and her nerves sparked.

'I'm at your home. I'm Marie Dumont from Crime, and I need your prints, Professor.'

'Can't this wait? I'm at dinner with my mother.'

'I'm afraid not. I can go to you.'

'No! I need twenty minutes.'

'I'll be here.'

Caitlin rubbed the stress from her face before she entered the kitchen. 'Mom, I have to go home for half an hour. I had work done on my front window, and the contractor wants to finish up. He has to get into the house. I'll be back in a flash. I'll reheat my pizza. You're in good hands with Carmen.' Caitlin was out the front door in a flash, cursing and swearing.

'What's all this about, Carmen?'

'Caitlin had the work done this past week. I thought it was finished.'

Maggie stopped eating. 'You and Caitlin have been friends so long that you lie alike. What's going on?'

Chapter Eighteen

Gripping her jacket against swirling gusts of wind, Caitlin rushed over to her new Golf GTI VII, and slammed the door behind her. 'Spring in Montreal.' She backed out carefully, then threw the clutch into drive and goosed the gas pedal. *That call was not routine. They're zoning in on me for God's sake. I'd have to be an idiot not to see their target. If Dad were here, he'd tell me to focus. What's that Euripides quote he uses as a mantra: 'Question everything. Learn something. Answer nothing.' I've blown the third rule already.* When she reached Sherbrooke Street, she blew a light and swore. On Wood Avenue, she drove carefully and was forced to park halfway up the street. She wasn't spotted until she turned into the short stone path that led to her front stairs.

'Professor Donovan?'

'Yes.' Caitlin turned to find Marie Dumont and a male partner.

'We're crime investigators. We called you a little while ago.'

'Follow me then.' Caitlin's voice was surly. Once they were inside the home, Caitlin led them to the custom-made knotty pine kitchen. It was exceptionally neat, giving Dumont the impression that the professor rarely cooked. There was a large fruit bowl, walnuts, and a water cooler. 'I'd like to get this over with as quickly as possible.'

'Let's get started then, Professor.' The prints took a few minutes.

'That's it?'

'Detective Damiano passed on a few questions, if you don't mind ...'

Caitlin began to feel the full weight of this visit. Damiano felt that Caitlin had motive and opportunity. She also had no alibi. She had no answer to put forward that would exculpate her from suspicion. Injustice was an everyday occurrence. 'I'd like to hear the first question.'

Standing, Dumont smiled and placed her hands on her ample hips before she spoke.

Was the woman trying to intimidate her? Caitlin put up her guard.

'You told Detective Damiano that Sanderson burst into your home. Did you notice if she touched any of the walls in the hall?'

'No, I don't think so, I was taken by surprise.'

'You said she marched into your living room. Did she touch anything in that room?'

Caitlin tried to recall. 'She was about to push my papers on the floor.

She may have laid her hand on the back of that chair.' Caitlin pointed to her favorite chair.

'May we dust for prints?'

Caitlin led them back into the living room. The male tech began his work.

'Professor Donovan, we are interested in eliminating you from the suspect list. Would you permit my tech to take prints in your bedroom?'

'What?'

'You are aware of the sexual harassment charge. This investigation will help clear your name and quash the charge.' Marie used her best persuasive tone.

Question everything. 'Has Detective Damiano told you what was behind this ridiculous charge?'

'Bogus assignments, I understand.'

'That's correct. The motive for her charge is the "incomplete" I gave as her grade.'

'All the more reason you should allow us a full inspection that can only work in your favor.'

Question everything. Answer nothing. 'Have you heard of infringement of privacy?' Caitlin could smell the incoming fire from Detective Damiano, and she had no intention of being burned by it.

Marie smiled. 'Your answer is no then?'

'Ms. Dumont, please leave my home. You asked for my prints and I provided them.'

'If we can't check for prints in the bedroom, we won't be able to clear you.'

'I have to get back to dinner with my mother.' *Dad would be proud.*

Once they were back in the car and driving to Lincoln Avenue, Marie Dumont called Detective Damiano. 'We just left the professor.'

'Bedroom?'

'No. The professor is intelligent and either righteously angry or a smooth sociopath. We did manage to dust for prints in the hall and living room.'

'Her father is one of the top lawyers in Quebec.'

'I thought you said the vic's father was...'

'Both are, and they know one another. Are you going after a warrant?'

'Yes. We want to be thorough. Now I have to get back to the office to pick up the notes and key. You dropped it off, right? I wanted to get to the professor's house asap. I'll backtrack. Remember me in your will.'

'I appreciate the work, Marie, above and beyond.'

Dumont was her best ally on cases. Damiano told Matte they'd had no luck. When her phone rang, she thought it was Marie. 'Toni, you have to come home. Luke went to school, but I don't think he's eaten in the past day and a half. He won't come out of his room, and won't let me in. He needs your help. You can't foist all this on me. He'll talk to you.'

'Well…'

'Never mind "well." You have a son who needs you.'

'I'm coming.' Damiano kept a nagging suspicion at bay that Luke needed more help than she could give him. Teenage emotions were fierce. 'Pierre, you'll have to cover for me tonight at the office. There's a problem with Luke. I have to go. Please set up an interview with Sanderson's ex, Andrew Weston, make contact with Glen, the tunnel man, and learn what you can on Donovan from Detective Remay. We also need a list of Sanderson's friends, probably from her phone. I'll be back as soon as I can.'

'No problem. Take your time with Luke. We also need some time in the office together to analyze what we have. We're scattered at the moment. I'm willing to stay late to study the leads we have.'

'You're right.' When they reached the Division, Damiano walked over to her Mini and drove to Anwoth Road. Jeff opened the front door before she reached it. 'Thanks,' he said.

'No need.' Damiano steeled herself, and didn't knock before she entered Luke's room. Luke had his head under the covers. 'Dad!'

'It's me, Luke.'

'Dad sent for the troops. I don't want you in here either. This is my room.'

'This is *our* house.'

Luke sprang up from under the sheets. The boy's face was haggard. He looked beaten. 'You want me to leave the house? I will! I don't want to be here anyway,' he raged.

'I don't want you going anywhere. I want you to talk to me – tell me what's wrong.'

'I'm not a kid. I'm not going to blab to my mother. I have to sweat this out myself.'

'You're not doing a good job on your own.'

'I went to school today, and I'll be back at that dumb place on Monday and Tuesday and the rest of the week. When I'm home – I want to be left alone!'

'Luke, when I was sixteen I fell for a "bad boy." He was cool when cool meant "neat and even dangerous." He was *my* first love, but he'd never fit in with my crowd. We met in places where my friends wouldn't be caught dead. His hair was dark and thick and slicked back, different from my friends. He always stood close to me, like he was protecting me. I got scared I'd be seen with him, so one day I stuffed a note in his locker: *I never want to see your face again.* I figured he had girls trailing after him, so my note was no big deal. Well, two years ago he called me. You can find anyone today. He said he still had the note, that it had ripped his heart open. For years, he never fully trusted anyone. He wanted me to know that. He's an engineer now and works in New York. He didn't ask or care about me. Twenty-seven years later his call hurt me, and I deserved to be told. We are all guilty at one time or another of hurting someone.'

Luke hadn't moved. He'd listened. Words tumbled from his heart. 'I liked the way her hands moved. I just liked to smell her hair. I was somebody new with her – my heart pounded when she kissed me...' Damiano watched blood creep up Luke's neck, and was touched.

'What happened, Luke?'

'I fucked up like I said before.' His tone was flat, lifeless. 'I lost her…' Luke fell back on the bed. 'I lost it all. I ruined everything.'

'We've both fucked up then.' Damiano saw the braiding of past and present with Luke's actions and her own. 'Thing is – you have to accept what you've done and get back on your feet.'

Luke wept. 'I'll never love someone that much again – I know it. I know what I lost.'

'Maybe you're right, Luke. A first love is never forgotten or repeated. When we're young, we don't think ahead, until it's too late.'

Luke cried like a kid, and Damiano gathered him in her arms. 'Maybe you're wrong too.'

She stayed with Luke until she felt a lightness in his body and knew he had fallen asleep. Her arm was pulsing. She pulled a blanket up to his chest and tiptoed from the room.

Jeff had caught the conversation from the hallway. When he was sure that Luke couldn't hear, he whispered, 'Good work, but you didn't need to make up a story – you've had your real share of "fuck ups,"' he whispered in her ear.

'Who says it was fiction? I'm sorry, but I have to be back at work, Jeff.'

'You can't talk?'

'Know what, I'm feeling bad that Luke takes after me. You're the better person.' She kissed Jeff on the mouth. 'I'm a poor role model. You're kind and gentle.'

'Well, thanks, I guess. Somehow, I feel we have our roles reversed.'

'Have to get back, Jeff.'

He stood alone in the hallway, and felt a familiar isolation. Being the better person didn't feel good. Jeff had been too busy and tired for girls in med school. Damiano was *his* first love, the one who ignited his heart. 'Guess I came second, just like I do now.' He smiled half-heartedly and stopped by Luke's door. He was still asleep. He went into the master bedroom and lay on the bed on his back with his fingers clasped behind his neck. His lips curled – he'd never known that jealousy was hot, as hot as love.

Chapter Nineteen

Detective Matte was on the phone taking notes. 'What's your final take on Donovan?' He listened; Damiano sat quietly. 'Might she be good for Sanderson? Right. Thanks for the time.' Matte looked at his notes. 'Short version or long version?'

'You should know me by now.'

'Alright. Donovan was devastated, blamed herself for her brother's death. She had suggested he walk home from her place on Wood. With her bud, Carmen DiMaggio, joined later by her guy, Mike, they worked tirelessly and tracked down the DUI driver. Remay says they closed the case for him. Didn't really get in his way – took risks – got the job done.'

'Is she a vigilante then?'

'Remay liked her.'

'Where does that leave us?'

'He also added she's not a woman to back down when injured. Donovan thinks Sanderson threw a brick that could have struck her on the head and left her severely injured. Yet, Donovan doesn't have an alibi. Coincidence?'

'You're forcing it, Pierre. Let's see where her prints go. What's happening with the prints on that cable at the entrance of the tunnel?'

'You've been running Dumont around the city.'

'She's not the only person working at the lab. I don't want to go over Dumont's head for results. It's taken time to forge a close alliance with her.'

'Let's leave that then. I did reach the ex and he should be here soon.'

'Good. Did you give him anything on the phone?'

'Nothing. He seemed nervous, but who isn't when the police call. I began the work on the vic's phone. I have the names and numbers of two friends she seemed to be in close contact with. One of them might know the identity of the throwaway. She must have shared that with someone. Most girls talk – guys too.'

'Glad you added that.' Damiano stood up, intending to get some water, but she added a groan.

'You should see someone about the arm.'

'Who?' she shot back. 'Eight months of physio! All two doctors, including Jeff, can tell me is I may have nerve damage. I'm stuck with it.'

'Don't sneak vodka or narcotics into work – if you do, I will report you. I can't go through the same shit a second time. If anyone had learned about your condition in the last case, we could have been suspended and had the case blown up.'

Damiano felt like knocking Matte off his chair. Instead, she walked out and returned with a bottle of Advil. 'Happy?'

'Relieved.'

She shook the bottle and dropped two in her palm. 'There is so much acid in these that they make my stomach raw.'

'Try Gravol.'

'Now you want me dizzy?'

'Half a pill is all you need.' The phone rang. The ex was waiting downstairs. 'I'll go and bring him up. Relax.'

'I have your permission?'

'You do, Lieutenant.' Damiano ditched the bottle in a drawer and threw out the two in her hand. She reached into her pocket for the half pill folded inside a Kleenex and swallowed it with a gulp of stale coffee that left her tongue stained. Pain beat out Damiano's vow.

A few minutes later, she saw Sanderson's ex with Matte. She was at that age, she admitted sadly, where every young person looked like a kid. Before they reached her office, Damiano remembered the throwaway and the 'stuff' Sanderson had told the professor. The owner of that phone took off. They needed him. He was an important key.

'Lieutenant Detective Damiano, this is Andrew Weston.'

Weston was about to extend his hand, but changed his mind. He wore the layered look over a blue hoody. Damiano liked the effect. Weston wore the stubble male look and that cement gel that kept his brown hair in tight brushed-back spikes. He had a kind face.

'Good morning, Andrew, sit there if you will.' She'd try the buddy approach. 'We need information on Taylor Sanderson. We hope you can provide us with a more complete picture of her. You don't mind if I record our conversation. It's routine. I understand you two were an item.'

Weston pushed his chair back and it grated on the floor. 'I want to help. Yes, for over a year.'

'But you broke up.'

Weston dropped his head and scratched above his ear. His hair didn't move. 'Taylor's exact words were "I'm done."'

'Were you taken by surprise then?' Damiano watched him closely.

Weston squared his shoulders then steepled his fingers. 'I felt taken. We had made long-term plans. I didn't see it coming. Then again if you're not looking for it, you don't see it.'

'Did you walk away?'

'Actually, Taylor didn't finish her shrimp gumbo. She left the restaurant and dumped me too.'

'You know what I mean, Andrew.'

'I called her, I swore a lot, looked for her on campus and gave up the day she passed me on de Maisonneuve and looked right past me.'

'You stalked her?'

'No!' he protested. 'I just wanted to see her, see if she was going to classes. I never went back to her apartment. I had some pride.'

'What happened?'

'Do I know? I suppose Taylor was bored. She hated routine.'

'Have you forgiven her?'

'Took a few months, but I did.'

'Are you seeing anyone now?'

'I'm partying some, but I'm not ready to commit, not near ready.'

'Have you had any contact with Taylor in the past few weeks?'

'Yes. She snail-mailed me an invite to dinner.'

This got Damiano and Matte's attention. 'When, Andrew?'

'I received it on that Tuesday. I don't know why – the note said not to contact her. She'd call me.'

'On the Tuesday of her murder? She just sent this note out of nowhere?'

'I guess. I didn't call her. I know her well enough to know if I called *her*, she'd say to forget the dinner. I never heard from her again.'

'Do you have the card?' Weston was using the present tense. Damiano saw it might be a natural slip or a deliberate ruse.

Weston stood and reached into his back pocket for his wallet. He pulled out the card. 'You can't confiscate it. The card is important to me. It's mine.'

'It's information in a murder investigation, Andrew.'

Matte was writing out a receipt. 'We'll have it sent to the lab, but we will return it to you.'

'I shouldn't have mentioned it.'

'You did the right thing.'

'Don't lose it, please. I love her. I guess I mean loved.' He handed the note over to Damiano, still in its envelope. Sanderson had mailed it on the Saturday before her death. The invitation offered nothing but the date and her name for the planned dinner. Sanderson had printed it.

'Do you recognize this printing as Taylor's?'

'Yes. She sent me invites when we were together, always printed.'

'You didn't think of calling her family when she failed to contact you?'

'I figured she changed her mind.'

'What about when the papers reported her missing?'

'We're deep in exams. I was freakin' busy. I didn't want her to tell me the invite was some joke. I stayed out of it. Bad move on my part, but *I* went through a bad year after she was "done." I was almost sorry I'd even heard from her. I was putting distance between us, feeling better.'

'You can leave, but we may call on you again, Andrew.'

'I've told you everything.'

'Just not at the right time.'

As Andrew rose to leave, Damiano's phone rang. She signalled Matte to take it while she led Weston to the elevator at the other end of the room. By the time she returned, Matte was saying: 'We will go to the hospital immediately.'

'What's this about?'

'Matthew Sanderson has been taken to the Montreal General Hospital.'

'I have to call the chief.'

Donat was in no mood to hear how they hadn't handled a dangerous situation properly. 'I bear the responsibility because I called him and believed he was in control. If Sanderson hurt his son again, arrest his ass. But check it out first! We can't have him crashing down on the department. And the case?'

'We have suspects Chief. It's only been a day and a half.'

'I need results, Damiano. I can't have the media suggesting we're dragging. Work it!'

'We have to check out the witnesses. The drop site threw us a curve, means more traffic.'

'Learn to hit curves.' Donat was rocking on his heels. 'I want an immediate update on the kid's injury.'

After Donat had left, Damiano asked Matte if he wanted to come with her to the hospital. 'No, I'll be here laying out our evidence. We need some thinking time.'

'I promise I'll be back. Order in some food.'

'Toni, I brought some with me.'

'On your monument will be inscribed: *He never missed a detail!*'

Chapter Twenty

Damiano caught a lucky break when she spotted a motorist leaving a parking space on Cedar Avenue. She nosed her car in as the driver pulled out. She used her credit card for the meter and held up her badge to stop two cars as she hurried across Cedar through the General's entrance. At the information desk, she discovered that Sanderson was in Emergency. Familiar with the hospital, Damiano walked briskly past the heavy hospital smells, thinking of the kid to block them out. Was Matthew all right? Was he still hiding something? Had he actually gone to the tunnel and abandoned his sister? Did Trevor Sanderson know? Was that the reason for the second assault?

Lawyers, like cops, had perks, and Damiano was not surprised that Matthew wasn't lying on a gurney in a hallway. He was in one of Emergency's four side rooms, each of which had two patients. His room had a window. A mother and young daughter were standing by the other patient, the husband, Damiano surmised. Neither Matthew nor his mother saw Damiano until she was a few feet from them. Trevor Sanderson was absent. She was about to say something when Matthew threw off his covers and awkwardly tried to leave, although he was sedated. His action triggered something deep in Damiano. Her panic was immediate. She couldn't breathe. Damiano grabbed the foot of the bed and almost passed out.

'Detective, what's wrong?'

Damiano labored to breathe.

'Sit on the floor, Detective,' Shari Sanderson advised. 'Put your head down, take deep breaths.'

Damiano tried, but her breathing was strained and thin.

'Do you need help?'

Damiano waved her off.

Sanderson knelt beside Damiano. 'Don't force – take one long deep breath.'

Air filled Damiano's lungs. Color rose to her cheeks. 'Thank you. I'm fine.' Damiano got up slowly, embarrassed and still shaky. 'It must have been something I ate…'

'Detective, I believe you've had some sort of panic attack.'

Looking around, Damiano was about to deny the attack.

Then she noticed, disturbed by the incident, Matthew had returned to bed while his mother's attenton was on her. He turned his head towards Damiano.

The words Damiano had shared with Luke flooded her mind. *You're not the only one who's damaged someone else.* She felt a sudden release from being the tough cop.

Although a delayed reaction she answered, 'You're right. I … I tried to… but I once lost a young man…'

'The story was in the papers.'

'Well, then you know.'

'You're human like the rest of us.'

'I am.' Damiano spoke to Matthew. 'I'm trying to help you. I'm trying to protect you. I have to know how this happened.'

Matthew was silent.

'Shari, let's put aside formalities. Did you see what happened?'

'I was on the phone with my mother, but I heard Matthew fall.'

'Was Trevor upstairs with him?'

Matthew looked hard at his mother, but she looked away. 'Trevor went up with boxes to tell Matthew to pack up the things he'd broken.'

'Was he shouting?'

'No, and that's the truth.'

'Did Trevor come back down before Matthew fell?'

Shari shook her head.

'Did…'

'Dad didn't push me.'

'What happened, Matthew?'

'I just tripped. That's all. No big mystery.'

His mother brushed the hair from Matthew's forehead. 'Did you fall on purpose, son?'

Matthew was about to speak the truth, but couldn't. 'I tripped. It would be better if I had died, and not Taylor.' He turned away from them. 'Just go. Dad never touched me.'

Damiano inhaled deeply and led Shari Sanderson from the room. 'I don't think Matthew is safe at home, with himself or with his father. Could he stay with your parents?'

'Trevor won't allow Matthew to leave, but I can ask my mother to come to us, if I feel I need her. Matthew said he tripped.'

'We both know that Trevor struck Matthew; please don't deny it. This second time, Matthew may have tripped or he may have thrown himself down the stairs. He's in danger, either way. As I've discovered, guilt can be over-powering. You don't want to lose your son.'

'Oh my God! No!'

'I'm trying to help you, but I have to act accordingly, and I must get back to the case.'

Shari Sanderson wept. 'None of us can believe Tay is gone. Blaming one another is a way of blocking the truth. It's so hard. My husband and son are so angry – so full of rage, and I'm numb. Will I ever forget Tay's eyes, already shrunken into her head… They're all I see now.'

Damiano's breath caught for a second when she saw the kid falling from her. How soon would she forget? 'Call your mother now. Ask, no beg her, to come to the hospital. You need her help. The tragedy is a heavy burden for you and your husband.'

'Trevor is so angry at me, at Matthew, at life and at himself as well. I will call my mother, because I obviously can't manage. I don't even want to manage anything. I want to lie down alone and weep for my little girl, but a refuge is not possible. Matthew needs me.' Shari had no intention of making that call. She hadn't the energy to comfort and console her mother. That's what she'd end up doing. Trevor would be furious – she couldn't cope with either of them. She was numb to any advice. Her body ached. It took what was left of her strength to speak to Detective Damiano. 'Thank you for your kindness, Detective. Take care of yourself.'

Damiano blushed. Once she was outside the room, she was flooded with emotion. Uneasy with them, she rushed back to her car and called the chief and brought him up to date.

'That was a good call. Come back and work the case.'

'I'm on my way. The Sanderson kid came out of this fall only with bruises.'

'Good. You don't sound right, Detective.'

'I'm a mother, Chief. This thing could have been worse.'

'On the job, you're my lead detective, unless you want to hand off.'

'I don't, Chief.'

'Be a cop then.'

Damiano sat in her car, favoring her arm. SAQs were easy to find. Just the thought of a few good shots made her mouth water. The problem was Matte. He had a nose, and that nose knew every mint she'd used. His threat to call her out was real. Biting her lower lip, she started the car and picked up a gluey pizza on her way to the Division. When she reached the second floor, she spied Matte still at work in her office. At least he had water bottles beside the files.

'Good to see you and the pizza. Give me the short hospital version.'

'What's up here? I saw a white Porsche pulling into the parking lot.'

'Might be our tunnel guy. He's actually Glen Gardiner, a computer programmer.'

'Well, he can tunnel, but he obviously can't find a buzzer.'

'Eat that thought. Here he comes, courtesy of Detective Fournier who brought him up.'

Damiano grudgingly put the pizza on top of a cabinet and opened the door. 'Lieutenant Detective Damiano and Detective Matte. Please take a seat.'

'Glen Gardiner.' He was tall and immediately personable, offering a hearty handshake. A handsome man who'd begun to lose his hair, he'd pushed his shades up on his head to hide the fact. There was no sun, so the ruse was his mask. 'How can I help you?'

'Was that your Porsche?'

'You bet. If you know cars, it's an analogue. That's a car that demands more of its driver by fusing feel and drive. Means the vehicle has the character, challenge and style of the better- made Porsches. I use my GTI to race though.' Gardiner relaxed with a driver's smugness.

'You mean when you're not contributing to the delinquency of minors.'

'Whoa! That tunnel is a city treasure, should never have been locked up. The kids weren't squatters – they just wanted a peek.'

'They're minors! You told them to bring a hacksaw.'

'You're right there, Detective Damiano. I wish I could have taken them, but I was out of town, and they were determined. I forgot to tell them to come with a new lock. No harm, no foul. You're not going to lay a charge on me. You guys are Homicide, correct?'

His charm began to irritate Damiano and Matte. 'I'll deal with that issue later. When did you check out the tunnel for the boys?'

'On the Friday, the week before the tragedy.'

'Did you scope the tunnel and the towers?'

'Didn't have time. I saw the lock on the tunnel entrance, figured the others were locked. I have obligations. When I'm not tunnelling, my wife wants me home.'

'Where's out of town?'

'New York, actually Manhattan.'

'When did you leave?'

'Drove early Wednesday morning – boss won't spring for flights – and drove back Friday night. I read about the student last night. It's Saturday, and I'm bushed, but I'm here for you.'

'You had no choice, Sir!' The man was galling.

'That's another way of looking at it.'

'You're a tunnel man, a car man, a program man.'

Gardiner smiled.

'Where were you last Tuesday from noon on?'

'At work and home. Is that the day…?'

'Witnesses?'

'You'd have to call my office, I wasn't counting heads.'

'Home?'

'Wife at seven, traffic. I live in Pierrefonds. Look guys, I'm tired, I had nothing to do with the murder. I'd like to leave.'

'You're free to go, for now.' Damiano turned her back and reached for the pizza and waited for the door to close. 'What do you think?'

'I'm not good with charm, or tunnels, or cars. He was in the city on Tuesday.'

'Gardiner's slippery. Run him and check his alibi.'

Chapter Twenty-one

By the time Caitlin Donovan was back in her mother's kitchen, all that was left of the pizza was the brown wrapping. Carmen threw up her shoulders, 'We realized you'd been held up and I was hungry. Italians and pizza! I've heated up the soup for you.'

'I need wine,' Caitlin said.

'Cait, Carmen won't tell me a thing, but I know something is wrong. What is it? Has this something to do with Taylor Sanderson? You balked when I asked if you had called the Sandersons with your sympathies. I have to call, and I don't want to be put in an awkward position.'

'Of course you can call them. Whatever is happening isn't serious. It's just awkward. Your health is far more important. You're my concern, Mom.'

Carmen looked from one to the other.

'Caitlin Donovan, I've changed your diapers. I know my daughter. You wouldn't be here tonight unless you were troubled. You know I'll be up all night worrying until I learn the truth.'

'Dammit, Mom, can't you let me deal with this problem alone? I want to take care of you. Are you that stubborn?'

'Caitlin…'

'Stay out of it, Carm.' Caitlin kneaded her hands, knowing she had gone too far.

Maggie smiled sadly at her daughter. 'I will not be sworn at in my home. It might be better if you both leave.' Maggie clutched her stomach when she rose from the chair.

'Sit down, Mom. See, I've already made everything worse, and I haven't said a word. I'm sorry. I'm trying to help though I'm not doing a good job of it.'

'Why can't you trust me, Cait?'

'I'm sorry I swore. It's complicated.'

'It is until you lay it out and we can analyze it.'

'Fine. Taylor was a student of mine. She handed in a plagiarized assignment. Following university protocol, I should have reported it. We knew the Sandersons, so I gave her a break. Then, she handed in a second bad assignment. I had to give her an incomplete for her final mark. She had the gall to barge into my home and demand a third break. I refused.

Minutes later, I believe she threw a brick through my front window, narrowly missing me. Before leaving, she warned me she'd ruin my life like I was "screwing" hers. She filed a sexual harassment charge against me at the university. She confided that she was in trouble of some kind. Maybe I should have helped her. But I was angry. Then, she's murdered.

'The police see me as a suspect. I have no proof she threw the brick – I was too freaked to open the front door. They have my prints. They want a warrant to search my house because I told them I handled Taylor's backpack when she ran away from the house. I tossed it to her. She must have been found with it. Worst of all, I have no alibi.

'I've always been fair with my students. I should have reported Taylor, and I should have been more attentive to her problem, but she was arrogant and hyper. I failed her. She did exactly what she promised she'd do. She's put me in a real bind. I don't know the dean or the director of Rights and Responsibilities at the school, they don't know me. I worry that they will judge me negatively and it's too late for me to file a charge against Taylor because I assigned her an incomplete for her grade. My job is on the line, along with everything else. The police have to find someone. They have their eyes on me.'

'That is some deep shit.'

'Thanks for that, Carm.'

'Where were you the day Taylor was murdered?'

'Where I always go when I'm scared – to the cemetery to be with Chris. I still believe in angels, I guess.'

'You need a lawyer, Cait. Call your father. Tell him what you've told me. He'll suggest the right person.'

'I have to hope the police are investigating the "stuff" in Taylor's life. I understand the university's prime concern is the students, but I'm left high and dry. That's how I feel.'

'First things first. Eat the soup. You look worse than I do. Would you like to spend the night here with me?'

'Yes, Mom.'

'Carmen?'

'I'm in. We all need a glass of wine.'

'An herbal tea for me, Carmen.'

Caitlin was hugging her mother. 'I'm sorry to bring all this on you.'

'Don't be, Cait. Mothers don't stop being mothers.' Maggie was excellent at note taking, as neat as a penciler for comics, as precise as Detective Matte. For the next few hours, she took notes of the events as they had happened on a legal pad. 'I've learned from your father that you must come prepared to meet your lawyer. The more we have, the more concise a report, the better their start.'

Carmen listened and took care of the wine. Monsieur had been lost in the seriousness. He tried to stifle his disappointment by moping at Maggie's feet. Caitlin had thought of something her father had once said. 'Actually, ninety-nine percent of people who seek out lawyers are guilty.' Maggie was exhausted; she left the two friends and retired.

Carmen had been waiting for an opportunity to speak to Caitlin. 'Do you have a plan?'

'What do you mean?'

'We're pretty good at amateur investigating. I'll help.'

'This is serious, Carm. I could lose my job. Worse case, arrested for first-degree murder.'

'Chris died. Wasn't that serious? Didn't stop us from finding the truth. You can't pull a lame duck.'

'If the sexual charge leaks out, I'm done.'

'It hasn't yet.'

'It's ignorant of me to lecture at Concordia for eight years and never read the code of conduct.'

'Who does until you need it?'

'There's a huge memorial for Taylor tonight at nine outside the Hall Building.'

'Bingo! You should go because all her profs will attend. It wouldn't look right if you weren't there. Stay away from me. I'll pose as a student and ask a few questions, teary-eyed. Easy, I cry at anything.'

'I don't know her friends. It's a risk.'

'Doing nothing is worse. You have to try something.'

'Taylor said there was "stuff" in her life as though that was the reason she couldn't write the assignment.'

'That usually means someone she was seeing, maybe someone threatening her. That's a hook.'

'It's after nine.'

'We're five minutes away, from the school' Carmen reminded her.

'I might learn something from her profs. Half an hour, then we head home. Stay away from me. No one should make the connection.'

'Good! Let's go. We should walk.'

'Not together!'

'I'll walk along Sherbrooke Street. You take de Maisonneuve, Caitlin.'

'Carm…'

'I promise to tread carefully.'

Chapter Twenty-two

Damiano was finishing her fourth piece of pizza while Matte was shaking his head.

'Are you on Lipitor?'

'No, and my blood's good.'

'Won't be for long.'

'I'll be a happy corpse while you'll lie in the ground longing for the nasty food you denied yourself.'

Matte gave their 'stop' signal and picked up his phone. 'Detective Matte, Major Crimes. Ms. Bernier, we had an appointment. Fine, I do understand. Before you go, are you free tomorrow? I know it's Sunday, but time is crucial. Do you know if Taylor was seeing anyone? Hmm, I thought friends shared. Did you wonder why she was so secretive? I see. But you didn't ask? Alright, then. I'll be in touch if we still need to see you.'

Matte swore; something unusual for him. 'This Nicole Bernier was not such a close friend. She knew nothing about the new lover. Dead end there. Toni, there's a memorial vigil for Sanderson outside the Hall Building. It began at nine, but we might still catch some of it. I'd be interested to see how many show up.'

'I imagine her friends are attending. I think we need time here for brainstorming.'

'How about we set to it right after the memorial?'

'Well, I'm driving.'

'No sidewalk hopping, no maniacal maneuvering. There will be students milling around.'

'Stop wasting time. Let's go.'

Damiano drove south on rue St-Denis and turned west on de Maisonneuve.

'There was a quicker route.'

'This is my route. I'm surprised Marie hasn't called.'

'I expected to hear from her tomorrow. It's only been two days, Toni; she's collating her findings as we will tomorrow. Gathering takes time, always has.'

As they approached Crescent Street, the congestion was obvious. 'Big crowd. I can see flashing lights, so that means officers have blocked off streets. I'll search for parking here.'

'Try the lot on Crescent.'

'Alright.' It wasn't a big lot and it was full. Damiano double parked and shot out of the car. Matte knew her moves, charm and punch. She ran back to the car. 'The student will take it. I palmed a twenty and it worked.' Matte got out of the car and together they walked the short distance to Bishop Street and Concordia's main building on de Maisonneuve. 'I'd rather have gut-wrenching cold than this dampness. It goes right through me.'

'If you'd dress properly then...'

'Put on a dress, Matte. Try it for a day.'

'Not my thing,' he smiled. 'Our vic drew a good crowd.'

The students stood quietly in small groups with candles. No one was speaking, but perhaps Damiano and Matte had missed the eulogies. They made their way slowly because Matte estimated about four hundred people had congregated to pay their respects. There was no music. As the front doors of the Hall Building came into view they saw the hill of flowers, all white, interspersed with candles and small photos. They were impressed. A large black and white photo of Taylor hung over the entrance, above the flowers, and under the name of the building. The Henry F. Hall Building occupied a whole city block between Bishop and Mackay Streets and was the hub of the downtown campus. It was a fitting place and storied locale for the memorial. Someone in the crowd began to sing, 'We Shall Overcome.' Matte smiled at Damiano and whispered, 'Some songs are timeless.'

The detectives did not notice one student in the large crowd who left the memorial suddenly, but they did spot Goldman when they heard his voice once the students had stopped singing.

'I'm telling you Major Crimes came to my place.'

'Why? Taylor never went with you.'

'She called me the day she died, wanted me with her then.'

'Really?' said a curious young voice.

'Yeah, I...'

'Mr. Goldman, I'm surprised you found the time,' Damiano said sarcastically. 'I thought you might be sleeping. And you are...?' Damiano flashed her badge.

'Gabriel. If Taylor Sanderson called Josh, I guess she was desperate.'

'Why do you say that?'

Gabriel felt no sympathy for Josh. 'He was hot for Sanderson, but she saw him as a total blow-off. Now he's just trying to torch up his importance.'

'You fucker!'

'You're a dickhead. You're still pissed at her and she's dead. Grow some balls.'

'Did you know her, Gabriel?'

'Casually, you know, "hi" and "see ya."'

'Do you know her crowd?'

'Emma Joly is in one of my classes. I saw them together with some guy. I didn't stalk her, like Josh.'

'I never…'

'Josh, I think you should leave.'

'It's a free country.'

'This is not a venue for gossip.'

'Who needs this? I'm outta here.'

Damiano and Matte moved on, trawling the gathering. 'Pierre, contact this Emma Joly first thing tomorrow. She must be here tonight.' Damiano studied the faces of the students, and her heart saddened. 'Memorials like this have a certain slickness because they're commonplace today. What a legacy for future generations.'

'I'm on Joly. I see Ms. Cupid, up there near the front with friends. She doesn't seem to be aware of them. Taylor's photo has her complete attention.' The detectives edged their way through the crowd toward her.

'Ms. Cupid!' Damiano shouted. When she turned, Damiano was shocked by a devastation she recognized from her own reflection eight months previously.

'For a time, she was my best friend,' Amira said through tears. 'Now, she's reduced to a photo. Josh wanted to come with me, but I would not allow it.' The women nodded. Matte tugged Damiano's arm.

'There's the prof with colleagues, it appears. She hasn't seen us. Should we leave it that way?'

'Yes, I'm waiting on Dumont's news. I think we need time together at the office. Do we trust tears, do we suspect callousness, or a professor who dealt with Taylor? We have nothing on the throwaway, or the "tunnel man." We're still fishing. We need a break.'

'Let's go.'

'Wait a sec, my phone.' Damiano picked up. 'Good, Marie, although Donovan said she'd handled the bag. It's a little progress. Serve the warrant on Sunday. Good work.'

As they started back through the crowd Damiano said, 'Let's drive back to the office and analyze what we've got.'

'None of our stories are complete. We have to sit down together, gather our notes and create a profile.'

'Isn't that what I just said?'

'I just broke it down better,' Matte suggested.

Damiano didn't pursue the twitch. She needed Matte's work, and he knew it. Traffic had thinned out, but they still battled the scourge of orange cones, detours and potholes – a Montreal reality.

The detective room was quiet. Only one other detective was at his desk working on a file. Matte went for coffee and took the empty pizza box with him. Damiano laid two large sheets across her desk and waited. She'd posit ideas and dictate to Matte. When he sat down, Damiano began.

'What was the motive for the murder?'

'Let's itemize what it was not,' Matte interjected. 'It wasn't a robbery, or a sexual attack. It wasn't a vicious assault. Our vic was struck once from behind and thrown into the tunnel to disguise the attack as a suicide. Her killer walked up on her from behind, or was already with her, took a step back, picked up the rock and struck. Repressed rage or impulse anger? Impulse I'd guess. The killer brought no weapon.

'Sanderson's notes told us she had been hurt: *How could you have done this to me? I was in love – what a fool I've been.* What had "X" done to her? We don't know, but it was an emotional injury *and* something that could have had our vic arrested. We still don't know what that was. The brick throwing? We can't eliminate that. Is there any foundation to the sexual assault charge Sanderson filed against Donovan? Only Donovan and Sanderson know the truth, and Sanderson is dead. We surmise our vic intended to end the relationship at the tunnel, and that got her killed. Who's "X?" We can only speculate it was the throwaway phone. That's not a given either. To conclude: we don't know who, we don't know why and we don't know what, in reference to "stuff."'

'Am I invited into your hypothesis?'

Matte laughed. 'Jump in. You *are* the lead detective.'

'We don't know if her killer was a "he." Right?'

'I'll add Cupid and Donovan to the speculative list.'

'Alright. We know she didn't choose the tunnel. She was afraid to go there. That's the reason she asked for help, so she wasn't going to meet Cupid or Goldman, but we have only their word they didn't follow her or go with her. We can't forget that Sanderson was always early. There is a chance the person who accompanied her murdered her.'

'A probability, not factual.'

'Are you getting these big words down, Pierre?'

'Have I ever failed you?'

'I'll order you a trophy. We have to look at "X." Who was our vic going to meet?'

'Whom?'

'Don't start. The throwaway? She called that number. He or she's our prime suspect for the meet. Without the throwaway, we have no handle. We have to find this suspect. The only person who might know him seems to be her friend, Emma Joly. We need Joly at the Division tomorrow. Make the call. Where the phone was sold? You said that's all we can manage, but we take what we can.

'As important, who knew our vic was going to the tunnel? Matthew Sanderson, Amira Cupid, Josh Goldman, the kid with the phone. Possibilities: Professor Donovan, Andrew Weston.'

'Before we deal with them, let's look at randoms: a homeless head case, or a troll, maybe the one or ones who set up the cable. The head case might not have sexually assaulted our vic, but he would have robbed her to buy booze. Dumping her doesn't fit. Do you agree?'

'Yes, her cash, cell, watch and clothes weren't taken.'

'The troll, one or more, fit the same scenario. Sanderson was a pretty girl, yet there was no sexual interference or robbery. They might dispose of the vic if they installed the cable, but what was their motive? We saw the cable. It was built for a purpose. Once the kids found our vic, their cable was shut down. No point – no motive. An outside random wouldn't have known about the cable or the opening. You have to climb down to see it behind the tree. He would have left her on the ground. Except for the single blow, she wasn't touched – no motive. Agree?'

'Perhaps the troll knocked our vic unconscious *with* a plan, but someone else was out walking. The plan was shelved, and our vic was dumped in a place the troll knew well.'

'I accept that as an outside possibility. Print it up like that, Pierre. Now to the principals. Matthew Sanderson – we only have his word he didn't go to the tunnel. He knew his sister was always early. Brother and sister didn't get along. Like his father, Matthew has a violent streak. Look how he trashed his room. There's a good chance he threw himself down the stairs. Question is – guilt because he abandoned her or guilt because they fought and he struck her down? No sexual assault, no robbery fits. He might have panicked and found the opening at the tunnel and dumped her, hoping we'd rule her death a suicide. The kid was hanging in the background when I informed the Sandersons about their daughter. He has a motive and opportunity. My first thought is that her murder was impulsive, not planned. Still a good fit for him.'

'A brother killing his sister, Toni? That's a stretch.'

'Has happened. That's something.'

'Speculation, at best.'

'Fine, Pierre. Amira Cupid – a hard-working young woman, certainly not a player. She's genuinely distraught. But there's a little something nagging me in the back of my mind. Cupid said they were close for a few months. Close? Young people experiment today and think nothing of it. Was that closeness some romp or real friendship? Was Cupid dumped like Andrew Weston? If it was a romp, was it much more to Cupid? Did Cupid catch up with Sanderson that Tuesday? Did she see some hope of renewal when Sanderson came to her for help? I just remembered the rocks she has in her apartment and her fondness for them. A rock might be our murder weapon.'

'I'm serious.'

'I'll write up another speculative. One point, did Cupid know that Goldman was home at the time of the murder and vice-versa. It might prove interesting to find out.'

'I agree. Now, Josh Goldman – the angry reject, yet Sanderson went to him for help. She must have been desperate. We know from tonight, he's still angry even though Sanderson's dead. Once Cupid went back in her room, did he throw some clothes on and follow Sanderson? Striking her from behind would fit his profile. we have to interrogate both of them.'

'You're right. Next, we have to find the kid with the phone. He's still in the mix. I hope Joly will help us locate him. I'll try her tonight.'

'Trying to finish a puzzle without a key piece is difficult. We can't give up on this. Next up is Donovan. Sanderson told her about the "stuff" in her life. We have her prints on the bag, but she had a reason for them being there. Did the charge against her have merit? The director didn't move it through when Sanderson was still alive. Sanderson cheated twice on her assignment, threw the brick I believe, and filed the charge threatening to "screw up" Donovan's life for the failing grade. Our professor didn't know about the tunnel, so we think. She must have been enraged when she discovered she had no proof for the assault and there was no charge to be made on an "incomplete" assigned to a student. Our vic took her prof to the cleaners. Her career is essentially over if this sexual harassment charge ever gets out. Maybe Sanderson opened up to Donovan. We'll never know. She doesn't have an alibi. It's like Sanderson infected her life. There's none so firm and all that. We are all capable of murder. Anger and rage are motives. Before you say anything, I know Donovan stays a hypothetical for now, Pierre.'

'We need to liaise with the footwork on alibis. We don't have the time. We're drowning in speculation. Will you ask the chief?'

'Tomorrow. He'll love a Sunday call. Now, Andrew Weston – he didn't know about the tunnel. Life was looking up for him if the invitation was still on. Let's let him sit for a spell.'

'Toni, I have been meaning to tell you something.'

'Go on.'

'I'll call Joly, but I won't be in till eleven tomorrow.' Damiano was irritated.

'Dylan came back last night. I have to spend some time with him or I'll lose him. The second time around is already a disadvantage. It's that simple. I have another chance. I need another chance. This last year's been hard. Being a cop can't be my whole life. There's nothing at the end of this job. I could have lost my best friend. You were that close, too, Toni.' Matte didn't meet Damiano's eyes.

Damiano had a sudden image of Matte's loneliness. 'See you at eleven. Make the call. And, I won't be in till eleven either. I'll have breakfast with Jeff and Luke. We need some distance to reboot.'

'Donat's chair isn't going anywhere.'

'Ha! Take off after the call. I'll close up.' When Matte left, she bolted to her locker and popped a Dilaudid that took about thirty minutes to take effect. Damiano would be home safely where she intended to creep into bed. Her arm was thumping and burning.

Chapter Twenty-Three

Damiano crawled into bed just after eleven. Jeff hadn't said a word as she undressed and washed up in the ensuite bathroom. When she rolled over onto her shoulder away from him, he turned on his bedside lamp. 'Your arm must be sore. I have the half pill and water for you.'

Damiano couldn't risk the extra dosage. 'I'm bushed. Give it to me, if I really need it, I'll take it during the night. By the way, I'm here tomorrow morning for breakfast.' It took an effort to pronounce her words without a drugged slur.

'Where did you get it?'

'What are you talking about?'

'The Dilaudid?'

'You are worse than a cop. My arm was killing me.'

'Answer the question!' Jeff demanded. 'You're not going to walk on this one.'

'Keep your voice down. Dammit. I hid an old prescript for emergencies. I took it after work tonight, and you're going to ruin its effect. I just want to sleep, please. We'll deal with my transgression tomorrow.'

'This is your health you're dicking with.'

'Take a breath.'

'You promised you wouldn't put me through this shit again.'

'I'm not. This is the first time. The day was long and wearing. I was sore and brain dead – I couldn't make it. It's one pill! You're exaggerating. How's Luke?'

'I'm not finished with this subject, but Luke's gone quiet again. It's our first bout with teenage anger and angst. He took off somewhere after dinner but was home by ten. I let him be.'

'How about giving me the same break tonight?'

'I love an ambitious cop. That's a package in itself, but I will not accept an addict.'

Damiano wanted to punch Jeff's back. 'I'm not an addict. Why did we ever commit to one another? We're such opposites. You knew what you were getting into when we married.'

'You were a piston alright. I didn't see then you'd want to be firing on all pistons every day. You're driven by something deep inside. One thing I know, you're still injured, still suffering traumatic stress, but you won't slow down. Narcotics are addictive and their effect weakens. It always has to be the difficult case, the top case. Did you ask for it?'

'Donat came to me. I told him about the nightmares and the arm.'

'I'm glad. He might think working this case will lessen the trauma. Maybe he's right. You're less hyper.'

'Pain does that to you.'

'You don't want to be thought of as a career opportunist, do you?'

'No, that's not it at all. I'm the best detective there.'

'Funny, you don't work at being the best wife. I want to be a good husband to you.'

'Do you still love me, Jeff? Don't give me that shit. *If you could, you'd leave me*. I'm not an easy person to love. I'm not kidding myself, but I want the truth.'

A slow moan escaped from him. 'Get over here.' Jeff took her in his arms, and they held on to each other.

'I have to move. That's my sore arm.'

'Roll over and give me a kiss.'

Damiano was frightened by Jeff's words. She lived in the moment, except for wanting Donat's chair one day. She made another vow. Only half pills from now on.

From the turns and pillow-punching, neither slept, and the hours dragged. At seven she dozed off until she heard Jeff in the kitchen. 'Eight-thirty! Is he trying to kill me?' She thought of her empty rented condo, but didn't dare mention it at breakfast. Jeff had made spinach omelets, a delicious fruit bowl and lightly buttered brown toast. The aroma of his favorite coffee filled the room. Damiano padded into the bathroom wearing her pale blue terrycloth robe and matching slippers. The roof of her mouth was dry from the pill. She threw cold water on her face, brushed her teeth, and did a quick job on her hair.

'You look almost human.'

'Thanks!'

'I have an idea for your arm. You need a sling. Part of the reason for the onset of pain is the pressure on your elbow because your arm is hanging down throughout the day.'

'Are you nuts? I can't go to work in a sling. Donat would flip me off the case.'

His eyes beamed. 'I thought you'd say that, so I have an alternate plan. Wear jackets with pockets, and keep your hand in your pocket whenever you can.'

'I'll look like Napoleon.'

'You're too tall. Anyway, he had big plans just like you.'

'He was exiled to Elba.'

'Right, but he returned to France.'

'What do we do about Luke?'

'Toni, he's a good kid. As far as we know drugs aren't involved. He's not out all night running around. Let's give him the time he seems to need.'

'I still can't figure out why a girl would break his heart. He's a beautiful kid.'

'He's your son.'

'I can see beyond that.'

'It happened. He's a kid – he'll bounce back. I checked on him earlier. He was asleep.'

The fact was that no one in the home had slept. Luke lay on his bed, staring at a wall.

Caitlin Donovan had sat alone in the Westmount mansion, waiting for Carmen to return from the memorial, praying that her friend hadn't made matters worse. At the end of the first term in early December, Caitlin traditionally invited members of her class for coffee and catered sandwiches. She was racking her brain trying to remember if Taylor had come. She had a bathroom on the ground floor, but had any of her students walked up to the second floor to use that bathroom? Spending the afternoon talking and serving, she couldn't lay odds that no one ever had. What did that mean for prints? She couldn't start wiping down her bedroom. The Crime technicians would find it odd there were no prints. At that moment, she felt no sorrow for Sanderson. She had been kind to the girl and stretched the rules. Where did any of that land her? Was the Dean about to call her to the office? What a mess! Caitlin was relieved when she heard Carmen's key in the front door.

Carmen threw her arms in the air. 'I tried to get something for you, but students were standing around quietly at the memorial. I couldn't impose myself. There was a pretty black woman at the front crying and being consoled by two friends. I was about to say something when two detectives arrived. I took them for detectives, so I edged off.'

'They were. You played it right.'

'I did hear something unrelated to the evening. Don't know if I should tell you.'

'I need all the information I can get.'

'Half a dozen kids were talking loudly enough for me to hear. Some students were planning to accuse two professors of sexual harassment by plastering their office doors with stickers and outing them. From what I heard, I think they were male professors. I'm sorry, Caitlin.'

'At first, it was only the brick Taylor threw that could have injured me. Now the harassment charge is going to ruin me. I can't get my head around this, Carmen. I have never felt so powerless. Taylor was right about one thing. I'm not a god. I'm hired help. I'd wring her neck if I had the chance. I'm about to hit the panic button. And Mom! I've got to call my father.'

Before Carmen could say a word, Caitlin began to cry. Eight years had passed since Chris had been killed. That was the last time Carmen had seen her friend lost and afraid. Carmen hesitated before she spoke gently. 'Maggie said she couldn't deal with consoling your father. She's trying to bank her reserves.'

'It's not right. None of this is right. What if Mom has cancer?' Caitlin's voice was thin. 'What then?'

'Choosing how she handles it is her decision, Caitlin. You should respect it.'

'It's not *your* mother.'

'I hope I'd act the same way.'

'Bully for you.'

'I'm sorry, I didn't mean…'

'Forget it. I'm prickly.'

Chapter Twenty-Four

[April 7]

Sunday morning, Damiano drove into snow mixed with rain and gusting southwest winds. The damp, drizzly day matched her state and mood. For a moment, she envied folks who chose to live off the grid, a simple, independent existence. She knew what part she had played in the miasma of her own life. There was fault and blame. She was part of each problem: Jeff, Luke, anxiety, her arm, Dilaudid and a case of leads that didn't go anywhere. The chief was about to have her in for a blast. Her eyes were dry from lack of sleep. Her arm had begun its burn early. When the station's steel door clanged behind her, Damiano felt the desolation of the empty gray building, until she spotted Matte who was bent over her desk, and her spirits calmed.

'Well, Pierre, I expected I'd arrive before you walked in all frisky from your first big night.'

'That word is beneath you, Toni.'

'Didn't sleep, so that's the best I could manage. What happened to you?' Matte hadn't been working on his murder book; he'd been drawing circles on a pad. 'Do you want to talk about it?'

'No,' he lied.

'Is Emma Joly coming in?'

'Elevenish, kids! And you? Is it Luke?'

'Amongst other things. At root, I don't measure up to personal obligations. I'm failing both Jeff and Luke. I'm forty-two, for the next few months at least, but I still haven't found my balance. I wish I had stayed at the condo.'

'You're selfish, you know.'

'Even with you?'

'At times, but you're also the best cop I've ever worked with.'

'Huh. Thanks, Pierre. Spill your thoughts – you have no one else to open up to.'

Matte rubbed his eyes and rolled his shoulders. 'I don't think I love Dylan anymore.'

Damiano watched Matte closely.

'Last night, you and I got home around the same time, so Dylan wasn't waiting for me. He hadn't so much as unpacked his clothes, but he went out to the bars in the Village. He crept into bed with me after three. At eight he's up popping Moët champagne and made breakfast: fresh, hot croissants, Gruyère cheese, apricot preserves and a Spanish omelette.'

What's so wrong with that?

'I was about to thank him, but he beat me to it. "I've left the receipts on the counter. I'm short, as usual."' Matte laughed sadly. 'What little hope I had, began to unravel. When we first met, paying for things didn't bother me. He was writing. I was happy. I felt needed, almost necessary. I had the funds, and a great looking young guy who was in love with me. In my world, time moves quickly. Dylan's not young in the gay world now. He'll be thirty in May. I don't even know if he's working. He's searching for security, and that's what I am to him.'

Aren't we all?

'Dylan sees me as weak. I'd forgotten I always paid for our time together, rent and groceries, but it's more than that. He ripped my heart open when he left. I was healing. But his leaving the receipts for the food re-opened the wound. I lost his love; what I also lost was my belief in who I thought we were. I don't think I'll ever be able to trust him again. I'm not up to being taken a second time by the same man. Have you ever felt alone with Jeff? Really alone?'

In the nine and a half years Damiano had known Pierre, he had never spoken so openly about himself. She thought carefully before she replied. 'Jeff has never supported my career, or ambition. He'd like me behind a desk. Do I ever feel really alone? No. Smothered, yes.'

'You're lucky. It didn't matter that he was across from me at the table. At breakfast, I felt alone and pathetic. I'm better than that, I hope.'

'You are. May I say one thing?'

'Go ahead.'

'Give it a week. I went back home and left the condo because of my surgery. My return home was easier last year. Jeff saw that I was too sick for recriminations. I got lucky. You didn't. You were still vulnerable when Dylan returned. We can both afford a week's trial at our age. We're not so old that we have to count minutes wasted. Give Dylan a chance. Don't walk away for pride – walk because you'll know what's best for you.'

'Sometimes you make good sense, Tony.'

'When it's not my own life. Ah, there's Joly ringing. We have to be hard on her. This case has to move. I think we have to interview Matthew again – he still might know more than he's given us.'

'I'll get her.'

Damiano changed her mindset and prepared for Joly.

Matte walked into the interview room first. Joly suited her name, although there was a studied look to her appearance. Her dark hair was long and parted off center. She was warmly dressed in a gray boiled woollen jacket that didn't cover her knees and tight-fitting black slacks. She wore a knotted scarf that fell to the bottom of her jacket. Her Uggs were gray. Joly scanned the room as they approached Damiano's office. Damiano made quick work of the introductions and gestured for Joly to take the seat in front of her desk.

'Would you like some water?'

'Yes, please. My mouth is dry.'

'There is nothing to be afraid of, Emma.' Damiano caught the eye twitch at the mention of Joly's first name.

Matte got up from where he was sitting beside Damiano to get the water.

'You're here because your best friend is dead and we need your help. We have to record our conversation.'

Joly played with her scarf. 'Alright.'

'How long have you been friends?'

'Since elementary school.'

'Have you always hung together?'

'Some short breaks in between, the usual fights. But, we were still tight.'

'Were you surprised Taylor didn't call you for help the day she went to the Wellington Tunnel?'

'We talked the day before. I told her she was an idiot to go there.' She suddenly broke into tears. 'Those were the last words I said to Tay. I was going to text her, but Tay's stubborn, I mean she was really stubborn. She ticked me off, and I didn't do anything. I'm a great friend!'

'You couldn't know.'

'That's what my dad says, but it doesn't change what happened.'

'Do you know who Taylor was seeing – or going to meet there?'

'That's part of what ticked me off. I knew Tay was seeing somebody. She told me she was in love. She said it was the real thing. I asked who it was. They wanted to keep the relationship a secret. "It's too soon to share," she said. 'I had the impression that Tay would have told me, but the guy wanted it quiet.'

'Do you know it was a guy?'

'I just figured… it wasn't?'

'Just asking. What happened?'

'I don't know. For a while, Tay was the happiest I've ever seen her. I mean that. Then she called me on Thursday…'

'That would be a few days before her death.'

Tears again. 'This is so surreal. Students die, I know that. You just never think it will be someone close to you. I'll never have the chance to say I wish I had gone with her. My dad said we only have one chance to stand up and be counted, and most of us fail, like I did. I knew how scared Tay was. I didn't even offer to help.'

'Tell us about the call.'

'I can still hear Tay. "I've been so freakin' stupid, Em. I've put myself in so much trouble. My whole fucking life could be ruined! I don't even know if I can get out of this." Then she just cried. I asked her if I could help. "No one can help me. I have to do this myself. I am so screwed." Tay was scared of dark places, so I don't know why she went to the tunnel. I told her not to go. It didn't look as though she had a choice. It probably was her best chance to get out of the mess, do things his way. But it wasn't, was it?'

'You know Matthew then?' Damiano veered off course, a habit of the last few years.

'We didn't pay much attention. He was always just a kid to me.'

'To Taylor as well?'

'They were okay, I think. I mean a younger brother is just a younger brother. Matt was a gamer, kept to himself a lot.'

'Did Taylor tell you about the school assignment she plagiarized?'

'No.' Joly dragged out the short word.

'Do you attend any of the same classes?'

'I'm in science; Tay was a psych major. I told her she wouldn't get anywhere with that. Her degree doesn't matter now, does it?' Joly was lost in thought and began to bite her nails. 'Nothing matters to Tay anymore.'

'What matters is finding the person who took her life.'

'How will that give me a chance to say I'm sorry? See what I mean?'

'Every victim deserves justice.'

'I was thinking of Tay and me. Tay does deserve justice.'

'You never tried to find out who the mystery person was?'

'The relationship began before Tay told me anything, and it didn't last long. I figured Tay would break and tell me, but she never did. She ran out of time.'

Damiano gave Joly her card in case she recalled something that might assist them.

Chapter Twenty-five

Caitlin hung on, but without sleep. Early Sunday morning, she showered without waking anyone. She made coffee, found some bagels and began to toast them. In all the years she had lived at home, she'd never brought her mother breakfast in bed. Caitlin loaded a tray with coffee, juice and a bagel with fresh strawberry jam. She paused at her mother's door and wondered if she was about to wake her. She placed the tray down on the hardwood floor and opened the door softly. Her mother was curled up in a fetal position.

'Mom!' her voice rang out in alarm.

Maggie's face was wet with perspiration. 'Cait, I'm not feeling well at all.'

'Oh my God.' Caitlin froze for a second. Her mother's face was blanched and her pillow was soaked. 'Alright, will you be okay for a few minutes? I'll get dressed and call an ambulance.'

'Can't you drive me?' Maggie was not one to make a fuss.

'An ambulance gives you priority in triage. Can you manage some juice? I have your breakfast in the hall.'

'I don't think I can.'

'Alright, I'll be right back to help you dress.'

'I'm not certain I can move.'

'Then don't.' Caitlin raced back to her room, tripped into some slacks and shoes, grabbed a shirt and jacket and ran for the phone. When she spoke to the 9-1-1 operator, she couldn't understand herself.

'Slow down, please.'

Caitlin spoke with what felt like cotton in her mouth. 'Ten minutes! This is an emergency! I can't drive my mother, she can't move. It might be cancer.' Her words horrified her. 'Dammit, please urge the driver to rush!'

Carmen heard the commotion from the guestroom and went to investigate. 'What's wrong?'

'It's Mom. It's really bad. Get dressed. We're waiting on the ambulance.'

Carmen ran to her room to dress. Caitlin hurried back to her mother and began to pack clothes and cosmetics. 'What meds do you take, Mom?'

'None.'

'Good.' Caitlin checked her watch. Ten minutes had passed. 'Dammit. Mom, if Carm and I carry you to the Lincoln, would you be able to lie across the back seat? The ambulance isn't here.'

'I can try.'

Caitlin called to Carmen. 'Get up here.' Caitlin lifted the packed bag and brought it to the landing. 'Good. Carm, stash this in the trunk of the Lincoln. The car's not locked. Then I need your help to carry Mom to the car. If the ambulance arrives, we use it. If not, we drive.'

By the time Carmen was back in the bedroom, there was no sign of the ambulance. They swaddled Maggie in a blanket and together, they carried her to the car. The task was not easy. Maggie was a big-boned tall woman, but they were pumped with adrenalin. Carmen ran to the other side of the car and pulled the blanket with Maggie across the seat. They took off. Caitlin called Emergency, said her father was a director of the Royal Victoria Hospital and that her mother was in grave danger. Her voice was frantic and her breathing erratic. 'Mom, what's your doctor's name?'

Maggie was shivering and her teeth chattered.

'Mom?'

'Franken.'

'My mother's physician is Dr. Franken. Please have him there.' Caitlin was weeping.

'For Christ's sake, slow down. You'll kill us all.' Carmen was a speeder, but Caitlin was driving recklessly even with the hazard lights flashing.

'Stop with the horn.'

'I can't let anything happen to Mom – what don't you get?'

'Cait, please…'

Caitlin was pulled over for speeding on Doctor Penfield at Peel. Caitlin jumped out of the car and spoke in French. The patrol officer escorted them to the Emergency entrance of the Royal Vic, and the officer gave Caitlin a warning. Carmen saw a gurney, and they lay Maggie on it. Caitlin never gave the triage nurse a chance to speak. Caitlin's voice was shrill and her words erupted in a pummelling torrent. She did manage to say she thought her mother's scans had been done already. Where was Dr. Franken?

The nurse verified the name and wheeled Maggie into a private emergency room. 'Dr. Franken is coming out of surgery and will be here as soon as he can. In the meantime, I'll have your mother set up with oxygen and make her comfortable.'

'Do you have any idea what's happening to her?'

'We'll have your mother's records here for Dr. Franken. I can't comment.'

Carmen whispered to Caitlin, 'Your mother can hear you. Calm down.' Caitlin spotted a facecloth, wet it and wiped her mother's forehead. 'Dr. Franken's coming, Mom.' Caitlin was holding her mother's hand when Franken walked into the room.

He was tall and broad with a face no one would notice, probably homely as a kid. Yet she also saw a toughened kindness in his face. 'Well, Maggie our date wasn't till next week. You couldn't stay away. I won't tell Frank.'

Caitlin had had enough of the banter. 'Dr. Franken…'

'You must be Caitlin. I'm taking Maggie to surgery. I want a PET scan first. I'll drain what I can to lessen the pain and avoid rupture.'

'You've done the biopsy – you still don't know if the mass is malignant?'

'Maggie's a friend of mine, Caitlin. She's in good hands. We'll know in due time what we're dealing with.'

Caitlin was about to cut in again, but Maggie spoke first. 'She's Frank's girl, Ben.'

'Oh boy, another stubborn Irishman. Let's get you down to surgery.'

'Mom!' That single word held fright and love and desperation.

'I know, Cait.'

'Mom could die, Carm – I have to call my father. I can't leave her.'

'I'll call him.'

'It's #2 on my phone.'

Carmen walked down the hall to the kitchen to make the call.

Caitlin sat down, staring at the floor tiles. When Chris died, her faith died too. She longed to believe again. Carmen came back inside rubbing her arms to warm them up and said her father would take the first flight out of New York. He knew about Taylor Sanderson, saw a brief newsclip on CNN. Caitlin and Carmen waited in silence and dread. Caitlin dozed off and woke immediately with a jerk. 'Carm, what were Mom's last words to me? I can't remember them!'

'She said, "I know." Maggie knows you love her. Try to calm down.'

'Jesus, Carm, you've never lost anyone – you don't know.' Caitlin's right foot began to tap and didn't stop. When her phone rang, she jumped to her feet. 'Dammit to hell! It's the Crime unit. I have to take it.'

Carmen closed the door.

Catlin paced the small room and bumped Carmen twice. 'I can't be there. My mother's in surgery.' Caitlin began to cry again. 'She might not make it. I can't leave her. Break down the door.'

'Professor Donovan, is there no one else who might have a key, a neighbor perhaps?'

'I'll go for you, Caitlin.'

'I have a friend with me. She'll drive down to my home and open the door. I have to turn off my phone. I'm at the Royal Vic.

'Thanks, Carm. Here are the keys. Call me when they leave.'

'Don't worry.'

'Be happy?'

'Sometime you're worse than I am. I mean, take care.'

'Sorry.'

'I know.'

Chapter Twenty-six

Damiano sat and waited for Matte to see Joly out. She played back the recording. Matte found Damiano with her fingers steepled and her head leaning on the stack. 'I'd forgotten how selfish kids are. Joly's main focus was the chance to get rid of her guilt.'

'At least she has the excuse of youth.'

'I'm of two thoughts: Professor Donovan is unlucky, or she's right for murder. Joly said Taylor's relationship was secretive and revealed nothing about the person she was involved with. Why? Because there was a woman involved? Why would a guy want secrecy? Why plagiarize two assignments? Why file the sexual harassment charge? Sanderson needed to end the relationship. Was that her way of ending it – destroy the professor? Why the meeting then? Why go somewhere that frightened her and ask for company? Dumont's executing the warrant at Donovan's house today. If the team finds prints, say in the bedroom…?'

'The valid point is the woman angle – the rest is problematic. Go to your second thought.'

'Fine. It was a guy she'd fallen for, but Sanderson discovered he'd been using her, wanted to pimp her out, to push drugs, whatever. She had to get out. Something was definitely motivating her to go to the tunnel with the mystery guy.'

'The "guy" couldn't be certain she'd come by herself.'

'True, but if he'd gotten to know her habits, he'd know she was always early…'

'So what, if she was coming with somebody, we'd have two bodies then.'

'Are we back to the idea that someone did go with her, or someone followed her? They fought, and we have an impulse murder?'

'That's a solid.'

'Sanderson was murdered by someone she knew, someone who had to disguise the attack and hope we'd rule it as a suicide.'

'Square one.'

'Round two of interviews. I want to question Matthew Sanderson for the reasons I've said.'

'We have to question him at the hospital.'

'Call to be certain he's still there.' Matte Googled the number.

Damiano took Marie Dumont's call. 'Finally.'

'It was difficult working in rain and ice. We're at Donovan's.' Dumont gave Damiano a quick rundown of the professor's story. 'Apart from prints are you looking for something special?'

'I was saving the best for last. Our techs found the faint outline of a boot on Sanderson's shoulder. The perp must have needed the boot to push Sanderson through the opening.'

'Is it a definitive print?'

'Faint is faint – not nine ID points. We have a herring bone print. I'm going through the professor's boots. I suggest you check your other suspects. We haven't found that pattern yet. The prof would have disposed of it is my guess – she has a brain. But your vic's neighbors, et al – you check that.'

'Any prints?'

'Too many – a long job to get through the matching.'

'The smear?'

'It's the vic's blood. The US lab is still testing for a print – they're pulling a thumb.'

'It's a bloody long process.'

'Technical data takes time.'

'You've checked Donovan's front window then?'

'Yep, it's newly replaced.'

'At least that wasn't a lie.'

'The rain was of great assistance to the murderer.'

'Too bad I can't charge the elements as accomplices. We're driving to the General to have a second go at the brother.'

'Really?'

'Something's out of joint.'

'Hamlet didn't have such great luck with his suspicions – he died.'

'I need something with points, Marie.'

'I know.'

Matte didn't want Damiano at her locker alone, so he had gone ahead and waited for her. His conspiracy didn't escape her ire. 'Let's go, bodyguard.' The traffic was easier on Sunday – the parking was still difficult. Shari Sanderson sat by Matthew's bed. He was awake, but they weren't talking.

Shari Sanderson sat like a ghost, white from fatigue and rigid with grief. Damiano thought of a shadow. She didn't have the strength to rise. 'Please let us be. Matthew hasn't said a word.' Speaking seemed to tire whatever reserves the woman had. 'Spare us the intrusion.'

'Mrs. Sanderson, we are trying to help you – please allow us to do the right thing for your daughter.'

'We are all guilty – I let Tay go out on her own, Trevor was too harsh, Matt didn't help, and friends evidently abandoned her – so arrest us all. What will that change, Detective? Do you receive a star for closing a case? Tay is still lost. Just leave us alone!' Sanderson's voice rose to a plaintive sob.

Damiano stood her ground. 'Matthew, I know you're awake. I'm glad you survived the fall. Did Taylor tell you who she was involved with? A simple question.'

Matthew turned his head towards Damiano. When confronted with deceit, Matthew always fought back. 'Play out your games. My sister wouldn't give me the time of day. Why would she tell me who she was bonking?'

'She needed you – she thought you could help – that's why she told you, even if it was just a bribe.'

Shari Sanderson began to rock back and forth moaning. 'Leave us alone.'

A nurse appeared. 'What's happening here?'

'Lieutenant Detective Damiano and Detective Matte. We're here to question Matthew Sanderson. It is very painful for Mrs. Sanderson, but we have a job to do. Matthew is quite able to answer my questions.'

'Are you, Matthew?'

'Didn't cut my tongue out.'

'You are driving us mad.' Shari Sanderson rose and tried to push Damiano from the room.

'Mom! You can't make this better. You guys really want to know if I saw anything that day – why don't you ask me. You want to know if I was there. You think I'm a liar as well as a chicken shit. Get to the point.'

'Were you at the tunnel, Matthew?' Damiano's arm hit high-throb, and sweat pooled in her armpits. She asked the question again, past the grief of Shari Sanderson. 'Were you there, Matthew?' There was an edge to Damiano's voice, the by-product of a sleepless night.

Matthew threw off the blankets and sheet and hobbled to the floor. His right hand clutched the hospital gown behind him. 'I went. Is that what you want to hear? I fucking went!'

A knock at the door threatened to wipe out the break in the case. A doctor in a white coat with a stethoscope looped around his neck pushed the door open. 'What's going on here?'

'The cops want to know if I killed my sister!' Matthew shrieked.

'I think you should leave,' the doctor advised the detectives.

Matte took a step to leave – Damiano stood her ground.

To add to the mayhem in the room, Shari Sanderson grabbed the bed for support.

'I fucked that up too! I got there too late. Tay was already gone…'

Chapter Twenty-seven

Shari Sanderson backed away from her son and covered her face with the back of her hand.

The doctor took a step back. Matte closed the door, and Damiano placed her hand in her pocket, grimacing. 'Let's all try to settle down. Matthew you did try to help your sister – you did stand up for her. Your father should know that. For Detective Matte and me, we have to know what you saw that Tuesday, every part of it. Please don't keep telling us that nothing matters. Be a brother and speak for Taylor. Help us find the person who took her life,' Damiano urged.

'Did you arrive at the tunnel at the time Taylor wanted you there?'

'I took off, mostly running and almost tripping. I was still ten, maybe fifteen minutes late. She didn't give me enough time to get there. It was her fault. It was that early shit of hers.'

'You looked for Taylor?' Damiano stepped back into control.

'Fuck, yes! She wasn't there. I figured she'd call me with her hysterical laugh. "I *punked* you!" It wouldn't have been the first time she'd put me down.'

'Did you see anyone around the tunnel?'

'Not at the tunnel, not at first.'

'Where?'

'I saw someone running. It looked like, you know, like away from the tunnel.'

'Can you describe the person?'

Matthew took time to think. 'He was tall and fast. I only saw him from behind and at a distance. His hoodie was up – not much to see.'

'Are you certain the runner was male?'

Matthew chewed his thumb. 'I don't know. Somebody in shape. I just figured it was some guy. No way could I have caught up to him.'

'You said, "At first." You saw someone else?'

'Yeah, I was still pissed at Tay, so I began checking out the graffiti along the side wall. I didn't want to climb the cement blocks. Tay would never go in there. The way I figured it, Tay was long gone. I checked out two old towers there. That's when I saw a guy back at the tunnel just standing there and looking around. Then he left, didn't stay long.'

'Was he there before you?'

'I don't know, I didn't see him, but I was walking around. My eyes were on the runner.'

'Describe him.'

'When I first saw him, I only saw his profile. I waited for him to turn. Before he did, he pulled on a woollen cap and his hoodie. And shades. When he turned around, he looked like any other guy, but taller than me.'

'Boots?'

'I don't know. Who looks at guys?'

'How old was he?'

'Like nineteen or twenty, I guess.'

'Hair color?'

'Dark. Thing is I just figured he came after me, but now I don't know. He didn't look suspicious. He was just standing there and then he walked off.'

'He could have been there before you.'

'Yeah, I guess.'

'Like he was waiting for someone?'

'Shit!'

'You think he was the one?'

'Shit! Shit! Shit!' Matthew angled his head in sudden thought. 'Tay was already dead. And I didn't get a description to help find the murderer. I was standing right there and she was dead in the tunnel.' Matthew's eyes burned into Damiano's. 'I fucked up.' He slumped back onto the bed. When Matthew could speak, he mumbled into the pillow. 'The guy at the tunnel had no gloves. He was blowing into his hands, like me.'

Shari Sanderson was eerily quiet, saddened beyond words. She didn't look up to see her son. She had withdrawn totally into herself. On her way out of the room, Damiano left her card with Matthew, who said nothing. 'If you remember anything more, you have my private number, Matthew.'

When they were outside the hospital, Damiano took a deep breath, trying to compose herself despite the pain. She wanted to scream. *I need a pill!* When she did speak, she spoke through gritted teeth. 'I hate hospitals. I'll keep my private thoughts of this kid to myself, but he may be playing us. He was at the tunnel, he saw two people, but couldn't describe either of them. Is the kid still lying? Is he trying to cover himself? Why not tell us the truth, if *this is* the truth today, when he was first questioned. Each time Matthew reveals something new, he isn't much help. Is this version the entire truth, or just another piece of the puzzle?' Damiano and Matte couldn't take the chance he wasn't. 'Is there something in his head telling him not to give it all away? Why? What do you think, Pierre?'

'Matthew wasn't the "stuff" in her life – then again maybe the "stuff" didn't kill her.' They walked to the car. 'The fact that we haven't got anything is troublesome. We gather facts – we try to get close to who or what we want. Matthew Sanderson is blocking us. We've looked hard at the murder – we see it as an impulse homicide. Anger and or passion were its cause. Our vic was struck from behind – a coward's act. Matthew Sanderson would simplify our lives if he's our perp.'

'The case would be neat and quick if he was, but cases are messy and depend on the force of fact. They're full of roadblocks like Matthew, at a time when *I* need something simple.' As they approached their car, Damiano saw the parking ticket on the windshield despite their cards on the dash. She grabbed it and tore it up.

'Do you want me to drive?'

'Thanks. Cold turkey is one thing when I've slept – it's the wide scream when I haven't. Why's the kid still in the hospital? She asked angrily. 'You saw him get off from the bed with miminal difficulty.'

'Psych evaluation is required, I imagine. They have counsellors available. The parents are worried about having him at home. He's volatile, maybe suicidal. If not for the parents' influence, he would have been tossed from the hospital by now.'

'So?'

'Some of the stress you're experiencing is elevating the arm pain. Maybe you should talk things out with a pro.'

'Are you practicing now, Matte?'

'I'm trying to help you, Toni. The stress of this case is detrimental to your recovery. This ghost on your back adds to the pain.'

'It doesn't – I'm just a bad loser. But a kid died! Jesus. Don't you get that yet?'

'That's exactly the reason you need to talk to somebody. You don't listen to me. You were cited for bravery – no one is suggesting otherwise. I regret keeping you from your hidden stash, but I shouldn't be in that position.'

'That's a low blow, Pierre.'

'What can I say that you'll hear? You did your best – let it go, or it will eat you up.'

'That's easy for you to say. You were outside the door – you didn't have to decide on a life.'

Matte fired up the engine without another word.

'Pierre, it's the goddam arm talking. I'm sorry.'

He didn't answer and picked up speed.

Damiano took a call and listened. She turned to Matte, but he looked straight ahead. 'Prints at least from the professor, Marie?'

'We'll run them, Toni. The throwaway phone was bought in the Montreal area. No great help. The tech in the US lab is using photogrammetry that will locate and define points in the smear. I expect to hear Tuesday or Wednesday. They're under-staffed and busy.'

'Sounds promising.' Damiano tapped off.

'Pierre, Marie told me that Donovan's mother is in the Royal Vic, seriously ill, but she was let into the house by a friend. They'll process the prints. No lead on the phone. Hope for the smear at the US lab.'

Matte kept silent.

'I think we should both go home. I need the rest. We need fresh eyes tomorrow for the chief. I am sorry, Pierre.'

Matte drove on.

Know what? When you're in the right – the grace period is not long.'

'Do you want another partner?' he turned to ask Damiano.

'Get over my warts and let's move on. Whether you see it or not, I'm trying to find my old confidence. That's humbling for me.'

'I know that, Toni, but you owe me respect. I'm not your secretary, I'm your partner.'

'I do. I will try to improve. Truce?'

'Ha!'

'Ha back.'

Chapter Twenty-Eight

Against her better judgement, after two in the morning, Caitlin Donovan had driven her mother home to Westmount. The cut-stone fourteen-room mansion sat comfortably on the north side of The Boulevard. The home was somber and quiet. Maggie was upstairs asleep in the master bedroom with Caitlin when Frank Donovan arrived. Caitlin slipped from the room and went downstairs to join her father. Now the wait for results began.

'Hi, Dad. Let's sit in the living room. I'll tell you what's been happening.'

Frank Donovan was accustomed to listening and he did not interrupt. Caitlin told him first about Maggie, then about her trouble. He was visibly stunned. 'What do you mean Maggie's not going to fight if the growth turns out to be cancer?'

'That's what she said.'

'Well, we have to change her mind. I can't lose her!'

'Dad, keep it down. Mom has just fallen asleep.'

'I won't bother her. I called Trevor Sanderson. There was no mention made of you.'

'The police executed a search warrant on my house today. I've been questioned. I've told you the whole story.'

'Why did you talk to the police in the first place, without first calling me? Never mind, Cait. What's done is done. We go on from there. I'll find the best person for you. Unless you are officially called in for questioning, do not have any further contact with the police. Partisan politics is a reality in most universities. If you're summoned to the Dean's office, you will not be going alone.'

Maggie called down from the upstairs landing. 'I'd like to join you, but I need a little help.'

Frank ran up to help his wife. First he embraced her. 'Oh my God, Maggie.'

'Help me down, Frank. I want to be where the action is.'

Caitlin managed a smile and waited. Frank helped Maggie into her favorite chair, and Caitlin covered her with a throw. Frank knelt in front of Maggie. He knew it was not the time to scold his wife, but he felt left out. 'I'm still trying to understand why you didn't confide in me, you or

Caitlin. I would never have gone to New York. No case is more important than you. Don't you know that? I feel I abandoned you, or you abandoned me somehow. I feel guilty for even bringing this up. It's how I feel. What's happened to us?'

Maggie smiled down at Frank. 'I've been sad for a long time, Frank.'

'Haven't we all been sad?'

'You and Caitlin threw yourselves into work, to lessen the grief of losing Chris. Cait tells me she hated coming home because Chris is too present here. It hurts too much. Frank, in simple words, you took off and you left me alone. This house is full of memories and sadness, so it was easier for both of you to stay away.'

'Mom, to be fair, I pass Wood and Sherbrooke every day, and I remember I told Chris to walk home. He'd still be alive if he'd taken a cab like he wanted to do. I didn't lose myself in work. I just tried to survive. We all did.'

'All you had to do was to ask me to stay, Maggie. I don't know your thoughts. I believed you wanted to be alone because you stopped working, or calling friends. But I lost my son, Caitlin lost her brother. I didn't feel you needed me.'

'Dad, we can't compare grief. Chris was the light of Mom's life. Why didn't one of us say something? Why didn't we help one another out? What's happened to us?'

'We suffered a death in the family, and it fractured us,' Maggie said simply. Maggie's pronouncement brought about a moment of silence until the guilt was unbearable.

Frank Donovan brought them back to the present. 'How long are you supposed to wait for this call from Franken?'

'A few more days.'

'I'm calling him first thing this morning. Someone must be able to reach him on a Sunday. This kind of waiting is inhuman. Those results are sitting in some file box.'

'Frank, don't make that call. I'm not his only patient. I'll wait. For now, let's go to bed.'

'Maggie, you have to fight if it's cancer. I can't lose you. We all have to start again, together, the way we once were.'

'Let's get some rest. I'm too weary to discuss this decision. Caitlin has classes today. Once more, to bed, all of us. No more talking. I've felt enough pressure for the last two weeks.'

'I'll stay home, Mom.'

'You'll see to your classes. Your father's with me.'

Caitlin went to her old bedroom, closed the door and called Carmen. 'Thanks for today. Dad's home with us. How long did the investigative techs spend in my house?'

'A couple of hours. I was stuck in the living room, so I couldn't see what was going on.'

'Did they take some of my things with them?'

'Not from my angle, but I didn't have the full picture.'

'Did you leave things you need here at Mom's?'

'I'll leave you guys alone. I'll collect my belongings another time.'

'Thanks, Carm.'

'No prob. Are you getting a lawyer?'

'Dad's calling his connections today. I'm not going to the Dean without a lawyer. The position I'm in now is untenable. I need support.'

'Good to hear. Catch you tonight.'

Trevor Sanderson had called Parthenais, the Montreal City Morgue, and learned they could take possession of their daughter's remains on Monday at noon. He made himself a stiff drink and had a second before he was able to call. He was seething with anger. He picked up the most recent family photo and held it tightly in his hands. His finger gently traced Taylor's face. She was waving in the photo. Trevor recalled the wave, a flick of her wrist, a little girl's wave. The arm raised high with the flash of her hand and a sudden smile. It seemed as close as yesterday. He wondered why it was that kids appeared invulnerable. Maybe it was their symmetry of youth and life that stretched far out ahead of them. The lie of it caught in his throat – lambs to the slaughter. He kissed the photo and left the house.

When Sanderson found his wife and son comforting each other in the hospital room he pretended not to see that his arrival disturbed them. He was on a mission. 'Shari, I'll need your help. We have to go home. I've called the Mount Royal Funeral Complex and have made arrangements. My secretary's begun work on the private invitations for the funeral. I don't want a media crush or hundreds of students who hardly knew Taylor at the church or funeral home. She's ours now – I don't want to share her with strangers.'

Shari didn't move, but twitched at the mention of Taylor's name. Matthew had crawled out of bed on the side where his mother was sitting and got dressed.

'The problem I can't get my head around is what to do with my little girl. Taylor died in a dark place all alone and abandoned. How can I put my girl in the ground or in the Sanderson section of the mausoleum that my father had arranged. I can't confine her to a box. The thought of that would haunt me for life. I don't know what to do… I can do a lot of things, but I can't do this,' he said forlornly.

Shari Sanderson had never seen her husband cry, or need support. His wail shook the room. Dumb with shock, neither Shari nor Matthew made a move to help him. A nurse's aide appeared, but Matthew swiftly ushered her out. 'Dad,' Matthew said timidly, 'Tay loved the ocean and the dolphins at Longboat Key. She loved the sunsets – she wouldn't have to be in the dark.'

'What?' Sanderson sobbed.

'Tay doesn't have to be in any box. She loved the waves and the sunlight. Remember, she ran early in the morning on the beach.'

Trevor stood and thought. 'You're right, Matthew, she did. She wouldn't be alone. Taylor hated being alone.' Tears ran down the sides of Trevor's nose.

'No! I can't surrender my baby.' Shari fought back. 'I need some of my daughter with me, or in a place where I can go to be with her. I'm not allowing you to give her up. I won't allow Tay to disappear as though she never existed. I must touch her. I couldn't hold her at the morgue. Now she's come back to me.'

Trevor reached for his wife. 'I understand – I want a remembrance of her too. Let's go home.' The silence in the car, while not comforting, had a certain warmth, not felt by either of them since the discovery of their daughter's body.

Shari Sanderson broke the silence when they were safely home. 'Mathew has something to tell you, Trevor.'

Matthew backed away from his mother, and she read the sense of betrayal in his eyes.

'What's happened now?' Trevor's sudden anger flashed.

Matthew backed away with each word, expecting another right hook from his father. 'I told the police that I did go to the tunnel that day, but I was too late.' Matthew spoke quickly before his father could break in. 'I walked around looking for her. I know now that she was already dead, but I didn't know that then, Dad. You have to believe me! I thought Tay had *punked* me. I was expecting her to call me laughing.'

Trevor frowned. 'Why the hell didn't you tell the truth in the first place? What are you hiding? I can't figure you out, Matthew. Why the lie? Did you see anyone at the tunnel?'

'I told the police about two people I saw there, but I didn't see them well enough for a good description, Dad. I was no help.'

'Why lie?'

'I got scared.'

'Of me?'

'I guess. You never screw up. I didn't want you to hate me, but you do anyway. That's why I came clean.' Matthew told his father about the two people he saw.

'You didn't think to look into the tunnel – the pathologist said Tay struggled to breathe for a few hours. Tay might well have still been alive while you walked around. You might have saved her.'

Matthew was white. 'Tay would never go into the tunnel, so I never thought…'

'Never thought? You bloody well knew she was in trouble – you knew she was scared! Why the hell didn't you use your head and explore the tunnel on the good chance that something had happened to her? You knew you were late, that she might be there against her will? What is wrong with you, Matthew?' Sanderson gathered his wits and asked his next question softly. 'Son, are you still lying to us?'

'I wish I was strong like you, Dad. I wish I had saved Tay, but I didn't. I wish I was dead.' Matthew ran up to his room.

His father rushed after him and stood looming in the doorway. 'Son, I've made mistakes. We all have. I'm begging you to allow Tay the time she needs in the next few days from all of us. Don't break your mother's heart. After the funeral, I'll arrange to get you some help. A real man lives with his flaws and accepts responsibility. If you want my respect, you'll have to earn it. A real man tells the whole truth. Have you told the whole truth?'

'You'll never forgive me, Dad, will you?'

'In time, I hope I can, but I can't fix you, Matthew.'

'I wish Tay had never called me.'

'She made the mistake of thinking you'd want to help her. I find it terribly sad that you might have saved her life.' Trevor walked away.

Chapter Twenty-nine

Jeff was busy catching up on his reading and had just opened *The New York Times* when Damiano walked into her home. The *Gazette* and *The Globe and Mail* she saw had been worked through. She smiled tiredly and pointed to Luke's room.

'He ran this morning. He's back in his room.'

'Is he talking, monosyllables at least?'

'*Yeah* and *no*.'

'I'll give it a try, Jeff, but I haven't slept and my arm…'

'Half a pill and I'll tuck you in, no more than three hours or you won't sleep tonight.'

'Yes, doctor.' Damiano smiled. *Jeff is too gullible not to realize that I have a stash for emergencies.* She was asleep in minutes, despite the pain. Damiano dreamt she was walking across the Champlain Bridge but on the outside of the barrier overlooking the St. Lawrence River. Holding onto it with both hands, a gust of wind caught her off guard and she lost her grip and… jerked up in bed, a sheen of perspiration on her face. She fell back into bed and pulled up the covers. Before she was fully asleep, she found herself back on the bridge, trying to climb over to the protected side.

Jeff opened the door when he heard the moans. He lay down on the bed beside Damiano and held her until the trembling stopped. When her breathing was soft and rhythmic, he inched off the bed. Jeff waited by the door for a few minutes until he felt she was safe, at least in her dreams.

Luke surprised Jeff in the kitchen. He was toasting a bagel. The cream cheese was on the counter. 'Dad?'

'That's me.'

'I had an argument at recess. Suppose you see a friend, say at Ogilvy's window, and you shout across the street for him to come over and go for a drink, something like that. The guy decides to come, but he's annihilated by a car he doesn't see.'

'Good description.' Jeff was taken aback that Luke was speaking. He tried not to see the dark circles under Luke's eyes and the pallor of his skin.

'I'm serious.'

'Alright, go ahead.'

'The friend is done. Is the guy who called him over responsible? If he hadn't called, his friend would still be alive, right?'

'What side did you take, Luke?'

'I want your opinion, Dad.'

'His friend would still be alive if he hadn't called, that's true. When crossing a street, like Ste. Catherine Street, his friend made the choice to cross, so *he* had the responsibility of looking both ways before he attempted to cross. The burden's on him.'

'So?'

'His friend might feel guilty, but he's not at fault. What did you think?'

'Like you kind of, but the friend still feels like shit.'

'Nice vocabulary from a private school boy. Did something like this happen?'

'Nah, we were arguing at recess. Robert, the philosopher, thought the friend who called was responsible, that he should be arrested or something.'

'Nothing ever happens in a vacuum. You might invite a friend here for gaming. If he has a fatal accident on the way, you're not to blame. There's no negligence on your part. If that story were true, the friend would feel badly for a long time, but arrested, a definite no.'

'Good that it isn't then. Why does everything fall into the gray zone?'

'That's an adult question. Life becomes more complex as we age. When you're a kid, you think only about yourself. An emerging adult, like you, begins to see the inter-connectedness of every action. We're all part of the human race, living on the blue planet.' Jeff knew to change the topic to keep communication open with his son. 'Are you going to eat that bagel?'

'You want it?'

'Maybe, it looks good.'

'I'll make another one.'

Jeff thought about the story. His son was talking. That was a start. It wasn't the time to probe. His question might not have a hidden component. Jeff still saw black and white. He liked life simple. Simple had a softer landing. Life with its edge of menace he left to his cop wife. Not for the first time, he wondered what it was that pulled Toni into dangerous paths that almost took her life and left her with nightmares. He knew it was not just the action – it was something more. Toni was trying to prove herself, driven to right wrongs. Were they hers, he wondered? Jeff hoped one day Toni would see her own clan and take fewer risks of losing them. As he'd said to Luke, we were all connected. He'd eaten half the bagel when he saw that Luke was staring at him.

'That's what bothers Mom, right? The decision she made in that last case.'

'Yes, but it's more complex than your example.'

Luke cut in. 'I don't know, Dad. Mom's not sure she made the right decision on the last case. She keeps her medal in a drawer. The man died.'

'In your example, the friend who called across the street didn't put his life at risk. Your mother knew she might die the instant she grabbed the young man. If he hadn't lunged back, they both would have lived. Your mother held onto him for half a minute. Actually, she never let go…'

'Right. Her arm imploded.'

'And he lost his grip. The government awards the Medal of Honor for deeds of valor. Your mom can't see how close she came to dying – she's deeply troubled by the man who died, as though she were to blame. Maybe your mother can't see the whole story of that night. She's afraid of being afraid, I think. That's why I said we have to carry burdens in this life. She has hers.'

'I think I get it, Dad. You're not so lame… that's not what I mean.' Luke gave his father a slap on his shoulder.

Jeff saw more clearly how tired Luke was, but he smiled and said. 'I have my moments. I'm going to make more coffee. You want to try some?'

'I'll go with milk. I couldn't wait to be sixteen, but I'm in no hurry now. Dad? Did you fall in love a lot, I mean before Mom?'

'My parents divorced. You know that. I was on my own since I was seventeen, always scrambling for money to get through school, to feed myself and pay for a room I shared with another student. I had no time and no money for girls. What girl would want to pay for her date?'

'Was Mom your first love?' he asked incredulously.

'First and last. You, you'll have many loves.'

'I gotta *bounce*.' Luke's cheeks seemed hollow.

I tried.

Damiano didn't hear any of the conversation between father and son, but after six bars of 'The House of the Rising Sun,' she reached over and padded around for the phone. 'Marie!' Her voice was groggy with sleep.

'We have a break. The professor told you that Sanderson didn't enter any other room but the hall and living room. We found prints there, but we also found her prints on the side of the fridge in the kitchen. We might be able to do something with those. Remember, she may still be at the hospital, the Royal Vic, with her mother.'

'That's good, Marie. I'll call today and have her in for questioning tomorrow. Nothing in the bedroom?'

'Prints, but not hers.'

'Good work.'

'Were you sleeping?'

'No sleep last night.'

'Lucky you!'

'In a way, it was good.'

'I won't touch that one.'

Damiano braved a cold shower and chattering teeth for one minute before she turned up the hot tap. Towelling and hair drying took fifteen minutes before she was set for late Sunday afternoon.

Jeff was waiting for her. 'Luke and I had quite a conversation about ethics. He didn't reveal much, but give me a minute. You're the cop. Help me read between the lines. Luke's lost weight and he looks haggard. The bagel is the first food I've seen him eat. He hadn't showered. The kitchen reeked of him this morning.'

Damiano sat and listened. The professor wasn't going anywhere. 'A few days ago, Luke said he had really "fucked up," that everything was ruined, done. Now he's wondering, via his analogy, if he's responsible. The analogy might mean that confiding in Dustin, I'm assuming it is Dustin his best friend, had no malice intended. Dustin betrayed his trust. Word got out and killed the budding relationship. The girl may well have been a virgin like Luke, a Sacred Heart or Trafalgar girl. She must have been hurt to the core and she dumped him. Luke was in love – why would *he* boast? It's so mean.'

'Males are stupid! We announce our conquests. Maybe Dustin guessed without Luke saying anything. What matters is Luke's heartbroken.'

'It's still so mean. I don't see it. What about checking his room?'

'Absolutely not! Luke would never trust us again. He takes after you, Toni. God knows you can be mean – you often don't think before you speak.'

'I hope I haven't influenced my son to that extent. If I have, Luke won't get over this love any time soon. We can't call Dustin, Luke would never forgive us for that either. No irate mothers have called. Let things play out, I guess.' Damiano locked eyes with Jeff. 'I used to be happy that Luke took after me, but that's not such a great thing. Know what, I wouldn't love me.'

'You're a challenge.'

'That's it?'

'When I see you sleeping, Toni, my heart's still overcome. Life seems new and fresh.'

'That's something. Then again, I'm unconscious. Where's Luke?'

'Out running again.'

'You should have stopped him.'

'I couldn't – he has to burn this off. He's just begun to communicate.'

'I have to make a call.'

'Do it then. We're fine.'

Caitlin Donovan took the call without checking the ID, believing it was Carmen. 'Hey!'

'Ah, Lieutenant Detective Damiano, Professor.'

Caitlin's stomach tightened. 'Yes?'

'I need you to come in for questioning tomorrow.'

Caitlin's forehead beaded with perspiration. 'I have morning classes. May I come at one-thirty?'

'I'm located at the Crémazie Division. It's…'

'I'll be there.'

'Detective Matte and I will meet you at the front of the elevator.'

Chapter Thirty

Caitlin had been sitting in the living room by the fire with both her parents. Frank Donovan immediately understood the intent of her visit. 'Dad, I need your help. We should go to the study.'

'Not on my account,' Maggie said. 'Problems can be a distraction. I could use some distraction.'

'The police want to question me tomorrow.'

'Not interrogate?'

'No, thankfully.'

'We have to move quickly, Caitlin. I have someone in mind. He has a varied portfolio, and I believe he's been on the board of some universities. That expertise should serve us well. Dino Mazzone is the man I want for you.'

Despite a rush of nerves, Caitlin laughed. 'Dad, an Italian lawyer?'

Maggie smiled. 'Frank?'

'What prejudice from my two favorite girls! Dino is not only an honest lawyer, he's a loving father and husband, a man very adept with the law and someone who can talk his way out of most trouble. He's a lawyer who puts his client first, ahead of billing hours. He has done work for our firm.'

'He has my vote,' Maggie said to Caitlin.

'I'll call him right now and invite him to dinner. We have no time to waste.' Frank walked to the study and closed the door. He was back in five minutes. 'He's on his way – he can't miss dinner at home and must be back for seven.'

Caitlin rushed up the stairs, showered, dressed and began to make notes. Between thoughts, she tapped the pen on her teeth. Her career was crashing. What would Detective Damiano think of the lawyer? *She's guilty of something.* But Caitlin had no choice. The police had something new. Each point added up. Caitlin racked her brain to remember everything that had happened. And then she thought of something. 'That must be it! Why didn't I think of it before?' Her frustration abated. She was still writing when her father called her downstairs.

No time was wasted on lengthy introductions. Caitlin, like her father, was not one to be easily impressed, but Mazzone caught her attention. She thought of Carmen when she assessed the lawyer. Like her Italian friend, image was important to Mazzone. His black hair was combed back. His suit was stylish and looked good without a tie. Caitlin liked a man who could wear a pink shirt. His dark eyes softened when he smiled. 'I'm pleased to meet you, Caitlin. I think we should get started.'

'The study is best. Dad, would you like to join us?'

'I want to be with Maggie, in case…'

Mazzone took no notice of the finely appointed study or its art. Sitting beside Caitlin on the dark leather chairs he reviewed and commented on Caitlin's summary. When he was through, he turned and said, 'It's good that you remembered the end of term gathering at your home. That's our trump card tomorrow. Your kindness is the main problem. In future…'

'I've learned.'

'I'll mention only one *if*. If you had opened the front door and spotted Sanderson, she'd have been detained. That might have saved her life.'

'Or, I might have been struck in the face by the other half of the brick.'

'True. Before we meet at Crémazie, my contacts in the university will have provided me with information regarding the harassment charge. If you are asked to see the Dean, call me immediately. I will attend that meeting with you. It's been seven working days since Sanderson made the complaint. Moving it forward is usually done in the first three days. The delay is good news. We have to hope they won't call you Monday. Concerning your alibi, have you driven to the cemetery to ask the men if they saw you that Tuesday?'

'I have. I'm there three days a week. I know the guys because it's been eight years. April is a lazy month for them. They're rarely on the grounds. One of the guys says he can confirm my presence.'

'Perjury is not on the table. Sanderson didn't give you a hint about the "stuff" in her life?'

'She was angry with me, but she was frightened, near hysteria, by the "stuff." Fear was driving Taylor that day. She took it out on me.'

'At Crémazie, allow me to talk for you; answer when you have the nod from me. You've said too much already. They know who Frank is by now, so they're expecting you to appear with legal help tomorrow. Don't talk to your colleagues about any of these issues. We keep a low profile. That's it for now. I'll look over the notes tonight. Are you here in case I need to reach you?'

'Yes, but here's my cell number. Thank you, Dino.'

'Remember, call me immediately if you are summoned to the Dean's office tomorrow. If not, I`ll meet you in the Crémazie parking lot or at the front door. Get some sleep. Ironically, you are the aggrieved party.'

'I'm better off than Taylor. It's the first time I've felt sorry for her.'

'Good to hear. See you tomorrow.'

Caitlin saw Mazzone to the door and joined her parents. 'It went well, I guess. The stress day is tomorrow if I hear from the Dean. How are you doing, Mom?'

The house phone rang. 'Give me the phone, Frank.' Caitlin saw her mother's hand shake. 'Why do you people call on a Sunday? I'm not interested! Everybody has to work for a living, but there are limits. Sunday!' After she hung up, she pleaded with Frank and Caitlin. 'Leave the phone with me. Why don't you two go for a walk? I'd feel better alone, for a while anyway. I won't hear from the doctor today, I'm sure.'

'I don't want to leave you alone, Maggie.'

'Frank, I love you, but hovering over me is getting on my nerves. Cait, you need fresh air.'

'Alright, Dad, let Mom be.'

'I don't think…'

'Dad, we're not helping.'

The phone rang again.

Maggie took the call. 'Shari, I am so sorry for all of you. I've been under the weather myself. I'd very much like that another time. Deepest sympathies. You're in my prayers.' Maggie looked at Caitlin. 'What could I do?'

'You handled the call well, Mom. Dad and I are off.'

The wind was strong and Caitlin pulled on her ear muffs. Above them trees bent and their branches tossed. Frank pulled on a black woolen cap and stuck his hands in his pockets. 'I don't feel good about leaving your mother alone.'

'It's what Mom wants that matters. We're just adding to her stress.'

'You have your own matter to deal with, but I fail to understand how you haven't convinced Maggie to fight whatever this ailment may be. We're the fighting Irish – we don't give up. Maggie has a good twenty to twenty-five years ahead of her. Cait, I'd be lost without her. Your mother is my best friend, my gal.'

'We're both selfish, Dad. How much support have we given to Mom since Chris was killed? I couldn't cope. I was of no help to anyone. I walked out on Mike and I see now that we both walked out on Mom. I visit Chris's grave more often than I see her. This is her life, not ours. We have to allow her the choice to choose how she wants to live, or not.'

Caitlin stopped and shook off the cold. 'I hope if we shower her with love, she might change her mind. Bullying won't help her.'

'Cait, if I have a vote, I vote we get back to her. I'm itching to call Franken.'

'Don't call, Dad!'

'Okay, I won't, Cait. What you said about your mother is dead on. Concerning you, listen to Mazzone. The less you say, the better for you. Call me when you can.'

'I'd rather to be home with Mom.'

'I'll be there. Don't worry. You must report for work *and* attend the police questioning. Apart from me, that's what Maggie would want.'

They buried their hands in their pockets, leaned into the wind and headed for home.

Chapter Thirty-one

Detective Matte and Detective Damiano were in Damiano's office completing paperwork when they were summoned to the chief's office. 'Pierre, how about I cover Matthew Sanderson – you take the professor and I finish up.'

Matte brightened up.

Donat was standing outside the office waiting on them. He closed the door after them and sat behind his desk, leaning across the top with both hands spread palms down. 'We've been lucky with the media so far. I chalk that up to Sanderson. But nothing lasts, so I hope you have something solid for me. Tell me everything,' he growled. He squinted, his pinched face a sign of the mounting pressure from the case.

Damiano outlined the details and her thoughts on Matthew Sanderson. She was still talking when the chief raised his hand. 'The kid's a suspect?' Surprise mingled with dread from the possible fallout.

'He is, Chief.'

'*Tabarnouche!* Sanderson's son killing his sister! You haven't grounds for an arrest, correct?'

'Not yet. I need him in here for questioning.'

Donat threw his hands in the air. 'Well then, do it, Damiano! By the book because Sanderson is a savvy and influential lawyer.'

'Matte will be questioning another suspect.'

The chief paced as Matte outlined what they had on Caitlin Donovan.

'Is this Donovan any relation to...'

'His daughter,' Matte answered.

'You better have the goods – this department cannot afford lawsuits from two of the top legal firms in the city. What else do you have?'

Damiano named the two tenants, the ex, Glen Gardiner, and the mystery man or woman. 'Chief, we need help checking the alibis.'

'Use Galt. He's a good tracker.' Tight-jawed the chief sat back down at his desk.

Damiano and Matte knew what that meant. 'We know we're stuck at square one,' she admitted.

'My thoughts exactly,' Chief Donat spat. 'Get out of here and close! Can you imagine the field day the press would have if they got hold of our two main suspects? My best team has nothing concrete. I don't have to tell either of you not to make an arrest without the guts we need to back it up. The public has little regard for us these days, already, because of the demonstrations. I won't give them cause to hone in on my department. Put Galt on it!'

Chief Donat immediately went back to the work on his desk, a blunt sign of his disappointment.

'Well, that went well. Nab Galt immediately. The chief is right – we *are* at square one.'

'Not precisely, Toni.'

'I was thinking…'

'Do you have to run everywhere?'

'We're in a rush, Pierre.'

'It's not a marathon.'

'Back to my thought. When the obvious are not bullseyes, look closely at the secondary.'

'You just made that up.'

'I'm serious. Amira Cupid with her rocks, Josh Goldman with his hatred, the throwaway who chose the site, and slippery Gardiner. We won't close in on the kid or the professor unless we have them locked into this murder. Something I'd forgotten, deep down, murderers are arrogant sociopaths who can kill without guilt.'

'It doesn't always work that way. If it did, Goldman would be in one of our holding cells. But I know you're referring to a hidden arrogance.'

'Exactly – the stealth of a murderer. In this case, a coward who struck from behind.'

'True. There's Galt.'

'Stephen! We need your help.'

Detective Galt smirked at his fellow cops as he swaggered into Damiano's office. 'Good to hear! How can I help?' He listened to their theories on the crime and tried to impress Matte with his notes. 'I'll begin with the cemetery, move to the tenants and verify that Glen Gardiner was in fact in New York. If you're right, and the tenants don't like one another, I can count on one telling me the truth. You want me on the road immediately?'

'On the double.'

'The way I like it.' Galt grabbed his lunch and left.

'What do you think?'

'I think we should eat and prep for the professor.' She lied. 'Does Sanderson's harassment charge hold water with you, Pierre?'

'I thought about it. If the professor is not called up on the carpet by the Dean, well…'

'Shuts it down, right?'

'That's like an acquittal. It's not declared innocence. The director is the judge and she's not infallible. We won't ever know is my guess. We've heard nothing from the techs on the vic's computer or phone. It's strange that our vic's relationship with the mystery man or woman remained secret. Kids talk. Why, if it was such a great love? The secret would make sense if it was the professor.'

'Agreed, but reaching. Let's prep, but first food. I brought my own. Just to tell you – my arm isn't bothering me, so I don't need a guard at my locker.'

'I can see you're in good shape today.'

Damiano took a call. 'That's improvement. Thanks for seeing him off. '

'Luke?'

'He finally showered.'

Caitlin Donovan walked to get her mail in the hallway. There was no letter from….. She read her email as she walked to her first class on the third floor of the Hall Building. The students were quiet – the mood was somber. Caitlin caught them looking over at Taylor Sanderson's empty seat. Caitlin's lecture rang hollow in her ears. Every second or two, she glanced at the door. A colleague had been called to the Dean's office three years ago. Caitlin recalled that he'd received a hand-delivered envelope during his class. Caitlin had two more classes. The next three hours would be torturous. And they were. After teaching she needed a shower, but there wasn't time. Her father said there was no news on his end. Caitlin couldn't eat. She drove through the noonday snarl of traffic and street closures that tore at her nerves.

In another sense, her body did not seem attached to her. It followed her commands as she drove, but *she* wasn't there. Her mother's precarious state, Taylor's death, her career stained with a sexual harassment charge, all merged into a running nightmare, particles of loss that she could not contain or control. She had spent much of the past eight years locked into her teaching, running from her brother's death. Caitlin never imagined she would be running from the present, a present as stable as Jell-O. 'Dammit to hell! I was doing Taylor a favor.' Taylor's words cut into Caitlin.

Screw up my life – I'll screw with yours.

Chapter Thirty-two

Detective Stephen Galt no longer used his nickname. "Prose." The would-be author had read his last three-line rejection letter. He shredded it with the rest of them and called his writing career a feckless illusion. He looked like a cop, tall and rangy, and still carried himself with the hint of a tight-end receiver who could once have run a football field. He was proud he had no paunch. He drove like a cowboy to the Notre-Dame-des-Neiges Cemetery. He threw a left and slammed on the brakes inside the gated entrance where he knew he'd find the groundskeepers in the graystone building. The seasonal workers were long gone.

Galt walked into a lunchroom where only men would eat. On one wall there was a felt board with names and tasks for the day written with colored markers, some half-erased. On another, a faded outdated calendar. Beside it a cork board with curling paper memos that had long passed their best-before date. The floor was muddy and littered; the table was a chaos of old newspapers and remnants of yesterday's lunch. The manager was eating homemade soup with crushed crackers and drinking coffee from a Thermos. Galt knew him.

'Figured to see you, Detective. The professor said you might be around asking questions. It's been eight years since her brother's death. We know her. We talk.'

'I'm only interested in one afternoon.'

'I know.'

'What do you have?'

'Professor Donavan is here three days a week, never on a Monday.'

'It's Tuesday, April 2nd, I want to know about.'

'Ninety-percent she was here.'

'You guys stayed in that day?'

'No snow, no plow; no freezing rain, no sand – we sit.'

'No one saw her?'

'Ninety-percent she was here. I'd bet on that, so should you.'

'Not good enough.'

'I coulda lied.'

'I get the message. Ninety-percent.'

'Go with it.'

'Don't strain yourselves.' Galt drove off. He was thinking about matching prints from the rocks. Seven to nine points met the requirements for court. Ninety-percent was essentially nine points of likelihood. He punched in Damiano's number and offered his thoughts.

'The chief says air-tight.'

'Utopia then?'

'With the professor and Sanderson, he's thinking lawsuits. Call Cupid and Goldman. Have them meet you at the apartment.'

'Yep.' Detective Galt got lucky, both students were home. It was too late for a lieutenancy, back stories and ratings had wiped out that chance. It wasn't too late to be included on major cases like this one. Galt figured he had to come up with something Damiano and Matte had missed the first time out. According to Damiano, Goldman was a 'prick' and Cupid was 'mysterious.' If he interviewed them together, something might pop. The fact that their vic was struck from behind told him more than cowardice. The perp might have felt Sanderson could get the upper hand face-on. Galt cursed when he saw the mess of cars on Lincoln and Fort. A ticket was out of the question. He grudgingly took time to validate his parking ticket and huffed back to Lincoln.

He called Goldman, and the kid opened the front door. Galt was a good head taller than Goldman. Advantage there, he thought until he saw Cupid. Drop-dead gorgeous. He kept his attention on Goldman so as not to be distracted. 'Ms. Cupid, mind if we use your apartment? If we're together, it'll save time.' Goldman smirked.

Cupid hesitated before accepting the proposal. 'There is not much room.'

'No problem. I'll stand,' Detective Galt told her, and he followed her into the room.

'What have you been doing, Amira?'

'A few touch-ups. I leave at the end of April.'

'If we don't all die first. Open a window.'

They weren't friends. Galt felt that was a good thing.

'We'll survive, Mr. Goldman.' Galt used his height to appraise the room. Books, files, and notes were stacked in piles anchored by painted rocks. Had Damiano seen these? He'd mention them. 'Well, Ms. Cupid, Lieutenant Detective Damiano has your recorded statement. I'm here to double-check your whereabouts Tuesday afternoon of April 2nd around four. Will you repeat exactly what you did after you told Ms. Sanderson you couldn't help her because you needed to study?'

'I went back to my notes. Then I changed my mind. I took my coat and hat and I ran out looking for Taylor.'

'What streets?'

'Lincoln to Fort.'

'Then you came back here?' Detective Galt kept his eyes on Goldman for his reaction.

Goldman was all eyes.

'I did not run back. I walked. I returned to study.'

Goldman's mouth opened, but he thought better and turned away.

'Ms. Cupid, is there a chance you stopped at Concordia for a book or coffee?'

Goldman looked up.

Silence. Then, 'I did return to my apartment, but I thought I saw Taylor just before I was about to walk back. I ran after her again, but I was mistaken. Yes, I returned later than I first said. It was an anxious day. Taylor never came back. I felt great guilt.' Amira bowed her head.

'Ms. Cupid, I have to tell you both that Detective Damiano...'

'You mean Lieutenant Detective, right?' Goldman corrected.

'She may call you in for further questioning, Mr. Goldman. Where were you after refusing to help Ms. Sanderson?'

'Nothing has changed with me. I threw on some clothes because she kept pounding on my door; told her I couldn't help, really wouldn't I guess, and went back to bed.'

'In your clothes?'

'Yeah, I guess so. I was half asleep. I sleep like the dead.'

'Did you hear Ms. Cupid come back in?'

'No, actually, but I was probably out cold.'

'Since you were already dressed, you weren't tempted to run after Ms. Sanderson?'

'She got herself in some shit – she was no butterfly. Taylor could handle herself.' Goldman's eyes burned into Amira's. 'Did you keep running after her, Amira?'

Amira rose to her full height. 'Like you, I was no help. I lost her.' Her large dark eyes had reduced to slits.

'She's lying, Detective. Amira did not come back till much later.'

Goldman's shot had Detective Galt's full attention. 'Is that true? Ms. Cupid?' he asked quietly.

Cupid ran her hand down her face. Her confidence dented, her beautiful face grimaced with rage. 'You are a snake! I could not come back because of you. Detective, he would not let us be. He hated Taylor because she ignored him, but he kept after me because I had no one to defend me. He has been terrible since Taylor's death. I returned when I was less afraid and thought he was asleep. Since that day, I have to sneak into the apartment with my key ready to open the door.'

'The bitch is lying. I wouldn't date an Amazon!'

'Why did you lie to Detective Damiano, Ms. Cupid?'

'I was afraid of trouble. I am frightened. I'm on a student visa. I did not want to say anything against Josh and give him reason to harm me. He did not go back to sleep. He was fully dressed; I saw him by his door. I have no other place to go. I must stay the month. What could I do? I could not tell the truth, you must see that.'

'You're a freakin' cop! You must be able to see through this.'

'You've both lied on record. Your alibis are not corroborated. Expect a call from Detective Damiano for questioning at the Division.' Galt concealed his excitement. He had enough to keep himself on the team.

'I cannot believe this!' Goldman growled.

'Ms. Cupid, would you feel safer with me?'

'Detective, this is ridiculous. I'll go to my parents, and the princess can have the whole place to herself.' Cupid could damage him, and his lie already had. He left the room and soon returned in a jacket, hiking boots and books. 'I'm leaving.'

Galt could see that the preppy was scared, so he stayed with Cupid till Goldman left. He'd report to Damiano in person. He wanted to be part of the case, but Damiano would have to wait till he met Gardiner. Galt made quick time to the Alexis Nihon Plaza's underground parking, paying the fourteen bucks he could have used. The Division paid for meters, but Galt was in a hurry so he ate the cost. He drove up to Sherbrooke Street, cut a left and snaked through the traffic and construction on his way to Westmount's Victoria Avenue. He parked high up on Victoria, the only place he could find parking. He walked down the hill to a modest gray office building that needed a facelift. His eye caught the specialty bike shop across the street. He had passed a bakery, and beside it a tiny children's clothes boutique. He liked the area. Gardiner's company was on the fourth floor. Galt took the stairs. The stairs and walls hadn't been painted in years. He knocked on the company door and was invited inside. He counted six rooms with old tables, desks and computers. The room had the appearance of a recent move or departure. Merchandise was packed in opened cardboard boxes. The walls were empty.

Since there were no nameplates on the desks, he asked for Gardiner.

'Bingo! Must be your lucky day.'

'Detective Galt from Major Crimes.'

'Figured you for a cop. Crime's another hobby of mine. I have my flight stubs. My boss, PJ Stewart, Paul actually, will be glad to verify my New York dates.' He reached into one of the drawers in his desk and pulled out an envelope. 'PJ, I need some help over here.'

Galt noted that the group of four men and two women were all in their thirties, gamers, he thought. PJ Stewart was another friendly sort. Tall, thin, balding and a fast talker.

'Detective, Gardiner's our best pitcher and spinner. He was in the Big Apple, got back Friday. I picked him up at Dorval. He only shares the news when he's back at home plate. News was good – like my guy here.'

'Tuesday, April 2nd. Pitching to a boardroom.'

Galt looked around skeptically.

'Don't let our office fool you – we make money that's going into our pockets for now. It's been nine years of hard work that's finally paying off. Anything else?'

'I'll let you know. I'll need the stubs.'

'My gift!'

One less suspect on their list. Galt tried to run up Clarke, but folded in two halfway up the steep hill, gasping, wheezing and rubbing his knees. 'Ha!' Galt felt an old excitement. The cop was back!

Chapter Thirty-Three

Caitlin Donovan sat in the small, cramped Crémazie parking lot. Dino Mazzone hadn't shown up. With only two parking spaces left, she hoped he'd arrive in time to get one of them. Her father generally arrived at the last minute; she expected the same from Mazzone. The tension she felt for her mother she could isolate, but she couldn't figure out if she was nervous or angry about having to be here. Mazzone finally pulled in and took the last space. She waited for him in her car. Before he reached it, she got out. 'Hi, Dino.'

'Caitlin, you're in good hands. I have good instincts about the cops I can trust. Nothing to report on that harassment charge, that's good news. I did some homework on this Damiano – ambitious, tough, arrogant, but straight. My advice to you is keep it simple. If I give you the nod, answer *only* what is asked.'

'Got it. Don't let them set me up. I don't want to be another exonerated client a few years from now with no career and no prospects. I've worked hard to get where I am.'

'Try to control the tremor in your voice. She'll hone in on that. Let's do this thing.'

Crémazie Division was a cold imposing gray building that faced the interminable traffic of a service road and the Metropolitan Expressway. From the noise to the air pollution, it was a building that rattled suspects before they opened the heavy front door. No one met them. They passed a display window with a uniformed mannequin on a motorcycle surrounded by police wares. Mazzone seemed calm and rang the bell at the right of the elevator. They waited.

Detective Matte appeared from a stairwell, followed by Detective Damiano in a tailored navy pant suit with a pale pink blouse; Matte also wore a blue suit and white shirt with a navy tie. Caitlin thought humorously that the outfits must be the tag-team rags. Both detectives nodded to Mazzone and did not appear to be surprised to see him.

'Please follow me,' Detective Matte said, as walked towards a door on their right, through a hall to what Caitlin thought was more like a boardroom than an interrogation room. At least she had escaped a formal interrogation. Caitlin and Mazzone walked to the opposite side of the long table and sat beside each another. Matte and Damiano chose the other and sat a few chairs apart. 'Lieutenant Detective Damiano will conduct the questioning. She will make a quick review of what we have on record. We intend to record this session as well.' The atmosphere was tense.

Mazzone nodded.

Damiano read Matte's notes, and he listened as though he didn't know every word.

'We have the plagiarized papers, the home visit, the problems Taylor referred to, the threat, the brick throwing, and your visit to the university's office of Rights and Responsibilities.' Damiano went carefully into each point. She looked up, about to continue, but stopped abruptly. 'Are you not feeling well, Professor?' Damiano rose, reached into a box, produced four bottles of water and offered Donovan one.

Caitlin opened her mouth, but Mazzone was quicker. 'My client has been at the hospital with her mother who is awaiting the results of a biopsy that might well be grim. She hasn't slept in two nights.'

'We're genuinely sorry, but that doesn't alter our work here.'

'Just clarification – but understood.' He had his hand up and nodded to continue.

'We did hear today from one of our detectives that you spend three days a week at the Notre-Dame-des-Neiges Cemetery, generally Tuesdays, but as you said, no one directly saw you that Tuesday in question.'

Mazzone nodded.

'I was there.'

'You do see our problem with that alibi. Now, you said the day Sanderson burst into your home, she was in the hallway and the living room.'

Caitlin looked to Mazzone. 'I did.'

'No possibility of any other room?'

'No.'

'Well, Professor, we did execute a search warrant at your home and found Sanderson's prints in your kitchen. So, I have to ask you again…'

Mazzone nodded at Donovan.

'Early December is mid-term. For the last three years, I've invited students to my home for coffee and sandwiches. Taylor and Emma were both there. Students went into the kitchen to restock the sandwiches and fetch more cream from the fridge. No students *ever* went upstairs.'

Damiano drummed her fingers on the table. 'We will check with Emma Joly.' Damiano felt a tingling in her arm and rubbed it. She hated having missed something she should have caught.

Silence.

'Is there a reason you have so many hiking boots?'

'Is there a relevant point, Detective?' Mazzone asked.

'It's odd to see four almost-new pairs. Yes, there is a point.'

After a nod from Mazzone, Caitlin answered. 'I walk to Concordia every day, no matter the weather, I walk in the cemetery for about an hour and I hike. I go through boots like water. It's the same with my sneakers in the summer months. I'm an exercise junkie.'

'We will conclude for today.' Damiano terminated the interview. 'I wish your mother good luck!' What disappointment she felt, she concealed. Damiano hadn't blundered on and made a sweeping accusation about the print or the array of boots. She intended to ask Marie Dumont about the number of sneakers. Damiano had kept herself in check. Small point.

Matte read the date, time and name of the suspect for the recording and then ushered Mazzone and Donovan out of the building. Damiano stayed with her papers and fumed. She began rubbing her elbow to increase the circulation. She didn't see that Matte was back.

'Are we going to persist with the professor?'

Damiano threw her hands up in surrender. 'I don't think we are going to prise anything further from the professor for the time being. We saw good lawyering today. My thought is that the professor remembered the mid-term party on her own. She hasn't changed her story, something guilty suspects do regularly. Yet she had plenty of time to wipe down prints in the bedroom. We don't even know what our vic accused the professor of doing. Today is Monday – we don't hear any further action on that either. It's Matthew Sanderson that I'd like to squeeze. He's like an onion; peel back one layer, there are others underneath.'

'Trevor Sanderson is claiming the remains today.'

'That means we have to have him in today or tomorrow morning before the viewing and service. Matte, would you call the hospital to see if the kid is still there?'

'Toni, the phone's beside you. Here's the number.' Matte pulled out his phone, scrolled down and found it.

Damiano grabbed the phone and had tapped in the numbers when she spotted Galt walking very deliberately towards her office. She stood and pushed the phone at Matte's chest. 'We may have something.'

Galt paid particular attention to his wording to impress Damiano. 'You know about the professor. Gardiner's alibi is solid. I have his plane stubs and the word of his boss.' Galt squared his shoulders. 'Both student tenants are lying. Their alibis fell apart. Goldman did not go back to sleep. He got dressed and had the opportunity to follow Sanderson and return to his apartment before Cupid returned.' His face glistened. 'Amira Cupid did not return to her apartment until it was quite late. Goldman told me that. Before you jump in, I chose Amira's apartment for the interview. I had the tenants boxed in together for better effect. It also gave me the opportunity to scope out the place. She uses rocks as paper weights and had been repainting them by the way. That's a tidbit. She claims that Goldman has been harassing her and worse since the murder, and she was afraid to go back until he was asleep. He packed a few things, said, shouted actually, that she was lying and went home to his parents.'

'I am impressed, Stephen.'

Matte was intrigued.

Damiano hesitated before speaking. 'Stephen, did you think of bringing her in with you?'

'I did, but I thought that was your call as lead. I can contact her again and drive back for her.' Galt's miscue deflated his hopes. He should have called. 'Look, you and Pierre, contact Cupid, then drive back and pick her up. We don't have grounds for a search warrant, but Pierre, snap a photo of those rocks while Galt is distracting Cupid. Do your best. Don't arouse attention. A closer look is better than nothing. I'll call the hospital.'

Damiano heard Matte saying they wanted to be certain she was safe. The ruse worked and they left.

Damiano learned Matthew Sanderson was home with his parents. The call put her on her guard and she delayed making it until she thought of her phrasing. Blowing the call was not an option. Damiano tapped in each number.

'Yes?'

'Mr. Sanderson, this is…'

'I know who it is. What do you want now? I presume you know this is a difficult day for us.'

'Yes, I do. I am truly sorry for this interruption, but we must to speak to Matthew at the Crémazie Division. You are well aware of my job here. I am working for you and your daughter.'

'Do you know my son's condition?'

'I know he's been released from the hospital, that he suffered some bruising.'

'*I* brought him home. Doesn't mean he's stable.'

'I believe that Matthew knows more than he has been able to tell us. Your son is very emotional, with reason. Please drive him down to see us. It is my hope to finalize the questioning today.'

'One nightmare atop another and you're part of it.'

'We need all the assistance we can muster to find the person who took your daughter's life. I know you want justice, Mr. Sanderson. I recall your words from that very first night. Your daughter is the focus of my full attention.' Damiano clenched her fists.

'Would seven tonight work?'

'I'll make it work. Thank you.'

Chapter Thirty-Four

Damiano didn't stew for long. At her locker, she reached into a spare shoe and withdrew a crumpled plastic bag. When she was alone, she swallowed the narcotic and took a few gulps of water and took the energy bars her husband had stuffed into the pocket of her coat.

Damiano began to organize the papers on her desk and the table against the wall. Her back was to the door, so she jumped when she heard the loud knock. *The chief!* Before she could respond, the chief let himself in and stood fixing her with a watchdog stare.

'You've not reported to me.'

'Only because things are moving, Chief. We've broken two alibis. I'm waiting on a tenant of Sanderson's as we speak. I'll deal with the other very soon. Tonight Trevor Sanderson has agreed to bring his son in to be questioned. The professor was in earlier this afternoon. I've been busy.'

The chief zeroed in on the main problem. 'The throwaway?'

'Matthew Sanderson comes into it. My gut tells me Taylor confided in her brother more than he's been willing to reveal. With each questioning, we learn more. He's frightened, stubborn and troubled. Not a good mix for truth, especially in front of his father. You have his back story. If I could have the kid alone…'

'Can't happen. You hear me, Damiano?'

'He's more frightened of his father than he is of me.'

'Is he good for this?'

'Possibility.' Damiano could almost hear the blood sizzling in the chief's brain.

'No deals or set-ups with this kid. I won't permit you to stumble into an arrest. No crumbs for Sanderson to use against us. If you make the arrest, you better have concrete proof. Hear me well. If the kid is guilty, I want his father to know we acted by the book.'

Chief Donat knew his detectives, their strengths and flaws. He also was meticulous in keeping on top every case that crossed his desk. He didn't miss much.

'I want news tonight, not tomorrow. I won't chase you again.'

'Understood.'

The chief left without a nod to the incoming group of Matte and Galt with Amira Cupid. Damiano rose and shut the white verticals. She'd thought of the boardroom, but had second thoughts.

'Good afternoon, Amira. Thank you for coming down. I wanted to know that you were safe. We just have a few questions I hope you might help us with. Detective Matte, please sit beside Amira. Detective Galt, could you stand near the table. Thank you.'

Amira Cupid could have passed for a typical brooding teenager in her gray tights and black hoody covered by a winter jacket. She wasn't wearing boots and her worn sneakers were soaked at the edges. She had a black woolen hat in her hands. Damiano could see that fear had taken hold of the young woman. She did not appear focused and there was an unsettling stillness about her. She was staring at the bottom of Damiano's desk.

Damiano began the questioning with a veneer of sympathy. She didn't mention she was recording. 'Has Mr. Goldman called you or threatened to return?'

Cupid looked up and her body relaxed. 'No, thank you. I feel safer now with the police protection.'

'That's good news. My feet are always cold, even with boots. You're lucky to be young and not need them.'

Cupid smiled and her face brightened, but she did not comment further.

'Hopefully, Mr. Goldman will not return. Where did you go that night you could not find Taylor?' Damiano had leaned forward, closer to Cupid's face.

A few drops of sweat trickled down Cupid's back. 'I just walked around – I had no money to spend. I looked in the shops and bistros on Crescent Street and passed many students. I walked across the street to the Montreal Museum of Fine Arts and read about their exhibitions. I walked until I was very cold.'

'How long would you say?'

The short pointed question snapped Cupid back to the reality of these questions. She sat bolt upright. 'I don't know the exact time, but I was tired and there were fewer people on the streets. I stood outside to see if Josh's lights were off, then I made my way very quietly to my room.'

'Did you try to call Taylor to see if she was alright?'

'No, because she was angry that I had not gone with her. I knew she would not have answered.'

'You knew Taylor well then.'

'I knew her moods.'

'But some time ago, you were close friends.'

'Yes,' she smiled, 'we were best friends.'

'Did you wait up for her to see if she was back safely?'

'No,' she blushed. 'I thought she had gone off with the person she was going to meet.'

'But you knew she was frightened, you knew that.'

'Of the tunnel – I did not know about the person.'

'Why did your friendship end – you were best friends.'

Cupid was more comfortable with tears; her face took on a serene beauty when she cried. Damiano envied that. 'I saw that she was not able to see anyone but herself. That knowledge hurt me and I saw we were not truly friends. She was my first Canadian friend.'

'What actually happened, Amira?'

Damiano backed off to give Cupid space. She was talking, musing was a better word.

'In late January there was a huge sale of boots on boulevard St-Laurent near rue Rachel, seventy-five percent off. The day was bitter with cold winds. Taylor was going to meet a friend not too far away on Hutchison. I asked for a lift, but she was in a hurry and didn't have time. Ironically, I left first. I walked up to Sherbrooke Street and stood shivering in a bus shelter. Five minutes later, she waved at me as she passed by.' Cupid paused, remembering. 'She destroyed our friendship that day.' Damiano felt a good buzz. Matte and Galt felt it too.

When did Taylor come looking for help, Amira?'

'The next afternoon.'

'How frightened was Taylor when she came to your door?'

'She couldn't stop shaking.'

'What did she say to you?'

Cupid smiled. 'She said, "I really need your help. I can't go to that tunnel alone. I can't." When I said I could not afford the time, I saw her face fall and something broke. I know that look, because that's what I felt when she waved at me and drove past.'

Motive? Opportunity and means, with the rocks?

'Did you ever buy those boots, Amira?'

The air was thick with silence.

Nothing moved but an involuntary flicker in Cupid's left eye. Then she spoke. No, the bus was late and it was too cold in that shelter. Since it was April the cold weather had to break soon, so I gave up on boots altogether.'

Damiano bore into Cupid. 'Did you catch up with Taylor that night and try to explain, Amira?'

'No. Someone else found her.' From outward appearances, Cupid had closed her door.

It was time to wrap up the session. Could Marie procure another search warrant? 'Detective Matte will drive you home, Ms. Cupid,' Damiano said. 'Thank you for coming down. We recorded the session, just a routine procedure for our files,' pointing at the recorder with her pen.

Cupid's eyes narrowed. 'You did ask the first time, Detective. You must do your work, I understand.'

Damiano felt only a slight tinge of guilt.

Matte was not happy to leave Damiano with Galt. He felt displaced. He was second on the case. A few minutes later, his phone beeped. 'Pierre, I need Galt here – he got a good view of the rocks. If you can somehow manage to step inside her apartment, try to check out the boots. You might get lucky.'

'Tricky, but I'll try.'

'Stephen, how big was the largest rock?'

'It was on a pile of papers tucked in that nook of hers. Hand-size, I'd guess.'

'Painted?'

'All five were freshly painted.'

'You didn't happen to see boots stashed anywhere, Stephen?'

'No, we were stuffed in there like sardines.'

Galt stood there, hanging on.

'We may still need your help.'

'Great!' Not as great as he'd hoped, but alright.

Cupid had referred throughout to Taylor as 'she.' Cupid had created a distance between the one-time friends that was not present at the first questioning. Cops read that as a guilty move.

Chapter Thirty-five

The mess Matthew Sanderson had left behind in his room had been cleaned up. Gouges and scrapes were evident on the walls of the oddly bare room. Matthew lay on his bed, listless and distant. When his father stood in the doorway, Matthew nervously got to his feet on the far side of the bed away from the door, his long arms hanging at his side.

'Detective Damiano has requested another questioning, this time at their precinct.'

'What's the point, Dad? Nothing I've said has helped them find the guy who killed Tay.'

'There is no choice. Get yourself dressed and meet me at the front door. You could bring that food tray down for your mother. Did you eat anything at the hospital?'

'I'm not hungry.'

'Try to throw out that food so your mother doesn't see. She's devastated and planning the funeral. Show some respect and sympathy for your mother who loves you. Don't break her heart any more than it already is.'

'Fine.' Matthew stuffed an entire roll into his mouth.

'Brush your teeth and put a move on. Be downstairs in ten minutes.' Trevor could not muster sympathy for his son. Downstairs, he found Shari at the dining room table, surrounded by papers. Her elbows were on the table and her head had dropped into her hands as he approached. Her hair was matted and she hadn't changed clothes. He laid a gentle hand on her shoulder and she jerked back on the chair. 'If this is too much for you, I'll take care of it.'

'I have to work, Trevor. I can't allow myself to think of Tay, or I'll...' Her voice rose to a nervous, angry wail. 'I just can't choose the hymns – Mozart and Bach seem too old for her. Tay shouldn't have died so young. What kind of music is suitable for a young woman, one who was murdered? What?' she cried.

Trevor helped Shari to stand. 'You need to sleep. Take something. Remember, Tay did like classical music when she was very young. She did those little dances for us when she was about three? Classical is just right. You love it – Tay is your daughter.' Trevor led Shari to the living room and onto a sofa. He covered her with a throw. 'Honey, I have to go out with Matthew. We won't be long.'

'Why? I can't be alone.'

'You need the rest. We won't be long.'

'Trevor, where?'

'The police think Matthew can help them.'

'Oh my God!' She sat upright and began to rock back and forth.

Trevor hurried to the kitchen and found the pills above the cupboard beside the sink. He dropped a tablet in his hand and poured water from a carafe on the side table. 'Please take one, Shari.'

Shari had no fight left and swallowed the tranquilizer and lay back down. 'Protect our son, Trevor. Promise me you will.'

From the upstairs landing, Matthew listened to the exchange between his parents.

Trevor bent and kissed Shari. 'I promise. Let this pill work. I'll help you when I get back. Get some sleep.'

Matthew crept to the front door and waited for his father.

Matthew stared out the side window as the Jag sped to the Division.

'Matthew, give the police whatever helps Tay. Just answer what's asked.'

Matthew continued to stare out the window in his own misery.

'Did you hear me?'

'Yeah.'

'Answer me when I speak to you!'

'I wish I was dead.'

'Matthew, I said that a lot when I was a kid.'

'Did you mean it?'

'Once I did, but I'm still here, like you.'

'You hate me, right?'

'You've disappointed me, son, but I don't hate you.'

Matthew rolled down his window.

'It's freezing, roll that thing back up.'

Matthew punched the lever and the window closed. They didn't speak again until they sat beside each other in the Crémazie boardroom. Damiano had turned on the recorder, named the people present and the date.

'I appreciate you and Matthew coming here at such a difficult time. I will make every attempt to move as quickly as possible so that you can go back home. Matthew, you said at the tunnel, you saw someone running, and you assumed the person had come from the tunnel. Think back to that day – try to figure as best you can if that runner could have been a woman?'

Trevor nodded to Matthew. He thought about the runner, but nothing sprang to his mind. 'First, I thought it was Tay *punking* me, but it wasn't her 'cause Tay doesn't wear black to work out. The runner was too tall for Tay.'

'It might have been a woman then?'

'I dunno. I only thought of Tay 'cause that's what I thought it was, a *punk*. I wasn't close. All I saw was someone tall, fast and dressed in black.'

Damiano rubbed her head. The hammer headache was starting, an effect of the narcotic. She reached for a bottle of water and drank half of it. 'Describe the second person you saw at the tunnel. Take some time to think, Matthew. Something might come to you.'

Matte worked his fingers. He knew what Damiano had taken. His entreaties meant nothing to her. She knew he wasn't a rat, that he was all threat. It would never even occur to Damiano that she was putting both their badges on the line.

'I have nothing to add. The guy looked nineteen or twenty, but I don't know. Before I saw his face, he pulled a watch cap down to his eyes.'

'You said he seemed to be looking around, like you were doing.'

'Yeah, I guess. He just stood there, walked to the other side and looked. Then he left.'

'You said he was tall.'

'Taller than me.'

'Did he check you out?'

'You mean like a pickup?'

'Like anything.'

'Shit no! He wasn't looking for me.'

'Did you not think of approaching the person and asking him if he was looking for Taylor?'

Matthew clenched his fist and examined it. 'Another fuckup. I thought Tay had never even gone there. Thought it was a *punk*. The guy must have been looking for Tay… must have been, and I didn't…' Matthew looked at his father, but there was no support there.

Damiano glanced at Matte before she made her next point. 'Matthew, you told us you never looked inside the tunnel or that opening with the cable. That seems odd to me since you were looking for your sister. I'd look before I left.'

'Dad! You know Tay hated dark places – she'd never go inside that tunnel in the first place. You know that, Dad.' Matthew pleaded for help, but Trevor shook his head and did not speak.

'But she was at the bottom of that tunnel, Matthew.'

Matthew pushed his chair back, scraping the floor. 'How many times do you have to remind me of that? I know, I know, I KNOW!'

Trevor finally spoke. 'Enough, son. Detective, what is it that you want to know? Stop beating around the bush!'

'I think you want your father to forgive you, Matthew, for not helping your sister when she needed you. Is this whole story about being there, just a story so your father will know at least you made the effort to go to your sister? The descriptions you've given me are vague and of no use to us. I can't believe you saw the nineteen-year-old and you still can't describe him. Makes no sense to me. Were you at the tunnel that Tuesday, the day Taylor died?'

Trevor grabbed Matthew's wrist tightly. Matthew winced. Matte stood up to intervene. Damiano raised her hand to stop him. 'Son, you didn't help Tay. For God's sake, tell the truth and don't obstruct the investigation from finding out who did murder your sister. Do you hear me – tell the goddamn truth! All Tay needs from you now is the truth.' Trevor pushed Matthew's wrist away in disgust.

Matthew held back tears. 'I was there. I swear to God. And I fucked up again.'

Matte opened his palms and gave Damiano the go-ahead.

'Matthew, I have to ask you this final question. Did you argue with Taylor and strike out and hit her? Did you dump her body in the tunnel to cover up what you had done?'

Trevor Sanderson stood and grabbed Matthew's shoulder. 'I don't want my son to answer that question – he's not thinking clearly. None of us are. We understand we are all to blame for what happened to my daughter.'

Matthew pulled away. 'Too late, Dad.' He sat back down. 'No, I did not kill my sister.' 'You can never prove I did – you're looking at the wrong person. I'm too much of a fuckup to do something that neat. I'm ready to go, Dad.'

To Sanderson, Matthew had become a stranger. That was how they left.

Chapter Thirty-six

Matthew Sanderson stared out the window and clenched both fists to be at the ready on the drive back home. When his father was pulled over for speeding, Matthew thought his father would argue but, uncharacteristically, he accepted the ticket without a word. When they were inside their garage, Matthew opened the door, but that was as far as he got.

His father grabbed his jacket and pulled him back inside the Jag. 'I haven't the emotional energy to try to figure you out. All I want, no, need from you, is peace and time to make the funeral arrangements. Your mother is on the verge of a breakdown. I know you love her. Have pity on her and leave us be. I want you at the funeral with us. It's our last contact with Tay. We have to show a united front. At the end of the week, I will arrange help for you. I haven't been the best father, but I never thought I wouldn't know my son. Can you do that for your mother, Matthew?'

'Yeah, whatever.'

'Is that a *yes*?'

'I 'spose.'

'Thank you.'

'Know what, Dad? You can't forgive me; I got that. You never will. Taylor did some pretty fucked up things herself. She cheated on her school assignments and tried to ruin her prof's reputation by filing a charge against her. She said you knew the professor. Yeah, Tay shared that with me to get me to go to the tunnel. You didn't know about that. She was a piece of work, your special girl. She got *herself* into some bad "stuff." That's what she called it. Then she went to a place that scared the shit out of her. Some princess, right, Dad! Next to Tay, how bad do I look? I'm just a coward.'

Trevor's first impulse was anger which quietly subsided. His own tears frightened him as he wiped them away with the back of his hand. 'Don't you see it yet, Matthew? She died, Matthew.' His voice was now gentle with no trace of anger.

'I'm not the only one responsible, Dad! Tay *made* mistakes didn't she? Doesn't she have to take some of the blame? Doesn't she?' Matthew cried. 'You tell me, Dad.'

'Your sister Tay is dead, Matthew.'

'Don't you fucking realize that I know that?' Matthew kicked the door, pushed out of the Jag and ran into the house.

Trevor moaned. 'Yes, son, Tay was partly responsible…' No one heard his admission, his acceptance. He sat and wept. The enormity of his own failure engulfed him until he began to shiver. He pulled up the zipper of his dark Italian jacket. Trevor had always gauged his life by his accomplishments and success. His family was part of his achievement. 'I gave them everything. I was out there setting up a life they could enjoy, a life I never had! I looked away for a moment. Now, you're gone, Tay. Just gone… and Matthew, is there a chance he might have…

'What did Matthew say Tay had done? Cheated and trumped up a charge against a professor that I know?' Sanderson's thoughts ran into each other. He resented his son for upstaging the tragedy of his sister's death and tainting the memory of her life. Was Matthew lying? Who did *he* know at Concordia University? His mind ground forward and faltered. Nothing was clear. His life had depended on clarity and order. Both had fractured. Who did he know? Whole minutes passed and no name surfaced. He wanted to abandon himself to despair, like Matthew. Each day was worse, empty. Nothing but grief mattered, or seemed real. Surviving the grief sapped his energy, but it was his driving force. He tried to think once again. Who? When the answer came, his heart sank to a deeper layer of sorrow. Matthew had told the truth, and Trevor lost another piece of his daughter. The professor was Caitlin Donovan. He remembered Tay telling him as much back in September. Trevor believed in truth, fought for the rights of his clients. What was he to do with the trumped up charge? The Donovans were acquaintances, friends at one time. Yet Tay deserved the next four days devoted to her memory. That was all Tay had left, all Trevor had left of her. After the funeral, he would contact Caitlin and inform her of the truth, and back her up if need be, not before. He would not inform Detective Damiano. She would interrogate Matthew again, and he could not permit another intrusion until after Tay had left them all behind and she was safe from human meddling and her own flaws.

He sat in the Jag until Shari found him still shivering. 'Trevor, what are you doing out here?' Shari had managed to shower and change. 'I need you, Trevor. Please come inside. The garage may be heated, but I feel the cold.'

Trevor sat envying Shari's strength. *I was wrong about that too.*

'What's happened?'

Trevor looked straight ahead. 'I don't think I can cope. Isn't that strange, Shari?'

'Matthew is back in his room. Come in with me. We'll help each other. You're a better organizer. Please come in with me, Trevor.'

Trevor stepped from the car and stood, his body heavy and listless. Shari took his arm and led him to the kitchen for coffee and toast. He ate without a word, without tasting a thing. No matter what he thought, Taylor was lost and he couldn't reach Matthew.

Shari sat and smiled at him. 'Trevor, I know you're in there. I'm glad the anger is gone. You're the husband I know.'

Trevor shook his head. 'I can't wrap my head around any of this – I don't understand.'

'I don't either, but we need each other. I have chosen the Notre-Dame-de-Bon-Secours Chapel. I've spoken with one of the priests and I've set the funeral for Thursday at eleven. I chose Mozart and Bach and Mendelssohn, beautiful, peaceful hymns for Tay. Will you set the times for the Mount Royal visitation?'

'I don't want to share Tay,' Trevor whispered. 'These few days are all we have with her.'

'I know. I've booked the chapel for us and close family friends. The funeral will be private. That's why I chose the chapel.'

Trevor did smile. 'That's a good decision, Shari. May I add one hymn?'

'Of course.'

'Be Not Afraid.' Trevor grabbed Shari's hands and held on. Life for the Sandersons had turned from order to chaos, tempered by tender moments he shared with his wife. 'Shari, I'll finish up the work. Go up and rest. We all need to rest. I'll join you as soon as I can.'

Shari appeared grateful for the escape.

Trevor's hand shook as he wrote the obituary. He smiled ruefully; he had believed that the Sandersons were the exception. They were successful and healthy and supposedly invulnerable to the culture of sadness that had now descended on their home. These horrors happened to other people.

Could he wait on this Donovan charge? Trevor knew legal loopholes and the importance of technicalities and he used them. Yet he had prided himself on eschewing dirty deals and shabby ruses – he was a reputable lawyer and well respected. Could he withhold information that could unjustly injure the daughter of a friend to save his son? Had Matthew… the pursuit of such a thought was horrible. Matthew had catapulted him into a legal and moral dilemma. Trevor went upstairs and looked in on Shari. She seemed asleep. He tiptoed to Matthew's room. His son lay on his side, quiet and very still. Trevor could not recall when he had last looked at the boy. He was a child, and it was another life.

Trevor poured himself some brandy and the tawny liquid felt rich and warm on his tongue. He poured another before he made the call.

Trevor's choice had left him with a deeper sense of failure. The calls would put their entire family in further jeopardy because he had chosen to do the right thing, for himself and his career.

It was almost nine-thirty when Frank Donovan beat Caitlin to the phone. Maggie held the wide armrests of her chair tightly. Caitlin stood beside her mother. 'Yes?'

It wasn't the hospital.

'Trevor Sanderson here.'

'I just read the ID on the phone.' Frank shook his head at Maggie and Caitlin. 'We're very sorry for your loss.' The late call surprised Frank and he could say nothing more.

'I apologize for the intrusion but I need Caitlin's cell number. I can't reach her at home. It's important, Frank.'

'She's here with Maggie.' Frank saw Maggie waving 'no.' 'I'll put her on.'

Caitlin took the phone and headed into the kitchen. 'Yes?' Caitlin answered awkwardly.

'I've just learned about the assignments and the charge…'

'My deepest sympathy, Mr. Sanderson, but I've had a very tough week because of…'

'That's the importance of this late call. Taylor confided to her brother that she had trumped up that charge to get back at you. Before you say anything, Caitlin, I need to tell you that the funeral is this Thursday. Is there any way you could inform the university that Taylor's claim against you was false without calling the police? If need be, I will vouch for you. I don't want the police informed yet. My son is in terrible shape. He won't survive another police questioning before the funeral and I need Matthew at his sister's funeral. I'm asking you to stall for three days. The family needs some peace at the funeral. Then you can call this Detective Damiano.'

'Mr. Sanderson, I have been subjected to two police questionings and a search warrant. If I don't inform the police, they might arrive at my door with handcuffs. This is my career. I gave Taylor two undeserved chances with those assignments because our parents are friends. Taylor thanked me by filing that false charge and throwing a brick through my front window that missed my head by inches.' Caitlin wasn't through. She walked deeper into the kitchen. 'Look, Mom is anxiously awaiting the results of a biopsy that might prove grave. She doesn't want anyone to know. It's been very hard here too.'

'I am deeply sorry.'

'So am I. Taylor was very frightened. I never had the chance to find out the cause.'

'I wish Maggie the best. Do what you have to do. Here's my private cell number if Detective Damiano wishes to speak to me.'

'Thank you for this difficult call.' As soon as Sanderson hung up, Caitlin went looking for Detective Damiano's card.

Chapter Thirty-seven

Detectives Damiano and Matte had briefed the chief about Matthew Sanderson and Amira Cupid. Donat had stayed behind to hear a full report and their progress. 'Lay down some fire on these suspects! I can't hold a press conference with empty hands.'

It was almost ten o'clock, and Damiano was in the living room watching her husband measure out two inches of U'Luvka Vodka. 'That's it for tonight, plus the half pill.'

'Forget what I said about being a cop. You're too tough. How's Luke?'

'He went to school, got home late. He ate.'

'That's some improvement.'

'Luke's behaving as we asked, but he's freezing us out again. He looks terrible. He's worrying me. He didn't speak at all tonight, said he had homework.'

'Your suggestion?'

'I'm as lost as you. It hurts to love, perhaps more when you're young and you open up your heart.'

'Jeff, this is our Luke. He'll come out of this. He's young, he'll meet…' Her cell rang.

Exasperation clouded Jeff's face. 'Can't they leave you alone for an hour?'

'You know I have to take it.'

He got up and left the room, but not before he scooped up the vodka.

'Professor Donovan?'

'Yes. I had to call.'

Caitlin described the call from Sanderson and gave Detective Damiano Sanderson's cell. 'I hope this will clear my name from your files.'

'You should inform the proper university authorities tomorrow morning. This information will help your position. In our case, I'm afraid nothing much changes. You always knew the charge was bogus, but the university administrators did not and it posed a threat to your position. Your anger with that and the brick throwing were very much in play at the time of the murder. The fact that the charge was false does matter to me, Professor, but you must see my position?'

'Seeing it and agreeing with it are two different things. Am I the only suspect then?' Caitlin's blood was pulsing in her ears.

'I cannot discuss this case, Professor. I can say we are closely investigating every possible lead.'

Caitlin exhaled. 'That's something.'

Damiano wanted to slam the phone down on the polished oak table, but held back. 'That goddamn little twit! He's still holding out against a father who's a tyrant, and police pressure. I have to admit the kid's got some stones! The chief will howl when I tell him we have to interrogate Sanderson's little bastard.' Jeff was standing by the door, holding the vodka. 'Have a heart! One more, please.'

'I do – I want you healthy. Call Matte and cheer him up with the news. That will change your ideas. Even better, call the chief.'

'I want to sleep tonight. If I were at the condo…'

'But you're not.' Jeff left Damiano standing alone with the phone. Interrogation was a more serious matter than questioning. What troubled Damiano, apart from the vodka, was that Matthew Sanderson might not give up anything. She trusted Matte's opinion and called him.

'What's up?' Matte answered brusquely.

'What's the matter, Pierre?'

'Usual.'

'Dylan? I suggested you give him a trial week.'

'I took your advice. He's not home, wasn't when I got here. No call – nothing.'

'You don't know that he's hooked up with someone, Pierre.'

'History doesn't lie.'

'He might have been in an accident.'

'Let's leave it – you're not helping. Why are you calling?'

Damiano brought him up to speed. 'Should I call Sanderson in tonight? I value your opinion. The funeral is Thursday.'

'We can't allow ourselves to be done in by a teenager. We're Major Crimes! It's after ten. Let them try to sleep tonight. Call tomorrow at eight. Have him in by nine, but run this by the chief tonight.'

'I agree, Pierre. Hang in there. You're a survivor.'

'I don't feel like one. Let me know if Donat wants us in tonight with Sanderson.'

Damiano had always admired that her chief was never put out about late calls. He listened and then he thought before he spoke. 'If this were just any kid, I'd want him in tonight. I agree with you. Make the call well before eight – shake the kid up.'

169

Damiano thought of the half pill and what little help that would be. Her arm was throbbing and the analgesic cream one doctor had given her worked for about twenty minutes. She'd be awake three times every hour. She missed the freedom of the condo and her stashes.

Jeff had returned. 'For a detective, you can be very transparent at times. Come up to bed and give sleep a try. Sometimes you've gotta bear the hurt.'

'Easy for you to say. You sleep through earthquakes!'

'I want you to see another therapist – come to bed. I do have a very generous half pill for you. By the way I pinched a nerve behind my shoulder blade on Sunday.'

'While we were…'

'Yep.'

'That's actually funny. Painful?'

'As a pinched nerve.'

'Take the spare quarter pill.'

'Let's go – the vodka's not even down here.'

'Damn!'

Damiano surprised herself and slept four hours without interruption. She showered early, dressed and grabbed some toast, yogurt and steaming coffee on the run. She was first to arrive on the Major Crimes unit. She preferred to stand while she made the call. A copy of the *Gazette* obituaries lay across her desk. She admired the simple announcement. Sanderson might well have used half a page, but he chose simplicity and a beautiful photo of his daughter.

Sanderson, Taylor. 1992 – 2014

It is with profound sadness that we announce the sudden and tragic passing of our beloved daughter Taylor… Taylor has left an indelible mark on our hearts…

It was not an easy call to make. Damiano read the obituary a second time. The visitation would take place at the Mount Royal Funeral Complex, Wednesday afternoon and evening. The Sandersons had chosen the Notre-Dame-de-Bon-Secours Chapel for the service on Thursday. Damiano saw Matte at the far end of the room and waited for him, perhaps for his support.

Matte walked in and laid an envelope on Damiano's desk addressed to him. 'Make the call. I'll explain that.'

Sanderson picked up on the first ring. He must have been waiting on the call. 'This can't wait till Friday, Detective? I'm not a man who asks for favors, but I'm asking for one now.'

'I've consulted the chief. Anybody else, we would have called you in last night. We must see Matthew this morning at nine.'

'My son is conflicted, Detective, troubled and burdened by his sister's death. God knows what else!'

'I understand, and that's the reason we did not have him in last night.'

'I have a long memory, Detective.'

'Please remember that I'm acting on behalf of your daughter who cannot speak for herself.' Damiano realized she had been talking to dead air. Sanderson had hung up. 'Nice.' She turned to Matte.

'Open the envelope, Tony.'

'Pierre, tell me – it'll be faster. I have to call Donat.'

'Dylan's book was accepted. He received a $500 advance and repaid the money he borrowed. He has a temporary editing job at a small Montreal publishing house and TA work at Concordia.' Matte smiled. 'You were right again. He was at Concordia last night. Maybe there are second chances.'

Damiano gave him a high-five! Her phone rang a few minutes later and she grabbed it.

'Matthew's gone! We checked every room in the house. He's gone! I thought he had done something to himself…' Sanderson said hoarsely. 'I truly thought he…'

'Mr. Sanderson, was there a note?'

Sanderson was out of control. Damiano could hear high-pitched wailing in the background. He must have been running up the stairs for his breaths were quick. 'No, I can't see a note. Matthew is suicidal… Oh my God! I knew it, but I couldn't help him. You have to get out there and look for him. Do your job! I can't lose my son.' Sanderson was weeping through his anger and fear.

'Mr. Sanderson, the Montreal police will set up a search immediately. Try to think of familiar places Matthew might hide, friends he might call. Lastly, recheck every room again, the bathrooms especially and the backyard and the drop-off at the back edge of your property.'

'He must have snuck back down last night and heard the call I made to Professor Donovan. Matthew likes to listen in…I should have seen this coming…'

'Is there a chance he's running – does he have access to money?'

There was silence. Of course, Matthew had access to money.

'Are you implying he murdered Taylor?'

Damiano sensed his horror and she waited.

'I don't know… I don't know my only son… I only know he's full of hate and fear, mostly of himself.'

'Detective Matte is setting up the search team. Please try to see what he's taken, what he might be wearing. Send me a photo, our officers need that. Please recheck your home and the clothes. Call me with anything you come up with.'

Matte stood by waiting on Damiano. 'We should have had that little shitter in last night. At least, he'd still be alive. Talk about a misfire. Our delay might have led to the kid's suicide.'

'Stop! Donat agreed with us. He was home with his parents. We're not responsible. It's not your fault that his family is influential. We acted accordingly. It wasn't our call.'

'Jesus, Pierre. Another suicide on my watch… I can't go through this again.'

'I don't think the kid is suicidal – he's running.'

'And you would know?'

'More than I like to admit.'

'Let's try to figure out where the kid might go.' Seconds later, her phone rang again. First she saw a photo of Matthew that she sent to Matte. Sanderson called back.

'His phone's still here, his ID and VISA. He didn't pack any clothes. All Matthew has are the clothes on his back. He may have some cash – he liked paper money. This is ominous, isn't it? If he were running, he'd have taken those things. Please find him.' Sanderson's voice trailed off, beaten. 'I'll start looking myself as soon as a physician friend arrives to tend to Shari.'

'Do you know what he was wearing?'

'His usual. Those clothes are gone. A black North Face jacket and black Merrells. He always wears a ratty gray hoody underneath. I called his best friend Timothy. He hasn't heard from him. He had a few more names and numbers for me. I'll try them. I just know that Matthew is alone. He takes after me in that at least.'

For the next four hours the search was on. Sanderson didn't want Matthew's photo in the papers or on news stations, but Timothy put Matthew's photo up on his FB page and word spread.

Matthew Sanderson knew exactly where he was going when he left his home on Summit Crescent. He walked with determination, blocking out any thoughts of hesitation. He didn't feel the cold. For the first time since Taylor's death, he felt nothing but resolve. He'd thought of recording his thoughts on his phone, but losers did that. It was dark when he reached the tunnel, but he had a flashlight. The police tape was still up, and the square was boarded up. He found a good-sized rock and went to work, splintering the wood. The work wasted some precious time. He wanted an end. Sweat beaded inside his hoody. Matthew used his foot to knock out what was left of the shattered wood. He stood and rubbed his jacket and jeans free of wood bits. He leaned inside the opening and shone his light into the tunnel. The chalk marking was eerily clear. Matthew wondered briefly how long it had taken Taylor to die. He shut that thought out. He watched the plastic flashlight burst into pieces when it struck the cement. Matthew eased himself through the opening and he fell...

Chapter Thirty-eight

By eleven o'clock there were no sightings. FB friends were calling the Sanderson home, but no one had seen Matthew. He wasn't at the airport; he hadn't boarded a train or Greyhound bus. The boy was not in any emergency room in Montreal hospitals.

Damiano and Matte had driven to the Sanderson home with two officers who scoured the area behind the house. Trevor Sanderson sat rigidly, white knuckled. The detectives examined Matthew's room again. Damiano went out to the garage and found an entire wall of tools. The contours of each tool had been drawn on the wall, not a task for the lazy. Two additional tool chests were set up one on top of the other. Aside from the panic Damiano was feeling with another impending suicide she could not avert, there was the case she might not close if Matthew died.

Damiano called Sanderson to the garage. 'Please examine the tools – see if anything is missing or out of place.'

'Apart from buying a few things, I haven't looked at my set in years. Nothing on the wall has been touched as you can see.'

'Try the boxes.'

Sanderson opened the top box. 'Huh! I recently bought that generator over there and a flashlight, small but powerful. I'm pretty sure I left it here in this drawer.'

Damiano was already on the phone. 'Send a bus and FD to the Wellington Tunnel. He's in the tunnel.'

Sanderson stood in shock. 'Come with us, Sir.' Damiano and Sanderson rushed from the house. Minutes later, with flashers and blaring sirens, they sped dangerously through the downtown streets. Matte nudged Damiano's leg, to no avail. They arrived on Ottawa Street at about the same time as the ambulance and the fire department.

Heedless of treacherous ice, Sanderson ran like a madman with Damiano close behind. He reached the opening first and leaned inside. 'Matthew, don't be afraid. I'm here. We have help.'

Matthew was crouched on the cement floor, hugging his leg. 'I just busted my leg. Why couldn't Tay…' He shouted up at his father. 'I also busted up my glasses.'

'Stand aside, Sir,' a firefighter said, moving Sanderson away. He inserted a ladder and manoeuvered himself skillfully onto it and descended. Another firefighter threw down a duffel bag before he too descended. While the men did their work, Damiano and Matte eyed one another. They had heard what Matthew said.

'Not much damage, Mr. Sanderson.'

'Thank God for that. I'll call my wife.' He wept as he spoke to her. 'He'll be okay, Shari. Don't worry – we have him back with us. I will keep in touch.'

What the detectives couldn't see was that one firefighter held Matthew under his shoulders and the other by his legs as he mounted the ladder. They carefully handed him through to the paramedics. 'Leg fracture.'

When Matthew was safely on a gurney, Sanderson held his son tightly and wept.

Matthew was crying. 'I guess I blew this too.'

'You're a stubborn little shit, but your mother and I wouldn't make it without you. That's all that matters for now. I don't even want to know why you did this – it's of no importance. I suppose there's too much of me in you.'

'You're not a fuckup.'

'Of the first order, Matthew.'

'We have to go, Sir. You can come along with us to the Montreal General.'

'Detective Damiano, stay away from us until his leg is set.'

Damiano had no intention of following that order, but said nothing. The death of a child changed a family's world. Matte and Damiano followed the ambulance to the hospital. Her job was making the arrest, and saving herself in the process.

'Toni, you heard Matthew. Is there a remote chance our vic's death was accidental? He did ask why his sister couldn't have… survived, I presume.'

'That they had some stupid argument and he pushed her down into the tunnel. Is that where you're heading?'

'Possible?'

'We haven't released the full details. Does the kid know that his sister was struck first before being thrown to her death? If he didn't know that then he didn't kill her. But we have to find that out. Pierre, do you believe the kid tried to kill himself?'

'He broke a leg. That suggests he fell feet first. It's a forty-foot drop. He might have hung on the side, cutting off six or seven feet. I can't say for certain. He's successfully wrenched attention away from his sister to himself. That's what he wants. Did they meet at the tunnel, fight, and she ended up stuffed through the aperture and died because of an awkward fall? Who knows with this kid? He hoards secrets. He's a self-involved adolescent, but is he a murderer? I don't know.'

'Remember, it wasn't an awkward fall. Taylor was pushed in such a way that it first appeared to be an accident or a suicide. The first strike was impulsive. The rock suggests that. That act wasn't premeditated, but the dump was planned and well executed while the girl was still alive. My immediate hope is that the kid's stuck in Emergency and not in surgery before we can question him. We'll charge the Division for parking and save time.'

Once inside the doors of the Cedar Street entrance to the Montreal General, Damiano began to run. Cursing Damiano, Matte ran after her. They found father and son still in Emergency. Sanderson walked towards them to block their way.

'Mr. Sanderson, I have to ask Matthew some final questions. I don't want to charge you with obstruction. Please don't force my hand.' Damiano shot a glance at Matthew who, though in obvious discomfort now that the adrenalin rush had worn off, was enjoying the confrontation. *Some kid!* 'Hopefully, we won't need Matthew at the Division.'

Clearly affronted, Sanderson stepped aside. Matte moved up beside him while Damiano approached the gurney.

'Matthew, these secrets have gone on too long. I have to know everything. You understand that now, I trust. Did Taylor tell you who she was meeting?'

Matthew winced with pain. She ignored that and her own pain. Sanderson eyeballed his son. Damiano figured she'd be lucky because the kid didn't want to risk losing his father's hard-won favor. 'Tay didn't tell me who, but she did say she had to end a relationship. She was freaked out and embarrassed and scared that she might be arrested.'

'Did she say what she had done to think that?'

'She said, "I was such a fool, an idiot." She wouldn't tell me anything else.'

'You let it go at that?'

'I figured I'd see who it was when I got there.'

'Matthew, the truth, finally. Did you really see those two people at the tunnel? It seems so odd you can't describe either of them.'

'I saw them.'

'Did you find Taylor in the tunnel that day?'

Sanderson stepped forward, but Matte caught his arm. The seconds stretched out.

'I was so pissed at Tay for *punking* me again that I didn't bother to look. I might have been a hero if I'd saved her life, but I wasn't, I'm not. I don't know anything else. I wish she had just broken her leg like me.'

The detectives left quietly. 'What do you think, Toni?'

'I'd rather be tripped up or punched than lied to. It's demeaning. I don't know about the kid. He's given us more information. He's made the right sounds, but he's playing the sympathy card for his father. It's working! He's gone from a coward to a decent brother. What do you believe, Pierre?'

'Matthew is a liar. I wish I could recall the source for this quote: "Liars are secret in their thoughts as snakes in their hole." I've had some experience with the best liars.'

'Matthew feels his sister was embarrassed by the relationship. Are we looking back at the professor or Cupid, Pierre?'

'If it's the professor, then it's the brick throwing with the intent to injure that, if proven, would result in an arrest. If this was an embarrassing relationship alone, it's the professor who'd be sanctioned by Concordia. And maybe not, Sanderson was of age.'

'A relationship with Amira Cupid is not an offence. It might have proven embarrassing for our vic if it got out to her friends, her ex, for example. I find no reason for a charge here, Toni.'

'You know where we are, Toni.'

'Of course I do, my dear Watson. We're back to the suspect with the phone – her date at the tunnel.'

'If we isolate the only charge we have – we're stuck with the brick. Our Sanderson may have been baiting the professor with the sexual harassment charge, threating to embellish it and destroy her career. If what? Our vic was the one, according to her brother, who needed out. Do you see our professor pursuing our vic?'

'I don't. Why tell her brother she'd fabricated the charge? They weren't close – he would then have that nugget for blackmail that I wouldn't put beneath him to use.'

'At square one, Matthew said he was there. He saw two people: the runner and the nineteen-year-old. Our targets are these two people. One of them at least. Our only clue is that one "might" have been a woman. Matthew's cleverly not certain about either one.'

Damiano was working her arm.

'I'll drive. We should get back.'

'Good. We have another clue. Our vic was in love, but she had to end the relationship or face an arrest. A second, she was frightened. Why? Forget the damn brick, was there something in the relationship that frightened her? Was it drugs she discovered? Something they did together that she did not want to continue?'

'We have to find these two suspects.'

'Matthew Sanderson is still a concern. The kid frightens me.'

'We keep him onboard. Goldman?'

'What the hell, keep the party going. We have no formal suspects. These two suspects might not exist. Everything we know is based on information from a devious liar. The chief will be pleased.'

'I have to remind you of another knot.'

'You're worse than a recording device. What?'

'Remember, I said it might not be the "stuff," one of the ghosts, who killed her. It might well be the person who accompanied her to the tunnel.'

'You're even lower than counsellors who tell you what you want to hear. You give me facts. Did you see how small Matthew's eyes are without his glasses? I saw something mean hiding back there. He's indifferent to anyone but himself. I'd like to get the supercilious little shit alone. Each time we interview him, he gives us something new as though he were doling out the tidbits of his sister's death. His information is calculated. There's an awful stench about him. If he murdered his sister, I'll drop him back in the tunnel myself and board it up!'

'You need food.'

'For a starter.' Damiano had bigger needs than food.

Chapter Thirty-Nine

Caitlin Donovan went back to work first before she called Dino Mazzone, rechecked her office box and was glad to find only the usual end-of-term notices.

'Do you want me to make the call to the director? I might add some weight to the information. The call's on the house. I'll get back to you,' Mazzone promised.

'Do you have Susan Wyman's number?'

'I do.'

'I'm off to my mother's. She must be very anxious. Waiting to hear from physicians is debilitating.' Caitlin walked back home, picked up her car and drove to The Boulevard. En route, she called Carmen. 'Sorry I haven't gotten back to you. It's been busy. Here's an update…'

'That's good news. I wouldn't worry about the detectives. That's routine.'

'Carm, in our best sleuthing – we weren't skilled detectives. What do we know?'

'We knew enough to track down that DUI driver before Detective Remay did. Remember? He was the lead detective who told us we were tenacious.'

'Depends on how you interpret the adjective.'

'I'm serious.'

'I wasn't a suspect back then.'

'Small point.'

'I'll pick up your things and bring them home. Mom still hasn't heard. There's no way she's up to visitors.'

'Understood. Wish her luck. Call if she hears.'

'I promise.' Caitlin's nerves knotted when she pulled into the Donovan's grand driveway. What if her mother had already heard? What if the news was the worst? Caitlin worked her temples before she got out of the car and walked up to the front door. Monsieur was scratching the door on the other side. She found her parents in the kitchen.

'Caitlin, please ask your father to leave me alone for an hour. His pleas and lectures are too much.'

'Dad?'

'What else do you want me to do, Cait? Also, I can't see why I'm forbidden from calling Franken. He's putting us through hell! There is no other word for this interminable wait.'

'Please, Cait.'

'Dad, let's go. We're adding to Mom's stress.'

'What about the telemarketing calls – are we allowed taking those for you?'

'I will take all calls. Now both of you – give me some peace.'

The phone rang. All three froze. Monsieur stood like a statue. Frank covered his eyes with a hand. Caitlin watched her mother pick up the phone. Her heart lurched. Her mother's hand was unsteady.

Maggie turned sideways. 'Yes, Dr. Franken, I'm still here.'

The silence felt like scalpels as Maggie heard the news.

'Yes, I understand, Doctor. I'll make a note of that date. Thank you for calling. It's been difficult. I know what I have now. I'll see you next Friday. Yes, I'm sure Frank or Caitlin will come with me. I agree with you. Knowing is everything. It's specific – it's a path.' Maggie turned as she put down the phone, breathed in slowly, deeply, and exhaled. She rested her chin in her hand, looking away from them.

Frank sank his hand into Caitlin's shoulder.

Maggie sat quietly, suspended in time.

Caitlin didn't move, but whispered, 'Mom?'

When Maggie looked up, her face was streaked with tears. Frank sank back, but Caitlin didn't. She could read her mother's emotions. She pulled free of her father and ran to her mother. 'I'm so happy for you, Mom.'

'Frank, it's just a cyst. I have a second chance.'

Frank couldn't move.

'I never knew till a moment ago how much I love you two – how much I want to live. I'd forgotten after we lost Chris.' Before she could say another word, Monsieur began to bark and Frank had scooped Maggie up in his arms. That was no easy task. Maggie wasn't tiny. They sat in the living room together. Frank re-lit a fire. Its warmth brought a softness to the room and a welcome moment of peace and clarity.

'I wish Chris were here to hear my news,' Maggie mused. 'I wish he'd had my good fortune.'

'We all do, Maggie,' Frank and Caitlin said with levelling peace. The rancor was gone. They sat quietly for some time.

'Are there developments, Caitlin?'

Frank listened attentively. 'The detective's actually correct, but the fabricated charge does dent their suspicions of you whether they admit it or not.'

Caitlin's phone rang. 'It's Mazzone. Shall I leave the room?'

'I'd like to hear what he has to say.'

'Director Wyman is a woman of few words. At least, that sexual assault file against you is closed. I still have work to do,' Mazzone told her.

Caitlin gave Mazzone what Detective Damiano had said before she was off the phone.

'Dad, Mazzone says the university dropped the assault charge and he agrees with you about Detective Damiano. He'll stay on my file until I'm off her radar.'

'What do we do about the visitation and the funeral, Frank?'

'We go for a short visit. I'd like you to attend the funeral, Maggie, if you are up to it. Caitlin, I'll leave that up to you.'

'I'll attend the funeral, but I wouldn't feel comfortable at the visitation. In hindsight, I have grappled with my conscience. I'm a teacher and I might have asked Taylor if I could help with her obvious anxiety. She was so agitated and belligerent that I found myself standing firm, trying to be fair by maintaining standards. More than that, I was angry – I had broken my policy by giving her those chances. I felt she had taken advantage of our family connection. That sounds so vacuous now, doesn't it? This isn't a pity party. I'm certain others are feeling a degree of guilt as well.'

An orderly took Matthew into surgery to set the fracture. Trevor Sanderson needed fresh air. He met a cloud of smoke from patients who huddled against the cold outside like vagrants, standing as close as they were permitted to the shelter of the emergency room doors. Some in wheelchairs; others stood hunched over, a cigarette in one hand, an IV pole in the other. They struck Trevor as pathetic. He walked across Cedar Avenue. He hated smokers. He took out his cell. The phone rang several times before Shari picked up. 'Did I wake you?'

'No. I'm trying to ignore the phone.'

'The examining physician said Matthew has a hairline fracture. I should be able to take him home tonight in a walking cast.'

'Was he trying to…'

Trevor was a perceptive man. Fears about Matthew were mounting. 'Trevor?'

Trevor wanted to unburden his doubts, but he could not hurt his wife. New worries would shatter her beyond repair. 'I think he wanted to be close to Tay. It's guilt, Shari.'

'I know he needs help, Trevor.'

'We'll get it for him. You and I must rebuild our family, with Matthew.'

I love you.' But for the last sentence, every other word was a cover-up. Trevor's attention was not so easily eclipsed from his daughter. Listening to the ongoing information that Matthew kept supplying, Trevor had gleaned that Matthew was mature enough for guile. That cold realization cut into his heart. He did not trust his son, and he did not love him. This sad prescience was crippling.

'There was one call I took. The man was very sympathetic. He asked if he might speak to you for a few minutes.'

'Was it some reporter?'

'He said his son was somehow connected to the tragedy.'

'It better not be a ruse.'

'I trusted him. Here's his number.'

Trevor made the call, ready to cut it off. 'M. Castonguay?'

'Oui, I mean yes.'

'This is Trevor Sanderson.'

Joseph Castonguay told his story. 'My son has not forgiven himself for not making the call at the tunnel. He did contact the police the minute he was home. I did not accept that he was influenced by his friend, Cameron. I taught him to know better at fourteen. But, as one father to another, my son found your daughter. Had he not disobeyed me that day, she might have been lost for days.'

'What is it you want, Sir?'

'I would like to take my son to the funeral. I want him to comprehend the enormity of this tragedy and his failure. I also want him to understand he did find your daughter. That was something positive. My son is a good boy – he has lost confidence in himself, and has not forgiven himself for not doing what was right. If you permit us to attend, I suppose I am hoping my son will learn something. If I am asking too much of you, I understand.'

Trevor lost the thread of what he was about to say. Since that Thursday Tay had been found, his days were marked by rage and misery. The sudden warmth from the family caught him off guard. He struggled for the right words. 'What's your son's name?'

'Liam.'

'Tell Liam he was the first person to help my daughter. She might, as you said, have been lost to us for days. You are welcome to attend. I would like to meet you both.' Trevor ended the conversation reluctantly. When he walked back to the hospital he bore the miserable expression of a hollow man who felt disloyal. If Matthew had hurt Taylor he knew what he would do. This hollowing, this emptiness, would stretch to the end of his life.

Chapter Forty

Damiano decided on Da Vinci's Restaurant on Bishop Street. 'It's my treat. The whole case has left a foul taste in my mouth. Adding bad food to the mix is out.'

'I have money, Toni.'

'I feel like treating, alright? We're at a stalemate. I can't move forward without squeezing Matthew Sanderson. He's the key. The chief won't stand for that – Sanderson will charge us with harassment.'

They ordered ossu bucco and a seafood platter and talked while they waited for the food. 'No wine, Toni. I thought we should have a sit-down with the chief. Let him decide the plan of action. You're right. We can't start looking for ghosts.'

'The chief will think I've lost control of the case.'

'False insecurity is unbecoming. We know the wealthy receive better treatment. We have to wait for that crack, as you call it.'

The food arrived and Damiano wasted no time on her ossu bucco, sucking down to the bone. When she saw the look on Matte's face, she flared. 'What? I enjoy my food. You have so little on the fork that you might be feeding an infant.'

'I still can't figure out how you keep fit.'

'Good metabolism. I'm active. You're as passive as a snail. That's mean. I take it back. Why are you so timid, Pierre? Why didn't you ever take the lieutenant exam, for instance?'

'You're a big help to my digestion. I'm not that timid. You burst into rooms without thinking. You get away with it because you shake things up. What's that song, "I'm sexy and I know it."'?

'That's bullshit!'

'Look around the room, on any floor, Domestic, Drugs, Gang, any of the seven, see how many ordinary female detectives are lieutenants.'

'Are you still suggesting my rack got me the promo?'

'No, I'm not. You have brains and boobs – the package. I don't mean to phrase it that coarsely, but that's it. Take a look around Major Crimes; do you think a gay cop has a chance at becoming a lieutenant? Think any of our group would want to partner with me?'

'You're an excellent cop.'

'Just a detective, Lieutenant.'

'I thought you'd change when Dylan returned, but I can feel you're still on edge. Answer me this. Why can't you look for a guy your own age? Guys are still hot at forty. Why do you need a thirty-year-old to stress you, even use you? You're a mature human being – why are you still playing games?' Matte considered the question. He looked preppy in his herringbone jacket, blue shirt without a tie, and gray pants. The only things missing were the pennies in his loafers.

'Tell me something, Toni. If Luke hadn't had his heart broken, would you be back at the condo with your vodka and pill stash?'

Damiano tried to suppress a smile. 'Maybe – so we are both fucked up.'

'I try to be less descriptive with my analyses. We work – I don't test the *why*.'

'With me as the boss lady. You're…' Their conversation nudging into an argument was interrupted by a call. 'Detective Damiano, Major Crimes.'

The voice was hysterical. 'Detective, I need help! Josh is back and threatening to break down my door. Listen.'

'Open this fucking door or…'

'He's drunk – I am so frightened. I have a knife and I will defend myself.'

'Amira, we will be there very soon. Move something heavy against the door. Don't take out any weapon.' Damiano threw too much money on the table. Matte had grabbed both coats. Had the roads been clear, they were five minutes away, but Montreal does not work on efficiency. Damiano rode the car dangerously, zig-zagging, curb-jumping until she drove the wrong way on Lincoln and double parked with her flashers on. The main door was locked. Goldman wasn't going to help them. Damiano had her weapon out when Amira opened the door.

'He broke the door. I had to defend myself.'

The apartment door had splintered, and the dresser lay overturned beside a wounded Goldman. 'The bitch stabbed me. She might have killed me.'

Amira had stabbed Goldman in the thigh. There was profuse blood loss. When Goldman saw the expression on Damiano's face, he grew frightened. 'Will I die?' He'd been too drunk to see the damage.

Matte called for a bus. Amira was standing by, shaking. 'What could I do? I did not want to kill him, but I needed to stop him.'

'Amira, get me a belt or two. I need towels.' Damiano reached for her gloves before placing both hands on the wound. Blood continued to ooze through her fingers. When she had the belts, she asked Matte for help.

Goldman hollered, 'It's too fucking tight!' The pain was bringing him out of his drunken phase. 'It hurts! Really hurts!'

'Josh, the femoral artery is compromised. Try to relax. Move as little as possible and you should be okay.'

'Should?' He began to cry. He looked like a ten-year-old.

'I'd bet on it, if you keep still.'

Tears smeared his cheeks. His head rested on Damiano's knee. 'She lied to you... Taylor and she, they...' He closed his eyes.

'Josh, stay awake! Help is almost here. You'll be fine. You have to stay awake.' Damiano shook his head, and he opened his eyes. 'Listen to me. Don't fall asleep. Wait for help.'

The paramedics worked quickly, and Josh was taken to the General. Matte and Damiano could hear the beep and blare of the ambulance sirens.

Matte had inched his way to the back of Amira's small apartment to get a good view of the painted rocks. One was the size he thought was right. The only problem, he noticed, was that it appeared old stock and dusty. Amira had painted a yellow heart with the word peace in its center. He slipped on a glove and picked up the rock. The back side of the rock was painted sky-blue. Only the top was dusty. 'Amira, why didn't you use this instead of the knife?'

Amira wiped the spittle from her chin. 'I, I did not think, I could not think clearly. I pushed the dresser against the door, but Josh kicked the door so hard, it broke and the dresser toppled. I grabbed the knife. I was frightened for my life. When he lunged through the door, his leg was high and I struck there to stop him. He gave me no time to think. I cannot believe he might die. Am I to blame? Is this my fault?'

'No, Amira. I can't say what Josh would have done if you hadn't defended yourself.' Damiano wanted Amira to think she was on her side. 'I'm trying to understand why Josh would call Taylor and you liars.'

'One time Taylor said she might go to dinner with him, but she had no intention of going. Josh began to call her a bitch and liar.'

'And you?'

'I am guilty of the same trick. We lied because he would not leave us alone.'

Matte held onto the rock.

'Amira, you were Taylor's friend. Do you know if she ever had a relationship with a woman? It's not uncommon.' Damiano had hit her mark relatively easily and she was surprised.

A wave of pain crossed Amira's face. The muscles beneath her cheek that supported such beauty pulled the face down. Seconds later, her face was composed again and soft. 'It happened in September on a Monday night. Taylor knocked on my door and walked in wearing a white cotton dress. She closed the door, came to me and gently kissed my mouth. "I've wanted to do that," she said. "You have a beautiful mouth." Much in my life is hard, earning enough money, studying and loneliness. That evening I fell into a cloud of curves and soft flesh and caresses. The month was a warm blur. I had not thought of such a love. I had not given myself to anyone. On a Friday, the first week in October, Taylor crept into my room and announced our "interlude" was over.'

'You had fallen in love with her?'

'Yes, but I have learned that nothing is ever what one expects it to be. My love changed to grief, and grief in time becomes an ache. I tell myself there was nothing to forgive. We made no promises. We have a saying in St. Vincent. If love does not live for two full moons, it is not love. No matter, it was my first love, and I will remember the peace of those nights.'

'Is that why you refused to help Taylor out when she needed you?'

'I have told the truth. I was still hurt when she passed me in her car, leaving me alone, waiting for a bus on a very cold night. I do not forgive meanness.'

'Why did you change your mind and run after her?'

'Taylor was truly frightened.'

'But you didn't find her, even though you knew where she was going?'

'As I ran, I grew angry and thought *let her fight her own battles*. That's the reason I walked around, feeling guilty and afraid of Josh as I have said.'

Matte had listened carefully and the word that stuck in his head was "peace." 'Amira, is this rock a remembrance?'

Amira answered with heartfelt lucidity. 'The yellow is for remembrance.'

'And the blue?'

'A month that was peaceful, clear skies I believe people call it.'

Matte wanted to have the rock tested. Damiano read his mind. Obtaining it was a problem. Amira was an intelligent young woman. The court would not validate illegally obtained evidence. 'Do you recall where you found this rock? The others are smaller in size,' Damiano asked casually.

'Yes. I found it at the Old Port by the Clock Tower. There's a space in a cement wall with steps leading down to a small beach.'

Damiano wasn't certain whether she saw a small puckering of Amira's lips or the hint of smugness. 'That's a real souvenir. We have to take the knife with us, you understand.'

Matte reluctantly replaced the rock, and took the knife by the blade and dropped it into a plastic bag he'd pulled from the inside pocket of his jacket. 'Call your landlord about the door.'

The detectives drove to the hospital. 'Our runner, tall and fit?' Damiano asked.

'We have no proof. I wish I'd figured out a way to take the rock.'

Damiano parked legally again and saved the receipt. Goldman, they learned, was in surgery and expected to recover. Damiano asked at Emergency if Goldman's parents had come to the hospital.

The triage nurse, a woman in her fifties, stocky and tired, pointed to a couple standing by a side wall. 'They're here enquiring every two minutes. See, here they come. I've told them I'll give them news when I have it, makes no difference.'

'Mr. Goldman, Mrs. Goldman, Detectives Damiano and Matte. We were at the scene of the dispute.'

'Then you know, Detective, my son was attacked by a wild bush woman. He could have died!'

I am too tired for this! Damiano thought. 'The good news is that your son will recover.'

'That woman came at Josh with a knife! I want her arrested immediately if you haven't already taken her into custody.'

'Mr. Goldman, your son kicked down this woman's door and knocked over a dresser. He threatened her and lunged at her. She protected herself which is her right. There will be charges laid, but against your son for assault with intent.'

'I don't believe you!'

'Detective Matte will show you photos of the scene.'

Detective Matte found the photos and passed his phone to Goldman who studied them.

'These two young women have made my son's life a living hell. This is rich, Suze, Josh is badly injured and *he'll* be charged.'

'That's why we would like to speak to him.'

'But not before you charge him, am I correct, Detective? My son will be represented before you can have one word with him.'

'Mr. Goldman, it was Detective Damiano's quick action that saved your son's life. She also kept him conscious. She deserves your politeness,' Matte said adamantly.

Goldman's expression changed. He looked to his wife for help, but she left him on his own. 'Well, I thank you, Detective. I was rude. Kids today! Entitlement! Who knows what they're up to?'

'We have to wait, Sir. Josh may be able to help our investigation.'

'I'm still calling our lawyer.'

'We'll wait,' Damiano said and led Matte to another crowded corner. 'Pierre, we've agreed that we're looking at a crime of momentary passion. Do you think that Cupid would have risked carrying that bloodied rock back to her apartment? Wouldn't she get rid of it? We want to know if Goldman saw her come back into the apartment, carrying anything, correct?'

'We also want to know if he detected any animosity between the women. He appears to have spied on them. Send Galt to the Clock Tower at the Old Port. Amira could be lying.'

'Galt will love that assignment. I'll remind him he wanted on the team. Look. The Goldmans are talking to a surgeon.' Goldman waved Damiano and Matte over.

The surgeon turned to the detectives. 'Whoever tied the belts to the boy's leg saved him from bleeding out. We have him heavily sedated, so he won't be talking for some hours.'

Reluctantly, the detectives left. Damiano took out her frustration on the hospital door.

'Push,' Matte advised.

Chapter Forty-one

Tuesday marked the eighth day without sun. The Sanderson visitation and the funeral loomed ahead for all concerned in the death of Taylor Sanderson. Detective Galt had driven down to the Old Port. Detectives Damiano and Matte sat dejectedly with Chief Donat who had pushed back on his chair and was cracking his knuckles. 'I can't say you haven't done a thorough job, but you are into your sixth day without a close. Thanks to Sanderson who's used favors, the media is not pressing us. But those dogs are out there in a scrum waiting to pounce. I won't have the wrong version sent to some editor who writes it up and pushes the Send button. Understand that! Get this right!' The chief's face tightened. He asked pointedly, 'If Galt finds rocks at the port, what does that do for you, Toni?'

'Although the rain that Tuesday destroyed evidence, Crime can compare the rocks from the tunnel with the rock Galt collects from the Old Port.'

'They won't compare,' the chief said, re-cracking his knuckles.

'I know that, Chief. The Sanderson kid ID'd the runner as someone tall and slim. Cupid has lied to us about her whereabouts that Tuesday; I think we can secure a warrant for her rock.'

'If she's as clever as you say, she's dumped it. You tipped her off today.'

Matte broke in, 'Goldman's a Peeping Tom. We have some odds that he saw her when she came back to the apartment. If he saw her with her backpack she might have kept the…'

Damiano jumped in before Matte finished his thought.

'Chief, Cupid might have kept the murder weapon as a keepsake. She admitted to having a thing for our Sanderson. Sanderson dumped her and treated her badly. If her rock matches what Galt finds at the port, then Cupid goes to limbo with the professor. If not, we have our warrant. We still look back at Matthew Sanderson and the disposable phone. Goldman is an outside shot.'

'You're nowhere with this throwaway,' the chief snorted.

'We know our vic's habit was to arrive early. We feel strongly that she was taken out by the person who accompanied her.'

'I want the case closed neatly. Find the phone.'

'Our best chance is tonight at the Mount Royal Funeral Complex.'

'I'm not with you there, Damiano. If this person has avoided scrutiny thus far, why would he or she jeopardize his identity now?'

'We know she was forced to break off the relationship with this person. That unknown, whoever it is, still has feelings for her – love, guilt or curiosity is the draw. Someone who doesn't fit in, provided it's not our professor or Cupid.'

'This is not the meeting I was hoping to have. Contact Galt. Tell him to bring the evidence directly to Crime. Contact Dumont – tell her *I* said asap. Get out there and find this person! Stop wasting my time,' he said, dismissing the detectives with the subtlety of a hammer.

Damiano left the chief's office feeling cast adrift. 'He's right, Pierre. We haven't been able to exact one overt action from this him or her.' She added another *wrong* to her list of miscues and began to feel an intolerable sense of failure. Damiano looked over at Matte and wished for the first time that she was as regimentally cautious as her partner. 'Will you see to Galt?'

'You can't just walk away – we haven't failed. We'll find this shit. You have to maintain your confidence or arrogance, whatever it is you use to keep us afloat. No meds, no vodka!'

'I need some time to rethink this case – we've missed something. Otherwise we'd have this suspect. It was stupid of me to suggest we might spot this person at the visitation. Do you realize we will be assessing a couple hundred students? Know what? I'm going home to shower and think. I'll meet you back here and go with you to the visitation.'

'Toni!'

'My arm's just quietly throbbing. I feel too bad to even drink. I can't abide failure. I have to figure this case out for my own sanity. It was a simple murder. We are not looking at randoms. We have suspects. That goddamn crack – I have to come up with a better word.'

'I trust you, Toni.'

Damiano drove home under an overcast sky that felt ominous and heavy. Looking for somewhere to hide, all she saw were orange cones and potholes, not big enough for her. She entered her home by the side door and thought briefly about a vodka hunt – *bad choice*. She thought of Chief Donat. *Bloody little midget – let him come out onto the grounds and test his skills.* Was she still a good cop? A top cop? Damiano walked into the bedroom and tore off her clothes and stepped into the shower and stood under a very strong hot spray, her form of consolation. This was her space – her hideout. *Tell me, Matthew, did you kill your sister?*

At three o'clock, Trevor Sanderson and his son Matthew left the hospital. Matthew was managing well on crutches. His walking cast was blue, and his pants had been cut to accommodate it. Trevor took the crutches and put them in the trunk when they reached their car. Matthew waited for his father to help him into the back of the car and he lifted his leg and rested it on the seat. 'I don't feel any pain.'

'You're medicated. That'll wear off.'

'Great.'

'I filled a prescription while you were in surgery. You should be fine.'

'I don't know if I can make it tonight, Dad.'

Trevor glared at his son through the rearview mirror. 'Do you think this will be easy for your mother or me?'

'No, Dad, but I have a broken leg.'

'A hairline fracture, Matthew. You have those bruises too, but we have to present ourselves as a family. Tay has only eight hours with us. Surely, we must make the effort to support her.' Trevor was adrift. His anger at Matthew had dropped to indifference. Trust to doubt. Love to distaste. His life drifted in and out from pain that was physical to an engulfing grief, to numbness. Where could he go from there?

Shari did not meet them at the door. The house was empty of sound, empty of heart. Matthew hobbled into the kitchen. 'Dad, I could use something to eat. I'm pretty much starving.'

'Help me out here, Matthew, make the sandwich yourself. I have to see to your mother.'

Matthew was disconcerted. Where had all the attention gone? They couldn't live without him. Well, he needed a sandwich. He was on crutches. Was that too much to ask? Matthew found peanut butter and slathered it on four slices of whole grain bread. He spilled honey from the jar on all four slices and slapped them together. He didn't bother cutting the sandwiches before he dug into them, and limped away without cleaning up.

Shari was still in bed, lying on her back with her eyes wide open, dazed and confused.

'I was hoping you might be able to sleep.' Trevor lay down beside her.

'I could stay here forever. It just seems we're destined to lose both children, so easily, like water through our fingers. I haven't the energy to save them.'

Trevor could see his wife was depressed, dulling her heart and perception. Was this what happened when you lost a child? You lost yourself?

'Matthew's eating. He's fine.' He knew only that they must not forsake Tay. He would see to that. The Sandersons would be at the funeral home for their beautiful daughter.

Warmth from Shari's body soothed Trevor, and he fell into a peaceful sleep for an hour before the nightmare took hold. *Tay was walking in a parade on Ste-Catherine Street. He was waiting to reach out for her and protect her, on the corner of Bishop Street. Tay saw him clearly and turned up a side street, as if to avoid him. He ran after Tay, but he lost her in a crowd of revellers. Why hadn't she come to him? He was frightened, but more deeply hurt by her deliberate choice to avoid him.* Trevor woke with a start and heard himself screaming, Tay was gone, even in his dreams.

Shari woke and held Trevor. She didn't speak. What words can heal such a loss? The balms she offered were silence and her arm across his chest. When his body shook with sobs, Shari held onto him, and he to her. The hours crawled by. Sleep did not return. Trevor eased off the bed before five o'clock and spoke. 'Shari, please take care in the shower. Do you need my help?'

'I don't think I can go, Trevor.'

'Let me help you. I need you with me tonight.' It took fifteen minutes, but Shari helped him and began to blow-dry her hair, and he felt he could leave. In the kitchen he found a garbage bag to wrap around Matthew's cast so he could take a shower. He climbed the stairs on heavy legs pausing briefly in front of Tay's room. He couldn't open her door, she had become a haunting dream that clings to the heart like flesh to bone.

He found Matthew asleep with his leg resting on a pillow. Trevor shook his son's shoulder. 'You have to shower and get ready for the visitation.'

It was odd, Trevor thought, how youth returns when children are asleep. Matthew raised his arms above his head, stretched and yawned. 'Dad?'

'You have to shower to get ready for tonight.'

'I just fell asleep. My leg hurts. I can't go. How can I even shower?' he asked pointing to the cast.

Trevor produced the plastic bag and proceeded to wrap the cast. 'There, get up. I'll help you to shower. I don't want to hear another word from you.' Trevor grabbed one of Matthew's arms and Matthew pulled himself up on one leg. He wound an arm around Matthew's back and Matthew squealed.

'What?'

'I don't know. My back hurts.'

Trevor waited until they were in the bathroom before he removed Matthew's t-shirt. 'What the hell is that?' There was an ugly yellow bruise, the size of a softball between his shoulder blades. 'Have you seen this?'

'No, I just know it hurts.'

'Take a look in the mirror.'

'Damn!'

'It's an old bruise, Matthew. You didn't get that from the tunnel. What happened?'

'I guess it happened when I fell down the stairs. I mean I don't know. I never looked. I hurt all over that day. Who checks a back?'

'It doesn't matter, but take care in the shower. Do you need me?'

'Come on, Dad.'

'Call me when you're finished.'

'Just give me the crutches and another pill.'

'No meds before you have some food. You cannot appear drugged. Are you able to use your mother's scissors to cut along the seam of your pants?'

'I can handle that.'

'Good, along the seam.' Trevor came back with the crutches and left.

At the bottom of the stairs, he turned and examined them. The stairs were heavily carpeted, the bannisters a smooth natural oak. He looked for a place that would leave such a mark. Perhaps Matthew had fallen on something the day he struck him. That made more sense. *He* barely recalled the events of that day. Still… Matthew had fallen backwards on the landing, on carpeted floor. Was his mind trying to distract him? Did he mistrust his own memory? The limo was coming at six twenty-five. He had to prepare some food that no one would eat and shower himself. Still… What ate away at him? As Trevor stood shivering under a hot shower, he knew. He wished that it was Matthew who had died. The soap fell from his hand and Trevor slipped and caught himself. Why wasn't it Matthew?

Chapter Forty-two

Caitlin Donovan was home, wondering if she had made the right decision not to attend the visitation. The Dean, many administrators, Susan Wyman, professors and students would no doubt attend, many of whom she knew. According to Dino Mazzone, Wyman had informed the Dean of his call. Then there was Taylor herself and Caitlin's guilt for not reaching out. When Caitlin looked at her front door, she remembered Taylor bursting in, pushing past her. Anger still surfaced. *Why didn't Taylor confide in me? I knew her as a kid. She never gave me a chance to help. The little bitch set me up and nearly maimed me with a brick, but I was the adult. I should have...* When her phone rang, she jumped. 'Carmen, you scared me.'

'Are you that bad? Change your mind and go. If you want, I'll go with you.'

'I'm angry at myself and I'm angry at Taylor.'

'Taylor's dead – she's paid her debts.'

'I can always count on your support, Carmen. Seriously, I came close to losing my job. If Taylor hadn't told her brother, I was halfway out the door.'

'You're right. I'm with you on that.'

'She broke my trust. I won't give second chances again – I won't ever have students back here for end-of-term socials. That's all finished. I like my students. I like what I do, most of the time.'

'Caitlin, having students to your home is not a great idea anyway. You're putting yourself at risk. Your mother's going to be okay. You still have a job and a best friend. Get dressed and I'll meet you at your place.'

'Alright. I'm just sad.'

'Imagine the Sandersons.'

'I know. I didn't mean to sound so selfish.'

Amira Cupid had dressed with great care. She wore black slacks and a long beige sweater. Gold earrings from her mother and a gold bag she'd found at Walmart set off the simple look she wanted and could afford. Regarded as a suspect, she felt fearful and edgy. Amira was no fool; she saw what the detective was after. With no sound in the apartment but hers, she grew frightened. She missed the hurried hustle and arrogant noise of Taylor and Josh. Their apartment had a heartbeat, a life that was gone. She missed Taylor. Her door had not been repaired. The landlord had said he'd get to it, but since she was the only tenant, it could wait. Amira picked up her peace rock and kissed it. If she could go back in time…

She had called the STM to find the best bus route, but she was unsure of the times. She reached for her heavy jacket and left. When she turned right on Sherbrooke Street, she found herself huddling in the same bus shelter that Taylor had driven past, waving and leaving her alone in the cold. Amira watched cars pass, looking for a blue BMW. A sharp gust of wind forced her deeper into the shelter and she began to shiver. When she thought of their love affair, her heart leapt. It was not a love affair for Taylor – it was an interlude. The love *she* had felt began to shrivel in the cold.

Matthew Sanderson balanced on one foot, was able to gel his hair and fingered the yellowing bruise on his left cheek. He hated ties, but he put one on to please his parents, navy blue, that was close enough to black. He'd done a good job on his pants. Taking one last look at himself in a full-length mirror, he liked being the injured brother. He felt bad for his mother. Something in her eyes had died, he'd seen that. Matthew was observant. He saw things and he listened. He also knew that things backfired, though he still did not understand how his father had gone from telling him he wouldn't survive without him, back to anger. He blamed the police. They kept at him, drawing out answers that he wanted to hide. Had he loved Taylor? It was hard to say. She was five years older, and she'd used him plenty. Still, she was his sister. He supposed he loved her, at times, at least. If only she hadn't called him. So much would be different for him. It was an awful feeling, Matthew thought, knowing his father wished he had died and not Taylor. He was the son! He had failed his sister, and Trevor Sanderson was not a forgiving man. But he was alive. That had to count. He stopped at Taylor's room and he heard her shouting. *You have to help me Matthew! I'm your sister. I really fucked up… Do you hear me? I'm fucking scared, please…*

Detective Damiano's mood darkened. She wouldn't have lab news from Galt that day. Josh Goldman was out of bounds for twenty-four hours. Her hands were tied. At the visitation, her eyes would be on Cupid and Matthew Sanderson. If by some good chance, Matthew saw Cupid, if he had told the truth and had been at the tunnel, he might spot her, and something in her fluid movement might spark a remembrance that she was the runner. *Ifs, always ifs!* The fact that the throwaway was still out there added stress to the pain in her arm. She knew that she became involved with people in her case, the way Matte kept his distance, his way of dealing. Matthew Sanderson had gotten into her head. It was wrong of her to take an active dislike to a seventeen-year-old, but she had. Yet she found his willful defiance and seeming indifference disturbingly admirable. And she'd grown to respect Trevor Sanderson despite his arrogance. He was a father who loved his daughter but was torn and broken by both his children.

Damiano usually left the cooking to her husband, but she began to make lemon chicken to get her mind off the case for a little respite. When Luke appeared at the kitchen door, he startled her. 'How come you're home this early, Luke?'

'Didn't cut! It's study hour. I chose to work at home.'

'Didn't accuse you, Luke. I was surprised that's all. How are you doing besides school?'

'I'm not hungry.' He turned to leave.

'Luke, get in here!'

Luke took a full minute to reappear.

In better light, Damiano was shocked by Luke's weight loss and the weariness in his eyes. 'You have to eat something.'

'It takes fourteen days to starve. It's only been a day.'

'Is that your goal – to starve?'

'What's the big deal, one day!'

'It hasn't been just one day. You're not eating most days. Nobody's worth starving for, not even your mother,' she said, trying to smile.

'I have to figure this out on my own.'

'I'm a detective. I'm pretty good at solving things. You've already told me you ruined this relationship. You're not the first person – you won't be the last.' She was shocked again when she saw Luke was near tears. 'You won't be, Luke.'

'You're too old to know what real love is.'

'That's a stupid comment from a smart kid of mine.'

'I loved her with every part of me…' Luke ran back to his room shouting, 'Leave me alone!' For emphasis, he slammed his door.

She wanted to fly after Luke, but she might lose him completely. 'Love! What the hell!' She didn't bother looking for the vodka. Jeff would not be in a mood to fight with her when Luke needed them. The chicken pieces received the brunt of her concern. Damiano believed in keeping her word, but she decided to break her promise to Jeff. Tomorrow or Thursday, she was going to the condo for her pill stash. Jeff's half pill and vodka regimen had become an irritant. She'd monitor herself with a combo that worked for her. It had been well over nine months since she'd been there. Ghosts travelled well, she knew. Damiano threw the last piece of chicken into the trash can. Like her case, it wouldn't have fit in the pan. She stood in the hallway, looking down at Luke's room.

Chapter Forty-three

Damiano called her husband to alert him about the growing crisis with Luke, and he promised he'd be home before six. Detective Matte was waiting for her in the underground parking at the Division. Damiano liked black and she wore it well. Her Jimmy Choo Anouk pumps – an over-the-top gift from her physician husband Jeff – caught Matte's attention because Damiano generally wore black designer sneakers. He thought of his partner as a powerfully feminine woman and the shoes reinforced that idea. They drove through Outremont, the affluent town surrounded by Montreal, to Chemin de la Forêt and the Mount Royal Funeral Complex. Attendance at such events took a toll on the bereaved and the cops too. Toni didn't say much on the drive until they arrived at the funeral complex.

'You're quiet, Toni.'

'Luke isn't any better, and I think this will be a waste of time. These events always make me feel like a leech, preying on the grief of others to give me something I can work with. How long has it been since we've seen any sun?'

'Nine days, I believe.'

'April in Montreal.'

Matte drove up the winding roads to the impressive complex. In spring and summer the arboretum and rolling hills were lovely The crowd they expected was there full force. He spotted media, but he also noted that there were four ushers at the door, speaking to each of the mourners. 'I think the Sandersons sent out private invitations. I see ushers collecting them. It's very formal.'

'I like that. Most students here are just curious. The Sandersons must have rented several salons. It's my guess that the family salon is private, invitation only. The students are permitted in the other rooms that have photos and flowers. I've seen another funeral very similar to this one. I'm pretty sure that's the arrangement."

'You don't know that.'

'Pierre, we're not on a Sunday drive. No matter how much money you put into a place like this, it's still a funeral home. To me the arched portals are cold. Humans seem smaller because of its scale. We're here for people. Back on point, Sanderson didn't have hundreds of friends, so we are looking at the curious.' When Matte tried to park, a valet walked over to them. Matte flashed his badge and the valet backed off.

The detectives spoke to one of the ushers and discovered that Matte was right. The visitation was to be very private. Apart from the room for the family and close friends, the Sandersons has rented three other visitation rooms for the mourners. As they walked down the corridor leading to the salons, they saw a single photo of Taylor and dozens of pink roses in each room. Students had already filled the rooms; others were waiting in the hall. As they approached the main salon with Taylor Sanderson's casket, they saw the formal plaque mounted outside the door with her name. Both detectives stopped. 'I don't know if we should disturb them, Pierre.'

'Toni, you should go in alone. We have to watch Matthew and Amira. That's what we came for, I believe. I'll stand out here and scan the other rooms.'

'I don't know if I'm up for this.'

'You are – go on in.'

Damiano tensed when she realized there were people lining up behind her and Matte. The room added to her stress. The casket was open. The Sandersons were seated close by. Friends sat quietly at a little distance. The room was still. Damiano felt she had dust in her throat as she walked to the casket, knelt and tried to swallow. She had seen Taylor Sanderson *in situ* and at the morgue. She had not seen the beautiful young woman who lay before her. She felt the tears before she knew they were there. A detective did not belong here, disturbing the quiet grief of the family. Damiano felt out of place. Thoughts of Luke lurked in the back of her mind.

When she stood, she was grateful to see that Trevor Sanderson had risen to greet her. He extended his hand and broke the silence. 'Now you see what I lost.' He looked at his daughter. 'Do what you have to do, no matter where it leads. My daughter wasn't refuse to be discarded. Please leave Shari alone today.'

Damiano looked back at Shari Sanderson. Her mother rested her hand on her daughter's shoulder, but Shari Sanderson was remote in her grief. Damiano noticed that Matthew was watching her. She nodded, giving him a false sense of security. He nodded back and Damiano sat alone. Shari Sanderson had not greeted anyone, but Matthew was in the thick of the attention showered upon him. Caitlin Donovan appeared with her parents and Damiano was on alert. Tall and fit, Donovan's parents were first to reach the family, the professor behind them.

To Damiano's surprise, Shari Sanderson rose unsteadily and reached for Mrs. Donovan. The women embraced. 'You know, Maggie, you know what it is to lose a child. I had no idea when…'

'It's alright, Shari. No one ever does until…'

They held each other and wept. Sanderson patted his wife's shoulder and turned to Caitlin's father. 'How did you keep it together, Frank?'

Their voices were loud enough to hear. 'You don't, Trevor. You try to pick up the pieces, but the pain stays with you.'

Caitlin Donovan shook hands with Trevor and whispered something Damiano couldn't hear. It seems to Damiano he nodded an okay to her. The scent from the roses was overpowering and Damiano suddenly wanted to leave when she spotted Amira Cupid at the door, pleading with an usher.

'I was her friend and roommate – I should have an invitation.'

Matthew leaned forward to catch everything while his father went to the door and spoke to Cupid, and then led her into the room. Matthew hadn't taken his eyes off her. Cupid knelt at the casket for a long time and wept openly with her head bowed. When she finally stood, she nodded to the Sandersons, noticing Damiano as she left the room. Matthew's eyes followed her.

Andrew Weston walked into the room of mourners alone. He walked directly to the casket and knelt as if there was no one else in the room. He leaned close to study Taylor's face, gripping the arm rest of the kneeler before the casket. He brought a fist to his mouth and shook his head at the unreality of seeing someone he had loved gone, forever. Damiano was surprised he knelt and stayed. No one bothered him. A good five minutes later, he stood, looked sadly at the family and left without approaching them. Weston stopped at the door holding back tears. Then disappeared.

The pain and grief combined with the overpowering sweet scent of the flowers unsettled Damiano. *The kid began to fall again. Luke was running away from her.* She held the sides of her chair and took a deep breath to settle her racing heart. It was Matthew Sanderson who managed to draw her back. He had seen her reaction and was amused by it. She looked towards the entrance of the room to clear her head.

Damiano knew the next couple, Joseph Castonguay and his son Liam. Damiano observed their stiff nervousness. Joseph wore a dark suit, Liam his school grays, a new white shirt and a blue tie that must have been his father's. Over his shirt he had a new black sweater that his father must have bought for the visitation. He reminded Damiano of Luke at his confirmation. Sanderson must have invited them and he guessed who they were and greeted them. Liam stood five feet from the casket. He could not believe how beautiful the girl was. He had seen Taylor in a brief flash of fear. Aware that he made a mistake by not coming forward sooner he balled his fists until his nails cut into his hands to keep from crying. His father turned to him and Liam squared his shoulders. 'I am Liam, Mr. Sanderson. I will regret my cowardice for the rest of my life.' Ironically, the words didn't seem prepared – they were spontaneous and heartfelt.

Both fathers smiled. 'Liam, you found my daughter. You did call the police. We all make mistakes, but you tried your best to correct yours. I respect you for that, son.'

Liam shook Sanderson's hand firmly and left immediately, before his father.

'Thank you, Mr. Sanderson. Accept my deepest sympathies. We feel your loss keenly.'

'You have a fine son, Joseph.'

Damiano saw Matthew grip the handles of his crutches, and she knew why she didn't like him so early on. Putting on a performance Matthew placed some weight on his injured leg, bent forward and kissed his mother's cheek. Shari turned to him, and he felt she had read the reason for his embrace. What did this Castonguay kid have that merited a smile from his father when he didn't?

Matthew saw that the little fuck didn't even own a jacket.

If looks could kill… Liam would be dead.

Chapter Forty-four

Detective Damiano found Matte back at the entrance to the funeral complex. 'Did you catch something?'

'Not sure.'

'Go on, Pierre.'

'I was in the hallway, checking the crowds because the rooms were too congested for me to see anything.'

'Drop the details, what did you see?'

'Alright. At the door a kid was either walking in or leaving. I stress *or*. When he saw me, I had the feeling he fingered me for a cop and left.'

'But he might have been leaving anyway?'

'That's why I stressed *or*.'

'Did you get a good look?'

'It's tough. There were students streaming in and out and I saw him for just a second. Tall, dark hair, good looking guy, well dressed – but hell, most of the males here fit that description. We did make eye contact. Might be our runaway, but Matthew Sanderson saw him in a cap.'

'Did you go after him?'

'No, I let him walk. Of course, I went after him! When I reached the exit, I bumped into a wave of students and lost him.'

'Maybe not all lost. He might show up at the funeral.'

'After he ran from me? Unlikely.'

'If the kid was in love – good odds he'll take the risk.'

'How did it go with you, Toni?'

'It was tough. Matthew Sanderson remains a prime suspect. The hatred, the indifference, the manipulation, the envy, the kid is oozing with all those vibes. He checked Cupid out, especially as she left the room. Cupid draws attention, front or back. He gave Donovan a good look, but not the same way he did to Cupid. If he's not lying about who he saw, he might be able to suggest she was the runner. His father told me to do what I had to do to close the case. I take that to mean we can interview the kid tonight after the visitation.'

'What does that mean? We sit in the car and wait till nine or later? What about respect for the parents on this day? Leave them alone, Toni.'

'I'm telling you what Sanderson told me, and we have less than half an hour to wait. I'm going to call home.'

'I'll step out and do the same.'

'Jeff, how's our wounded boy?'

'Don't get angry, I was held up by an emergency at the hospital. When I got home Luke had left a note to say he needed air. He was fine and would be home soon. In large script: "Don't worry you guys! I just want to think."'

'We have to have this out with him, Jeff. It's his health I'm worried about. When he does appear, try to get some food into him.'

'Yes, Detective. I'm on the job.'

'This is serious.'

'I know. Hold on. He's home. He used the back door.'

'Thank God!'

'I'll leave him be for a few minutes and then I'll have a go, a serious go, Toni. I'm worried too, but at least he's home and not wandering the streets. Kids act up one day – the next day it's a whole new ball game. Just a sec!' Jeff was back in seven seconds. 'He said we are driving him into paranoia. Let's try to let him be.'

Damiano checked her watch. In ten minutes, she'd approach Sanderson outside the main salon and impress upon him the necessity of asking Matthew two more questions.

Matte was still on the phone. His body language told her the call wasn't going well. He slid back into the car without saying a word.

'I guess we both have problems at home.'

'I need to work this out on my own, Toni,' Matte said, giving her his back-off shrug. Matte was upset.

'No problem.'

'How's the arm?'

'The concern for Luke is distracting it. I'd give my life for Luke. He's a good kid, and it's tearing my heart out to see him so troubled.'

'Look, stay in the car, Pierre, I'll go back in to interview Matthew.'

'Toni, I hope you're right about this.'

'If I'm not, it's on me. Your murder book, our murder book, is bursting with photos and reports and recordings that have amounted to nothing. I have to press.' Damiano had given up on the note-taking on the third day of the case.

'Cornering the vic's brother in the funeral home is low balling.'

'Do you think it's better to follow them back home and interview Matthew there? It has to be done tonight, Pierre. If I wait till tomorrow, you'll have the same reason for waiting. Then there's the funeral.'

'You're going to do what you want anyway.'

Damiano shot back. 'It's not what I want! It's what needs to be done.'

'It's your case.'

'Folks are starting to leave. We won't have that long a wait. I'm heading back inside to see if the director has a free office we can use. Coming?'

'Sure.'

From the director's expression it was clear he sided with Matte, but led them to his office. Matte took out his notes and sat. Damiano waited by the door, glad to people were being gently shown out. Twenty minutes later she saw the Sandersons and their parents making a slow, reluctant departure. Matthew spotted Damiano and he angled closer to his mother. When Sanderson saw her, he left the family and came to join her.

'I appreciate your time and your willingness to help, Mr. Sanderson. I'm hoping Matthew may have seen something tonight that might assist us. We can speak to him here in this office. Afterwards, Detective Matte and I will see you and Matthew home. I felt it would be easier on the family than doing this in your home tonight.'

'Matthew is still a suspect, isn't he, Detective?'

'We don't even know if he went to the tunnel, Sir. We are trying to establish what really happened...'

'Let me see Shari and our in-laws to the door. I'll be back with my son.'

Matte said nothing when Damiano walked into the office. They waited quietly. Matthew hobbled into the room, and took his time to sit and arrange his crutches against the nearest wall. He undid his tie and placed his elbows on the table. Trevor Sanderson sat a seat away from his son.

'Matthew, did you see anyone tonight who in any way might resemble the runner or the man you saw at the tunnel? To be more specific, is there a possibility that Professor Donovan or the woman in black might have been the runner? Did something suggest they resembled the person you saw that day?'

'I never said it was a woman. You suggested that. All I saw was a runner dressed in black. I wasn't even sure the person was running from the tunnel. Professor Donovan has blonde hair. Wouldn't I have seen some of her hair?'

'Not if she had bunched it under the hat.'

Trevor Sanderson was sceptical of the question.

'What about Amira Cupid, the black woman? You were examining her closely.'

'With every other guy who was there – she's hot!' Matthew added, smirking.

His father rolled his eyes.

'She's also very fit.'

'I could see that,' he smirked.

The questioning was going badly, but Matte did not jump in. Damiano wanted this interview. It was her job to clean it up.

'Matthew, I have to say that I still don't believe much of what you have told us.'

Matthew pulled his elbows off the table and sat up.

'I'm trying to find the person who murdered your sister. You still can't tell me the truth that might help us. Did you actually go to the tunnel that day?' Damiano's voice rose with the last question. 'Are you just making up this story of being there and seeing two people that you can't identify just to get attention? Isn't that what this is all about, attention?'

Sanderson looked hard at his son.

'If everything is a lie, you're obstructing justice in the murder of your sister.'

Matthew bit his bottom lip.

'How did you find the exact place in the tunnel with your fake suicide attempt?'

Matthew hopped to his good leg. 'I found the police tape and I saw the marking of Tay's body on the tunnel floor,' he said with gritted teeth. 'I wasn't going to kill myself – I wanted to see where Tay died. I don't care if you believe me. I was there that day. I saw those two people. Why is all the blame coming on me? Why am I the hated one? My sister caused her own death, didn't she? She cheated, she tried to injure Professor Donovan. Then she gets caught up in a bad thing with a guy who kills her. She got herself killed. That's how I see it.'

No one said a word. His father kept his eyes down.

'What's with you, Dad? Tay was no princess – she did bad shit that got her killed. Why do you hate me because of what *she* did? Why are you so blind? Maybe she did something that day and the guy hit back. Maybe it was an accident. Could be, right?'

Sanderson stood abruptly, knocking down the chair behind him. 'Is that what happened, Matthew? Tay dominated you again like she did when you were younger and you, the brave man you are, struck back. Is that finally it, Matthew?'

'You'd love that, Dad, right? Is that why you hate me?'

'I can't believe you're my son. Take us home, Detective. I can't listen to any more of this.'

'Was it an accident, Matthew?' 'Is that what happened?' Damiano asked.

Trevor Sanderson remembered the bruise on Matthew's back. 'That's what happened, isn't it, Matthew?' Sanderson could not reveal the bruise to the detectives. The thought that Matthew might have murdered his sister was so odious that he felt physically ill.

Matthew gave a slack grin. He had his dad's full attention. 'Don't get so caught up with words, Dad. Tay messed up her own life. I had nothing to do with that. You can't get rid me of me that easily. That was just a theory. How the hell do I know how Tay died?'

Just an accident, Damiano thought. 'Mr. Sanderson, is Matthew safe with you tonight?'

'Matthew, you have nothing to worry about. I'm disappointed with you, Matthew, but your mother loves you. Help her survive the next two days. We're ready to go, Detective.'

The Sandersons didn't say a word to each other all the way home.

Chapter Forty-five

'What choice did I have, Pierre?' Damiano knew her partner thought the questioning of Matthew in the funeral complex was disrespectful.

'If his mother had heard her son, she would have been further traumatized. In the end, I suppose you had no choice.'

'Is his suggestion of an accident, something we can work with?'

'Might be.'

'Behind those owlish glasses is a kid in a very dark place. All the slights he's experienced over the years as the number two in the family have come to a boil. It's obvious Sanderson favored his daughter. He has labelled him a coward and disavowed him. There's also survivor's guilt.'

'In simpler terms, Toni, the kid's suffering a breakdown?'

'Am I grasping at straws to think he is also a murderer?'

'If his sister provoked him, Matthew is very capable of murder. He was jealous of his sister, and he's explosive. We've seen sparks in our interviews. And let's not forget how he trashed his bedroom. By the way, at the funeral complex I received a text that I just read now. Crime says the rocks don't match.'

'We follow our plan. Get a search warrant for Cupid's apartment. She's too sly to keep the murder weapon and taunt us with it. It's the boots I'm after. The only solid clue we have is the sole's herringbone pattern. She doesn't have the money to throw those out. That's a guess on my part. Few laymen understand about trace transfer. We have to find a way to search Goldman's apartment as well.'

'I'll try to figure out a way for that.'

After leaving the funeral home Damiano pulled over to the side on Côte St. Catherine Road in obvious pain. She got out of the car and began to pace and rub her arm. 'Shit! Shit!'

Matte got out of the car, went around and slid into the driver's seat. Damiano hated offers of help when she was in distress of any kind. He'd learned from experience to keep quiet, so he waited while she swore and stamped her right foot.

'Get me back to the Division. Need to work on the warrants.'

'Sooner or later you have to do something about your arm.'

'Don't go there, Pierre!'

They drove in the silence that was customary when Damiano wanted to suffer alone. They parted at the Division, and as soon as she was in her Mini, she sped from the lot and headed for the condo. If ever there was a night she needed her stash, it was tonight. Promises be damned! By the time she reached Hutchison Street, the spasm was threatening. In great pain it took Damiano several manoeuvers to squeeze into an allotted parking space using one hand. She hurried from the car and took the stairs running. Ghosts and guilt be damned as well! She pushed the door at the top of the stairs so violently that it crashed against the side wall.

A condo door opened, '*Mon Dieu!* Ah, Toni it is you. I was frightened. Good to see you. Are you alright? *Vous-êtes blanche comme un drap!*'

'I have to rush, so sorry.'

'*Allez-y!*' Her neighbor said, throwing up her arms. '*Quelle femme!*'

Damiano struggled with the key to the condo, the door slamming as she ran for her stash taped under the kitchen sink. Unscrewing the top of the plastic container with her teeth, pills spilled on the counter. Managing to get one to her mouth she gulped water from the tap. To establish control she picked up the pills one at a time, returning them to the container. Taking deep breaths, she paced the apartment, oblivious of her surroundings. Since she hadn't eaten, she began to feel the effect of the pills quickly.

She walked slowly to the bedroom and lay down on the bed, being very careful of her arm, and closed her eyes. And then opened them. There was a smell in the bedroom that wasn't hers. *Be quiet – let the pill work!* But her nose stayed on its job. Waves of codeine began to wash over the spasm. *Relax – forget the smell. It was probably Jeff who hired someone to clean the place.* Something wasn't right. Odours didn't last for over nine months, but Damiano stayed put, afraid to move her arm. The smell could wait. She closed her eyes and fell asleep. Her cell woke her. Like a mother attuned to the sound of her infant's crying, Damiano would never miss the ring of her cell. 'Damn.' She rolled off the bed and went back to the kitchen. Clearing her throat, she reached into her purse and fished out her cell. 'Jeff, it's been a long day. I should be home in half an hour.'

'Are you alright? You don't sound right.'

'Arm spasm.'

'Give me your location and I'll come and get you.'

'No problem, I can make it.'

'For God's sake, be careful.'

Damiano growled when she got off the phone. She really didn't want to leave. In the bathroom she splashed water on her face, still feeling woozy. The mystery smell was stronger here. 'What the hell is that?' She opened a cabinet over the sink and found nothing. She threw open two cupboard and couldn't find anything. Nothing. She got down on her hands and knees and opened the cabinet under the sink where the smell was stronger. Behind rolls of toilet paper she found the Azzaro Chrome cologne that she had bought for Luke. For Luke! Had Luke and his girlfriend been meeting at the condo and using her bed for their lovemaking?

It wasn't anger that Damiano felt as she drove home. It was something worse, something like impending doom. Her heart raced, but she drove home slowly, making full stops at intersections. Even in her drugged state, her elbow began to buzz. She was afraid to learn the truth, and furious at Luke's deception. When she pulled into the driveway, Jeff came out to help her.

'Thank God you're home safely.'

'Is Luke home?'

'Lying on his bed plugged in to his music.'

'Let's get inside. We have to talk.' Jeff followed Damiano into the kitchen. 'Check on Luke and shut the door when you get back here.'

'How serious is this?'

'I don't know yet.' Damiano had her own confession first. Jeff wasn't going to take it well. He'd see it as a breach of trust.

Jeff closed both kitchen doors. 'Okay, Toni.'

'Before you jump, I have a confession to make that led me to our deeper problems.'

Jeff studied Damiano's face. 'You went to the condo.'

'Yes.'

'You made me a firm promise.'

'I was closer to the condo than home. I'm sorry and I won't go back.'

'You had pills there although I looked and didn't find them many months ago.'

Damiano lied to turn Jeff onto their real problem. 'There weren't any pills. I ran my arm under cold water. Then you called.'

'Toni, don't lie to me.'

'Damn it to hell! Alright, I found pills. I'm an adult and I'm not popping pills every few hours. I had a spasm and I *was* closer to the condo.'

'I told you, Toni, I will not feed your addiction. Give me the pills, now!' Jeff had his hand out.

'You're out of luck. I left them there.'

'Enough. Make the one you've taken last, Toni. That's it for tonight.'

She'd gotten away with a half-truth. 'Fine. We have a deeper problem. Luke has been using the condo with his girlfriend. I found the cologne I gave him for Christmas in the bathroom.'

'Toni, it's not the end of the world. Maybe his deception is a reflection of yours. What's really bothering you?'

'I don't know yet, but I'm scared.'

'Help me out here.'

'I have to talk to Luke alone.'

'As a mother or a detective?'

'I'm both, Jeff.'

Damiano transferred her concern to Jeff. Perhaps that was worse for a doctor who needed clarity. 'I should be with you. I want to protect him. He'll need a full parent.'

'You will be, but I need some time alone with him. I have to question Luke.'

'You're a mother first, for God's sake! Get your priorities straight.'

Chapter Forty-six

Luke had his eyes closed lying on the bed fully dressed when Damiano walked into his room without knocking. He ripped out his earbuds and jumped to his feet. 'Mom? What about knocking first?'

'I've been to the condo.'

Luke sat back down on his bed and dropped his head.

'How long were you using it?'

'About a month.'

'And the relationship ended?'

'Yes.' Luke chose to stand defiantly with a hand on his hip.

Damiano walked over to Luke's dressers and began to open one drawer after another, rummaging in each.

'You can't do that!'

'Watch me.'

When she spotted his khaki bag, she went for that.

Luke lunged for the bag, but Damiano reached it first. 'You can't fucking do this to me! It's my private stuff!'

'Language, please! This is our house. I bought that bag, not you.' Damiano emptied the contents onto the bed. She'd seen his iPhone on the dresser. When the second phone dropped from the bag, Luke threw himself across the bed and snatched it.

'That's none of your damn business – this is my life.'

'Let's try to be calm,' Jeff said, coming into the room.

'I want to see your phone, Luke.'

'It's mine. *I* bought it. It's all I have left.'

Damiano made a quick grab and wrestled the phone from Luke and saw Taylor's number.

It can't be… It's not possible…

'What's going on?'

'Jeff, please leave us alone.'

Tears were running down Luke's cheeks.

'I can't, Toni, we're family.'

'Please, let me handle it, Jeff.' Damiano turned away and began to scroll through Luke's calls. Taylor's name came up several times. Damiano looked at him aghast, her breathing ragged. 'You? Oh my God! How is this even possible?' 'You?'

Luke screwed his eyes shut.

'Luke, you have to explain this to me. I can't understand it.' Her arm began to spike.

'I demand to know what's going on, Toni.'

'Please, Jeff, you must leave us alone. Please!' Damiano nerves were raw. 'I'm serious! You have to leave.'

'This is our home!' Jeff saw fear in Damiano's eyes. He knew her breaking points. He raised his arms in surrender but stopped at the door.

'Luke, you have to tell me.'

'Give me the phone, Mom. It's all I have left of Taylor. I didn't hurt her – I only loved her.'

Damiano's neck and back felt stiff. She struggled to be the cop. 'This phone is evidence. I can't give it to you. How did you even meet Taylor?' Damiano trembled as she asked the question. *It's Luke.*

The fury Luke felt over the loss of his phone dissolved into fear of what he had done. He had no fight left. He answered dully, 'At Concordia.'

'What were you doing there?' She heard her own straining voice. *How can it be Luke?*

'They have social events and other stuff. I just went to check it out. Taylor was there.' He smiled woefully. 'She thought I was a student there. I told her I was at McGill. I never thought anything would come of the lie. I never thought we might hook up. It was a no-account lie. We went to the caf and had coffee and we talked for over an hour. It just started… I began to skip classes… There was something electric between us – she felt it too. I knew right away she did.'

'You don't even drink coffee.' Damiano shook her head, and yet, she had a feeling, something in the back of her head. The timing, the depression. 'Didn't she ever figure out you're only fifteen?'

'Every kid has a fake ID… and I had the condo. Once I told the first lie, I couldn't undo it. We fell hard. I mean she loved me, and I loved everything about her. It wasn't just sex. We talked forever. I just listened to her. I loved being with her, looking at her. I never met anyone like her.'

'What happened?' Damiano's heart was shaking. Luke was the throwaway. All the signs were there and she had missed every one of them. How could she have been so blind, so stupid?

'We were at the condo. I'd ordered pizza from La Pizzaiolle across the street. I was in the shower when it came. I told Taylor the money was on the counter, but she went to my wallet instead and found my Loyola High School student card.'

'And noticed your age.'

'It freaked her out. She just cried and cried. I couldn't stop her. She kept saying, "How could you do this to me? How? I loved you... You're underage! How could I not know? How could you do this to me?" And she cried some more.'

Damiano's body tensed again.

'I told her I never meant to hurt her. Then she said that she could never see me again. I begged her to wait just two months. I'd be sixteen. We could be together. She ran out of the condo and I ran after her. You won't understand this part. I ran after her and I said if she left me, I'd report her to you. You were a detective, and she could be arrested because I was underage. She backed away from me like I had punched her in the stomach. She looked so sad when she left and she was scared of me. She backed away and then she ran, crying real loud.'

Luke's words finally reached Damiano though she was still torn between being a mother and a cop. 'Oh, Luke... don't you see? Taylor would never have dated a sixteen-year-old, she was twenty-two; she was a young woman – you're still a kid. You were trying to blackmail her, hurt the person you just said you loved.' Her tone stung Luke.

'I wouldn't have done it, Mom,' Luke pleaded. 'I never would have told on her, but I couldn't lose her. Can't you understand that? It was the only way I thought I could keep her.'

Disappointment fell on her every word. 'Because of you, Luke, she cheated on a paper and threatened a professor. She couldn't think straight. She was that frightened of what you might do. With the second phone – you just made everything worse.'

'I know what I did. I loved her, Mom.' He raised his voice. 'I *never* would have told you. Not *ever*! When I asked her to meet me, she only agreed because she was afraid I would tell and she'd be arrested. I got to the tunnel late because I wanted her to be a little scared. She'd need me then, right?'

'Why there? She was afraid of places like tunnels.'

'She said she'd go with me before they tore it down. She'd feel safe with me. She went that Tuesday because she thought I'd tell you if she didn't. I'm the reason she died. I killed her. I killed the only person I'll ever love.'

Jeff was listening to everything from the doorway.

Damiano's hands shook. 'Tell me what happened at the tunnel, Luke.' Damiano could not believe she was interrogating her son.

'That's just it, Mom, she never showed. I looked for her, but I didn't stay because I knew she hated me, and she never came. I never thought to check the tunnel because all the entrances were boarded up. Taylor would never go near them.'

'But she did, Luke.'

'I know that now.' Luke rubbed both eyes. 'Was she still alive in that tunnel when I was there?' he rasped.

'Yes, Luke. She was dying... she was struggling to breathe for a good hour.'

Luke jumped up from his bed with a piercing, plaintive howl. Damiano and Jeff rushed to him, but he pushed them both away screaming. Jeff wrapped his arms around Luke as they struggled and fell back onto the bed. Luke wept uncontrollably.

Damiano stood frozen. *Luke can't own up to the whole truth – he can't. He'll ruin his life. He might have trashed my job. The throwaway phone was under my nose, and I'm supposed to be the lead detective.* Damiano stepped back when she realized she had bitten her tongue.

When Jeff released Luke, he rolled into the fetal position and began to moan. Jeff kept his hand on Luke's back.

Jeff might not know the full repercussions of Luke's act, but she did. Taylor Sanderson had lost her life, Matthew Sanderson might be damaged for life, and the parents would grieve forever. Professor Donovan might have lost her position and been arrested. On her side, Luke could be charged with harassment and endangerment and she'd be taken off the case. Trevor Sanderson might sue them personally. Damiano sat beside Luke and gently placed her hand on his shoulder. 'Luke, did you see anyone at the tunnel? I know you are upset but I need an answer.'

Luke moaned. 'You say you loved Taylor, help us find her killer. Did you see someone there? Please look at me, Luke.'

Jeff turned to Damiano. 'Toni, this is probably not a good time.'

'Yes, now, Jeff.'

Luke shouted back at Damiano. 'I want to confess everything. Taylor's dead because of me and my threat. I owe her that. I don't care what happens to me. I don't care about anything.'

'Luke, just answer my question, please, son. It's very important. What you did was deceitful, but someone else killed her. That's why I need to know if you saw anyone else there that day?'

'Another guy was there.' Luke was able to focus.

'Was he looking in the tunnel?'

'He was rubbing his arms. It was cold and I put on my cap.'

'Did you see anyone else in the vicinity?'

'No. Taylor hadn't come – she had left me. That's all I could think about and I left – I left her to die alone…' In between sobbing, he shouted at Damiano. 'Did the other guy kill her?'

'That was her brother. She'd begged him to come with her.'

'Because she was afraid of me?' he croaked.

'Yes.'

'Don't you see, Mom, I have to confess. I have to!'

Chapter Forty-seven

Damiano left Jeff with Luke and sat alone in the kitchen. Reaching into her pocket she broke a tablet in two and popped a half and struggled to breathe deeply. Luke and Taylor fell in love despite the age difference. Luke was late for their meeting at the tunnel. He felt Taylor decided not to come when he didn't find her. He didn't hang around. Damiano had a problem; too many people knew about Taylor's reluctance and fear of going there. If Chief Donat went at Luke, he'd coolly eviscerate him. She pictured the swarm of media: *Lead Cop's Son a Suspect in Sanderson Murder.* Outside, the wind was gusting and moaning like Luke. She had to coach Luke to protect him when he was questioned at the Division.

It was almost midnight when Matte's phone rang. 'Toni, do you know what time it is?'

'I have an emergency and I need your help.'

'Are you alright?'

'Pierre, I won't be in in the morning. I trust you with my life.'

'And mine with you, goes without saying. Why are you getting into this?'

'I need you to come to my home tomorrow about eleven. What I'm going to tell you is off the record. I need your help.' Damiano did not miss a detail.

Matte was very quiet on the other end.

'That's my plan, but I need your thoughts and quiet discipline.'

Matte was sorting out the story and thinking of his career. Kids were natural tattletales. It's going to be very difficult.

'Are you there, Pierre?'

'I am. I need the night to think this out.'

'I know it's withholding evidence, but it's my son and his life's at stake.'

'Trust between you and me is a done deal – Luke sounds like he's determined to confess that he threatened Sanderson. I need time. I'll see you about eleven.'

'Thank you forever, Pierre.'

'Don't thank me yet. I have to think about your plan for the interview. You have to work with Luke. You know what I mean. There's a lot at stake. Personal problems. Career. I'm alone again.'

'I understand. I trust you'll come up with something, and I'll continue discussing this with Luke. My kid's life hasn't really started yet. We need a break. He's a mess.'

'We need answers for all the facts already known – I'll work on that, Toni.'

'I'm sorry about Dylan. I don't know what I'd do without Jeff although you wouldn't know it sometimes, the way I treat him. I can't believe he's stuck with me. I'm not easy, even when I try to be. I'm really sorry for you, Pierre.'

Jeff was standing at the door and heard the conversation. 'I gave Luke a sedative and he's out, but I'll sleep in his room to make sure he doesn't take off. What about you, can you sleep?'

'I have to figure things out. I can't allow Luke to ruin his life.'

'I heard.'

'What do you think?'

'If Luke is not truthful, he'll live with that regret for the rest of his life.'

'If he protects himself somewhat, he still has to live with what he's done.'

'What kind of an example are you setting for him? Luke threatened the girl. He's just a kid and he was desperate, but you're the adult. You're a cop and you're willing to break the law? You haven't been the best mother to Luke. You know that's the truth, but Luke has always admired and respected you. His pride made up for your frequent absences. You have a lot to lose, something to consider.'

'Jeff, you're naïve where the law is concerned. I'd bet my badge that Trevor Sanderson has information about his son that he's holding back. He won't be the father who turns in his own son. He's given me free rein with Matthew, but he wants *me* to make the arrest if need be. Parents protect their children. Cops protect their family. I want Luke to tell the truth, all of it, except the threat. That's it. He didn't mean to carry it out. He was in love and in danger of losing Taylor. He's suffered for what he's done. He didn't just lose Taylor. She was murdered. Now he knows he was feet away from her when she was dying, and he didn't bother to check the tunnel.'

'Track what his threat did to the young woman – she lost her life.'

'I'm not forgetting Taylor, but nothing we do will bring her back. How many lovers say stupid things? How many make idle threats? I'm a high-profile cop – the Sandersons are high-profile too. Luke's threat will be blown out of proportion. His photo will be in every newspaper and all over the Internet. It's a juicy story. Blackmail, passion and underage sex:

the *Romeo and Juliet* of it all will play well. Luke's life will explode because of my work and the influence of the Sandersons. Orwell's allegory got it right. The world isn't black and white, it never was.'

'Mine has worked well within those colors.'

'I respect you for that, but this is life and death – taken together, dirt and grime. I work with them every day.'

'You said that Sanderson had muzzled the press.'

'Yes, for his family. I've come down forcefully on his son. He's human. He'll want the same treatment for Luke. If I were him, I'd want the same.'

Jeff stood. His shoulders tensed. 'I intend to be part of the decision. I'm Luke's father. Try to get some rest. I'll stay with Luke.'

Damiano couldn't sleep. She saw Luke in the crosshairs of the law, his adolescence lost, her beautiful son forever changed. When she finally slept, it was not a restful sleep. She woke to the noise of showers, Jeff's and Luke's. For a nanosecond, she didn't remember last night's events. They struck then with additional force. Jeff had allowed them to sleep past nine-thirty. He was fully dressed when he walked into the room. 'I'm working on breakfast. I'll wait with Luke until you're ready.'

'Thank you for letting us sleep.'

'You're the only one who did. I knew you needed it.'

Damiano rushed through everything, dressed quickly and was at the kitchen table in fifteen minutes. 'You call me at noon, both of you.' Luke sat motionless and Damiano nodded.

When the side door closed, Luke said, 'What happens now?'

'The day will be busy for both of us. Please try to eat some breakfast? We may not have another chance to eat today.'

'I'm not hungry. I know what you must think of me. I want to confess – do you record my statement, or do you take me down to Crémazie?'

'Do me a favor and eat, Luke.'

'I don't want to eat. I don't care if I die.'

'I do and your father does. For us, please.'

Luke grabbed his fork and stabbed the scrambled eggs until the fork was full. He stuffed his mouth and then he inhaled the toast. He grabbed six bacon slices, broke them in two and stuffed them in his mouth till both cheeks ballooned. Somehow, he managed to chew through it all. 'Are you going to eat yours?'

Damiano slid her plate across to Luke and he repeated his act. She ate the toast and drank the orange juice before Luke got to those. She had an awkward urge to laugh, but didn't. Luke grabbed a handful of napkins and wiped his mouth and drained the orange juice from the carton.

One mission accomplished! Damiano thought.

'What's next?'

'Before we go to the Division, I need the story to be very clear.'

'I'm ready.'

'For the record, did you murder Taylor Sanderson?'

'NO!'

'You met casually, you both fell in love, you deceived Taylor about your age and you hooked up in my condo without my knowledge. Taylor found your student card, discovered your age and left you.'

'Yes.'

'Off the record. You can tell all of that to the police, nothing more. If you tell my chief on record that you threatened to accuse Taylor with statutory rape, you could be taken into custody. Your threat might be called reckless endangerment because it led to a murder. You could face juvenile detention and a police record. Your face will be everywhere – the course of your life will be drastically changed. You won't finish your school year.

'On the other hand, if you confess to the police that you told Taylor I was a detective and she figured you might tell me – the situation is better for you. I know you never meant to carry out your threat, Luke. I'm trying to help you. You'll have a lifetime to grieve for Taylor and your part in her death.'

'Mom, you forgot the most important part. I lost Taylor. If I had been truthful when we met, she'd still be alive. I…'

They were interrupted by the doorbell. Matte was early. Damiano went to the door.

'I handed off the Cupid work to Galt. Dumont secured a warrant. Good on that front. Galt will try to see Goldman with our question, but no guarantees there.'

'Thanks. Let me take your coat.' She led Matte into the kitchen. Damiano cleared the table. 'Pierre, this is my son Luke.'

Luke stood and offered a hand. 'We almost met,' Luke said.

'At the visitation, I know, Luke.' Matte turned his attention to Damiano. 'Where are we, Toni?'

'Mom wants me to kinda lie, not a whole lie, a sorta lie, and she's a detective!'

'Toni, we have a problem. Taylor might have told Matthew about Luke's threat and whoever went with her. We still don't know who that is.'

'It will be Matthew's word against Luke's. I think the chief will believe Luke. Matthew has told so many lies. Same goes for whoever went with Taylor. We both know truth gets twisted.'

'I think we can trust the chief to be fair. He has children,' Matte said with authority.

Luke's heart pumped faster. 'I don't care what happens to me. I don't care if I'm sent to detention. I don't care if I die. I want to tell the truth! I won't lie, not now. Why can't you hear me, Mom?'

Chapter Forty-eight

Matte took Damiano aside. 'I'm heading back to bring the chief on board. I suggest you bring Luke down with you to the Division. Call Jeff, he might want you to have a lawyer. Discuss the pros and cons with him. You be present at the questioning as guardian, actually, you or Jeff.' Matte saw Luke was already tensing up and he left them.

'Luke, while I call your father, go and dress. Put on your school clothes.'

'Why?' he asked sullenly and nervous. 'Do you want me to look younger?'

'I want you to look your age. If you had... never mind.' Luke didn't put up much of an argument. Jeff picked up immediately and listened. 'A lawyer? Really?'

'Yeah, Jeff, really. Luke is determined to tell the whole truth. He's your son alright.'

'He's duplicitous and honest – like you. What are you thinking?'

'I think Luke and I should go it alone, or you and Luke. I'm hoping Matte will soften the chief's approach. There's no telling. I'm still coming to grips with the gravity of the situation.'

'I think you and your *gray* will do better than a black and white approach. I thought about that driving into work. My work is relatively simple; yours is more complex.' Jeff had grown up in Virginia. He pronounced complex *cumplex*.

Luke sat beside Damiano on the drive and fidgeted, tapping the floor of the car, drumming his fingers, adjusting the heat vent, and moving on his seat.

'Stop all that, Luke. I'm nervous enough.' She called Matte. 'He's handling it? Did you try to talk him out of it, Pierre? Fine, where? Great.'

'What?'

'Chief Donat will be questioning you. I'll tell you one thing, Luke. Answer the questions you're asked. Don't add anything. Be brief; be as truthful as you're determined to be.'

'I will.'

Damiano parked in the visitor parking, and Matte met her at the front door and led them to the questioning room. Chief Donat was already there. The recorder was set up. There were glasses and a water pitcher. Matte sat near the chief. Damiano and Luke sat on the other side. No one spoke until the chief took command of the interview. Matte turned on the recorder.

'April 10, 2014. Interview No.11, Chief Richard Donat presiding. Detective Pierre Matte assisting. Subject: File No. 2714: Taylor Sanderson: Homicide. Present: Luke Shea with guardian Antoinette Damiano.' Chief Donat turned his attention to the suspect. 'Luke, I have been briefed by Detective Matte. Speak when asked, understood?'

Luke nodded.

'Speak up for the recorder.'

'Yes.'

'You met Ms. Sanderson at Concordia University. You told her you were a McGill student, correct so far?'

'Yes.'

'That was a lie.'

'Yes.'

'Why did you purchase a second phone?'

Luke, on edge. 'To keep our relationship secret.'

'Ms. Sanderson thought you were about the same age and you wanted to be what, romantic? Am I correct?'

'That's what I told her.'

'Another lie.'

'It was our secret…'

'But a lie as well.'

'Yes.'

The chief read Matte's notes. 'Ms. Sanderson did discover your student card and realized you were only fifteen.'

'Yes.'

'At that point you began to tell her about yourself. You wanted her to wait two months till your birthday. You told her you went to Loyola – you told her your mother was a detective – that the condo was hers. Are these facts correct?'

Luke sat rigidly and Damiano could hear him breathing hard. 'Yes, but…'

'The answer is yes, correct.'

Luke nodded, and corrected himself. 'I mean yes.'

'Did you think that Ms. Sanderson was slow, not very intelligent and not as smart as you?'

'No! She was super smart. She was interesting. She knew things I never heard of.'

'She must have known right off she had committed a crime when she found out your age. When she learned that your mother was a detective, she must have been deeply hurt and scared.'

Luke swallowed. He dropped his head and wiped away tears with both hands before he looked up. 'My lies destroyed everything.'

'I have learned that Ms. Sanderson was afraid to go to that tunnel. Did she go because she feared you might tell your mother about her and she'd be arrested?'

'Yes,' Luke wept openly. 'But I never would have told my mother. I loved her – I loved her.'

'Your love was based on lies.'

'Yes.'

'If you loved Ms. Sanderson, why were you late getting to the tunnel?'

'The bus was caught in traffic. I got off and I ran the rest of the way.'

'I don't think I believe you, Luke. If you were so deeply in love and you didn't want to lose Ms. Sanderson, you would have srrived there early and been planning what you wanted to say to convince her not to leave you.'

Luke wiped his nose. He kept his head down. 'I wanted Taylor a little scared so she'd feel she needed me and not walk away.'

'Instead, she was early and she was murdered. She did need you, but you weren't there.'

'Don't you think I know that now?' Luke whispered between nose wipes.

'Speak up for the recorder.'

'I know that now.'

'Did you look for Ms. Sanderson when you finally reached the tunnel, look for this great love of yours?'

Damiano wanted to lash out at Donat, but she saw that he was doing her a kindness, guiding Luke past his threat. She thought of *Hamlet*, "I must be cruel only to be kind." She'd never seen the merits of that line till that day.

'I looked around a bit, but I thought she had decided not to come. Maybe she never intended to. I called her when I was a few blocks away, but she didn't answer.' Luke dropped his head on the table. 'If I had called her at the tunnel, I might have saved her – but I didn't think… I didn't think…. All I did was love her. I didn't want to lose her. I never thought… I never thought I was putting her in danger. And now, and now…' Luke hid his face.

Chief Donat signalled Damiano not to console him. The three adults waited for Luke to compose himself. 'You saw someone else at the tunnel, correct?'

'Yes, I didn't know it was her brother.'

'Did you arrive before he did?'

'I don't know. I was looking for Taylor.'

'You didn't think to ask him if he'd seen a young woman?'

'No, no, I didn't. All I could think of was that Taylor had left me.'

'Did you murder Ms. Sanderson? You've told us a lot of lies, Luke.'

Luke leaned forward shouting, 'NO! NO! I'd never hurt Taylor – I loved her, and I ruined her life. Am I under arrest? I should be under arrest because she died because of me.'

'Not at this time. Not if you have told the truth. May I have our crime unit examine your boots?'

'Yes.'

'That's good. Detective Matte will see to that. I'm giving you a direct order, Luke. You are to attend school and come right home. Do not go anywhere near the funeral service for Ms. Sanderson. Do not attempt to call their home. That is a direct order.'

'But I want to go to Taylor's funeral tomorrow.'

'You are now under police orders not to attend, Luke. If you disobey my orders, you will be picked up and brought back here. Intended or not, you played a role in the death of this young woman who trusted you. Ms. Sanderson did not misrepresent herself to you. You took advantage of her trust. You're not wanted at the funeral. Neither her father, nor her mother, nor her brother, would want you there. You have done enough damage for a fifteen-year-old. Love is our strongest emotion. It's also our most destructive emotion. At fifteen, you have experienced both sides of it. The interview is concluded at 1:27 PM.'

Damiano stayed with Luke as Donat and Matte left. Donat had been kind and she was grateful. She held Luke as he wept with a growing knowledge of the devastation he had caused. 'I really killed her, Mom. All my lies, the tunnel, getting her scared, telling her about you... I never meant...'

'No one ever does, Luke. Let's go home. You heard Chief Donat. You have to stay away from the funeral.'

'I never meant...'

'What you meant doesn't matter anymore, Luke. What matters is the Sandersons are burying their daughter.'

Chapter Forty-nine

Detective Galt had attempted to see Josh Goldman first. Amira Cupid was definite that she could not meet with him until three that afternoon. He expected to find Goldman in a private room in the hospital and that was exactly where he found him. He felt lucky, Goldman was alone. Galt did his slow swagger. He felt it created a friendly approach. 'Josh. I'm still working with Detective Damiano on the Sanderson case.'

'So?'

'First, Detective Damiano wanted to know how you're doing. She helped you out, right?'

'Damn straight. Saved my life.'

'What the hell happened that night?'

'Know what? Those bitches lied about me. Taylor's dead, I know, doesn't change the fact they exaggerated everything. I asked them out, but I never stalked them like they try to pretend.'

'Alright then. What about that night you were injured?'

'You mean the night Amira stabbed me, yeah. I know I had a full head going, but when I saw her come in, I lost it. She told the cops I frightened her. She's one fine liar with her smooth velvety talk. Doesn't fool me. I wanted to tell her face to face that she'd lied about me. I was loud. I admit that, but a fucking knife!'

'True.'

'I could have died!'

'You got lucky. I have one question for you, Josh. Amira admits she ran out after Taylor that night. You've said she came back to the apartment quite a bit later. Was that because you heard her at the door?'

Josh's brow wrinkled in thought. 'I went out to pick up a quick bite and came back to eat the sandwich at my place. I told the cops I stayed in bed, but I was only gone twenty minutes at most. I was awake.'

'That's a small change in your story then. You both went out.'

'Yeah, but like I said, I was back in change – she wasn't.'

Galt let that go. Damiano would want a second bite at him. 'Do you know what time Amira got back?'

'Around eight o'clock, I think. Didn't check the time.'

'Did you see her – like did you open your door?'

'Just a bit, to see if it was Taylor.'

'So you saw Amira.'

'Yeah.'

'Did she have a backpack, do you remember?'

'Never goes anywhere without it.'

'Did it look bulky to you?'

'Ha! So pretty girl is a suspect! It's consistently bulky. She always carries books and what good shit she has with her. Amira has a problem with trust, among many other things.'

'Did she see you?'

'Nah, my light was off but I could still hear.'

'That's it for now. How's the leg?'

'A bitch. They cut the pain meds. They give me Tylenol; does nothing.'

'Good luck with it! By the way, do you wear winter boots?'

'Merrell boots. Why?'

'Routine questioning.'

'Yeah right.'

Goldman had given Galt nothing on Cupid, but he had admitted to being out that Tuesday. He'd just shot down his alibi. He had time to kill Sanderson. Galt had opportunity and motive that he liked to deflect onto Cupid. He'd have Crime check the boot pattern.

Cupid was on time. Galt met her on the street. He had the warrant out, but she didn't ask to see it. Galt followed her into the apartment. The door was still broken. 'What is it exactly that you want, Detective?'

'I have to look, Amira. Have you been painting?'

'I hope that is not a crime, touching up the walls. I am leaving at the end of April. The landlord will inspect the room. Is it my favorite rock you want?'

'We'd like to test the rock for one thing.'

'I found it in a parking lot at the Old Port – the beach just sounded better.'

'Just the same.'

'I have it ready for you.' The bag was by the door.

'You have boots now, I see.'

'From a thrift shop. I have the receipt.'

Galt picked up one of the boots. She'd taken them off at the door. He found no herringbone pattern and replaced it. Amira had tossed the boots she'd worn that Tuesday if she had murdered Sanderson. The question remained, had she? Galt began a methodical search through the apartment. When he found the letters under the sheet on Amira's bed, she yelled out.

'Those are my private letters! You have no right!' She lunged for them, but Galt turned and dropped them into a plastic bag that he'd pulled from his pocket. 'They're evidence.'

Amira stamped her foot. 'You have no right! Thoughts are private. Those letters have nothing to do with Taylor's horrid murder.'

'There is no privacy in a homicide, Amira.'

She was furious. 'If I had money, I would have hidden them in a safety deposit box, safe from curious eyes. I have already informed Detective Damiano that Taylor and I were once lovers. You don't need those letters. They are precious and they belong to me.'

When Galt opened the one kitchen cupboard, Amira ran at him. 'This is my room. Nothing here has anything to do with a murder.' On the top shelf, against the front wall, near the door that made finding it from floor level difficult, was a letter that Galt missed.

Amira relaxed.

Chief Donat signalled for Detective Matte to follow him back to his office and pulled out a chair for Matte as he walked around behind his desk. 'What do you make of Luke Shea?'

'All teenagers are selfish. He was possessive and controlling. The kid thought that was love. Wanting Sanderson frightened so that he could "save" her was misguided. Luke kept their relationship a secret. Revealing his age made meant possible legal implications. Sanderson acted the way she did because she was frightened. That was the "stuff" she threw at Professor Donovan. He…'

'Enough detail, Pierre. Could he have killed the girl? That's what I want to know.'

'Details may seem a bore, Chief, but they become immensely interesting in their totality.'

'Answer the question.'

'No, I don't believe he killed the girl. Matthew Sanderson saw him. Luke was simply looking around for Taylor. Matthew didn't tell us that Luke was agitated. He didn't run, he just walked away.'

'I'm keeping an open mind. Call Damiano. I want to meet with you both today.' The chief was interrupted by a call. Matte rose to leave, but the chief waved him back down. 'Yes, Sir. I can arrange that for four o'clock. I'll have Detective Matte meet you at the front door.' Chief Donat hung up the phone. 'Get Damiano back in here asap. That was Trevor Sanderson and we are to meet with him here at my office. Naturally, he wants an update on the case. He also wants to know how his son figures into our investigation.'

'Are you going to inform him of Luke Shea's connection to Toni?'

'Who else knows about this?'

'There's a problem.'

'Get to the answer, Pierre,' Donat barked.

'Sanderson may have told her brother – the kid keeps doling out new info.'

'*Fils de pute!* Get Damiano back here!'

Chapter Fifty

As they pulled into the garage, Damiano asked Luke if his father had called the school.

'Yes, he said he would.' Luke hadn't said anything on the drive home. As soon as they were inside the house, he made a beeline for his room.

'Luke, hold on a minute.'

He walked into the kitchen like a schoolboy going to detention and dropped onto a chair on the other side of the table. 'I still want to go to Taylor's funeral,' he said sullenly. 'No one will spot me. I have a right to say good-bye.'

'Do you have a hearing problem? Did you not hear Chief Donat?'

'Did you hear me? I don't care if I'm arrested – I don't care about anything anymore.'

Damiano reached across the table and took Luke's wrists. He was about to yank them back. 'Don't, Luke. I'm your mother and I listened very carefully to your answers at the Division.'

'I know the chief was letting me off by not allowing me to say I threatened Taylor – so what! Why don't adults listen? I don't give a fuck what happens to me.'

Damiano's hands held firm. 'Watch your language. I listened alright. Do you hear *me*?'

'Yes, I… I want my phone back. Can't you get it for me?'

'I told you that the phone is evidence in her murder. You won't be getting it back. Remember, you threatened her on that phone too.'

Luke removed his hands, but he didn't leave. 'I loved her!' His voice broke.

'In your own selfish way, Luke, I believe you did. But that's not a great love. You began it with a lie, you deceived us, you snuck into my condo, you kept Taylor all to yourself, and then you threatened her if she left. You ended by having her go to a place that scared her and you hoped her fear would compel her to stay with you. Real love begins with honesty.'

'She fell in love with me too. Don't forget that. You're twisting everything around. I never meant for any of this to happen.'

'But it did happen. Taylor is dead. What have I twisted around, Luke? Tell me!'

'What's the point? I loved her – I wanted to be older – but I wasn't.

I didn't want to lose her. I tried to hang on. That's all. I didn't plan to be such a shit.' Luke didn't bother to wipe his tears away.

Damiano smiled in spite of her disappointment. They both turned when they heard the door. 'We're in here, Jeff.' She turned back to Luke. 'Before I drive back to the office, I want to know that you heard what the chief said about tomorrow's funeral.'

'He said that no member of the family wants me there.'

'Do you understand why, Luke?'

'Maybe, but what about what I need?' he asked with less force.

'You destroyed her life even though you didn't kill her – leave Taylor to the Sandersons who love her without lies. Begin to acknowledge what you did, Luke.' Damiano's phone rang. 'I'm there. I have to go. Jeff, please talk to Luke. Talk to him. You're good with him.'

'I will – I won't just try.'

Damiano sped back to the Division. Something was up. No matter what occurred, Damiano had felt she could communicate with Luke – she understood him. A cloud of devastating depression shrouded her heart. She'd wondered how Sanderson had so misjudged his son. Now she understood. Luke was blind to his actions. All he saw was what he felt he'd lost. He did not even grasp the full tragedy of Sanderson's death. Damiano felt a chill as she drove. Where was Luke's guilt for what he had caused? Whatever grief he felt was for himself. Damiano was struck with the depth of her own failure with Luke, her frequent absences and work distractions. Most pointedly, she thought of her own selfishness for the badge that came first in her life.

Matte and Damiano thought along the same lines. What new information had Matthew Sanderson told his father? Sanderson had never come to the Division. Why now, on the afternoon of the last visitation for his daughter? What story pitch should she offer? If he already knew about Luke and a mother who was a cop or detective, if she'd tried to withhold information Sanderson already knew, she'd face immediate suspension. Allow Sanderson to take the lead and plan her strategy from there. By the time she'd parked and taken the elevator, Matte was already at the front door waiting on Sanderson. Chief Donat was sifting through paperwork, channeling his frustration. When Detective Damiano knocked, though the door was open, he waved her inside. 'You had no clue?'

At least the chief wasn't spewing his litany of swear words. 'No,' she muttered in apology. 'I never thought to connect,' she heard the tremble in her voice. 'He's fifteen years old, Chief.'

'Quite a little hustler!'

Damiano didn't comment. The chief took a call. 'They're on their way up. Are you ready, Detective?'

'I'll follow Sanderson's lead. I want to know what he's discovered before I commit myself.'

Sanderson walked in first. He was dressed in a dark tailored suit with a pale gray shirt and a muted gray tie, the suit he'd wear that night. 'Trevor Sanderson.' He extended his hand to the chief as though the office was his. The office was large enough for the four adults not to feel crowded. The chief had had a file cabinet removed and two good chairs brought to the office. 'I should begin,' Sanderson said with authority, 'because I called for this meeting.' The anger Damiano had witnessed on the first night of their meeting seemed to have dissipated. Sanderson's eyes were darkened by circles. He looked weary. 'What progress have you made in the case, Detective Damiano?'

'We've narrowed the suspect field to three, principally two.'

'Is Matthew one of the two?'

'As soon as an arrest is made, I will inform you, Mr. Sanderson. Beyond that...'

Sanderson thought of the bruise on Matthew's back. He was awake in bed all night thinking of that bruise. He could not be the father who turned in his own son. He could not. 'I have cooperated with you, Detective Damiano, as far as my conscience allows. Do me the courtesy of factual information. Don't insult me with delaying tactics.'

Damiano looked at the chief and turned to Sanderson. 'Matthew is one of the two.'

Sanderson bowed his head and rubbed both his eyes. 'I thought as much. Matthew also told me that Taylor revealed that she had unwittingly fallen for an underage boy. When she discovered the truth, the boy begged her to stay. He said his mother was a cop.'

Chief Donat took over. 'We have more than 1,660...'

'Actually, the boy said, to be specific, his mother was a...' he turned to Damiano.

Damiano finished the sentence. 'His mother was a lieutenant detective.' 'She'd taken a hit discovering she was searching for her own son. She couldn't hide the truth because she couldn't bear to be found out. It was demeaning. The suspension she'd face seemed secondary for the moment.

'My son said he had a good laugh at that before he said he'd help Taylor out. She wasn't laughing. She told him she had been in love and now felt stupid and used.'

'Mr. Sanderson, the boy was my son, Luke. I learned of this relationship one night ago, and I brought Luke in for questioning…'

'You were permitted to question…' Taylor's death had drained Sanderson's shock. He stood looking weary. He hadn't even raised his voice.

'Chief Donat conducted the interview. I was present as a guardian.'

'And you never suspected?' he asked contemptuously.

'Luke was devastated over his first love, but I thought it was some high school girl. Luke is fifteen. I never made the connection – I can't believe I didn't see it. He wouldn't eat; he stayed in his room. I made the mistake of thinking he was a kid and stopped probing when he said he'd follow house rules and return to school. I just never made any connections.'

'Is your son a suspect?'

'Not a principal, as of yet.'

'Why not?'

'Matthew saw Luke at the tunnel. Matthew said the guy just looked around and left. Luke told Chief Donat that he'd called Taylor a few blocks from the site, but she didn't answer. He was pretty certain that she never intended to meet him, that's why she hadn't answered, so he left, heartbroken.'

'Luke and Matthew were about forty to sixty feet from Taylor and not one of them thought to look for her in the tunnel or even call her? They're idiots who might have saved her life! My daughter's tragedy worsens every day. I thought I'd been negligent with my children because I didn't know what was going on in their lives.' His lips turned into a sneer and challenged Damiano. 'Here you are a top detective and you knew nothing of your son!'

Damiano wasn't angry. The scope of her failure engulfed her. 'I have no answers, Mr. Sanderson. You're right. I thought I knew my son.'

'Chief Donat and Detective Matte, may I have a few words with the detective? I want to understand the story, how they met, how my daughter ended up dying. Everything will be off the record. You have my word.'

The chief realized that Damiano wanted to speak with Sanderson alone too. They left the office and closed the door.

'Did you bring a photo of your son?' Sanderson sat back down when the chief left.

Damiano had thought to bring one. She reached for a folder and handed the photo to Sanderson. He studied Luke's face and rested the photo on his knees. 'I can see the attraction,' Sanderson said quietly. 'He doesn't look fifteen; even Matthew thought he was older. How did they meet?'

Damiano told the story as Luke had outlined it for her. Sanderson listened with his eyes on the photo of Luke. 'A simple, harmless lie, "I'm at McGill," set the tragedy in motion.' Damiano continued. Sanderson's face hardened. 'How did you not know about your condo?'

'I was injured nine and a half months ago. I kept it, but I've never been back.'

'No neighbors saw them, or called you?'

'No.'

Damiano explained how she discovered the lovers' nest and finished the sad tale.

'Matthew tells me that Taylor was crying when she called him. He thought she was putting him on. As frightened as she was, Taylor said she'd been in love, for the first time.'

'And it was the same for Luke. He wept when he told me he would never love anyone that much, not ever. That was the one thing he said that I believed.'

'All this emotion was based on his lie.'

'It was. When we got home yesterday, Luke said, apart from not caring if he's arrested or dies, he said, "I wished so hard that I could be twenty-two and not be the shit I was."' 'Were we that selfish at that age?'

'I'm still guilty,' Damiano admitted. 'Luke would never have told me about them.'

'Doesn't matter after the fact. The threat or the fear of it led her to that tunnel. I couldn't comprehend Taylor's cheating at school or her assault on Caitlin Donovan. I felt I didn't know her at all. I understand now. Maybe she was so frightened that she struck out.' Sanderson tore Luke's photo to shreds, slowly and methodically and held the pieces in his fist.

'I am truly sorry, Mr. Sanderson.'

'I'm afraid to go to sleep at night because the morning always comes and with it, I can feel the edges of my memory one day older, one day farther away from Taylor.'

In her mind, Jean Pauzé was falling from her grasp. Damiano flinched. 'I am so sorry.'

'For the next two days, lock your son up, Detective. If I see him tonight or anywhere tomorrow, I won't be responsible. We have so little time left with Taylor. I pray that Matthew is just troubled and guilty and selfish. That he did not… Well, you know.' Sanderson stuffed the pieces in his pocket, rose and walked to the door. 'Way past "sorry," Detective.'

Chief Donat and Detective Matte found Detective Damiano slumped in her chair. They left her in peace.

Chapter Fifty-one

Matte was walking back to Damiano's office when Galt intercepted him. 'Pierre, where's Toni?'

'She'll be here in a minute. She's talking with Trevor Sanderson in the chief's office.'

'I have information.'

'Good. Here she comes.'

Damiano composed herself and appeared to be in control. She made none of her usual wisecracks to the cops' sidelong glances that usually elicited a put-down from her. 'Stephen, any success?'

Damiano closed her door.

'I took Cupid's rock to Crime. The wait period is two days. Marie Dumont told me they have to remove the paint layer by layer from the rock, and there were a few coats. I have love letters that might tell us something, add a stronger motive.'

'Good. Did you manage to see Goldman?'

'I did. He's one angry student. He also admitted lying about his alibi. He did go out that night for a sandwich, he says. He hated both women. You said he knew where Sanderson was heading. When I asked about Cupid's backpack, he said she's never without it, fully loaded. She's worries about being robbed. I'm not even certain Goldman really saw her. His light was off when she apparently returned. Could be *he* was still out.'

'Interesting. Look, tonight, I need you both at the visitation. Sanderson has threatened Luke if he shows up, although Luke is under orders from the chief, and me, to stay away. Jeff will watch him at home. I'll send you both a photo of Luke, just in case. Hold on a minute.' Damiano grabbed her phone. 'What? How, Jeff? Shit!' Damiano hung up quickly. 'Luke slipped out when my husband went to the bathroom. I can't believe it. I'll run off some photos, and we can pass them around to patrolmen there tonight.'

'What are you talking about, Toni?'

'I'll fill you in when we're in the car, Stephen.'

'You're not driving, Toni.'

'Let Stephen drive, then.'

'No, I'll drive.' Matte was not about to be relegated to the back seat.

Damiano was back on the phone with her husband. 'Have you figured out what he's wearing? Dammit! How did he manage that, Jeff? Weren't you with him?'

'Calm down.'

'I won't calm down. Sanderson has threatened to hurt him if he catches sight of him. The chief will have Luke arrested. How calm can I be?'

'He said he didn't feel well and kept making trips to the bathroom. That's when he got dressed and left. I'm calling his friends; they answer, but I get nowhere. He might be with one of them, and they're not being straight with us. Do you want me to drive to the homes of his three best friends? I'm betting he has no plans to be home tonight. He's made up his mind to attend the funeral. I'm sure of that.'

'That's a good idea. Go to his friends. This is serious.'

'I'll do my best.'

'I know this isn't your fault, Jeff. He got by me as well.'

'He's in love, Toni, or what he thinks is love.'

'I'll call if I have news.'

'Me too.'

'Stephen, Pierre can fill you in later. I can't hear Luke's story one more time. I'm ready to shoot the kid myself. He'll try to hide himself in a large group and enter with them. Pierre, I need you to stand outside the family room. I'll do the halls and the other rooms, and Stephen, hand out the photos and scan the groups outside. We have time to set up before the visitation.'

Before Trevor Sanderson arrived home, Shari lay on her side, half drugged with sleep that wouldn't come. Comforting her parents, having them in her home was beyond her strength and will. Although well intentioned, her attempts at counselling her patients would be of little help to anyone. Theories make sense when they applied to others. Locked in the hollowness of own grief, Shari couldn't offer any she actually believed. What Shari wanted, no one could give her. She wanted her daughter. She wanted the world she knew two weeks ago. She did not hear Matthew limp into the room.

'Mom, are you awake?'

'Yes.'

'Do I have to go tonight? My leg is aching. I'll be at the funeral, but I just need a break.'

Shari had her back to Matthew and she didn't move, so Matthew hobbled over to her side. 'Mom?'

'It's two hours, Matthew.'

'Yeah, but it's more like three because there's the drive there and back. Dad doesn't even want me there. It's all for show.'

'Make the effort for Tay and me, then.'

Shari found it hard to look at her son and she kept her eyes closed. 'None of us have been there to comfort each other. It's nobody's fault. It's too painful to think of anyone else.'

Matthew searched for the right words and said awkwardly, 'I didn't hate Taylor, Mom.'

'I'll never see Tay married…'

'Mom, did you hear what I said? I didn't hate her. She was okay, sometimes.'

'Tay will never have a child…'

'Mom? I'm not feeling good. I don't want to go tonight.' Matthew heard his father at the front door, and he skittered back to his room carrying his crutches, hoping his father would leave him alone. Nothing worked for Matthew.

His father didn't knock when he walked into his room. 'Matthew, don't wear the same clothes as last night. I'll see you in ten, then. By the way, the fellow you saw at the tunnel was the boy Tay was seeing.'

Matthew brightened at the exchange. 'He looked nineteen or twenty, Dad.'

'That's what Tay thought. You're not the only teenager to make bad choices. Someone should label adolescence the fumbling years. There will be some influential people present tonight. Your mother needs me. I want you to represent the family and be responsible for greeting people. Will you take charge of that for us, Matthew?'

'Yes, Dad.'

Trevor Sanderson wanted desperately to ask Matthew about the bruise on his back, but he could not bear the answer. He left without another word and went in to see his wife and bent down and kissed her. 'I've learned about the boy Tay was seeing.'

'I can't hear the story – nothing you tell me will bring my baby back. I have one favor to ask of you. Sit with me tonight, Trevor. I don't care about anyone else. Hold my hand or I will pass out.'

'I'll hold you all night, Shari. I won't leave your side. I need you too.'

Sanderson had ordered a limo, and the family appeared somber but more comfortable with one another on the drive to the Mount Royal Funeral Complex. They were also grateful to be driven to the side entrance, avoiding the large crowd that was slowly streaming into the building. Sanderson noticed that Matthew had quickly changed into the best suit he owned. That night he stood to the right of his mother, beside the casket. Patrol officers and the detectives were on alert.

Damiano had positioned herself inside the second room because it was closer to the family. When she spotted the window in the second salon, she walked across the room to see that it was locked. A few seconds later, she joined Matte and whispered something to him. Matte walked into the main room quietly and checked both windows. On her way back, Damiano saw Amira Cupid and quietly intercepted her and guided her back to the second room. Cupid bristled when told she could not make a second visit.

'But I have no invitation to the funeral tomorrow! That is not right.'

'There are eighty seats for university friends. You'll have to get there very early.'

Cupid sat close to Taylor's photo and kept her eyes on it, ignoring Damiano as she left.

Damiano stood quietly as the Who's Who of Montreal arrived to pay their respects: the mayors of Montreal and Westmount, city councillors, the CEO of the McGill University Health Center, presidents and deans of Concordia and McGill universities, and the heads of many of the city's exclusive clubs, including the Saint James, Forest and Stream, and the Royal Montreal Golf Club. Matthew surprised his father. He stepped forward and shook hands with each and every mourner. The entire room was immersed in a respectful silence. Those present rested a hand on Trevor's shoulder, and each touch conveyed what words could not. *We mourn your loss – we are with you.* In the second hour, Shari lay her head on Trevor's shoulder, and he put his arm around her waist and held her up, for she had collapsed very quietly. Sanderson was surprised that she felt like a warm feather on his shoulder. The only firmness in her body was Trevor's hand, which she gripped tightly.

With no sightings of Luke, Damiano felt some relief. She summoned Matte and Galt. 'I don't think Luke intends to come tonight. Luke knows you, Pierre. He's also aware that I'm here. He wouldn't take the chance of being caught tonight. I think he's laying low. Would both of you read Cupid's letters? I'll still keep on looking out for him anyway.' She called Jeff. He had had no luck in his search for Luke. 'His plan is the funeral tomorrow. He's my son and he's as stubborn as I am. He will be at Notre-Dame-de-Bon-Secours tomorrow without fail. You have to get to him first, Toni. I'm thinking of Luke and the Sandersons and what might happen.'

'I'll find Luke, Jeff. I'm still trying to come to grips with the grief he's already caused.'

In fact, Luke was already at the church in Old Montreal. He'd walked in with tourists and had been clever enough to find a bathroom at the back of the church. When the tourists left at six in the evening, he'd hidden until the church was locked up. He had his water bottle. Until darkness fell, he took full advantage of the majestic view of the Saint Lawrence River. He felt close to Taylor. He chose the darkest corner, curled up and fell asleep, locked in his own box, as she was in hers.

Chapter Fifty-two

[April 13]

The sun took most Montrealers by surprise. Its brightness swept across the city, illuminating the east side of Notre-Dame-de-Bon-Secours Chapel, the historic jewel of Montreal also known as the Sailors' Church. The sun's warmth seeped through the stained glass windows of the church. It woke Luke Shea who had no time for the two cameo paintings of Paul Chomedey de Maisonneuve, founder of Montreal or Marguerite Bourgeois, the first teacher and founder of the Congrégation de Notre-Dame. He needed the bathroom and a new place to hide. Panic had struck. Where could he hide now?

Police patrols were on duty as students gathered in front of the church before nine in the morning. The three detectives arrived at nine-thirty. Rue Saint-Paul in Old Montreal was cobble-stoned and narrow. The police foresaw a massive traffic jam and kept the early traffic moving. West and east, streets would be closed off at ten thirty.

Luke moved to the choir loft and waited. A loud knock on the red wooden doors at the front of the church startled him. The choir had arrived with seven altar boys trailing behind them. Luke flew down the stairs, dropping a broom he had picked up for protection. While the older priest was ushering the members of the choir to the loft, Luke took the initiative. He offered seventy dollars to anyone who would let him take their place in the coming ceremony. The boys looked at one another. 'She was my cousin,' Luke threw into the mix, and 'I'd like to carry the cross.' Luke felt he could hide behind the cross.

'Ninety.'

Luke was prepared for that and fished out a twenty. The deal was made. The altar boy left with his money, and Luke joined the six boys. He was grateful he wasn't the tallest. Luke had learned from a movie that hiding in plain sight was supposed to work. No one spoke to him as they followed the priest to the vestry to change. Pleased that there was a bathroom, he washed his face and did his best to part his unruly curls dead-center. It did give him a different look. He met with a few stares from the boys, but no one said anything. He sat and waited and listened to the instructions from two priests who appeared. Luke was not a neophyte.

He had served mass when he was eight and nine. He had only to listen and wait.

Men from the funeral complex wearing white gloves positioned themselves at the main doors of the church. Detective Damiano spoke to them and gave each a photo. Behind her a student crowd was growing. Luke could be anywhere among them. At least the front door had not been officially opened. Fifteen minutes later, it was. The narrow street was soon clogged with limos. No one without an invitation was permitted to enter the church. Damiano walked among the students, trying to outthink Luke. Where would he hide? *He's here; I know it.*

Detective Matte found her. 'I can't see him and I've scanned the crowd, believe me.'

'Luke is here somewhere. He could be waiting near one of the doors to sneak inside with the few kids who had invitations. He might have arranged for a friend to signal when the time is right.'

'He's that cunning?'

'He's that desperate.'

Twenty minutes later, determined students still jostled one another for a chance to get inside the church. The funeral complex people were as resolute and barred all attempts.. Damiano and Matte stood dumfounded outside the door on either side. Damiano asked one of the men if they were going to close the doors, once everyone was seated. The answer was no. The day had warmed; the packed church needed air. Fine, Matte and she wouldn't leave the front door. 'Galt?'

'He's still out there.'

Damiano brought Galt up to speed and told him not to phone, but to text her if he found Luke. She and Matte scarcely noticed the dignitaries and the beauty of the historic church. Both remained outside the church and drew long breaths when the hearse arrived with the family following behind it. Damiano couldn't watch, but Matte followed the casket covered with a blanket of pink roses as it was lowered onto a rolling gurney and wheeled to to the main entrance of the church. Trevor stood between his wife and Matthew, with their parents behind them.

A procession of the cross bearer, six altar boys and the officiating priest joined them. One of the pallbearers removed the roses. The priest laid the pall across the casket. The roses were replaced, and the priest laid a crucifix on top of the casket, said prayers and together they welcomed Taylor into the heart of the church. All the altar boys piously kept their eyes lowered in respect. The procession turned and walked slowly down the aisle to the altar. The organist began to play Mendelssohn's Funeral

March. The music filled the air as the sun sent laser flashes of light into the church. There was no coughing, no movement but the music.

The mass began and the choir sang Bach's 'Bist du bei mir,' and tears fell. Shari was remote in her sadness but heard the music she had chosen. Matthew was as quiet as one of the famed historic statues in the chapel. Trevor was distinguished and somber in a tailored pin-striped suit and white shirt. He kept his eyes on the casket. Everything else faded away from him. When communion was received and the mass ended, he rose from his pew, kissed the casket, walked to the pulpit and raised the microphone. He smiled down at his daughter and spoke without notes. 'In my life, I have been fortunate and have received many accolades. No one prepares you for the miracle of birth. No reward, no achievement comes close to it. When I saw this little bundle of life lying on Shari's chest I knew I was seeing a miracle. When the infant was offered to me, this flower rested on my chest and I felt the flutter of her heart, her tiny hand clutching my thumb, and the tickle of her breath. There is no moment in life to equal this joy – innocence, purity, a jewel of perfection. We promise to protect them – to guide them – to love them. I was surprised to know immediately that I would die for this little fluttering heart. I had that capacity...'

Trevor bowed his head and tried to compose himself. 'But they grow up, they fly away, in and out of our lives, and we watch, worried, but astounded. At times, Taylor's energy tired me, but it brought me back to thoughts of my youth. I marvelled at hers, the wonder of it, the promise and the hope.' Trevor wavered. 'I have learned that love played a part in Taylor's death – I have found some comfort there.'

Listening to Taylor's father's words, Luke pursed his lips, trying to stem his tears. He did not move his head as he sat in the pew at the side of the altar. When he heard the word 'love,' tears streamed down his cheek. He bowed his head. His love had taken Taylor's life. Her funeral brought him face-to-face with the misery of that truth. His curls unfurled and fell on his forehead. The cross offered him no shelter.

'No one prepares a parent for the loss of a child, my little girl. The searing, shocking pain is matched only by the joy of her birth. Taylor was always afraid of the dark. The sun shone for her today. I used to carry her outside at night when she was an infant and point to the stars. She grew to love them and learned their names. No one prepared me to lose the light of my life. Taylor, today, you have the sun, its first appearance in nine days. Tonight, you have the stars to light your way into eternity.'

Trevor gripped the pulpit to steady himself. As he turned to return to his seat, one of the altar boys caught his attention. A weeping Luke did not see him. Trevor instantly knew the identity of the server, but he did not waiver, and walked unsteadily back down the steps, kissed his daughter one last time and joined his family. Matthew sat very still, dry-eyed. Along with the mourners, Detective Damiano, standing by the front door was not untouched by Trevor Sanderson's eulogy. With a cop's eye she'd seen him glance over to where the altar servers were sitting and saw her son. Luke had outwitted her but she rejoiced that he was still alive. When the mass ended, the altar boys and the priests positioned themselves behind the casket. The priest circled the casket with incense and blessed it with holy water. The pallbearers turned the casket to leave the church. Luke walked first with the cross trying as hard as he could to hide his face behind the cross. Sanderson was aware how close Luke was to him, but his only interest was his daughter. As the procession walked down the aisle, the choir sang, 'Be Not Afraid.' Sanderson, Shari and Matthew kept their eyes on the casket. At the back of the church, the roses and pall were removed, the roses replaced and the casket blessed one last time. The crucifix remained on the casket. Later, at the funeral complex, the priest would offer a final commendation; a funeral director would remove the crucifix and hand it to the priest to be blessed and then offer the crucifix to Trevor Sanderson.

But at that moment, Damiano manoeuvered around the back of the church and followed the procession towards the front door and took hold of Luke's arm before they descended the stairs to the street. He handed the cross to another altar boy and stood quietly beside his mother. She caught Sanderson's eye but he looked away. She and Matte led Luke back into the church, off to the side.

'Mom, I loved Taylor with my whole heart. You can arrest me later. That's what I want anyway. I have to pay for what I did.'

'Detective Matte will take you back to Division and I will follow you, Luke. I know you loved her, Luke, but I am still a police officer. The chief will decide what's best. As far as paying for what you did, son, it may take a very long time for reconciliation. You're just beginning to perceive the scope of this tragedy.' Damiano left Luke with Matte. She walked quickly from the church and saw that Sanderson was standing with Shari and Matthew as the casket was lifted into the hearse. She hurried by the mourners until she was directly behind him.

'Mr. Sanderson, we tried our best, I'm sorry, Luke was…'

When he turned, he stepped away from the family. The last nine days had aged Sanderson. 'I believe you,' he said, with no hint of accusation. 'It was oddly comforting to see that your son wept for Taylor, that he loved her.' Sanderson walked back to his family, waiting in the black limousine.

Chapter Fifty-Three

D amiano and Matte left Luke alone sitting in the back of the car. 'What do I do with him, Pierre? Sanderson actually told me that seeing Luke's concern for his daughter was some comfort to him. Do we take him to the chief?'

'You're lead. There's been enough deception. Let's take him with us and let the chief decide how to proceed. Luke has to answer to him.'

Galt spotted them and hurried over and stopped dead. 'Where was he? Where the hell was he?'

'Never mind,' Damiano said. 'Any other news?'

'While I was out patrolling, I called the Goldman home. I figure you want to see him. His father told me he's planning to take his son to the Cayman Islands for further rest and a holiday.'

'Oh no, he's not. You said his alibi got flushed. Of course, I have to question him. Let's go. Pierre will drive. You have the number?'

'Yep. I also took photos of the dépanneurs and any other convenience joints down St-Marc and St-Mathieu Streets. Goldman said he bought a sandwich from one of them. He'll tell us he doesn't remember which one, but he'll have to choose from one of the photos. I can take his photo from FB and do some footwork.'

'That's good thinking.' Damiano made the call, asking to speak to Josh.

'He's resting, Detective.'

'That's good to hear. Unfortunately, I have more questions for him.'

'Well, that might…'

'I also heard about the vacation. This is a homicide investigation. Josh is a suspect. He can't go anywhere until I'm satisfied with his answers. How about five tonight?'

'I don't think I have a choice.'

'See you at five then.'

'Stephen, tell me you have his address.'

'I do, boss.'

'Pierre, will you rustle up some food, enough for our suspect as well? As soon as we reach the Division, I'm taking Luke to see the chief.'

'I'll canvass as many of the stores as I can,' Galt said a second time, reminding them he was a partner.

As soon as they had parked in the Division's lot, Damiano marched Luke up and over to Chief Donat's office. 'Wait out here, Luke.' Luke heard the chief swear more than once as Damiano explained. 'Didn't you think of checking the church? Never mind – it's clear you didn't.'

The chief opened the door and gave Luke a nasty wave into the office. 'Don't you dare sit down. I want you standing. Did you hear my order?'

'Yes, Chief Donat.'

'You went right ahead and disobeyed it.'

'Yes, Chief.'

'I'll have an officer drive you down to Place Versailles, headquarters for major crimes. You can cool your heels in a holding cell.'

Damiano knew enough not to interrupt.

'I'm arrested then?'

'In a manner of speaking – you are detained.'

'Mom?'

'Chief, may Luke have something to eat before he goes? He's been a day and a half without food.'

'Get him something in the vending machine, Detective. You willfully disobeyed my orders! I don't take that lightly, son. I want you to stand up against that wall till Detective Damiano's back with something to eat.'

Damiano gave the vending machine two swift kicks. She returned with three packages of peanuts, a coke, two water bottles and an old apple she found in her locker. She made a quick call to Jeff.

'It's harsh, but Luke might benefit from this experience. I don't know. I feel for him.'

'It's not up to me, Jeff.'

'I know.'

Chief Donat stood in the hall waiting for Damiano. Luke drained a water bottle in a single gulp.

'Chief, I'll call Detective Marchand and tell him I'll handle the paper-work.'

'Toni, there won't be any. You can pick him up at ten tonight – I'm doing you a good turn. Luke contravened my direct orders – love or no love. Beware of Romeo, Detective, he definitely has your markings.' The chief gave Damiano a thin smile.

'I was afraid of that, Chief. Thank you.'

'Get back to work.'

'I have an interview tonight.'

'Don't waste your time here then. Go and prep. The funeral's over. We need to close.'

The three detectives ate quickly. Galt inhaled Luke's peanuts. 'Do you think Goldman's good for this murder, Pierre or Stephen? Have I been looking at the wrong people?'

'Goldman's a short, angry guy who hated both women. He's trying his best to point me toward Cupid, but he was out that day as well,' Galt said.

'If we can find the dépanneurs where he bought his sandwich, we'll push him back a slot. Stephen, I'll keep you in the loop.'

As Matte and she drove north on Cote-des-Neiges to Granville Street in Hampstead, Damiano was irritable and tired. 'Are we wasting our time, Pierre?'

'I don't know. We're thinking Cupid or Sanderson. What if we're wrong? We can't take that chance and let this kid leave for a vacation. There it is, the place with the circular driveway.'

The large, white two-storey house had a wide stone balcony and was built on a corner lot. When Matte rang the front bell, a wave of weariness engulfed Damiano. She felt she was back where they'd started with nothing to show for their efforts. She was relieved that Josh Goldman opened the door. She wasn't up for another parent.

'Detectives, come on in. My father said we could use the dining room.'

The courteous approach, Damiano observed, was for his parents who were standing by a fireplace to their left. Surprisingly they didn't say a word. Damiano expected to meet a lawyer in the dining room, but found they'd be alone. Goldman sat at the head of the table, and they had no other choice but to sit on either side of him. Matte took out his notes and recorder.

'Josh, I'd like to work this interview smoothly. It's been a difficult day.'

'Right, I thought of going to the funeral, but I didn't want to be a hypocrite.'

The introductions for the recorder were made with names, times and date. Damiano began the questioning. 'Josh, you've admitted you went out that Tuesday night, correct?'

'Briefly, yes.'

'For a sandwich?'

'Yes, and a drink.'

'You're an intelligent young man. You do understand you've declared your animosity towards Taylor Sanderson. You also knew where she was going that Tuesday. That's motive and opportunity. As we speak, Detective Galt is canvassing the dépanneurs on St-Marc and St-Mathieu. He has your photo with him. Now, you did lie about that night the first time we questioned you. If you are not truthful tonight, I will arrest you on suspicion of murder. Am I clear? I want to be very, very clear, Josh.'

Silence. Goldman tensed and rubbed his face with his hands. When his father appeared at the door, Matte stood up immediately. 'Mr. Goldman, you cannot be present. Your son is an adult. Please leave, or we'll take Josh to the Division and question him there.'

His father backed off, but said forcefully, 'I was not given to understand the seriousness of this questioning. I would have had Josh represented. You have my son at a disadvantage.'

Matte walked Goldman back to the living room and returned and sat. Perspiration glistened on Goldman's forehead and chin. 'I lied.'

'Speak up for the recorder.'

'I didn't buy a sandwich.'

'You ran after Taylor Sanderson.'

'I was curious, that's all.'

'And?'

'I run pretty fast. 'I saw her in that blue jacket on Ste-Catherine Street.'

'And?'

'I was going to tell her I'd go with her. That's the truth. She did seem scared.'

'Josh – spit it out!'

'I stopped.'

'Why?'

'Cupid was closer to her than I was.'

'Did you see them actually join up?'

'No. I knew Cupid would be with Taylor in a matter of seconds, so I left.'

'Why didn't you tell us this the first time around?'

Josh ran his hands over the smooth wood of the table.

'Josh? If you don't answer, I'm taking you down to the station.'

Josh rapped his fingers on the table. 'After what happened to Taylor, and seeing Amira almost meeting up with her that day, I thought I could…'

'Use that knowledge to get into Cupid's pants!'

Josh kept his eyes down. 'Something like that.'

'That's what you wanted when you kicked in her door. Had you succeeded you would have raped her.'

'No! Not rape. I just wanted her to stop lying about me. She owed me. I didn't rat on her.'

'Josh, you'll have time to think all this out. I'm arresting you for obstruction of justice. I'll advise your father to engage a lawyer. Detective Matte will take you to the car.'

'This is ridiculous. I didn't kill anyone! I didn't rape anyone either. *I* was stabbed. You're wasting taxpayers' time. My father won't let me spend a minute in a cell! Dad? Dad, get me help!'

Detective Matte placed Goldman in the back seat of their city car. Damiano felt a buzz of satisfaction seeing Goldman sitting small in the car. As they stood behind the car Damiano spoke. 'Have you figured it out, Pierre?'

'I never predict till I write up the last note in the murder book. And you?'

'Still wavering.'

Chapter Fifty-four

Far from a sense of closure, funerals cast a pall; for a few days we are gentler, reflecting on our own mortality. The untimely death of the young rattles our hearts. The Donovans went out for brunch together, but their conversatin was quiet and reserved weighed down by the loss of their son and brother. 'I will call Shari. I never thought I would use our tragedy to help a friend.'

'Shari will feel a kinship with you, Maggie. You'll create a lasting bond that she'll never forget. You know that we ran from one another, stumbling around in our grief. You'll be there with her to help keep the family together.'

'I wonder why we recognize needs when it's often too late.' Caitlin asked.

'You were face to face with moral responsibility, fairness if you will. Taylor was angry and cruel to you. There wasn't much room for you to offer help. She was unintentionally blocking you.'

'I should have been more human – I was playing the role of her professor.'

'That's what you were, not a guidance counsellor.'

'Hindsight's just a horrid tease and a waste of thought.'

'Or a reminder that there was a better way of acting,' Frank added.

Detective Matte was bone-tired when he drove home. He had no answers for the case and that was unusual for him. Doubt ate away at pride in his work. That he had missed the possibility, the most obvious possibility, that Luke would hide in the church irritated him. The slip demonstrated a lack of focus. He found Dylan leaning against the front door of the condo. In the darkness, he looked young and beautiful.

'I lost the editing job. I was late with my work. The editor just said thanks for what I'd done and wished me better luck in the future. The joke of it is that editors I've known in the past are rarely on time themselves. This fellow is the exception. I didn't see it coming.'

'Huh,' Matte smiled and rubbed the back of his neck. 'It didn't take this editor long to read you, Dylan.'

Dylan ignored criticism of any kind. 'Is there a chance of a warm bed tonight?'

'I'm wasted. I need some time to think and sleep.'

'Last chance!'

Damiano's words echoed in his head. 'I think we've had our share. I have to go.' Matte left Dylan at the door. He was forty-two years old, too old for high maintenance. Matte had to think – he was good at details.

Detective Damiano drove to Place Versailles on Sherbrooke Street East. The Major Crimes building was attached to a larger mall and stood at the west end of it. She was buzzed up by the detective on call, Denis Pichette. 'Where is the truant?'

'Trying his best to sleep on the steel mattress. He's been quiet. I'll go get him.'

'I'll go with you.'

Damiano peered through the tiny window high up on the door and saw Luke rolling from one side to another and mumbling words she couldn't hear. He scrambled off the bed and nearly fell, blinded by the bright fluorescent lights Pichette had turned on. 'Okay, Luke, let's go home.'

Luke said nothing but he followed his mother.

'Easy 'spect, no shoe laces, no belt,' Pichette said to Damiano.

'And no pillow,' Luke added sullenly.

Jeff was waiting for them at the door. 'Look Mom and Dad, I stink. All I want is a shower. I have nothing to say. I had to be at the church.'

'What about pancakes and sausages?' Jeff asked.

Luke had his 'no' on the way when it was interrupted by a 'maybe.'

The front door was still broken when Amira Cupid arrived at her apartment. She showered and packed up the room. She was prepared for her last exam on Friday. The police would have to wait until after the exam. . Her painted rock was being examined. The police were not finished with her. Montreal seemed to have offered her not only an education but a new life in the city of tolerance. Offended that she had not received an invitation to the visitation, Amira was more deeply wounded when she was again forgotten at the funeral. Despite telling an usher that she was a close friend of the deceased she had to stand outside the church during the service. Outside, hidden and dismissed from Taylor's life, that was her place. Amira had no regrets for her actions. She reached into the kitchen cupboard and took the letter. She sat down and reread it.

The Sandersons and their in-laws returned to Summit Crescent. They walked in a silent file into the living room, locked in their own thoughts

and sat like ghosts until Dorothy Tellett, Shari's mother stood and spoke.
'Do you have enough food in the house, Trevor?'

'You know your daughter, Dorothy. We can last for a month with the two packed freezers downstairs.'

'That's good to know. I'd like to take Shari home with me for a few days. I'm her mother. I know I can get her to eat and rest. I'm very much afraid for her.'

Sanderson was about to protest.

'We're not far. She'll only be a half hour away. I know what's best right now, Trevor. This house, with all its memories, is not a good place for Shari. Trust me.'

'Shari?' Trevor entreated, hoping she'd stay.

Lost, Shari looked from her mother to her husband.

'Maybe it's for the best. I'll go up and pack some things.'

Even when she left with her parents, Shari had nothing to say.

Trevor and Matthew were alone. Matthew shifted uneasily on the sofa.

'Well, Matthew, we finally have some much-needed time alone, together.'

Chapter Fifty-five

[April 14, 9:00 a.m.]

Friday morning, the sun made an early appearance but disappeared behind low-lying clouds. Damiano was showered and dressed, talking with Jeff at the kitchen table. They'd decided Luke would go back to school on Monday.

'The condo's been on my mind, Toni.'

Damiano's phone rang, and she gave Jeff a *what can I do?* gesture and picked it up from the table beside her cup of coffee. 'Finally, I thought you had forgotten us, Marie.'

'Try working with rain and bacterial contamination, and overtime, I might add. Even the US lab couldn't make a five-point match.'

'Thanks for the hard work. I do appreciate it, Marie.'

Jeff was waiting to continue the condo discussion, but Damiano's phone rang again. This time, Jeff gave up what small leverage he'd had. He brought the mugs to the sink, rinsed them and left the room. Damiano covered her ear with hand so she could hear.

'Detective Damiano, are you there?'

'Yes, Ms. Cupid. It's quieter now. Go ahead.'

'Josh Goldman called. I was frightened. I thought he might have come back to the condo, and my door is still not repaired. I was about to make a run for it when he laughed and told me he was still at home. The police wanted to see me, he said. He wanted to unsettle me with his news and he did. I know you wish to speak with me,' Cupid said, reaching out awkwardly. 'I write my final exam in a few minutes. I implore you to allow me to finish it. It's been a long year of study. I will be free at eleven o'clock.'

'Where is the exam room?'

Cupid readily gave Damiano the information. 'This exam is extremely important to me. I will be true to my word. It is time to talk to you.'

Damiano's head was dizzy with all the lies she'd heard. 'Fine. We will be waiting outside your classroom.' She called Matte. They alerted Concordia Security and had an officer sent to the exam room to wait for them and to ascertain that Cupid was indeed there. Damiano was out the door before Jeff could say another word. 'This could be it!' She shouted back at him. Damiano and Matte drove down to Concordia in their own cars to save time.

Five minutes into her reckless drive to the university, Security called, assuring her that Cupid was in the first row, second seat. Damiano took a lungful of air and exhaled loudly. *All I needed on the case is a runner!* At Concordia she had no choice but to double-park, blocking a Honda and part of a Lexus SUV. She left her card on the dash and ran up the escalator to the third floor. Security was easy to spot and she hurried to a fiftyish stocky grump who surprised her with a warm smile. 'Thanks for this. You've been a big help and I need you again.' She told 'Alex,' whose name was written on his pocket, where she'd double-parked, handed him twenty bucks and asked if he could move her car to a better spot and call her with its location. With a quick peek at her phone, she saw they had over an hour to wait.

Matte arrived ten minutes later. 'Where did you park?'

'Had no problem.'

'How so?'

'Alex the security guard.'

'Figures.'

'When did a perp ever call us to take him in?'

'Never.'

'I'm only half-buzzed. I need something…'

'Don't go there. Toni. Stay in the moment. She called us – she wants to talk.'

The hour passed relatively quickly. The detectives stood by the door and decided not to use cuffs. Fifteen minutes later, true to her word, Matte guided Cupid to his car because it would better accommodate her height. Cupid sat up in the car like an African goddess, Matte thought as he glanced back at her in his rear view mirror from time to time on their way to the Division. Once there, the detectives wasted no time setting up the interview in the claustrophobic 'box' set up with cameras and hidden recorders. Matte sat in the video booth noting Cupid's body language. Damiano made the formal introductions before she began the interview. The small room was an awkward fit for the two tall women. 'Ms. Cupid, we know now that you did go to the derelict Wellington Tunnel with Taylor Sanderson. Why did you change your mind and accompany Ms. Sanderson to the tunnel?'

Cupid's beautiful face creased. 'I know that one never gets back what was lost, but I loved Taylor. She was really scared. I wanted to be friends again at least, perhaps even more. I had hoped, I suppose, because she said she needed me.'

'Did you talk along the way?'

'She confided in me about the boy who had lied about his age. She truly thought she might be arrested for statutory rape if he told the police. She was crying, almost hysterical. My hope grew that I still mattered. I had never seen Taylor frightened of anything.'

'What happened when you reached the tunnel? Were you alone?'

'Yes. We were quite alone.' Cupid tensed and began to tremble.

'What happened, Ms. Cupid?'

'Taylor said if she got through the breakup, if the boy accepted it, she was going to call Andrew and tell him that her dinner invitation was real, and not some joke.'

Damiano could sense where this was going.

Cupid's voice rose. 'Taylor had betrayed me yet again. I meant nothing to her – *I* was not the one she invited for dinner! I was to be used by her again. I was simply an interlude, for her messages and for that infernal tunnel. Taylor betrayed me on every level.' Cupid rose, glaring at Damiano.

Damiano clenched a fist under the table, and watched Cupid closely. 'What did you do, Amira?' she whispered.

Cupid was startled at the mention of her name. 'I wanted to slap Taylor's face right then and there, but I remembered shivering in the bus shelter and my loneliness as she drove by ignoring me. I looked squarely at Taylor, waved in her face and then I ran. She called after me, begging me to come back, but I kept running, from her and the misery she had brought into my life. I did not hurt Taylor – I just abandoned her as she had me. Do not bunch me in with your common murderers, Detective.'

Damiano fought her own control and disappointment. 'Did you not look back, Amira? You knew how frightened she was.'

'At that moment I felt no love for her at all. I never wanted to see her again. I tried to leave, but love is not so easy to sever. I stood by the road across from the tunnel and watched. Taylor was pacing and crying, I think.'

'Did you leave then?'

'I waited, tempted to return.'

'Then?'

'A man appeared from the far side of the tunnel. He stopped about forty feet from Taylor. I thought it was her young lover. He was the only one speaking. I just assumed he was pleading with her to be forgiven because Taylor always got what she wanted. He stood and threw his head back. I wasn't close enough to hear their exchange or tell if he was crying or laughing.'

'And?'

'Taylor ran at him and pushed him to the ground. She left him there and walked off. I couldn't see clearly because of the trees, but it appeared he got up with difficulty.'

'Amira, please go on.'

'She never once looked back at him. It seemed seconds later. It couldn't have been more then a few seconds. Taylor crumpled to the ground. Just collapsed. The man hurried over to her...'

'And?'

'I ran away as quickly as I could.'

'Why didn't you go back and try to help her?'

'I did not want to be involved. The man was kneeling with her. No. I had to think of myself.' Cupid's eyes glazed with tears. 'My life counts too.' Cupid began to cry.

'Could you make out who the man was?'

'He was too far away.'

'Could it have been Josh?'

'No, he was much taller, but he looked young.'

'Why didn't you tell us the truth when we first spoke with you, Ms. Cupid?'

'From the beginning you thought I had murdered Taylor, didn't you? I am a black woman and this is not my country. Josh Goldman attacked me. Was he arrested for that? He shattered the door to my apartment. Was it repaired by the landlord? Taylor's family did not even know my name. Am I to be arrested because I left Taylor to deal with her own problem?' Cupid reached into her bag and produced a letter. 'It is the one note Taylor wrote to me, telling me she cared. It is too personal to read aloud. It belongs to me. Detective Galt did not find my hiding place for it.'

'Wait here, please.' Damiano did not care about the letter at that late juncture.

Damiano and Matte met outside the soundproof room. 'I'll have a car to take Cupid back,' Matte said, taking out his phone.

'What the hell just happened?' Damiano swore. Her face was flushed.

Chapter Fifty-six

[April 14, 9:00 a.m.]

Trevor Sanderson hadn't slept. His muscles ached and his eyes were bloodshot. He stood under a blistering hot shower spray before switching to ice-cold water and turning his face to meet its stinging relief. Towelling off was work. His legs were heavy and slow. The last three days had been a passion play of unrelenting grief. Sanderson had read Shakespeare when he was a serious young man. The bard had been right once again. After the heraldic obsequies of death, what remained was air and *Amen*.

He dressed, called his office and phoned his mother-in-law to ask about Shari. Dorothy didn't want to disturb her daughter because she'd just then fallen asleep. Sanderson envied her that sleep. He thought of the day ahead of him and he wavered. Where did loyalties lie? To the daughter he'd lost, or to a son he didn't trust? He found no answer. At four, he'd attend the cremation of his daughter alone. He would be her witness. He would shed tears for Taylor and he would remember her, and like *Laertes*, demand more ritual. *Amen* was not enough. To whom did he owe his loyalty? He wondered, agonized. When does one turn from the dead without betrayal?

He made a strong cup of coffee with the DeLonghi coffee maker. He grabbed a large plastic garbage bag from a kitchen drawer and brought it to Matthew. His boy was awake. 'Here, Matthew, let me cover your cast so you can shower. Do you need help?'

Matthew was rubbing his eyes and stretching. He looked so young, Sanderson thought.

'Nah, I'm okay, Dad.'

'What would you like to eat?'

Matthew sat up with interest. 'Really?'

'Absolutely.'

'A grilled cheese sandwich, like the ones you used to make when I was young, remember?'

'With that old black iron that I hid from Mom, I remember. How many?'

'Three, and let the cheese drip over the side. That's the best part.'

'Done. Cheese?'

'Sharp cheddar. And Dad, chocolate milk.'

'If I can't find that milk?'

'Regular's good.'

'Get yourself up and shower. I'll begin our breakfast.'

'What about school, Dad?'

'Monday.'

Sanderson tried to recall the last time he'd seen Matthew smile. He tousled his hair and left.

The smell of familiar food warmed Sanderson's spirit. His great-grandfather had owned that iron and braved the wrath of his wife when he'd made toast. Sanderson could soon see why. He was ruining one of Shari's frying pans and would have to hide it. The toasting bread and burning oozing cheese scarring the pan was adding to the mess. The kitchen smelled good overlaid with nostalgia. He wanted Matthew to remember their breakfast together.

Matthew made good time, as most hungry kids do. He was sitting at the table drinking chocolate milk that left a line on his upper lip. Sanderson served up the hot grilled cheese and set one down for himself and sat across from Matthew. 'You did a fine job at the visitation. I was proud of you, Matthew.'

'And the funeral?'

'Son, I was thinking of Tay and the life she's lost. I had such hopes.'

'All that great stuff you said about her…' Matthew had scarfed one sandwich. 'Did you feel that way about me when I was born?'

'Your mother and I both did.'

'Not as much, right?'

'It's just different, son. One can never repeat a first, like your first bike, or your first kiss.'

'I was your first son, though.'

'Certainly there was that. You're right.'

Matthew made short work of the second grilled cheese and poured himself more milk. He tore the third sandwich into irregular pieces, pulling the cheese apart. 'Dad?'

'Yes, son.'

Matthew's face bore a miserable expression. He took off his glasses. 'Why didn't you ever love me as much as you loved Tay? I never got that. I was your son! She was a girl.'

Sanderson felt his throat dry. Unwelcome truths diminished both concerned. 'I do love you, son, but the truth is that some children are easier to love than others. It's not something a parent plans. We're human and imperfect. Mom took to you because she saw herself in you. Life's like that. I guess I saw something of me in Tay.'

'You never once took my side from the time I was a small kid,' Matthew complained.

'What do you mean?'

'You and Mom knew that Taylor bullied me. She began when I was three. Why didn't you punish her, stand up for me, Dad?' Matthew's voice rose. 'I was a kid and I couldn't defend myself.'

'I thought you'd get up one day and give her a good smack.'

'Tay was five years older than me, Dad. She really hurt me at times, and you thought it was funny.'

'Matthew, you're exaggerating. I don't remember many times.'

Matthew began to shake with rage. 'You were never fair to me, Dad. You're not being fair right now. Anyways, you're always busy. That's what I remember of you.'

'I'm forty-four years old, son. When you were young I was twenty-seven, just out of law school, trying to support a family of four. I didn't have time for myself back then.'

'For once, be truthful. You don't much like me. I'm a nerd. The only thing I have going for me are good grades.'

'Are you edging for a fight, son? No one has it easy in life. Look around you. Be a man.'

'I saw you with that kid who had no jacket. You liked him – it showed.'

'Yes, I liked him because at fourteen, he owned up to his mistake. He was brave enough to admit his mistake and regret it.'

'I don't want the rest of this sandwich.'

'Son, it's time.'

'For what?' Matthew shouted, grabbing his glasses. He pushed his chair back against the wall, expecting a beating.

Sanderson's breaths were shallow and his heart beat wildly, like Matthew's. He'd hoped he'd feel resigned, but he wasn't. He was furious.

'When did you know?' Matthew backed further against the wall.

'It took some time to get my head around it. When I spotted the large bruise on your back, I began to wonder.'

'But you didn't know then?'

'No. I watched you at the visitation. You never shed a single tear, Matthew, not one that I ever saw. You frighten me. I don't believe you care for anyone but yourself. I've watched you closely and I see no emotion. I did see a semblance at the funeral, but I'm not certain I believed it.'

'If you could have loved me… if just once you had…'

'If I didn't love you, Matthew, I would have turned you in to the police.'

'I didn't hate Tay. I went there to help her. You have to believe that I never hated her.'

'I do.'

'Alright then.'

'What went wrong, Matthew?'

Matthew stood unsteadily, tucking his head into the side of his shoulder. His words stretched out before him, attaching their story to the wall. 'I got there. Tay was crying. For some stupid reason, I laughed. I mean how stupid could she be to fall for a fifteen-year-old. It was funny – I couldn't help laughing. How many times had Tay laughed at me – you and Mom laughed at me. All I did was laugh.'

'Go on, son.'

'Tay flew out of control. She ran at me and pushed me down hard and I fell on a rock. I thought I had broken my shoulder blade. Then I thought, what if I had landed headfirst on that rock? She could have killed me. I could have died, from just laughing at something stupid.'

'Son…'

'I'm lousy at sports, but I have a good arm. I got up and I wanted to throw a real scare into Tay because she'd hurt me. Tay has never once turned back and apologized when she's pushed me down. That day was no different. She turned and stomped off. I aimed to throw the rock close to her, not at her. You have to believe me. I didn't aim at her!'

Sanderson felt chills down his spine.

'She turned unexpectedly, right into the path of the rock and it hit her. She fell down, just like that. She didn't scream – she just went down. I ran to her, Dad. I tried to shake her. Her eyes were wide open. I tried mouth-to-mouth.' Matthew was screaming, 'She wasn't breathing – she wasn't breathing. I never meant. I tried to save her! I didn't just give up. She wasn't breathing. I put my hand against her mouth and nose to feel her breath. Nothing! She was dead…' Matthew's face bore a look of horror.

'And the tunnel, Matthew?' Sanderson had risen.

Matthew edged away, hopping toward the door. 'I panicked. I couldn't just leave her there for dogs or rats at night. I couldn't just leave her there. She was dead, Dad. I lifted Tay in my arms and dropped her into the tunnel. The dark wouldn't bother her then. She was dead, by accident!' Matthew shrieked. 'I went to help her! You have to believe that, Dad.'

Sanderson walked up to Matthew, grabbing him by both shoulders. 'Tay wasn't dead, Matthew.' He pressed his face close to Matthew's. 'She was unconscious. She was still alive! You could have saved her life,' he roared. 'Don't you understand what you did? You left her alone – you didn't call for help. You stuffed her in that tunnel and Tay died alone in that hole!'

Matthew sank to the floor. 'I know that now – I thought she was dead.' He stared at the floor. His expression was flat. 'I thought she was dead.'

Sanderson let go of a shoulder and brought a closed hand above Matthew, as Abraham had done with Isaac. Matthew shut his eyes, waiting for the blow. 'Taylor threw that brick, and that kid scared Tay into going to the tunnel in the first place. Tay pushed me down, and *she* hurt me on purpose!' Matthew battled for his life. Sanderson was suddenly tired. He knelt and pulled Matthew deep into his arms, crushing the boy against his chest.

'I believe you, son. You're going to call Detective Damiano and turn yourself in. Involuntary manslaughter is not murder. I'll hire the best lawyers, you're a juvenile. We'll work for a ten-month sentence. It's a first offense. But you'll be as much a man as that other boy. You'll be a son I can respect.' Sanderson held Matthew tightly with both arms wrapped around his son's neck. He did not feel his son struggle. Matthew's efforts to break the hold soon weakened and stopped.

When Sanderson heard the door bell, he released Matthew. 'You'll be a man, Matthew.' The boy crumpled to the floor, but Sanderson was already at the front door. *I'll respect my son.*

'Detective Damiano and Detective Matte, Matthew was about to call you. He wants to speak to you. My son knows it's time.' The detectives stood in the hallway while Sanderson took their coats and hung them in the front closet. Damiano followed him and spotted the boots inside.

'May I take a quick look, Mr. Sanderson?'

'Of course. Matthew has nothing to hide now.'

Damiano turned the boots over. The herring bone pattern was easy to see. Detective Matte gave her a familiar *oops* look. 'Where is Matthew?'

'He's waiting in the kitchen. We had breakfast together and we talked. Follow me. Matthew is waiting for you.'

Detective Matte rushed to Matthew, turned him over on his back and immediately began CPR. Detective Damiano called a bus.

'I don't understand, Detective, I didn't strike Matthew. I held him in my arms and I promised him I'd hire the best lawyer. I assured him that he'd only serve a matter of months… He knows I wouldn't abandon him.

I'm his father. It's not easy being a good parent. Without Shari, I'm lost, but I know that Matthew needs me now. My son finally understands what he has to do, and he will do what's right.'

'You had Matthew in a choke hold, Sir.'

'What?' Sanderson shouted.

Detective Matte continued CPR. Matthew coughed, his head moving from one side to the other. Sanderson fell to his knees beside his son. 'Matthew, I never meant to hurt you. Matthew?'

'Mr. Sanderson, I need the room,' Detective Matte said angrily.

Damiano grabbed Sanderson's arm and led him from the kitchen while he protested and scowled at her. He wanted her to treat him with some deference, but Damiano hadn't time to waste on formalities. She couldn't lose another kid on her watch. 'Mr. Sanderson, sit down please, and don't move.' Damiano rushed back across the hall while keeping a close eye on Sanderson. In less than a minute, Matthew sat up with help. Matte coached him to take deep breaths before he helped the boy to his feet and onto a chair. While clearly shaken, Matthew was breathing without difficulty and appeared fully conscious. Damiano stepped back into the room. 'Do you remember what happened, Matthew?'

Matthew sat quietly, content to be breathing easily. Without Damiano blocking him, Sanderson had come to the door and Matthew saw him. 'My dad said he would find the best… then I couldn't breathe. I passed out.'

Damiano turned then to Sanderson for the rest of the story pitch, but Matthew cut back in. 'I think it was a panic attack because my father grabbed me before I fell. That's the last thing I remember. Right, Dad?' Matthew offered his father the mercy of a lie in exchange for his forgiveness. Sanderson could find no words. He stepped closer to Matthew and laid a hand on his shoulder.

Damiano was about to frame another question to draw out the truth, but she paused. Matte waited on her. She was the lead detective. Damiano thought of Luke and Pauzé. Filing an assault charge against Sanderson seemed wrong, indecent. She was there to arrest his son for the murder of his sister, his father's only daughter. The family had suffered unspeakable damage. Matthew was protecting his father. Damiano respected that. 'Well, I'll have the paramedics check you out, Matthew, and then…'

'I will accompany my son to the Division and act as his legal counsel in this accident.'

'Detective Matte and I will take the statement. The crown prosecutor will examine the findings and make that determination.'

'I will engage another lawyer tomorrow. Will you permit us to change first?'

'Yes.'

As soon as they climbed the stairs, Damiano told Matte to bag the boots. 'You made the right decision, Toni. The loss of young Jean Pauzé almost broke you and left you with a physical injury, but Pauzé also taught you a measure of kindness. That's something good.'

Damiano and Matte took Matthew's statement at the Division. The trade between father and son didn't sit well with Damiano, kindness or not. Involuntary manslaughter did not nearly cover the tragedy of events that led to the death of Taylor Sanderson. The closure of the Sanderson case did not sustain her. It saddened her and added a deeper layer of mistrust of others and their quiet compromises.

Epilogue

It was a week before Trevor confided the news to his wife. Shari Sanderson did not return home for six months, unable to cope with the depth of the tragedy. She made no attempt to understand or appreciate the sudden bond between Trevor and Matthew, except to observe that it appeared artificial, perhaps coerced. A year later, she and Trevor quietly divorced. She never spoke to Matthew again. She simply couldn't. Shari found she was unable to accept Trevor's secret deal – she determined to hold fast to the truth of her daughter's life.

The story appeared on page three with no photo of Matthew. The headline read: DEATH OF CONCORDIA STUDENT RULED INVOLUNTARY MANSLAUGHTER. It was a two-column story that spared the Sandersons. Trevor Sanderson had used all his contacts with the media. According to inside sources, important friends used their leverage in the effort as well. The Montreal 'clan of influence' saw to it that the vultures never landed on the full story.

AMIRA CUPID graduated with honors and left Montreal to join her sister in Toronto. She took Taylor's only letter with her. JOSH GOLDMAN moved to another apartment building and left the women on Lincoln Avenue behind. He could do that.

LIAM CASTONGUAY went back to school and dreamed of another chance to prove himself. One day he saw Cameron walking home alone and joined him.

CAITLIN DONOVAN supervised a final exam. She looked around, feeling she had lost the comfort and security she once felt at the university, until a student called out to her as she walked home. 'I had a great year, professor!' Her mother's surgery had gone well, so Caitlin agreed, it was a good year, considering.

DETECTIVE MATTE invited his partner out for a drink and Damiano accepted. It was a first. 'You told me to look for people my own age!' His eyes twinkled. They were friends, soulmates. He finally had the last word.

Closing another high profile case meant increased success for Detective Damiano and Detective Matte, although they were both scarred from the experience. Damiano's intense involvement in the case only highlighted her deep maternal failure. The condo sold within a week – she took the first offer. Damiano, Jeff and Luke went to family counselling. Jeff was surprised that Toni and Luke were not only receptive but they both reached out for a lifeline he guessed they'd needed. Damiano signed up again for physio and quit on the second day. Her arm hurt more after the therapy than it had before she'd gone. Damiano was stubborn, and driven, at times she begrudgingly admitted, by insecurity. She couldn't change, she'd hurtle through life. Work would remain a problem. There weren't enough hours in a day. Her rush to Chief Donat's chair lost a step. She was the lead on the Sanderson case and had missed her own son's involvement! That misstep bruised her confidence. That night Damiano sat alone recalling that all the damage had begun with a simple lie. The ghost had no intention of leaving Damiano. *Hell! It was April and it was snowing. Besides, this cop with unresolved issues meant he'd found a long term host.*

ACKNOWLEDGEMENTS

The research at the Wellington Tunnel became quite a story in itself. I met Montrealer Robert Idsinga at a book signing. He suggested I visit the abandoned Wellington Tunnel with him. There were prerequisites: we needed the cover of night, a hacksaw, good lights, and hiking gear. He'd saw through the single lock and we'd take photos of the intricate graffiti on the walls of the tunnel. Was there a question of trespassing, I asked? I was told not to worry, but I did. A friend Louis Castonguay drove me down. It was a miserable, rainy night, and we met in a fifties bar on Ontario Street shrouded in heavy mist.

We crossed the street, equipment in tow, and met with mounds of sheer ice between us and the tunnel. Forming a human chain, we slid and nearly fell as we approached the tunnel. When we reached the entrance, Robert saw that the lock had been replaced by a four-foot cement triangle of squares. Undeterred, I climbed to the top of the blocks and snapped photos with Robert, forgetting that climbing 'up' is much easier than climbing 'down.' We then slid to two small towers on either side of the tunnel and met with the same blocks and I climbed and snapped and jumped. At the second tower, someone had already sawed a two-foot square opening and securely attached a steel-reinforced cable from a tree into the tunnel. I had the 'drop' site for my victim!

Glen Graham is not only a good friend; he's also the best Montreal guide I've ever met. Lachine was my goal, particularly, the setting for two male characters who'd live close to a French and English high school and minutes from the bike path. I wanted to know precisely, door-to-tunnel, the time it would take fourteen-year-olds to cycle the path in heavy rain and possible snow, but free of cyclists. I needed to identify the danger points along the path and the landmarks the boys would pass. Glen had answers. I took notes as we studied the path and the history of Lachine.

Louise Shiller is Director and Senior Advisor on Rights and Responsibilities at Concordia University. I am grateful to Louise for her time, explanations and the conduct code that outlined the course of action that takes place when a student files a charge against a professor, verbally or formally. It was an eye-opening experience.

My visits and interviews at the Crémazie Division, Place Versailles, and Parthenais have been valuable as visuals and helpful in police procedures. The offices, the holding cell, the 'real' cells, the intake room, the interrogation 'box,' the examining room at the morgue, the fridges that occupy two rooms, and the autopsy theaters create a certain atmosphere of dread and mystery on their own.

Rev. Dr. Pearce J. Carefoote, librarian, Thomas Fisher Rare Book Library University of Toronto, was kind enough to help me with liturgical information concerning the religious ritual at a Catholic funeral. I appreciate his detail. It was important to be accurate since the service took place in the 360-year-old chapel of Notre-Dame-de-Bon-Secours.

I would like to thank the following friends: Louise Morin, for her generous support, her patience with my calls for the 'best' French word and her technical savvy. Most important is her friendship. Mary Kindellan, my little sister, is the best sales rep in TO who makes it a point to home deliver. I owe you, sis. Kathleen Panet, thanks so much for our friendship and your generous backing through the years. Claire Coleman, what a pleasure it's been to reconnect with you and to enjoy your valued support. Brenda O'Farrell is a remarkable friend whose affirmation I'm fortunate to have and respect. The Kindellans encourage me and have for every book – many thanks!

My faithful team: Irene Pingitore is not only a second reader; she's also the book counter at the signings. Thanks for addressing the invitations too, Irene, and the greeting smiles. Cynthia Iorio is a special friend who somehow makes time in her busy life to work every signing with her good cheer and charm and is irreplaceable at each event. Your generosity humbles me. Gina Pingitore was the friend there when I first began writing. She was the first member of the team and she and Cynthia work their magic and make each signing a success.

Margaret Goldik is not simply an editor and stylist, but a wise friend whose counsel I appreciate. Margaret has always offered her enthusiasm and support from *Sheila's Take* to *Where Bodies Fall*. She is an integral part of the process and a very dear friend.

From the memoir to the last mystery, Gina Pingitore has been my first, second and third reader, surrendering weekends to proofing, making time, being punctual and a cheerleader during the various stages of every novel. I feel an overwhelming sense of gratitude for her loyalty and friendship.

The relationship I enjoy with Simon Dardick is a privilege I treasure. His trust, humor, gentle ways, insight and knowledge are generously given to his authors.

www.vehiculepress.com